P9-BZV-090

BABYLON RISING

The EDGE *of* DARKNESS

BOOKS BY TIM LaHAYE

Tim LaHaye Prophecy Books—Nonfiction

Are We Living in the End Times?
Charting the End Times
Charting the End Times (study guide)
End Times Controversy
Perhaps Today (90-day devotional)
Merciful God of Prophecy
Revelation Unveiled
The Rapture
These Will Not Be Left Behind
Tim LaHaye Prophecy Study Bible: NKJV & KJV
Understanding Bible Prophecy for Yourself
Understanding God's Plan for the Ages (chart)
Bible Prophecy: Quick Reference Guide (booklet)

Tim LaHaye Fiction

Left Behind® (volume 1)
Tribulation Force (volume 2)
Nicolae (volume 3)
Soul Harvest (volume 4)
Apollyon (volume 5)
Assassins (volume 6)
The Indwelling (volume 7)
The Mark (volume 8)
Desecration (volume 9)
The Remnant (volume 10)
Armageddon (volume 11)
Glorious Appearing (volume 12)

Babylon Rising® (book 1)
Babylon Rising® (book 2)
Babylon Rising® (book 3)
Babylon Rising® (book 4)

Left Behind®: The Kids—Youth Fiction Series (volumes 1-40)

The Soul Survivor—Youth Fiction Series

The Mind Siege Project
All the Rave
The Last Dance
Black Friday

Additional Bestselling Books by Tim LaHaye

Spirit-Controlled Temperament
How to Be Happy Though Married
The Act of Marriage
How to Win over Depression
Mind Siege
How to Study the Bible for Yourself

BABYLON RISING

The EDGE of DARKNESS

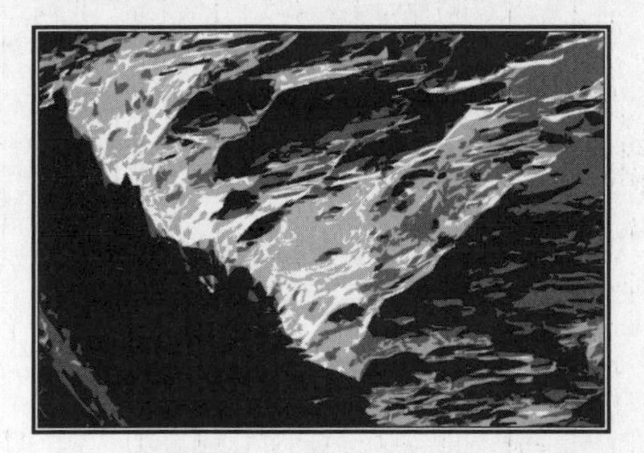

TIM LAHAYE

AND BOB PHILLIPS

BANTAM BOOKS

NEW YORK TORONTO LONDON SYDNEY AUCKLAND

BABYLON RISING
THE EDGE OF DARKNESS

Published by
Bantam Dell
A Division of Random House, Inc.
New York, New York

This is a work of fiction. Names, characters, places, and incidents either are the product of the author's imagination or are used fictitiously. Any resemblance to actual persons, living or dead, events, or locales is entirely coincidental.

ISBN: 0-553-80325-5

Printed in the United States of America

Dedicated to those who realize this world
is in an irreversible mess and want to believe
there is hope for a better world tomorrow

FOREWORD

from Tim LaHaye

A famous scientist gave this forlorn view of the future when he said, "I see no future for this world as we know it, beyond the year 2025." Another, more optimistic scientist set his doomsday at 2050! There is scant hope for today's teens.

In our time, there are weapons of mass destruction in the hands of unknown terrorists, renegade countries like North Korea that make no pretense of giving up their quest for nuclear weaponry so they can blackmail the world, rising ruthless dictatorial regimes that have already proven they have no regard for human lives other than their own—and now the rise to power of an Islamic madman who even told delegates at the UN that it was his destiny to create world chaos so his prophet will return to earth and establish a worldwide Islamic dictatorship.

At the risk of sounding negative, there is even more in the field of nature: earthquakes at unprecedented levels (some above 9 on the Richter scale), hurricanes at unprecedented numbers, out of control plagues like AIDS that threaten to decimate all of Africa, the threat of an "Asian flu" epidemic . . . and the list goes on. We are indeed approaching THE EDGE OF DARKNESS.

Yet this is not the end! The Hebrew prophets and Jesus Christ and His apostles warned many times that such days would come. That is why I started this series of action thrillers based on Bible prophecy, to show that even at the edge of darkness there is much hope for the future.

Dr. Michael Murphy, the exciting hero of our Babylon Rising series, is the perfect person to interpret these times in the light of the Bible's ancient prophecies. An academic expert in archaeology and an ardent student of prophecy, one of his greatest joys is proving the accuracy of the Bible archaeologically.

This book could not be more timely. It offers an intriguing answer to the problems of our globe that is extremely relevant for this age.

Tim LaHaye

BABYLON RISING

The EDGE *of* DARKNESS

ONE

CALL IT INSTINCT, intuition, or just plain street smarts—whatever it was sent a tingle down Murphy's spine. The clicking noise caused him to leap off the seat of the roller-coaster car as fast as his six-foot-three-inch frame would allow. He sailed over the back, clutching the seat with both hands. As his feet landed on the bumper that ran around the car, he hunkered down and held his breath.

It was not a moment too soon. A rush of wind tousled his hair as two eighty-pound blocks of cement smashed into the seat where he had just been sitting.

Another millisecond and I would have been dead, he thought. *How do I keep getting into things like this?*

It was one of those days when everything inside of Murphy said *Don't go to work.* It was too beautiful a day to be inside a classroom teaching biblical archaeology. As he reluctantly gathered his papers and stuffed them into his briefcase, the words of Mark Twain echoed in his mind: *Do something every day that you don't want to do; this is the golden rule for acquiring the habit of doing your duty without pain.*

Murphy never tired of the scenic drive to school and the campus of Preston University. There was something deeply attractive about the lush greenery of the South and the beauty of the magnolia blossoms. Parking his car in the teachers' lot, he meandered up the tree-lined walkway toward his office near the Memorial Lecture Hall. The smell of jasmine in the air filled his senses.

Students were sitting under the trees. Some were studying, but most were just talking with their friends. One group tossed a Frisbee back and forth. Murphy recalled his days as a student. *Life was so much simpler then. They don't even realize how great these years are.*

The unbidden image of Laura swept across his mind, the moments of joy and laughter they had shared during their marriage. Those happy years before she had been murdered by Talon. The pain tore at his insides, and a sigh escaped his lips. He shook the memories away, unwilling to let the grief overwhelm him.

He reached his office, opened the door, and groaned. His desk was stacked high with student test papers and book reports that needed to be reviewed. *I think I'll delegate those to Shari. She'll hate me, but isn't that what assistants are for? Doing all the jobs you don't like?*

Shari had been in the laboratory for almost an hour. She was peering through a microscope at an envelope when Murphy entered.

"I know, I know. You're wondering what I'm doing here so early."

Murphy smiled a Cheshire cat grin as he looked at Shari. Her very light complexion and sparkling green eyes contrasted with her black hair. The ponytails coming out from each side of her head were hanging down, almost covering the microscope. She had on her favorite white lab coat.

"I know you love it here," he said. "Maybe I should move in a bed and then you won't have to go home at night."

She looked up at him and wrinkled her nose. "Like you don't get involved in *your* work!"

"Who, me?" Murphy set his briefcase down. "What are you looking at?"

Shari sat up with a guilty look on her face. "Oh, just something that came in the mail for you."

"For me? Why are you looking at my mail through a microscope?"

She smiled, with a twinkle in her eye. "I'm just trying to protect you."

"Protect me from what?"

"From what I think might be inside."

"This all sounds very mysterious. What are you talking about?"

"I think it's a letter from your admirer," she said with a smirk.

"Let me guess. Does my admirer's name start with an M?"

"Not bad, Doc, for so early in the morning."

Shari handed the letter to Murphy. "I was comparing this handwriting with some of the other letters you've received from your deranged admirer. They're the same."

Murphy held the envelope up to the light and saw what looked like a three-by-five card inside.

"So why don't you open it?"

Murphy smiled. Shari was forever curious about anything that might be mysterious. He opened the envelope, took out the card, and began to read.

Row, row, row your boat gently around the lake
Walk and talk and have a piece of cake

Ride, ride, ride the trolley
Be sure to stop and visit Molly

Dance, dance, dance the choo-choo
Visit the zoo and casino too

Round, round, round you go
Don't be depressed by the big tornado

Search, search, search and find
Be sure not to lose your mind

Seek, seek, seek, like a mouse
You may even find a fun house

"So much for poetry!" said Shari. "What in the world do you think he means? Maybe he's finally lost it."

"Well, Methuselah is strange, eccentric, even sadistic . . . but he's not crazy. His clues and riddles have led us to many archaeological finds in the past." Murphy stroked his chin, lost in thought. "He must have some new trophy for us to search for."

"Can you make heads or tails of this one?"

Murphy ran his fingers through his brown hair and paced around the room. Shari just smiled and watched her boss. She knew it was best not to disturb him once the mental wheels were in motion.

Murphy went to his computer and got on the Internet. Shari stepped behind him and watched dubiously as he typed in the words "Amusement Parks." After another fifteen minutes of searching, he turned to her.

"I think I may have the answer to the riddle."

"Well, pray tell, Mr. Sherlock Holmes. Don't keep me in suspense."

"The first clue for me was the word 'trolley.' At the turn of the century, one of the main modes of transportation in larger cities was the electrical trolley line."

"So? What does that have to do with the rest of the riddle?"

"Hang on to your ponytails. It says here: Electrical companies in the early 1900s charged the trolley companies a straight fee for the use of electricity. Regardless of the number of people that rode the trolley, the electrical fee was the same. Owners of the trolleys tried to devise a way to get more customers to ride. The plan they settled on was to build amusement parks at the end of the trolley lines. This would encourage more travel and generate more revenue. Not a bad idea, huh?"

"I think maybe you're off *your* trolley this time."

"Cute, Shari. Just hear me out. The phrase 'visit Molly' is the key to the riddle. In 1910, Lakewood Amusement Park was built at the end of the trolley line in Charlotte, North Carolina. At that time it was three miles west of the city. Its design was similar to that of Coney Island and it became one of the most attractive parks in the South."

"How do you know all of this?"

"Genevieve Murphy."

"Who is Genevieve Murphy?"

"My grandmother. She used to live in Charlotte and I would visit her in the summers. She would tell me stories about growing up in the South. One of her stories was about a trolley park with a lake. I remember her talking about riding on a roller coaster. She loved it. She would ride it two or three times each time she visited the park."

"Go on, I'm still listening."

"Lakewood Park had a lake with rowboats—*Row, row, row your boat gently around the lake. Walk and talk and have a piece of cake.* The lake had a walkway around it with concession stands. They also had a half-mile-long roller coaster formerly called the Scenic Railway. Its nick-name was *Molly's Madness.* My grandmother sometimes referred to it as 'riding old Molly.' The park also had a *merry-go-round* that could seat a hundred people. They had a *shooting range.* They had a *petting zoo.* They had a *dance hall* that was over part of the lake, and they had a *casino.* All of those attractions tie in with Methuselah's riddle."

"What about being *depressed by the big tornado*?"

"I think that's the clincher, Shari. In 1933, the Great Depression bankrupted Lakewood Park. People didn't have money to spend on rides and games. In 1936, a large tornado hit the area and trashed the park. The heavy rains that followed washed out the dam and caused the lake to overflow. Repairs were never made, and the park closed for good."

"Bummer. Is there anything remaining from the original park today?"

"No. I believe they built over that area years ago. There is one thing, however. There were rumors that the owners of the park were in the process of constructing an underground amusement area in the form of a fun house. It was supposed to have rolling barrels, slides, roller bridges, a human roulette wheel, a maze of mirrors, and a ride called the Tunnel of Fear."

"And all of that was going to be built underground?"

"That was the rumor. Maybe they did build it but didn't open it to the public. Maybe that's what the phrase *Seek, seek, seek like a mouse—you may even find a fun house* means. Methuselah is telling me to look for something. Probably old building records that date back to the 1930s. The fun house may still be there somewhere underground in Charlotte."

Shari recognized the glint in Murphy's eye. "You're not really going to try and find out, are you? Need I remind you that Methuselah has tried to kill you on a number of occasions?!"

"I know, I know. But his clues have helped us find the golden head of Nebuchadnezzar, Noah's Ark, and the famous Handwriting on the Wall. I'm curious as to what new archaeological find he might lead us to."

"That's just the problem. You're too curious."

She might as well have been talking to the wall. His mind was already made up.

Murphy's alarm sounded at 5:00 A.M. He moaned a little and shut it off.

Well, time for a new adventure.

He wanted to get up early enough to have breakfast and make the two-and-a-half-hour drive from Raleigh to Charlotte. He had called the day he received Methuselah's riddle and found out that the Hall of Records opened at nine in the morning.

No telling what the old coot has in store for me, he thought. *I'd better be prepared.*

Murphy loaded his backpack with water, a knife, a hatchet, a first-aid kit, a compass, some rope, and a few other items. He looked around the room trying to think of anything else he should bring along.

Laser, he thought.

He went to the closet and pulled out a black, five-foot-long by one-foot-wide, impact-resistant case that contained Laser. He opened the case and smiled. His hand glided across the laminated carbon-fiber-compound bow. Instinctively he checked the draw system of cables and eccentric pulleys mounted at the limb tips. They gave him the power to shoot an arrow, as straight as a laser, at up to 330 feet per second.

This may come in handy. Who knows what Methuselah is up to this time?

Ever since Murphy was a teenager, he'd been interested in archery. It was a precise discipline and he had become a serious bow marksman. His perfectly aimed arrows would shoot like tiny guided missiles at their target. Laser had helped him on more than one occasion—even against one of Talon's falcons in the Pyramid of the Winds.

A dozen arrows, he thought. *That should be enough.*

The trip to Charlotte gave Murphy time to think. He cringed as he remembered how Methuselah pitted him against a lion in the warehouse building in Raleigh. He still had the scar on his shoulder as a reminder. Then there was the Cave of the Waters, where he'd almost drowned trying to save the two German shepherd puppies. And the time when Methuselah cut the cable he was walking on over the Royal Gorge in Colorado. Oh, yeah, and the rattlesnakes that dropped on him in the Reed Gold Mine.

Methuselah is one very strange man, he thought. *He must sit awake nights dreaming up these traps for me. And I just keep playing the game his way, risking my life to try to solve his riddles. So who's the crazy one?*

Murphy stopped first at the main library. He spent an hour looking through old newspaper clippings from the *Charlotte Gazette.* He was about to quit when he saw a small article dated April 12, 1929.

TUNNEL OF FEAR

> Jesse P. East and Roland Kalance, owners of the Lakewood Park and Trolley Company, have planned a new attraction at their park. It is to be called the Tunnel of Fear. It will be a ride only for the brave of heart. It will be part of a new underground fun house. Construction will begin in September and should take no longer than a year and a half to complete. This reporter has been told that the construction cost may mount to an astounding $53,000.
>
> Floyd Cornford—Reporter

Murphy took a deep breath. *Well, Methuselah said to "Search, search, search and find."*

Murphy spent the next four hours in the county Hall of Records, mostly working his way through the endless red tape and the frustration of government bureaucracy. He had to invoke the Freedom of Information Act with a number of different people before he finally got to look at some plans.

He gradually realized that the names of streets on the old maps were not the same as the current ones. He asked one of the clerks to assist him.

"Mr. Murphy, as far as I can tell, Lakewood Park used to be located between what is now called Lakeview Street and Norwood Drive to the north, Parkway Avenue to the east, and Parkside Drive to the south."

"Do you have any idea what is now in that area?" asked Murphy.

"Well, my map indicates an electrical substation and what looks to be about ten warehouse units where the lake was. They are north of Parkside Drive. There are now four large warehouse buildings south of Parkside. They would have been outside of the lake."

Murphy smiled. "I get the impression from these old building plans that the fun house that Mr. East and Mr. Kalance were supposed to build would be located under one of those new warehouses. Right?"

The clerk examined the 1929 plans. "I think you may be correct. Look over here on the west side of the fun house. It looks like a shaft was to have been dug into the ground. If they did build it, that's how the workers got in and out while they were digging out the area. It was to become the entrance from the casino down to the fun house."

"Do you have any idea if they ever completed the project?"

"That was about sixty-five years ago. I wasn't even born yet," said the clerk as he sifted through some old and yellowing papers.

"Here's a note from one of the inspectors, a Mr. Fritz Schuler. He indicates that most of the project was completed. All they had to get was a final inspection, but it was put off due to insufficient funds to complete the project."

Murphy smiled to himself.

"That seems to be all the information we have. I hope this has been helpful to you, Mr. Murphy."

"Yes, you've been a great help. Thank you for your time and patience."

TWO

MURPHY DIDN'T FIND anything that looked like an entrance to a shaft around the four warehouses south of Parkside Drive. He clenched his jaw and struggled to restrain his mounting frustration. Patience was not one of Murphy's redeeming qualities.

Maybe they built the warehouses over the shaft.

He pulled out the crude map he had drawn of the area while at the Hall of Records. To the west of the last warehouse was a grove of trees. He surveyed the area, trying to imagine where the dance hall and casino might have been located in 1929. He then looked again at the grove of trees.

I'll bet that's it, he thought.

The ground under the trees was layered with fallen leaves from countless autumns. For half an hour he searched the area, finding nothing. He ran one hand through his hair while the other pulled out Methuselah's card.

"Seek, seek, seek like a mouse." If Methuselah has been here there will be some sign.

Murphy crisscrossed the area, trying to envision where a shaft might have been located.

It would probably be in some type of clearing. They would need to have a road to bring in equipment.

He noticed a large open area in the grove of trees, wide enough apart for equipment to pass between them. As he reached the center of the clearing, he saw that the matted tangle of leaves there had been disturbed. He began to kick back the leaves, revealing old eight-by-eight-inch timbers. He kept removing leaves until he saw the hinges to some kind of door. He cleared away more leaves, until he spied a latch and what looked to be a fairly new padlock.

Methuselah.

Murphy was glad that he had loaded his backpack. He removed a hatchet and chopped away at the wood around the latch and lock. It took him about ten minutes before he could loosen the latch enough to pry it off the wood. He pulled up the door, revealing a set of stairs about ten feet wide, disappearing down into the earth.

East and Kalance must have been very close to finishing their fun house. You sure you really want to go down there?

Murphy put away his hatchet and took out a large flashlight. He started down the winding stairs into the darkness. Alongside the stairs was a cast-iron hand railing. The wood on top of the railing was weathered and covered with a growth of moss. Running the flashlight beam along the railing, Murphy could see a number of places where the moss had recently been knocked away. It was as if someone had grabbed on to the railing to steady himself. He shined the light on the stairs, revealing innumerable footprints in the dirt and dust. Murphy guessed he was about two stories underground.

Methuselah, he thought, *what are you up to now?* He squinted in the darkness. *I'll bet there's more than one entrance to this place.*

At the bottom he shined his light around. He could see a large archway about fifteen feet wide. Above the arch was an old signboard with faded colored paint. It read:

Welcome to the Lakeside Fun House
Come in for the time of your life

As Murphy stepped under the arch, dim lights came on. He shined his flashlight back toward the arch and located a pair of sensors. He could see that he had broken a beam of light that must have activated the power for the fun house. He then heard the whir of some kind of machinery going on.

That old man must have money to spare to fix up an old fun house buried underground.

As he pressed on, there was a startling sound. Shining his light upward, he saw a large mechanical clown with its head rocking back and forth in laughter.

It's not funny yet, Methuselah.

He moved through a doorway under a sign that read:

Have a barrel of laughs

The only way forward was through a series of three large barrels that were lined up on their sides in a single row, like a tunnel. Each barrel was about eight feet in diameter and about fifteen feet long. The first barrel was rolling to the left, the second barrel to the right, and the third barrel to the left. Grinding motors and chain drives made the barrels roll over and over.

Murphy remembered another fun house he had gone through when he was about ten years old. It was in Denver, Colorado, and also had rolling barrels. His father had shown him that the only way through was to walk in the opposite direction from the roll of the barrel, like being on a giant treadmill. Otherwise, you would end up rolling around the inside of the barrel.

The dim light illuminated the inside of the fun house, so Murphy put his flashlight away in the backpack. He held the pack in his left hand to balance the impact-resistant case that contained Laser in his right. Murphy took a deep breath and entered the first barrel, walking in the opposite direction of the roll.

As Murphy reached the center barrel, an Asian figure in a black ninja outfit entered the third barrel. He resembled a young Bruce Lee and moved toward Murphy with the agility of a cat. He did not look too friendly.

Okay, here's where it gets interesting, Murphy thought.

A quick glance behind Murphy revealed another Asian, dressed in a dark brown outfit. He had entered the first barrel after Murphy and was quickly gaining ground.

Oh, great! Double the fun. That's all I need.

Murphy also glimpsed a shadowy form lurking at the entrance to the first barrel. *Could it be . . . ?* A moment later, the familiar cackling laugh of Methuselah confirmed his suspicions.

"This will be fun to watch, Murphy!"

Murphy was not going to allow Methuselah to distract him. The two Asians looked like professionals. Fast, confident, deadly. And out to do him some serious harm.

The man from behind was almost upon him. *Divide and conquer,* thought Murphy. He turned and ran in the same direction that the barrel was rolling, rising quickly up the side. As Murphy felt himself starting to lose the battle against gravity, he shoved backward as hard as he could. All of Murphy's one hundred and ninety-five pounds dropped down on the man in brown and drove his head hard into the thick wood.

One down, thought Murphy. The fall knocked his backpack and impact case out of his hands, and they began to tumble on the floor with the unconscious Asian. Murphy had just regained his shaky footing when the impact case ricocheted into his midsection, knocking the wind out of him. He fell again, gasping for breath and struggling unsuccessfully to get to his feet.

The assassin in black leaped over his unconscious partner and landed a kick on Murphy's shoulder. Murphy rolled with the blow, still trying to catch his breath. He scrambled to his feet just as the assassin sprang through the air, kicking Murphy in the chest, and again knocking him to the floor.

"Bravo! Bravo!" shouted Methuselah with a laugh.

Murphy knew that he could hold his own if he could ever catch his breath and get his feet under him. His aptly named impact case kept rolling against his body, making it difficult to get up.

The man in black came in for a third attack, aimed at Murphy's head. Instinctively Murphy grabbed the impact case and swung it in front of him, knocking the assassin off balance. He went down on his back next to Murphy. Murphy brought his elbow down as hard as he could on the side of the Asian's head. Murphy finally rose to his feet. It was all over except for the tumbling of two bodies, one backpack, and an impact case.

He gathered up the backpack and Laser, and stumbled out of the last barrel. He looked back at the two bodies tumbling over and over like rag dolls in a washing machine. Methuselah had disappeared.

THREE

"I THINK WE NEED to make a toast to Mr. Bartholomew. He has selected another wonderful location for our meeting place. Cape Town is always beautiful this time of year."

"Hear, hear!" said Sir William Merton, the oldest member of the Seven. "I couldn't agree with you more, General Li. It's much warmer than China this time of year, wouldn't you say?"

The portly English cleric lifted his wineglass high as he slouched on a lawn chair like a white-collared sea lion. He was physically repulsive but quite brilliant.

Everyone lifted their glasses. General Li gave a slight bow, his powerful frame hidden by his finely tailored suit. His manner was unfailingly gracious and polite, but there was something cruel and relentless in his eyes.

Ganesh Shesha cleared his throat. The bright sun had turned his usual cold stare into a squint. His gray hair was deeply contrasted by his dark skin and hatchet nose. Massive corruption and shrewd manipulation had enabled his rise to prominence in India's Parliament.

"Most beautiful. Although India is not very far away, this is my first visit to South Africa." Shesha looked out across the harbor and pointed. "That island in the distance. Do people live there?"

Jakoba Werner smiled. Her blond hair was tied back in a bun. In fact, no one in attendance could ever remember seeing her with her hair down. She was half laughing as she responded, her curt tone and German accent punctuating each word. "That is Robben Island, the home of a maximum security prison. It is no longer in use and has now become a tourist attraction. It is similar to Alcatraz Island in the San Francisco Harbor, only Robben Island is much larger. Nelson Mandela spent a number of years incarcerated there."

"It's too bad they let him out of prison," stated Bartholomew. "I've grown weary of his rhetoric about apartheid and his suffering through racial segregation. For the life of me, I can't imagine why they awarded him the Nobel Peace Prize."

Viorica Enesco nodded in agreement, brushing her red hair out of her eyes. "Enough about that." Her Romanian accent was strong. "I have no desire to visit the prison on Robben Island or anywhere else. I've personally seen enough prisons."

"How about a ride up toward Table Mountain, behind our estate?" asked Señor Mendez. "I hear there's quite a view of the Cape from up there. And then perhaps we could drive over to Lion's Head. It is quite famous."

"This is not a vacation," said Bartholomew. His British accent had a chilling tone to it. He was tired of all this useless banter and anxious to start the meeting. "We are here to discuss business. Our attempt to blow up the George Washington Bridge did not succeed quite as we had hoped. It did, however, fulfill our plan to drive the leaders of the United Nations out of America. They have started their relocation plans to Babylon. The European Union is functioning well, Europa is rising, and we are still on course."

"Well, I must add that the George Washington Bridge plan did put quite a scare in the Americans. That was a great bonus for us."

"True, Jakoba. That, along with Talon eliminating Stephanie Kovacs. That reporter was getting too inquisitive for her own good. She was on the verge of finding out about our payments to the U.N. leaders. Besides, she was giving too much information to Murphy."

Sir William Merton quickly sat forward. His face began to change and his eyes flashed with hatred. "We have two loose cannons to be concerned about. The first is Dr. Michael Murphy. He knows too much about the Bible and has discovered too many ancient artifacts that can help to prove the Bible to be true. But what worries me the most is his talking with Dr. Harley B. Anderson. There's no telling what information he acquired from him before Talon killed him. We don't know what he learned about the birth of the Boy from reading Anderson's notes."

"The Boy!" said Viorica. "You know he's not a boy anymore! He's a man, and it's almost time for the Friends of the New World Order to expose him and unite the people of the earth under his leadership!"

"And the second loose cannon?"

"Yes, Ganesh, that is our old enemy Methuselah. His hatred for the Seven is matched only by his great wealth. We have been unable to get close to him. He has too many bodyguards. Yet he keeps getting information about us somehow." He studied the faces of his six compatriots for several moments before continuing. "There has been a breach of security in our organization. You will recall that we had Talon steal the tail of the Bronze Serpent from the Parchments of Freedom Foundation and bring it to our office in France. We were going to then transport it to the castle. However, someone stole it from the safe in the office and sent the tail back to the Parchments of

Freedom Foundation. I've instructed Talon to get it back. Whoever did this is through. Once we discover who it is . . . he's a dead man.

"Or woman! Who do you think that might be?"

"I don't know, Señor Mendez. But you can be sure that we will find him or her. It's just a matter of time. We'll all have to be on the alert for anything suspicious. Meanwhile, we need to focus on the future. It would be good to eliminate Dr. Murphy, but for now, we must concentrate on empowering De La Rosa."

"What do you suggest?" asked Mendez.

"We shall invite Shane Barrington for a visit. We will get him to promote De La Rosa through the vast Barrington News Network. Between his television stations, his newspapers, and his magazines, we will get excellent coverage."

"Will he cooperate? After all, we did have Talon kill his live-in lover . . . Stephanie Kovacs!"

"That is true, Señor Mendez. But remember, we also killed his son. He betrayed his own blood relation to obtain enough money to keep the Barrington News Network from going bankrupt. He is not a man of morals. He is as greedy as Midas. He wants everything he touches to turn to gold. And if it does not turn to gold, at least he wants power and control over it. His own pride and arrogance and lust for money will keep him under our control."

"I hope so," said Merton. "If he turned on us, he would be a powerful enemy."

"He wouldn't dare. He has too much to lose." Bartholomew took a long sip from his wineglass. "And speaking of losing, Talon has lost some articles from Noah's Ark. We need to send him to see if he can retrieve them from the Black Sea. They may contain the secrets of the Philosopher's Stone, and we need to know more about Potassium 40. I don't know about all of you, but I find the possibility of extending life very intriguing."

Sir William Merton's eyes seemed to glow again. "Yes, we all want to live to see De La Rosa and our Master come to power."

FOUR

MURPHY SHRUGGED OFF the pain in his gut and looked around. The faint illumination revealed a sign pointing to a doorway. The sign read:

Having fun yet?
How about a game of roulette?

The next room contained a large spinning wheel like a merry-go-round without any animals or poles. The wheel was low to the ground and covered with polished wood. He had a vague recollection from childhood that people would sit on the wheel and it would turn faster and faster until the centrifugal force threw the riders off the wheel and into a low, curved wall. The only way anyone could remain on the wheel was to be in the exact middle. Murphy could see that something was in the center of the spinning wheel. It looked like another one of Methuselah's three-by-five cards.

The next clue.

As Murphy started forward, he heard a grunt. An enormous man in crimson emerged from the darkness. At least, Murphy *thought* it was one man. He was dressed in red wrestling tights and must have weighed in excess of three hundred pounds. He was at least six and a half feet tall and looked like he had been lifting weights since the age of five.

Murphy took a few cautious steps backwards. He had been trained in boxing and the martial arts, but had never faced an opponent of this size. He had to stay out of the giant's long reach.

Murphy hurled the impact case at the wrestler, and he batted it away without flinching. But it bought Murphy a few precious moments to open his backpack. *Water, compass, first-aid kit . . .*

As he fished inside for a weapon, the man charged. Murphy's fingers brushed against the handle of the knife just as the wrestler barreled into him like a Mack truck, sending him to the ground and his backpack flying onto the roulette wheel.

A pair of huge hands grabbed for Murphy. He rolled and kicked at the man's muscular legs. It was like connecting with two tree trunks, but he somehow managed to sweep the wrestler's legs out from under him. He went down hard.

The bigger they are, thought Murphy. He leaped onto the man's back and held his face against the spinning wheel. The enraged giant roared and swung, and suddenly Murphy found himself airborne.

He landed a few feet away. Before he could recover, the giant seized Murphy, lifted him over his head, and slammed him against the wall. Through a dull haze of pain, Murphy saw the wrestler moving forward and reaching for him on the floor. He scooted between his thick legs and rose to his feet. He looked for his backpack, and finally spied it in the center of the roulette wheel. *The one place where it won't spin off. Just great.* He had to get to his weapons or he was done for.

Murphy ran over and hopped onto the wheel, staggering forward in a low crouch. He reached for the backpack, just nicking it, but could not maintain his balance. He flew off and spun into the curved wall.

The wrestler charged, and Murphy was in no position to defend himself. He waited for the crushing blow, but instead something crashed into the wall nearby and burst, spraying them both with liquid. The wrestler looked behind him, and the squashed water bottle landed at Murphy's feet. Then his first-aid kit skidded across the floor. The open backpack had fallen on its side and its contents were flying out at great velocity. The wrestler turned back to Murphy and moved in for the kill.

A sickening sound of metal meeting bone echoed through the chamber, and the wrestler cried out. He fell to the ground, Murphy's hatchet lodged in the back of his leg.

This was Murphy's chance. He grabbed the wrestler around the neck and squeezed. The wrestler caught an arm in his crushing grip, and Murphy knew he couldn't match the man's strength. He put his foot on the hatchet and pushed it in deeper, as blood splattered everywhere. The giant howled and released Murphy's arm. He tightened his chokehold and finally the man ceased struggling and collapsed to the floor.

Lucky, thought Murphy. *That hatchet could just as easily have hit—*

He hit the deck as his knife flew overhead. Another water bottle rolled in his direction. He glanced about and saw his belongings scattered around the room. He sighed and picked everything up. Lost a couple of water bottles and the compass was smashed, but everything else seemed to be okay.

Now he just needed to get that backpack.

Now empty, the backpack continued to spin in the center of the roulette wheel. Murphy tried to get to it once more, but it was spinning too fast, and he was thrown again.

There must be a way to do this.

Murphy ran his fingers through his hair and looked around.

Laser.

He grabbed the impact case and took out his bow and an arrow. He then tied his rope to the arrow and took aim. It was an easy target. The arrow shot between the backpack and one strap, and lodged into the opposite wall. He gently pulled on the loose end and guided the pack off the wheel.

Something fluttered and flew out from under the backpack. *The next clue!* Murphy had forgotten all about it.

A corner of the index card landed in the pool of blood oozing from the giant's severed tendon. Murphy retrieved the card. It read:

IN THE TOWN
OF KING YAMANI
A GREAT MYSTERY
HAS BEEN SOLVED.
I Kings 8:9

Murphy frowned. *Who in the world is King Yamani?* He turned the card over and read the other side.

RIDE YOUR FEARS
TO THE END.

It made no sense. He tucked the card into a pocket and gathered his belongings into his backpack. All except . . .

Ugh. He reached down and reluctantly dislodged the hatchet from the giant's gargantuan leg. He wiped the blood off on the man's red outfit, and put it into his pack. The blood ran freely from the gaping wound and Murphy's stomach turned.

And they say professional wrestling is fake.

FIVE

MURPHY ENTERED a dimly lit hallway that twisted a couple of times until it came to another entrance. The sign above read:

Mirror, mirror on the wall
Who's the fairest of them all?
Those who can escape the hall.
Welcome to the Hall of Mirrors

Murphy let out a sigh. *What next?*

He entered and was greeted by . . . himself. Dozens of Murphys were reflected back at him. Most of them were normal but there were several that, under better circumstances, might have caused Murphy to smile. One of them was curved and made him look fat. Another made him look skinny—he really liked that one. There was one that endowed him with a tiny head and big feet, and another that gave him tiny feet and a big head.

He opened his backpack and rummaged through it. He pulled out an energy bar and then strapped on the backpack. He switched the impact case to his left hand. He then began to walk around the room, touching each of the mirrors until he found the passageway that started the maze of mirrors. As he moved forward he would occasionally break off a small part of the energy bar and drop it on the floor.

Hansel and Gretel have got nothing on me, he thought.

As he worked his way through, Murphy was on the alert for the next attack. At each corner he became more and more apprehensive. Then he heard the cackling laugh of Methuselah echoing through the maze.

"Bravo, Murphy. This is turning out to be more entertaining than I'd hoped."

Murphy held his tongue. He didn't want to give Methuselah any more satisfaction than he already had.

I wonder if he can see me. Maybe he has some hidden video cameras set up in here.

Murphy looked up at the line where the mirrors met the ceiling, and saw a very small red light about twenty feet away. It would occasionally blink on and off. He cautiously approached.

Suddenly, he found himself dropping into a hole in the floor. But even as the realization struck, the impact case carrying his bow and arrows straddled the opening of the trapdoor, wrenching his left arm and shoulder. He was now hanging in the air, barely holding on to the handle of the case. And his fingers were beginning to slip. . . .

The sudden fall had caused him to drop the energy bar, and Murphy heard it hit water somewhere in the darkness below him.

Adrenaline pumped through his body. He struggled to grasp the impact case with his right hand and pull himself up. As he did, the case slipped a little.

Whoa. Easy now.

He had to work carefully and slowly. It took all of his strength to pull himself up, all the while expecting a minute shift of the case to plunge him into the abyss below. He finally crawled over the edge, exhausted from the effort, his shoulder throbbing. He lay there for a while to regain his strength and derived some small satisfaction from the fact that he had again escaped Methuselah's gauntlet. He rubbed his aching arm and shoulder.

Close one.

It took Murphy another ten minutes before he exited the Hall of Mirrors. And it was none too soon as far as he was concerned. In the passageway outside the maze, he noticed another sign with a red arrow. It pointed down a wide hallway to his right. He was growing weary of this game, but there was nothing to do at this point but press on.

At the end of the hallway, Murphy found himself in a large room. To one side he noticed small railway tracks and a brightly colored two-seater roller-coaster car. The car had a bumper that ran around its perimeter. The railway tracks disappeared under two wide swinging doors. Above the arched doorway was a sign:

Tunnel of Fear

Near the roller-coaster car was a red button and the words: PUSH TO START.

You've got to be kidding me.

Murphy tossed the impact case and backpack into the rear seats and climbed into the front. The next clue had to be here somewhere. He looked all over and even felt under the seats with his hands. *Nothing.*

He climbed into the second row and continued to search.

Murphy was thrown back into his seat as the car lurched forward. The bumper hit the swinging doors, and they popped open and then closed behind, leaving him in darkness.

He could hear the wheels on the track and the car jerked on the turns. He stuffed the backpack down on the floor of the car to make room to sit back in the seat. He felt strings brush across his face and an occasional burst of air. Every now and then lights would flash as some Halloween-monster reject would pop up and let out a scream. He could hear the sounds of wild dogs howling and eerie music.

Tunnel of Fear, huh. Not so much.

Yet something made him apprehensive. Call it instinct, intuition, or just plain street smarts—whatever it was sent a tingle down Murphy's spine. The clicking noise caused him to leap off the seat of the roller-coaster car as fast as his six-foot-three-inch frame would allow. He sailed over the back, clutching the seat with both hands. As his feet landed on the bumper that ran around the car, he hunkered down and held his breath.

It was not a moment too soon. A rush of wind tousled his hair as two eighty-pound blocks of cement smashed into the seat where he had just been sitting.

Another millisecond and I would have been dead, he thought. *How do I keep getting into things like this?*

Murphy held on as he rode the bumper behind the last seat. Methuselah had a way of playing for keeps in his little contests.

After a dozen more turns of the track, Murphy could see streams of light around the edges of two swinging doors ahead.

The exit.

As he hurtled toward the double doors, something didn't feel right. *Too easy,* he thought.

He jumped off the car a moment before it shot through the doors. He rolled to soften the fall as he tumbled along the track.

He looked up as a loud crash filled his senses. He got to his feet, walked toward the doors, and carefully opened them.

About ten feet outside the doors the railway tracks had dead-ended into a block wall. The roller-coaster car was crumpled in a heap. His backpack was inextricable from the wreckage and this was one impact that his impact case couldn't handle.

So much for Laser. Knew I should've insured the darn thing.

Then Murphy saw it. It was another one of Methuselah's three-by-five cards, taped to the block wall above the destroyed car. He took it off the wall and tried to make out the familiar handwriting in the dim light.

Well, you must be alive
if you are reading this card.
Since you have come this far,
you deserve your reward.

Murphy turned the card over.

Thirty degrees northeast
of the altar . . .
press the king's head.

SIX

Jerusalem, A.D. 30

THE MARKETPLACE WAS TEEMING *with vendors selling their fruits and vegetables. Weavers of purple cloth were yelling and holding up their materials, hoping to gain the attention of passersby. Shepherds led their sheep to be slaughtered, skinned, and hung up with other meats. The pungent odor of perspiration was heavy in the hot, dusty air.*

Caiaphas was nervous. He looked around to see if anyone was watching him, hoping he would pass unnoticed since he was not wearing his normal priestly robes. He sighed and stepped under the shade of one of the arches that led toward the temple. He raised his hand and motioned for the men to approach.

Eshban poked Zerah in the side.

"Stop that!" said Zerah with irritation in his voice.

Eshban pointed. "He is giving us the sign to come."

Caiaphas watched the two swarthy men approach. He was beginning to have second thoughts. Would anyone really believe them? They were poor men of little influence. Well, better to fail in the attempt than not to try.

Eshban spoke. "How may we be of service to you, Your Excellency?" There was a sarcastic curl to his smile.

"I want you to follow the teacher. The one they call Jesus. I want you to listen carefully to everything he says and then report back to me each evening."

Eshban and Zerah nodded their heads in agreement and exchanged conspiratorial glances.

"Now go. I must not be seen talking to you." He then turned and walked away into the crowd.

Zerah looked at Eshban. "How much did the high priest give you?"

Eshban opened the small leather bag. "Four silver coins. Two for me and two for you."

Zerah eagerly took the coins and put one of them between his teeth and bit down to test it. It was real silver. He smiled. The remnants of his last meal were visible between his teeth and his breath reeked of garlic.

The teacher and his followers were walking toward the eastern gate. Zerah and Eshban followed, moving steadily closer.

"Who is the big one talking with the teacher?" Zerah muttered.

"I heard someone call him Peter. A few more steps and we shall be able to hear all."

"Master, look at these tremendous buildings! The stones are massive. I wonder how they ever moved them into place! It must have taken many years."

"Yes, those are magnificent buildings, Peter. But I will tell you a truth. One day these buildings will be completely demolished. The destruction will be so great that there will not be one stone left on top of the other."

Zerah looked at Eshban and shook his head in disbelief at what they had just heard. He opened his mouth to speak, and Eshban motioned for him to remain silent. They were within earshot.

Eshban and Zerah followed, blending in with the other people going to and from the city. Their dirty and torn clothing made it easy to remain inconspicuous. No one paid them any attention.

The climb up the Mount of Olives took about thirty minutes. Eshban and Zerah watched as the teacher and his four disciples sat down on a cluster of rocks overlooking Jerusalem and the temple courtyard. They concealed themselves behind an olive tree within hearing distance.

"Who is the one talking to the teacher now?" whispered Zerah.

"One of the other followers called him Andrew."

"Master, you mentioned that the temple would one day be destroyed."

"The temple will fall. The rivers will boil. The Day of Judgment will come, and it shall be a sign of my return."

"Can we tell when the end of the world will come?" asked Peter.

"Others will come in my name, claiming to be the Messiah. They will lead many astray. Wars will break out near and far, but don't panic. Yes, these things must come, but the end won't follow immediately. Kingdoms will wage war against one another, and earthquakes will swallow up entire nations. Terrible famine shall follow. But all this will be only the beginning of the horrors to come."

Eshban and Zerah looked at each other in disbelief.

"It sounds terrible, Master!" said one of the followers.

"Will anyone survive this devastation?" asked the fourth member of the group.

"Who are those two followers?" whispered Zerah. "They bear a resemblance to each other."

"They are brothers. Their names are James and John. I've seen them on the seashore of Galilee. I think they are fishermen."

"Yes, people will survive. But when these things begin to happen, be

cautious! You will be handed over to the courts and beaten in the synagogues. You will be accused before governors and kings of being my followers. This will be your opportunity to tell them about me. And the Good News must first be preached to every nation and then the end will come."

"It sounds as if it will be a terrible time of tribulation."

"Yes, Peter, it will be. At that time if anyone says to you, 'Look, here is the Christ!' or 'There he is!,' do not believe it. For false Christs and false prophets will appear and perform great signs and miracles to deceive the majority of people. Even some believers will be tempted to follow these false teachers who seek financial gain, glory, and power.

"Beware of false prophets who come disguised as harmless sheep, but are really wolves that will tear you apart. You can detect them by the way they act, just as you can identify a tree by its fruit. You don't pick grapes from thornbushes, or figs from thistles. A healthy tree produces good fruit, and an unhealthy tree produces bad fruit.

"Not all people who sound religious are really godly. They may refer to me as 'Lord,' but they still won't enter the Kingdom of Heaven. The decisive issue is whether they obey my Father in heaven. On judgment day, many will cry out, 'Lord, Lord, we prophesied in your name and cast out demons in your name and performed many miracles in your name.' But I will reply, 'I never knew you. Go away; the things you did were unauthorized.' Be warned, Peter. I have told you ahead of time so that you might be prepared."

Eshban leaned over and whispered into Zerah's ear. "I am sure that the high priest will want to hear about all of this. It almost sounds as if there is going to be some sort of insurrection against the religious leaders."

Zerah nodded his head in agreement.

SEVEN

MURPHY WAS SITTING at his desk when Shari entered, carrying an armful of papers. She smiled and her eyes twinkled at the sight of him.

"So, what's the occasion?"

Murphy looked at her curiously.

"What do you mean?"

"I usually get to the office way ahead of you. You must have some burning project you're working on."

"I just needed to do some thinking."

She plopped the papers on his desk. "Here's one less thing you'll have to think about. It's all the book reports and test papers. I was up till two this morning grading them for you."

"Thanks, Shari. That's a real help. Above and beyond the call of duty."

"Well, I know how much you hate grading papers. . . . almost as much as I do. Since I've finished your dirty work, maybe I could get off a little early this afternoon?"

"To get some sleep?"

"No, to do some shopping."

"Now, that sounds real restful." He stifled a yawn and Shari studied him closely.

"Speaking of restful. You look a little tired yourself."

Murphy nodded his head.

"Oh, I get it. You must have been off having fun with your friend Methuselah. He plays a little rough."

Her eyes noticed the turnip-sized bruise on his forearm and the slight swelling around his left eye.

"Those bruises look like they hurt." There it was. The protective, motherly tone. "Well, don't keep me in suspense. What happened?"

Murphy recounted his trip to the Hall of Records in Charlotte, and the discovery of the shaft that led to the fun house. He omitted some of the gory details, knowing that she would not be pleased to hear how close he had come to death. He handed her the strange messages on the three-by-five cards that Methuselah had left for him.

"This is weird. Who is King Yamani? What town is he talking about? And what does that have to do with I Kings 8:9?"

"No idea. Methuselah doesn't ever make anything easy."

"What about the Bible reference?"

"The passage in Kings refers to the Ark of the Covenant."

"You don't think he's found the Ark, do you?" Shari's eyes were wide with excitement. "That would be one of the greatest archaeological finds ever!"

"Let's not get ahead of ourselves. Here's what it says in that verse: *Nothing was in the ark except two tablets of stone which Moses put there at*

Hoeb, when the Lord made a covenant with the children of Israel, when they came out of the land of Egypt."

"So where does that leave us?"

"Well, you have to refer to several passages to get the clue. In the book of Exodus, God instructs Moses to put the Testimony—you know, the Ten Commandments—into the Ark of the Covenant. He then instructs Moses and Aaron to collect an omer of manna and put it into a pot and place it in the Ark along with the Ten Commandments.

"Manna, that's some sort of food, right?"

"Yes. Manna was the food that God fed to the Children of Israel as they wandered in the wilderness. It was like a white coriander seed, supposed to taste like wafers made with honey. It was to be kept in the Ark as a reminder of how God had provided for all of their food requirements."

"I still don't get it."

"Have patience. In another passage in the book of Numbers, God instructs Moses to put Aaron's Rod into the Ark along with the Ten Commandments and the jar of manna. But, if you remember, the Children of Israel started to rebel against the leadership of Moses and Aaron. The leaders of the twelve tribes came together for a showdown. They each brought their rods (or leadership staffs) with their names on them. They placed them in the tabernacle of meeting to determine who would be the leader. The next day, when they looked at the rods, they were all the same—except for Aaron's. During the night, it had sprouted and put forth buds and produced blossoms and yielded ripe almonds."

"I guess that settled that."

"Yes. Aaron and Moses continued their leadership. Aaron's Rod was to be kept in the Ark as a miraculous sign against the rebels."

"Okay, I'm following. There are three things in the Ark."

"Right. There is one more detail. In the book of Hebrews we are told that the jar that held the manna was made out of pure gold."

"So?"

"So, the Ten Commandments were given somewhere around 1445 B.C. Solomon's Temple was completed in 959 B.C. When the temple was completed, they brought the Ark of the Covenant to be housed there. I Kings 8:9 informs us that at that time, the Ark contained only the Ten Commandments. Sometime in the roughly four-hundred-eighty-year interim, Aaron's Rod and the Golden Jar of Manna were removed from the Ark of the Covenant. What happened to them remains a biblical mystery."

"Do you think that Methuselah has discovered where they are?"

"I think that's a strong possibility. The next question is, who in the world is King Yamani? And what does it mean? *Thirty degrees northeast of the altar . . . press the king's head.*"

"Would you like some help?" A knowing smile played across Shari's face.

He hesitated for a moment. "Of course. Do you have the answer?"

"No. But I think I know someone who might."

"And who would that be?"

"I'll give you a clue. Stunningly beautiful. Red hair. Sparkling green eyes." Shari seemed to delight in seeing Murphy blush.

"Isis McDonald."

"You've told me that she is one of the leading experts in ancient cultures and languages. The name King Yamani sure sounds ancient to me." Shari was still smiling. She knew that she had got him and she intended to savor the moment.

EIGHT

MURPHY TAPPED HIS FINGERS on the desk as the phone rang. He found himself wanting to hear that familiar voice and thought back to the first time he met Isis. It was in the hospital, as Laura lay close to death. She had entered the room wearing a black coat and looking a little sheepish. She had brought a section of the Bronze Serpent that Moses had lifted in the wilderness. Moses had used the serpent to save the lives of his people, and somehow Isis thought the artifact might help to heal Laura.

After Laura's death he had not allowed himself to think of any other women. Then Isis reappeared. At first he thought that she might be an ice maiden. She seemed preoccupied much of the time, interested only in her work. After her father's death, she had lived her life in hiding. Perhaps in an effort to avoid dealing with her loss, she holed up in her office at the Parchments of Freedom Foundation in Washington, D.C.

Isis's skills as a philologist were astonishing. She could read and write Chaldean, Terammasic, a dozen varieties of Arabic, and ten other distinct Near and Middle Eastern languages. She had been extremely helpful in uncovering clues that had led Murphy to discover a number of ancient biblical artifacts.

His feelings for her had started to grow during the expedition to Ararat. They had spent a lot of time together talking and planning for the trip. They had also spent many memorable moments talking around the campfires on the mountain. His mind began to drift back to his rescue of Isis from the bandits. Ever since, he had begun to feel protective toward her.

He thought about how his battle with Talon on the ark had nearly killed him . . . and how Isis nursed him back to health in Azgadian's secret cave. He feelings for her grew stronger on their search for the Handwriting on the Wall in Babylon. Now he found himself excited at the prospect of speaking with her again.

"Parchments of Freedom Foundation. How may I direct your call?"

"Isis McDonald, please."

Murphy drummed his fingers some more as the hold music played. He found himself smiling and wishing he could be there in person . . . to hold her. For now, he'd have to be content to just hear her voice.

"This is Isis McDonald."

"Isis."

"Michael!" Isis sounded genuinely happy to hear from him. "It is so good to hear your voice."

"Isis, I have really missed you. I'll be flying up to Washington in a couple of weeks. Will you be free?"

"Oh . . . let me see . . . I think I might be able to work it in." She laughed, and he suddenly wished he could arrange the trip sooner.

"I'm glad you have an opening in your busy schedule."

"Michael, how have you been? Overworking yourself as usual?"

"Probably no more than you."

"Have you been staying out of trouble?"

There was a pause. "Well . . ."

"Come on. What's going on?"

"I've gotten a couple of notes from Methuselah."

"Aha," she teased, "so that's why you called. Okay, what is it this time?"

"King Yamani."

"Who?"

Murphy's heart fell. "King Yamani. Have you ever run across his name before in your studies?"

"No. But his name has a definite Middle Eastern sound to it. Would you like me to do some research?"

"That would be great. Anything you can dig up on him would be helpful."

"Sounds mysterious. Are you planning some new expedition?"

"Not this time. I'm just trying to find out who he is."

Isis paused for a second. "Is that a class bell I hear in the background?"

"I'm afraid it is. I'm on in about five minutes."

"I'll try and see if I can run it down for you, Michael. In the meantime, you get some rest."

"I'll try. I can't wait till I see you."

"Me too."

Shari not so subtly wandered over to Murphy's desk. "Well?"

"Well, what?

"Well, how is she doing?" There was a sly grin on her face.

"Are you trying to play matchmaker?"

"The thought never crossed my mind," she protested with feigned innocence. "By the way, Professor, Bob Wagoner called my cell phone while you were talking with Ms. McDonald. He said that he tried to reach you on the other line but it was busy, and he would like you to call him at his office. He sounded a little agitated."

"Thank you, Shari. Say, have you heard anything back from the FBI about that fingerprint I sent them a while ago?"

"The one you took off the signboard in the Reed Gold Mine?"

"That's it. I think it might be Methuselah's. If it is, it will be his first mistake. It might help us find out who he is."

"They haven't responded yet. I'll give them a call for you. They've certainly had enough time."

"You would think so." He shook his head. "Never underestimate government bureaucracy."

Murphy gathered some papers and put them in his briefcase. As he turned to leave, his phone rang. He reached back and answered it.

"Michael Murphy."

"Michael."

"Oh, hi, Bob. I was going to give you a buzz after class. Shari mentioned that you called."

"Could we meet for lunch?"

"Sure. Is there something going on?"

"I think there may be, Michael. I need your advice."

"My class won't be over till noon. Could we shoot for a quarter to one?"

"That'll be great, Michael. Would the Adam's Apple at twelve forty-five be all right? I know you like the food there."

"Best chicken sandwich in town. See you there."

NINE

MURPHY INCREASED HIS PACE as he neared the Memorial Lecture Hall. If there was one thing he hated, it was being late for anything. He didn't like it when other people were late for meetings with him, and he was fanatical about promptness himself. He had traced this idiosyncrasy back to an experience in fifth grade. It was the day a field trip was planned to the Hershey factory. He loved chocolate and was excited about going. He had arrived at school about five minutes late, only to find out that the class had boarded the bus and left without him. It was devastating.

Murphy looked at his watch. *Three minutes.*

The lecture hall was almost full when he entered. Most of the students chatted in small groups. Some were on cell phones and a diligent few were in their seats reviewing their notes from the previous week.

Murphy acknowledged a number of them with a nod on his way down to the front. He placed his briefcase on the desk, took out his laptop, and hooked it into the cable for the PowerPoint projector. Once the program booted up, he clicked on the morning's lecture.

"Okay, gang. Let's take our seats."

He was about to begin, when Clayton Anderson entered, dropping his books loudly as he looked for a seat. Everyone turned to look and then laughed. The class clown had arrived with his usual entrance. He turned up his palms and opened his mouth in mock shock. *What's the problem?* he mouthed as he looked back at them, eliciting another appreciative laugh from his fellow students.

"I'm glad that Mr. Anderson has graced us with his presence . . . we can now begin. Today we will be examining the subject of pagan gods. As you will recall from previous lectures, the worship of various gods was central in ancient cultures. This was an attempt to explain and deal with the forces of nature that everyone experienced. In Babylon, Enlil was the god of the weather and storms. Ea was the god of wisdom. Shamash was the god of the sun and justice. Gaia represented Mother Earth and Kishar was the Father of Earth. Presiding over all of them was Marduk, the national god of the Babylonians."

Murphy clicked on the PowerPoint projector.

"Today we will look at a few more of the pagan gods."

Nebo	**The god of education, literature, writing, and arts**
Baal	**The god of the productive forces of nature**

Asherah	**The favorite goddess of women**
Ra	**The sun god**
Bes	**The grotesque god who watched over childbirth**

"Each god had a number of priests or priestesses who would direct their followers in worship, and dedicated temples where the people would offer sacrifices. Some of the sacrifices would be in the form of grains and fruits. Others would be animals, like cows, sheep, and turtledoves." He paused dramatically. "Occasionally the sacrifices would be human. The god of the Moabites was named Chemosh, and parents would offer their children on the altar to him. The same thing would be done for the Canaanite god Molech. In his temple, they would burn the children as a sacrifice."

Murphy heard groans from the students and many of the women were making faces. A chorus of such comments as "Gross!" and "Sick!" swept through the lecture hall.

Murphy smiled. "If your parents had believed in these gods, maybe some of you wouldn't be here today enjoying my lecture."

That got a good laugh from some of them. Murphy was about to click on the next slide when the door to the lecture hall opened again. As he looked up, the words stuck in his throat.

She was tall, shapely, tan, and athletic-looking. She was wearing a baseball cap and her long blond hair flowed out the back of the hat in a loose ponytail.

All the students turned to see who had entered the room. Murphy noticed them whispering to one another. Whoever the blonde was, she was the type of woman that both men and women noticed.

She seemed older than the college students in the class. Whoever she was, she certainly looked like a professional model.

Murphy forced his thoughts back to his lecture.

"This next slide will indicate how the various gods were pictured to the people."

Nisrosh	**Assyrian god with human body and eagle's head**
Horus	**Human figure with a falcon's head**
Hathor	**Goddess with cow's body and a woman's head**
Set	**Man's body with animal head**
Amon Ra	**Supreme deity of the Egyptians, man's body and head of a hawk**
Dagon	**The Philistine god with the head and hands of a man and the body of a fish**

"Many of the gods on this slide have been pictured on ancient artifacts, like jars and plates. Some were imprinted on coins. Others can be seen in paintings or reliefs on the walls of buildings. And yes, this will be on the test."

Murphy saw a hand go up.

"Dr. Murphy? Is that Dagon god sort of like a male type of mermaid?"

"I guess you could say that, Clayton. The likenesses that have been found show him as a fish from the waist down. The upper body is like a man. He is depicted with a beard and wearing a tall and rounded hat, or crown, of some kind."

"What kind of bait would you use to catch him?"

Murphy smiled.

"Well, personally, Clayton, I'd use wisecracking Preston University students."

Everyone laughed and went "Oooooh."

"He got you, dude!" said one of the students. Murphy gestured for quiet.

"Some of you may recall the story of Samson from the Bible. He gave the Philistines a lot of trouble and they plotted to capture him. His girlfriend Delilah betrayed him and his captors blinded him. Later they took him to the temple area where the priests were offering sacrifices to Dagon. They were celebrating the fact that he had been caught."

Many who knew the story nodded their heads.

"The Philistines then brought forth Samson to make sport of him. While Samson was waiting to go before the people, he asked one of his guards where he was. He was told that he was in the temple area, standing between two pillars. Samson then pushed with his mighty strength against the two pillars, literally bringing the house down. The building collapsed, killing at least three thousand people, including Samson himself, and destroying the house of Dagon."

Murphy continued with the lecture until the bell rang. Immediately the students jumped up and began to leave. As Murphy began to gather his things, he scanned the lecture hall.

The striking blonde had left.

Murphy was still thinking about the blonde when he entered his office. His attention was diverted when Shari spoke up.

"Guess who called while you were in class?"

"It must have been the president of the United States. I told him that I would be in class at that time. He must have forgotten."

"You're quite the comedian today . . . but don't quit your day job. It was Levi Abrams. He said that he's back in Raleigh and would like to get together with you. I told him that I would call him back with a time you both could meet."

"Levi! That's great! After he was shot, I got him to the hospital and then he just disappeared. That was months ago. Did he say anything else?"

"No. He sounded like he was calling from a pay phone. There was lots of noise in the background. He gave me a number to call. He said it was an answering machine and he would pick up the message later."

Murphy consulted his calendar for a good time to meet with Levi.

"By the way, Professor, I also received a call back from your friend at the FBI. He said that they could find no match for the fingerprint you got from the Reed Gold Mine. Methuselah remains a mystery. When you meet with Mr. Abrams, why don't you ask him to see if he can help with the fingerprint? He may have some international contacts unavailable to the FBI."

"Good thinking, Shari. It's worth a try."

TEN

MURPHY PARKED his old, beat-up Dodge in a spot outside the diner. As he approached the door, he smiled to himself. *I'll bet they haven't spent a cent on improvements since they opened thirty-some-odd years ago.*

It was moderately crowded. The décor left much to be desired, but the food was great. He paused for a moment and looked around. Rosanne, the gray-haired waitress, was moving as fast as her heavyset body could. She was in the process of clearing a table when she looked up and saw him standing there.

"Good afternoon, Professor. There's an empty booth in the back. I'll be with you in a moment."

"Thank you, Rosanne."

Murphy made his way to the back, slid across the green vinyl bench, and sat down. There was no need to look at the menu. He was going to order his old standby, a chicken sandwich and a cup of coffee.

After a few minutes, Bob Wagoner entered, wearing tan slacks and a polo shirt that mostly concealed his slight paunch. His white hair was thinning but his face was tanned. He looked more like a golf pro than the pastor of the Preston Community Church.

Murphy waved and Bob nodded as he walked toward the booth. He did not appear to be his usual jovial self. They shook hands and he sat down.

"Sorry I'm late, Michael. I got a phone call just as I was about to leave the church."

"No problem. I haven't been waiting long." Pet peeve or no, Murphy was too concerned to hassle him about his tardiness.

"Good. I . . ." He trailed off as Roseanne waddled up to the table.

"Good afternoon, Reverend. Do you and the professor want your usual?"

Both of the men nodded their heads.

"You got it," said Roseanne as she turned and yelled to the kitchen, "Cheeseburger and chili fries and a chicken sandwich!"

Murphy chuckled. There was no one quite like Rosanne.

But Bob was in no mood to laugh. He got right to the point.

"Michael, I'm glad you could meet with me. I need your advice on something."

"I'm glad to help if I can."

"During the past few weeks I've had a growing concern about some of the people in the congregation. I think someone could be leading them astray."

Murphy's brow furrowed. "What do you mean?"

"Well, have you heard about the tent evangelist that has come to town? His name is Reverend J. B. Sonstad."

"I read something about it in the paper."

"Some of the people from the church have gone to his meetings.

When I've discussed it with them, they've told me disturbing things about what goes on there."

"Disturbing things . . . like what?"

"I was told that he walks around the audience and then all of a sudden stops. Then he'll say, 'What, Lord? Yes, I hear you. You say that someone named George has a kidney problem that needs to be healed.' Then he'll look around the audience and say, 'Is there someone named George that has a kidney problem?' Then George will stand up and go forward to be healed. The whole thing bothers me. I don't think that is how God works. Do you have any thoughts?"

Murphy sat there for a moment before he responded.

"You know, Bob, the Lord works in mysterious ways."

"So you believe in all of this?"

"Not for a minute. It sounds to me like some kind of put-up job. You know the Bible says that in the last days there would be many false prophets. He sounds like he might be one of them."

"Exactly my thoughts, Michael. Which leads me to the next question. Would you go with me to one of his meetings? I'd like to find out firsthand what's going on."

"Sure, Bob. Let's get it straight from the horse's mouth. Besides, I've always been curious about these so-called faith healers anyway."

"The other thing is, I've heard that some of the young people might be experimenting with the occult. You know, things like using a Ouija board and table tipping."

"That's a starting point, Bob. I've seen it before." Murphy had witnessed table tipping when he was in college. Several of the students had gathered around three sides of a small square table. At one end of the table they placed a chair, ostensibly for the spirit who would answer their questions. Then they lightly placed their hands on the table and looked toward the empty chair. They would ask yes-or-no questions. The table would lift off the ground and then come down with a slight noise. One knock on the floor for yes and two knocks for no.

"What happened?" Bob interrupted his recollection.

"It was eerie. All of the answers were correct. I remember that when a new person came into the room they did something different. They asked the new person to pull out his wallet and his Social Security card. They then asked the spirit to tap out the third number on the Social Security card. None of the students around the table knew what the number was. The table lifted off the ground and came down three times. It was the correct number."

"What did you do?"

"I just watched and thought they were all crazy. I thought it was some type of trick. Now that I'm older and have a lot more experience with ancient gods and pagan worship, I think that some of the things are fake and some of them may be real."

"Well, I can't ignore it, Michael. My people are beginning to ask questions and more and more of them are starting to go to the meetings. I would like to nip this in the bud if possible. Faith healing, table tipping . . . it's all very disturbing."

Roseanne came by with coffee and overheard. "Did you say table tipping? At this table, you should tip twenty percent. At least."

Even Bob had to smile a little. Nope, there was nobody quite like Roseanne.

ELEVEN

EUGENE SIMPSON PACKED the last piece of luggage into the trunk. He closed the lid of the ebony Mercedes and used his coat sleeve to polish off his fingerprints. He wanted everything to look perfect. His boss was a real stickler for details and hated to ride in a car that was the least bit dirty.

Simpson had a primo job as driver for Shane Barrington, one of the richest and most powerful men in the world. It paid extremely well and he did not want to lose it. He snapped to attention and opened the door when Barrington came down from his penthouse.

The huge athletic frame of his boss was imposing, to say the least. That, along with his high cheekbones, thin lips, and flint-gray eyes sent chills down Simpson's spine. He knew that his employer did not appreciate small talk and had zero tolerance for weakness of any kind.

"Where would you like to go, Mr. Barrington?"

"To the airport, Eugene."

A half hour later, Simpson parked the Mercedes next to a Gulfstream IV jet owned by Barrington Communications. He unloaded the luggage and put it on board.

"Eugene, I'll be back on Thursday. I don't know what time. Call the airport for our time of arrival."

"Yes, sir. I'll be here."

Simpson let out a long sigh as he watched the Gulfstream taxi down the runway and take off.

The flight to Zurich gave Barrington time to think. Maybe too much time. His mind began to drift back to Stephanie. He hadn't thought that he would miss her as much as he did. He laid his head back on the leather seat, closed his eyes, and tried to sleep. But sleep would not come.

Instead, he kept reliving that day. His assistant Melissa had come running into his office.

"Mr. Barrington, Mr. Barrington, did you see the latest news flash?"

"What are you talking about, Melissa?"

"Look, I'll turn on the news."

"This is Mark Hadley reporting for BNN. I am standing outside of the apartment building of Stephanie Kovacs, a former investigative reporter for Barrington Communications and Network News. Our information is sketchy at this time, but initial reports indicate that her throat was slit early this morning by an unknown assailant."

Barrington gritted his teeth. He knew it was Talon that had killed her, and that the order came from the Seven. His stomach tightened with raw hatred and a longing for revenge. But just how would he be able to do it?

He was jarred back to reality when the plane hit some turbulence.

The Seven were so powerful that Barrington wasn't sure if he could ever avenge Stephanie's death. But he desperately longed to see all seven of them with their throats slit, to watch them die in the same way they had murdered Stephanie.

The twisting mountain road into the Alps was wet with a fresh rain. The gray and overcast sky mirrored Barrington's mood.

Why do they always have to send that creepy, sallow-skinned chauffeur without a tongue to pick me up? Oh well, at least I don't have to listen to some idle chatter.

The closer he got to the castle, the more apprehensive he felt.

Come on, Barrington. Get it together. Never let your opponent know that you are afraid. Remember what General Patton said: Courage is fear holding on a minute longer.

As the limousine rounded one of the turns, Barrington saw the castle in the distance. Ever since he had first laid eyes on the castle, he thought it looked like an evil gargoyle, a cancer growing on the mountainside.

The closer they came, the more he could see of the massive granite walls holding up spiked turrets. Candlelight danced behind several of the ancient leaded windows.

This would be the perfect place to film a horror movie.

The chauffeur opened the giant wrought-iron door of the castle and Barrington crossed the large entry hall. The flickering light of a dozen torches lit up the hallway that led to a large steel door.

As Barrington approached, the door made a hissing sound and opened, allowing him to step into the elevator. Once inside, it hissed shut. The elevator automatically began its descent into the deep recesses of the castle.

Next stop, hell, he thought.

The doors hissed open and Barrington stepped into the medieval gloom that was the meeting place for the Seven. As his eyes adjusted to the dim lights he could see the familiar chair he always sat in. It was ornately carved with gargoyles on the arms. A light shone down upon it.

There's the hot seat.

His eyes shifted to the table that was about twenty feet in front of the chair. It was covered with a bloodred cloth that hung down to the floor. Seated behind it were seven high-backed carved chairs and the silhouettes of the seven members waiting for him.

"It's good to see you are punctual, Mr. Barrington. Last time you were late," said John Bartholomew. "Did you have a pleasant trip?"

Barrington wanted to throw up. None of them cared about his welfare. They were just using him.

"Of course," he said with a forced grin on his face. "Always a pleasure to be with you again."

Two can play at this game, he thought.

"We're glad you feel that way. Today we want to discuss with you a very important project. We want your media organizations to promote an up-and-coming individual by the name of Constantine De La Rosa."

"Who? I've never heard of him before."

"He is a very religious man who will unify the various religions of the world."

That will be the day, Barrington thought.

"Underneath your chair is the first of many announcements to come. We want you to print it in your magazines, talk about it on the radio, and produce special television programs about him. We want to introduce him to the entire world and we feel the best way is through your media companies."

Barrington reached under his chair and picked up a manila envelope containing a news release.

NEWS RELEASE FROM THE BARRINGTON NEWS NETWORK

World Unity Summit

Dr. Constantine De La Rosa, founder of the Religious Harmony Institute based in Rome, Italy, has announced a World Unity Summit. The Unity Summit is planned for the first week of September in Rome. This summit is designed for everyone interested in world peace and religious harmony. It is hoped that religious and political leaders from around the world will attend this historic conference.

Dr. De La Rosa has indicated that there will be a number of goals that the World Unity Summit hopes to achieve.

- The celebration of religious unity in the midst of diversity—with the understanding that all religions are seeking to reach out to God and to assist their fellow man
- The creation of a culture of peace and security for all peoples of the planet
- The expression of divine love for every human being
- The ending of religion-motivated violence
- The striving to heal the earth environmentally
- The honoring and encouragement of cultural differences—and the experiencing of the richness received from various values and beliefs of every nation
- The discouraging of absolutism and the encouraging of religious tolerance for all sects, cults, and methods of expressing worship
- The discouraging of groups who stress discrimination with regard to sexual preferences, race, or age

- The establishment of seminars and training in conflict resolution and negotiation to help end religious intolerance

- The creation of discussion groups related to matters of human reproduction and the overcrowding of the earth

- The training of methods to uncover the positive aspects of the human potential of mankind—the celebration of man's ability to achieve

- The planning of methods to reduce poverty, starvation, and health care needs of every nation

Dr. De La Rosa has also announced that the Religious Harmony Institute will be establishing Harmony Centers on every continent. Also planned are Youth Harmony Programs for children eighteen years of age and younger. Along with the Harmony Centers, the University of Unity will begin operation within a year. This school is intended to attract students from around the globe who want to dedicate their lives to world unity.

Dr. De La Rosa is also suggesting that each nation adopt a new national holiday. It will be called World Unity Day. A second holiday to consider would be World Year of Thanksgiving. For further information, please contact the Religious Harmony Institute at the following address: 18 Unity Boulevard, Rome, Italy, or visit our website at *www.religiousharmony.com*.

Barrington read the article and then looked at the Seven.

"Come on! You don't really believe all this, do you?"

Even at twenty feet away, Barrington could see the angry spark in the eyes of Sir William Merton. His voice was low and guttural and definitely unfriendly.

"Mr. Barrington, we are not asking for your opinion. The Unity Summit will take place. And you will do exactly as we say. Do you understand?"

Barrington understood but he didn't like it. He didn't like anyone telling him what he could or couldn't do.

"And if I don't?"

Jakoba Werner began to laugh, a truly horrible sound.

"Let me ask you a simple question, Mr. Barrington. Do you wish to live?"

So there it was. Do or die. That was his choice.

Discretion is the better part of valor, he thought. *I need to get out of here alive.*

"As you wish."

"That is a very, very wise decision," responded Ganesh Shesha.

"Is there anything else?" At this point, Barrington was more than eager to part company.

"That's all, Mr. Barrington. We will expect a massive promotional campaign within the next month."

Barrington rose from the chair, entered the elevator, and left without a word. The only sound was the gentle hiss of the elevator door.

Señor Mendez turned to the group. "I do not like his attitude. I think he is a dangerous man. Are you sure we can trust him?"

"He will do what we ask, or he will be eliminated like the others," responded Bartholomew. "Besides, he has gotten used to our money and he doesn't want to give that up."

"I agree with Señor Mendes," said Viorica Enesco. "He almost said no to us here today."

Bartholomew cautioned, "We need him for the time being, to promote De La Rosa. The public holds his news network in high regard, and any reports coming from them will be taken seriously. So, we will use him as long as he serves our purpose."

The other members nodded begrudgingly. Impertinent or not, Barrington was a valuable asset. And if he became too disobedient? Well, there were ways of dealing with that if and when the time arose.

TWELVE

MURPHY ENTERED the Out West Steak House at 6:00 P.M. He was looking around for Levi when the hostess came up.

"May I help you, sir? Would you like a table?"

"Yes, a table for two. I'm meeting a friend."

"Your name?"

"Murphy."

As she jotted his name down on the wait list, Murphy saw Abrams waving from the other side of the restaurant.

"Excuse me. I see that my friend has already arrived."

The hostess smiled and nodded and proceeded to cross off his name from her list.

As Murphy approached the table, the six-foot-five Israeli greeted him with a big grin and a warm embrace. "It's great to see you, Michael," he said as they sat down.

"You look a lot better than the last time I saw you, Levi." He tapped his temple. "There's hardly any scar at all from the bullet."

"No, I was very fortunate. They told me later that you saved my life."

"You know what that means? According to Asian tradition, you now become my servant for the rest of your life."

They both laughed.

"Michael, help me out. I have no memory of what happened in the warehouse after I was shot. All I remember is waking up in the hospital at Et Taiyiba."

Murphy's mind quickly flashed back.

"Well, we were in the warehouse looking for Talon and his men. They started firing at us with handguns. Then one of Talon's goons fired an RPG at the warehouse from a building across the street. The front of the building went up in flames, then you caught a bullet and it was lights out."

"The last thing I remember was the fire."

"I was in a different aisle, behind some boxes, pinned down by their gunfire. Uri had crawled up to you and was checking for a pulse when a second RPG went off behind Uri. His body protected you from the blast. He was killed instantly."

Murphy paused as an expression of guilt and sadness crossed Levi's face. This was his first true glimpse into the events of that day.

"He was a good friend."

Murphy nodded. "There was nothing I could do for Uri. You were bloody but still breathing. By that time, the building was engulfed in flames. Talon and his men were gone, having taken us all for dead."

Levi was listening intently, his eyes focused on Murphy.

"I dragged you over to where they had been firing from and found an escape tunnel. I pulled you into it, looped our belts together to create a rudimentary harness, and used it to slide you through the tunnel."

"That must have been no easy task."

"You're no lightweight," Murphy concurred. "Then there was an enormous explosion."

"Explosion?"

"Yes. They must have wired the building to destroy any evidence or to discourage any pursuers. It collapsed part of the tunnel and pinned us both for a period of time. I was lucky to be able to dig us both out."

"Were you injured?"

"Not badly. The claustrophobia was the worst part. The darkness, the dust . . . I couldn't see, couldn't breathe. I had no idea if the other end of the tunnel had collapsed, trapping us in between. All I could think about was getting you out." That wasn't quite true. Murphy had also realized at that moment how much he wanted to see Isis again. Levi looked at him expectantly and he continued. "After several hours we emerged into fresh air. Your bleeding had slowed, although you didn't look so hot." Murphy laughed. "I guess I wasn't such a pretty sight either."

"Where did the tunnel lead?"

"We emerged inside a building down the street. I looked out the window, back at the warehouse. It was a blackened, smoldering heap. Firefighters from Et Taiyiba were still in the street and were dousing hot spots with water. I couldn't see any of the other members of your party. Uri was dead, and Judah, Gabrielle, and Isaac were gone. I got the firefighters to call for an ambulance and I rode along with you to the hospital."

"I don't remember any of this."

"At the hospital, they patched up some of my scrapes. The police came and started questioning me. That didn't last long. Some Mossad agents took me away to another building and questioned me for a long time before letting me go. The next day I returned to the hospital to see how you were, but you were already gone, and no one had any records that you had ever been there. I felt like I was in a spy movie."

"You're not far off. They took me to a special hospital that very few people in Israel know about. Once I recovered, I was sent to a safe house in South America, where I remained out of circulation for about sixty days until things quieted down. I just got back."

"What about Judah, Gabrielle, and Isaac? What happened to them?"

Levi smiled. "If I told you, I'd have to kill you."

"That's some gratitude for you," Murphy said with a smirk. He could tell that he was getting into issues that Levi would not reveal. He let the matter drop.

Toward the end of dinner the conversation took another direction.

"Levi, I have another matter I could use your help on."

Abrams smiled. "Well, since I'm your slave forever, how can I refuse?"

"I may have a lead on Methuselah. I found a fingerprint that might belong to him. I was wondering if you could check it out for me."

"What about your friends at the FBI?"

"Actually, they have looked at it and came up with zilch."

"What makes you think that I can?"

"Well, Levi, you have friends in high places. I just thought that it might be worth a try."

"Sure, send it to me. We have access to lots of fingerprints. No guarantees, though."

"I understand . . . but he's got to make a slip someday."

THIRTEEN

THE FLASHLIGHT BEAM hovered around the large entry hall of the Parchments of Freedom Foundation. The light danced over the reception desk . . . swept to the elevators . . . then glided across the floor to the front doors.

It was 2:30 A.M. when Greg Graham rattled the front doors. They were locked. He couldn't remember how many times over the years he had checked those doors on his rounds.

It must be in the thousands, the security guard thought. *All in a night's work.*

Then he heard something.

He listened intently to the hushed voices in the distance. He turned off his flashlight, put his hand on his automatic, and quietly began to move in the direction of the voices.

Why would someone be in the Hall of Ancient Artifacts? As he drew closer, his heart started to race. Even though he had been a guard for many years, he'd never had occasion to use his gun. He saw the beam of a flashlight shining on one of the cases in the center of the room, and the dark silhouettes of two men standing in front of the case.

Greg took a deep breath and turned on his flashlight.

"Hold it right there! One move and I'll shoot!"

"What in the world? Greg, get ahold of yourself!"

The men turned around and glared at him, and he could now make out the security guard insignias on their chests. It was Tom Meier and John Drake.

"And get that light out of our faces," said John.

"What are you guys doing down here? You're supposed to be checking the upper floors."

"We got through early and thought we would come down and see how you were getting along," Tom said.

"What were you looking at?"

John turned his light back toward the case. "Come over here and see for yourself."

Greg directed his flashlight beam into the case with John's.

"I can tell that it's bronze, but what is it?" he said.

"It's the tail section of a bronze snake," John replied. "It's supposed to be part of the snake that Moses lifted up in the wilderness. You know, real old."

"How do you know all that?" Greg asked.

"Ah, I overheard some of the curators talking."

"What happened to the rest of the snake?"

"One of the curators said that the middle section was in the museum at the American University in Cairo, Egypt. The head section, he said, was lost somewhere in the Pyramid of the Winds . . . wherever that is."

"Well, you guys can stand here and look at the rear end of a snake, if that turns you on," Tom said. "I'm going to step outside for a smoke."

Tom had been working for the Parchments of Freedom Foundation for less than a year and he was ready to move on. Walking around looking at old jars of clay, mummies, decaying pieces of paper, and broken stone pillars was not his idea of fun—especially at night, when he could be home in bed or out partying somewhere.

He lit his cigarette and took a deep drag. The half-full moon shone brightly in the clear night. The parking lot was empty except for four cars. He recognized his old, beat-up Volkswagen, John's Toyota, and Greg's Ford pickup. But it was the black SUV that caught his attention. Whose vehicle was that?

Hmm. I'd better check that out.

He turned on his flashlight and shined it on the vehicle. It looked empty. He checked the doors. They were locked. Through the back windows, he saw what looked like two metal cages of some kind.

Strange.

He took out a pad and a pen and wrote down the license number.

I'll check it out, just in case. I'm sure that Greg will want to know about it.

He started back across the parking lot and tossed his cigarette on the asphalt. He crushed it with the sole of his right foot.

He heard a soft whistling and looked around. Nobody there. Maybe he'd just imagined it.

He had taken about five steps back toward the front doors when he heard a strange flapping noise next to his right ear.

It was the last sound he ever heard.

Greg and John were beginning to wonder what had happened to Tom, when they heard his footsteps coming toward them. He was shining the flashlight into their eyes.

"That was a long cigarette break," said John. "What did you do, smoke a whole pack?"

"Hey . . . get that light out of our eyes," Greg snapped.

"I'll be glad to," came the reply.

Greg hesitated. *That wasn't Tom's voice.* Instinctively he reached for his gun, but too late, as the knife slit his throat from ear to ear.

John fumbled for his gun, but as he removed it from the holster, the man fired off a side kick that crushed his fingers. He cried out and the gun clattered to the floor.

John staggered sideways, then rushed forward with a front kick that caught the stranger in the chest and knocked him back. He pressed his advantage, reaching for the nightstick in his belt with his left hand. In a moment, it was out and swinging.

The man dodged the blow effortlessly, planting a fist into the side of John's neck. He went down to his knees, dazed, and felt the stranger's hands on his head. There was a quick jerk, followed by a snapping sound . . . and then all was silent.

Murphy reached for his cell phone.

"Murphy here."

"Michael. I'm glad I caught you. Where are you?" It was Isis, and her voice was trembling.

"I'm in the car on the way to school. What's wrong?"

"Something terrible has happened at the Foundation. There was a break-in last night and three of the night watchmen were murdered."

"What?"

"One was killed in the parking lot. It was terrible. His throat and neck had been ripped to pieces. The coroner said it looked like some animal had done it. He even found some feathers around the body."

"Talon."

"What?"

"It sounds like the work of Talon. He uses his pet falcons to do his dirty work for him. That's where he got his name."

"The two guards inside were also dead. One had his throat slit and the other had a broken neck."

"Is there anything missing?"

"Yes, there is. The tail section of the Bronze Serpent of Moses. The one we found in the clay amphora jar, with the message scratched on it from Dakkuri."

Dakkuri, thought Murphy. *The high priest in Nebuchadnezzar's court.*

"Why do you think he took it?" Isis asked.

"I don't know. Maybe he wants to return it to the cult we discovered in the sewers below the city of Tar-Qasir. They weren't too happy when we took the middle portion of the snake. . . . Isis, were you injured in any way?"

"No. I'm just scared to know that Talon was that close to me again."

Murphy's heart hurt to think that Talon could kill Isis like he did Laura. He knew that would be unbearable.

"Isis, I want you to promise me something. Don't go out alone. Keep your cell phone with you at all times. And if you don't have a weapon, get one, and bring it with you everywhere you go."

"Oh, Michael. You really think Talon might come after me?"

"I hope not. But I don't want you to take any chances. You hear me?"

She promised to be careful, but it did little to quell the uneasy feeling in Murphy's gut.

FOURTEEN

In a field near the town of Ebenezer, 1083 B.C.

THE DIN OF SWORDS *and spears beating against metal shields swelled to a deafening pitch. It was augmented by men stomping their feet up and down, shaking the dusty ground. Soon it was accompanied by the shouts and chants of thousands of soldiers. The battle cry of men readying themselves for war echoed throughout the valley.*

General Abiezer clenched his jaw and appraised the men. The lives of these soldiers were in his hands. He knew that all of Israel was looking to him for leadership . . . and for victory.

The soldiers shook with anticipation, their eyes glued on the gray horse and rider on the hill holding the battle flag high above his head. Emotions were at a fever pitch and adrenaline began to flow. Fear gripped their hearts and each man wondered if he would be alive to see the new morning. The moment of battle was close at hand. They awaited only his signal.

This was not the first time the Israelites had to face their enemies, the Philistines. They had been engaged in many conflicts during the past three hundred years, and thousands of countrymen had died in those battles. They could trace their encounters with the Philistines all the way back to their ancestors Abraham and Isaac.

Bazluth knelt down to tighten his war sandals. He looked up at his brother Neziah.

"Are you afraid?

Neziah scowled down at him, but then his expression softened.

"Of course. To fear death is natural. But courage comes when you don't run from your fears, but face them directly. You must not think about the pain of death, little brother. You must keep your thoughts on protecting our families and our nation."

"But I have never fought in a battle before like you have."

"Then focus your thoughts on all that I have taught you. Think about how to best swing your sword and block with your shield. Take courage and think about our enemy's death . . . not yours."

"I know, but I—"

"Enough of that talk! Stay close by my side and we will fight together."

Neziah helped Bazluth to his feet and embraced him.

It did not take long for the rumbling noise of the Israelite warriors to reach the ears of the Philistines. They had been encamped near the city fortress of Aphek for nearly a week, preparing for battle. Their deep hatred for the people of Israel was fueled by, the desire for revenge. The anticipation of the seized fortunes and the capture of slaves—especially the beautiful women from the tribe of Benjamin—those were just the spoils of war.

Commander Jotham of the Philistine army lowered his arm and the sound of trumpets rang out throughout their ranks, followed by the battle cry of the Philistine warriors. They surged forward, pounding their shields with swords and spears in like manner as the Israelites.

At the sound of the Philistine trumpets, the rider on the gray horse lowered the battle flag. An enormous yell went up from the Israelites and they moved toward their enemies.

The archers from both sides of the conflict readied their weapons. Moments later, arrows sailed into the sky, answered by screams from both the Israelites and Philistines as the arrows found their marks. However, their raised shields protected most of the warriors.

The warriors yelled at the top of their voices as they charged into the fray like madmen, their swords and spears held high. It was now a matter of kill or be killed . . . and no one wanted to die.

As warriors from both sides merged, screams of agony could be heard everywhere. Wounded men desperately tried to stop the flow of blood from their limbs or torsos. The dust swelled, making it difficult to see or breathe. Soldiers stumbled over the bodies on the ground and slipped in the blood. It was almost impossible io tell one soldier from another as they butchered one another.

The initial, brutal foray lasted for almost an hour. Then the sound of the withdrawal trumpets began to blast. Both sides retreated to opposite ends of the valley to rest, regroup, and reevaluate battle strategies. It was also a time for counting losses and assisting the wounded back to camp.

General Abiezer was in his tent with his advisors when the messenger brought word from the battlefield. "Sir, the Philistines have killed about four thousand of our Israelite warriors. There are about another two thousand wounded. It is estimated that we killed only three hundred of their soldiers."

Abiezer was speechless. All of his advisors dropped their heads in despair. There was a long silence. Captain Gaddiel was the first to speak.

"Why has the Lord allowed us to be defeated before these Philistine dogs today? Let us bring the Ark of the Covenant of the Lord to the battlefield. It will protect us and give us victory." Gaddiel thought that the sight of the Ark of God would encourage the disheartened soldiers.

The advisors in the room nodded their heads in agreement.

Gaddiel continued, "The Ark of the Covenant is under the care of Hophni and Phinehas, the sons of Eli the priest. They are in Shiloh. It would not take long to get the Ark and bring it here." He nearly choked on his own words. He had heard too much about the sordid lives of Hophni and Phinehas.

Commander Hadoram joined in. "The Ark is the home of the Lord of Hosts. He dwells between the two cherubim on the top. If the Ark comes among us, it may protect us from the hand of our enemies."

General Abiezer gave a questioning look at all of his advisors. He was not yet convinced. He issued a silent prayer. "Oh, God, I need your help in this decision. We must win the battle tomorrow."

One by one, all of the advisors voiced their agreement with Commander Hadoram, until Abiezer finally acquiesced to their suggestion. A new sense of courage and hope arose in their hearts.

Abiezer spoke: "Captain Gaddiel, I want you to take a group of soldiers with you to Shiloh. Bring back the Ark of the Covenant, along with Hophni and Phinehas. I want them to pass through the warriors and bless them as they go out to battle. I am confident that the Lord will give us a great victory."

Gaddiel bowed and left the tent. He quickly gathered fifty of his elite soldiers.

"Men, we have an urgent mission. We must travel through the day and into the night to Shiloh. Our orders are to bring back the Ark of the Covenant and the sons of Levi, the high priest."

The men looked surprised, but Gaddiel pressed on. "We have about eighteen hours to do this. We must return in time for tomorrow's battle. Our brother soldiers are depending on us. We cannot again suffer so great a loss as we did today."

This resonated with the men. They stood ready to do whatever was necessary.

Gaddiel swelled with pride. With the Ark at their side, how could they fail?

FIFTEEN

MURPHY HAD GROWN to adore his course in biblical archaeology. His students seemed alert and eager to learn. Word of mouth had made the class size increase each year. Everyone seemed to enjoy the lectures, except the dean of the Arts and Science faculty, Archer Fallworth. Maybe he was jealous because his classes seemed to diminish in size. Or, maybe it was the fact that he just didn't like Christians. He often said that the Bible was for "bubbleheads." And he referred to any athletes who shared their faith as "Jocks for Jesus." Murphy just found him boring. Anyone who published a paper on "Button Materials of the Eighteenth-Century Georgia Plantations" needed to get a life.

Murphy entered the lecture hall and joked with a number of

students before he set up his PowerPoint presentation. He flashed the lights once and everyone got the message to sit down and stop talking.

"Good morning. In our last class we spent some time looking at various pagan gods."

He had barely gotten started when the back door opened and in stepped the mysterious blonde beauty he had seen in his last class session. This time, her hair was down and a pair of sunglasses sat on the top of her head. She did not carry a purse or notebook. She found a seat and looked up and smiled. Murphy could see some of the men in the back row nudging one another and pointing at her. It was everything he could do to keep his train of thought.

"The, uh, the belief in these gods strongly influenced the daily actions of the people, as evidenced not only by their sacrifices of crops, animals, and humans, but also by their art. Many ancient civilizations illustrated their gods in physical form by the making of idols, paintings, and reliefs on buildings, pottery, and coins. This was also true of their belief in angels. They would often place characterizations of angels on artifacts. The Ark of the Covenant is a classic example of this. On the top of the Ark there were two angels with their wings spread protectively above the chamber that held the Ten Commandments."

A voice chimed in. "Don't forget that some countries use angels on television programs to increase their television ratings."

The class laughed and Murphy noticed the blonde smiling.

"That's a good example of the belief in the afterlife, Clayton. There are basically two types of angels: good angels and evil angels. Both of those types are displayed in television programs. Under the category of good angels they go by the following biblical names."

Murphy clicked on a slide.

GOOD ANGELS

- **Announcing Angel—his name is Gabriel**
- **Archangel—God's lead angel, named Michael**
- **Celestial or Heavenly Beings—a general title**
- **Cherub or Cherubim—chiefly guardians of God's Throne**
- **Heavenly Host—a general title for good angels**
- **Seraph or Seraphim—angels who lead Heaven in worship of God**
- **Thrones, Dominations, Principalities—ranking divisions**

"The two angels on the top of the Ark of the Covenant were called cherubim. In a number of passages in the Bible, angels are seen taking on a human form and conversing with men and women. This concept is also the basis for many modern television programs and movies."

Murphy clicked on another slide.

GOOD ANGELS

- **Angels punish God's enemies.**
- **Angels execute God's will among men.**
- **Angels do not get married to each other.**
- **Angels have been revealed in bodily form.**
- **Angels have great wisdom and strength.**
- **Angels guide the affairs of nations.**
- **There are a great number of angels.**
- **Angels seem to protect followers of God.**

"You will notice on the second-to-last point that there are a great number of angels. That concept comes from several different passages. One is found in Revelation where it states:

Then I looked and heard the voice of many angels, numbering thousands upon thousands, and ten thousand times ten thousand. They encircled the throne and the living creatures and the elders.

"The last point suggests that angels protect the followers of God. This comes from the book of Psalms where it says, 'The angel of the Lord encamps around those who fear Him, and He delivers them.' "

As Murphy continued he became aware that the striking blonde in the back row seemed to have her eyes riveted on him. On one hand it was exciting and on the other hand a little unnerving. He felt like he was having one of those Shirley MacLaine out-of-body experiences, giving a lecture and at the same time thinking about the beauty in the back of the room.

Murphy expounded upon good angels and how they tied in with many biblical artifacts that had been found. At one point he reached down to advance to the next slide. As his eyes came back up to the students, he saw the blonde leaving the lecture hall and felt the sting of disappointment.

Who was she?

He glanced at the clock on the wall and realized that the bell would soon ring.

"You may need all the help you can get from angels this next week," he said with a grin. "On Tuesday, you will be tested on the material we have gone over during the last three weeks."

There was an audible groan from the class, followed by the ringing of the bell.

He raised his voice a little. "After the test, we will begin to look at the influence of evil angels in various cultures."

As the class filed out, Murphy found his thoughts dwelling upon the mysterious blonde.

SIXTEEN

IT WAS MIDAFTERNOON when Murphy decided to get an ice-cold strawberry lemonade at the Student Center. He sat down at a table that was a good distance from the crowds of students. Sometimes it was good to just be alone and relax.

He was sipping the lemonade when he heard a familiar but unpleasant nasal-tone voice behind him.

"Just what kind of poppycock are you teaching now, Murphy?"

Murphy turned to look into the pallid face of Archer Fallworth, dean of the Arts and Science faculty. He was as tall as Murphy but much thinner and looked like a walking mummy. *He could use a little sun*, thought Murphy. *But then, vampires didn't like to go out in the daylight.*

"'Poppycock.' That's a pretty big word for you, Archer. Do you know how to spell it too?"

Fallworth did not acknowledge the comment but went right on talking. "I understand that you're now teaching about angels in your class. Next thing you'll be teaching is that Satan is alive."

"That's a good idea, Archer. Thank you. I'll do that in my next lecture." Murphy wasn't trying to egg him on, just to knock him off his high horse. But he couldn't. Fallworth was too good of a cowboy to dismount.

"I'm getting tired of you always trying to promote some type of Christian viewpoint in your classroom."

"Why is that, Archer? Have you given up on freedom of speech for everyone except you and those who think like you? It's only your atheistic views that must be accepted and not those of someone who believes in a Creator? Did you hear about the dial-a-prayer for atheists? You dial a number and no one answers. I was going to be an atheist, Archer, but I gave it up. They don't have any holidays."

"I'm not an atheist!"

"What exactly are you, Archer?"

"I'm . . . mmmm . . . I'm more of an agnostic."

"So you'd rather submit to a life of ignorance and uncertainty than accept the existence of a higher power? Seems pretty lame to me. . . ."

Fallworth's usually ashen face was now turning red.

"Murphy, your kind of teaching has to end."

"I get it, Archer. You can have a course in Greek Mythology, or lectures on the beauties of being a Wicca witch with white magic, or have health classes where you teach yoga and transcendental meditation, but the world will come to an end if the name of God or the Bible is mentioned. Have you forgotten that Harvard, Yale, Cambridge, Princeton, and many other universities were originally started as theological institutions?"

"They are not that today!"

"And that's not something to be proud of, Archer. Look at what they have produced. People like you. People who talk about openness, acceptance, and intellectual interaction of ideas . . . but attempt to squelch it at every possible turn when it doesn't agree with their point of view."

"I'm going to do everything in my power to shut down your stupid class on biblical archaeology. Do you hear me?"

"You're shouting . . . everyone in here can hear you. But you were the one who mentioned you were an agnostic. Do you know why atheists and agnostics cannot find God? They can't find Him for the same reason a thief cannot find a policeman. They don't want to. You're doing better than Satan himself. At least he believes there is a God."

Fallworth turned in a huff and walked off.

Murphy let out a big sigh. *I'm getting so tired of all of his flak.*

He did not like confrontation but met it head-on when it came. He would use pointed humor to throw his opponent off balance, and then support his argument with a more serious line of reasoning. He sat there, staring at the magnolia trees in the distance, trying to process what just had happened.

Way to go, Archer. You certainly know how to ruin a perfectly good strawberry lemonade.

"What was *that* all about?"

Murphy's thoughts were interrupted by a soft and feminine voice behind him.

He turned and was somewhat startled to look into the deep blue eyes of the mystery woman who had been attending his lectures. Her warm smile caught him a little off guard.

"Forgive me. Let me introduce myself. I'm Summer Van Doren."

She reached out her hand. Murphy stood up and shook it.

"I'm Michael Murphy." He couldn't believe how firm a handshake she had. *She must work out.* "Please, sit. Is there something I can get you?"

"No, thank you. I have a class starting in a few minutes."

"Did you recently enroll at Preston?"

Summer laughed. "Thank you for the compliment. No, I'm the new women's volleyball coach. I started a couple of weeks ago."

"I saw you in the Memorial Lecture Hall."

"Yes, I was just trying to get oriented to the campus and some of the classes. The title biblical archaeology caught my attention. I thought I would drop in and see what it was all about."

Mystery solved, thought Murphy. He felt complimented by the fact that she had shown up twice.

"Please forgive me, but I couldn't help hearing part of the conversation between you and the other professor. Who is he?"

"That's Archer Fallworth. He's dean of the Arts and Science faculty. He sort of oversees my area of study."

"It doesn't sound like he's too happy with your class."

Murphy cocked his head back and laughed.

"That's putting it mildly. He doesn't like anything that has to do with Christianity. He's very outspoken against it."

"That's good to know. I'm a Christian too."

Murphy perked up. "Really. Have you found a local church you would like to attend yet?"

"I think so. I've gone to the Preston Community Church a couple of times."

"That's where I attend," said Murphy in surprise.

"I know. I've seen you there. Pastor Wagoner seems to be a very good speaker."

"Yes, he is. He's also a good friend."

Summer looked at her watch.

"Excuse me, but I have to go. I don't want to be late for my class. It was nice to meet you, Professor Murphy." She rose to leave and Murphy stood up.

"Call me Michael."

"All right. It was nice to meet you, Michael."

Murphy watched her as she walked away, and then downed the rest of his lemonade. Somehow, all the ice had melted.

SEVENTEEN

THE TRAFFIC BECAME extremely heavy the closer Murphy and Wagoner came to the large tent. Men with orange vests were directing cars to turn into a field that had become a temporary parking lot. People could be seen walking toward the site of J. B. Sonstad's Faith in God Crusade. They parked and joined the hundreds who were headed toward the entrance.

Along the way, signs were placed for everyone to see.

COME EVERYONE WHO WANTS
THEIR FAITH STRENGTHENED.

GOD WANTS YOU TO BE WELL—
THE DEVIL WANTS YOU TO BE SICK.

GOD HAS ONLY GOOD PLANNED FOR YOUR LIFE.

GOD WANTS TO BANISH POVERTY—
HE WILL MAKE YOU PROSPEROUS.

TURN YOUR ENEMIES INTO FRIENDS.

ENJOY EMOTIONAL HEALTH AND WELL-BEING.

WITH GOD NOTHING SHALL BE IMPOSSIBLE—
ONLY BELIEVE!

Murphy turned to Wagoner as they walked along.

"Well, Bob, I can see why some of the people of your church are coming to these meetings. Those are some pretty big claims."

"I know, Michael. Everything is *me* focused. It's what can God do for me? How can God help me? It has a strong appeal, especially if you are in ill health, need more money, or want everyone in the world to love you."

"That sounds better than winning the lottery."

"That would be funny if it weren't so tragic. There are many people around the world who are living in desperate conditions. There are wars, famines, crippling diseases, and political unrest. In some countries, tribes of people are slaying other tribes of people. Is it because the believers don't have enough faith? I don't think that Sonstad's message is completely legitimate."

"Well, Bob, you know that statement *Error always rides the back of truth*. The truth is, God does care for people but He hasn't always given them an escape route or a free pass on trouble. Think of the Christians eaten by lions in the Roman arenas."

As they approached the tent, they could see a number of large, brand-new semi trucks painted with the words: J. B. SONSTAD—FAITH IN GOD CRUSADE. One even had its own generator setup. Another had antennas and aerials placed on the roof.

"Look, Bob, they have their own television recording and broadcasting truck. I'll bet that cost a pretty penny."

"Yes, they broadcast his various crusades on one of the TV networks. He seems to have the ability to draw large crowds. And today we'll be part of the crowd."

The tent, large enough to hold at least five thousand people, was absolutely filled to capacity. Rousing organ music played as people found their seats. Large television monitors were placed at various locations for those who were quite a distance from the platform. Murphy noticed a special section that seemed to be reserved for those in wheelchairs and those with crutches or canes.

A lively song leader began to engage the crowd in singing, which went on for at least a half hour. Most of the time, the people were on their feet swaying back and forth with their arms in the air. They sang choruses that repeated themselves over and over with an almost mesmerizing effect.

The people were asked to sit down and the music changed. Stage lights were turned on and smoke machines cranked up. With great fanfare, J. B. Sonstad made his entrance. Everyone was on their feet, yelling and clapping.

"It reminds me of the entrance of one of those wrestlers in the World Wrestling Federation," said Murphy as Wagoner nodded. "And this is just as phony."

Sonstad was wearing a bright white suit, in contrast with his tanned complexion, jet-black hair, and deep blue eyes. He raised his hands and the people grew silent. He had on a microphone that hung over his ear and was almost invisible as it came alongside his face.

For the first thirty minutes, his message sounded quite common. It was similar to almost any minister with a radio program or a pastor in a local church. It was filled with quotations from the Bible. He talked about God and Jesus and living a godly life. The audience became involved, laughing at his illustrations, clapping and praising God when he made a point, and responding with the occasional "Amen!" and "Preach it, brother."

Then there was a transition. As he kept on speaking, the organ music started to play. The volume seemed to increase as he made various points. The audience was beginning to get worked up emotionally. Sonstad began to raise his voice and shout.

"Are you tired of being sick? Do you want to be healed?"

The audience cheered and clapped in approval.

"Do you want to get the bill collectors off your back and have extra money to spend?"

Again the crowd hooted and yelled.

"God wants to protect you from trouble. He has sent His angels to protect you. You have all heard about Michael the archangel and Gabriel the announcing angel, but there are other special angels that will minister to your needs. There are the angels of protection and guidance . . . and also the angels of success and energy. You may need the angels of happiness and good times to bring you joy and satisfaction. Or you may be feeling very lonely tonight. God has the angels of love, romance, and good relationships to encourage you and satisfy your heart's longings. Or you may be saying I need wisdom and knowledge as how to improve my financial condition. God has angels that will help you to become prosperous."

The crowd was on its feet again, yelling and clapping and dancing up and down.

Murphy had to raise his voice for Wagoner to hear him.

"It's a shame that he's distorting the truth about angels."

As Murphy looked around, he could see the men behind the television cameras hard at work. He noticed that some of Sonstad's other workers were getting the disabled people organized to go up on the platform.

Soon Sonstad began to talk of God as a God of miracles. He shared one story after another with the crowd, preparing them for the healing service that would soon follow.

"God is going to do great miracles here in Raleigh tonight like he did last week in Greensboro. Why, we had a man come into the service who had a terrible problem with cavities in his teeth. Some kind of disease had affected him. He came to the service and was healed. His teeth were transformed. Just to confirm it, he went to his dentist the next day. The dentist was shocked as he looked into his mouth and saw that all the cavities in his teeth had been filled with gold. The dentist told the man that he had never seen gold as pure as this in his entire life. He asked the man who put the gold into his teeth. The man shared with him that he had been healed, and his cavities filled by God. Do you know why the dentist had never seen gold like that before? Because it came from the heavenly city—where the streets are paved with gold."

The crowd yelled uncontrollably. Murphy leaned over to Wagoner. "Why didn't God just put the enamel back in his teeth?"

"The book of Revelation tells us that the gold from the heavenly city was as pure as glass," added Wagoner. "I'll bet the dentist hadn't ever seen that before. How would he recognize it?"

It wasn't long before some in the crowd seemed to get really worked up, leaving their seats and running up and down the aisles. They then began to run toward the back and outside around the tent.

Just out of curiosity, Murphy decided to get up and follow them to see where they went. Wagoner shot Murphy a questioning look as he stepped into the aisle. Murphy gave him the sign that it was okay and that he would return.

Outside the tent, Murphy saw the people disappearing around the side of the tent. Those inside could hear the excited shouts as they ran around the tent and back inside.

Murphy started to go back inside but hesitated. He saw a great number of tables that had been set up while everyone was in the tent. There was something on the tables covered with white cloths.

He walked to one of the tables and lifted the cloth. Underneath was a cash register, credit card machine, T-shirts, sweatshirts, and various literature.

It looks like they plan to make a killing.

As he started back into the tent, two bulky men stopped him.

"Don't do that again!"

Murphy was caught off guard.

"Do what?" he replied.

"You know what. Don't follow the people anymore. And keep your hands off the tables."

Murphy rejoined Wagoner, who was intently watching how Sonstad kept working the crowd up. Wagoner looked relieved when he saw Murphy come back.

Sonstad quieted the people and walked around the stage, looking up in the air and nodding his head up and down. It seemed like he was listening to a conversation with an unseen person.

"Yes, Lord. I am listening." Sonstad began to speak to the sky. "You want to heal someone today. Thank you, Lord. That's wonderful. You say that the man you want to heal is named Clyde . . . and that he has a kidney problem. I hear you, Lord."

The people in the audience were spellbound, watching him seemingly talk to God.

"You want to heal this man named Clyde tonight if only he will exercise his faith in You."

Then Sonstad turned to the audience and looked at them.

"Is there anyone in the audience named Clyde that has a kidney problem?"

One man stood to his feet waving his arms and tears began to flow from his eyes.

"Yes, I am Clyde and I have a kidney disease."

"Please come to the platform," invited Sonstad.

Clyde came forward and Sonstad met him as he came up the steps of the platform. He then asked him if he wanted to be healed. Clyde said yes, he would like to get rid of the disease that had bothered him for years. Sonstad touched the man on the forehead and he fell backwards. Two of Sonstad's men caught him and eased him to the ground. After a few moments on the ground, the men helped him to his feet. Sonstad then proclaimed him healed and there was much excitement and rejoicing in the audience.

Murphy leaned over to Wagoner and whispered, "I'd like to see a doctor verify that healing."

Wagoner was shaking his head.

"That man is Clyde Carlson. He has recently started attending our church. I'll talk to him later."

Sonstad spoke for a few moments about healing and then took an offering. Sonstad's workers collected the money in large containers.

After the offering Sonstad continued his conversation with God and healing more people. Then long lines of people wanting to be healed flowed up to the stage. They, too, were touched and would fall to the ground. This process continued for another hour, accompanied by rousing organ music.

The meeting finally ended and the people began to disperse. Murphy and Wagoner remained behind.

"What did you think of all of that, Michael?"

"It was quite a show. However, I think there's more here than meets the eye. Something's not quite right. Let's get the car and see if we can follow Sonstad."

"What do you expect to find?"

"I'm not sure. But my gut tells me that this whole program is not on the level. I think his actions could give honest ministers a bad reputation. Remember that the Bible suggests that in the last days there will be many false teachers and prophets that will lead many people astray."

Murphy and Wagoner had to wait about fifteen minutes before Sonstad and a number of his workers left the tent and got into a black limousine with tinted windows.

Murphy gave them a small lead and then began to follow the limousine. He had not driven far when a large SUV suddenly pulled right in front of him and stopped. Murphy had to slam on his brakes to avoid a collision.

A moment later, a second SUV pulled up behind him, boxing him in. The doors of both SUVs opened and a half dozen large men got out and surrounded Murphy's car.

"What's going on, Michael?"

"I get the feeling they don't want us to follow Sonstad, Bob."

"Do you think we're in any danger?"

"They're a mean-looking bunch, but I think they'll just block us from following him. They can't risk any bad publicity that would get into the newspapers. As it stands now, it would just be our word against theirs. How could we prove anything?"

The large men surrounded Murphy's vehicle and pushed down repeatedly on the hood and the trunk. The car rocked back and forth, jostling Murphy and his nervous passenger.

"Michael . . ." Bob said.

"Don't worry. They're just trying to intimidate us."

The shaking stopped. One of them pointed through the window at Murphy and shook his head menacingly. Murphy just glared back at him. After a few more seconds of this staring contest, they got back into their SUVs and drove off.

"This confirms my gut feeling. I think we need to come back again. Are you up to it, Bob?"

"You bet I am. We need to find out what is going on here. It looks like this whole meeting is planned around selling products and taking offerings. Even though there is a lot of God talk, I agree that this whole thing is a sham."

"Good, because I've got an idea," Murphy said. "I think I know how to expose J. B. Sonstad."

EIGHTEEN

MURPHY'S CELL PHONE began to ring as he drove into the teacher's parking lot at Preston University. He glanced at the caller I.D. display and smiled.

"Good morning, Levi. To what do I owe the pleasure?"

"Michael, I've got some good news and I've got some better news."

Murphy laughed as he got out of his car and started to walk. "Far better than bad news and worse news. Fire away. What's the good news?"

"The good news is . . . if you can break away around twelve o'clock, I'll buy you lunch."

"I'm free. Where would you like to meet?"

"How about the Shaw Towers Dining Room? I'm working on

some security issues with the owners there and part of our deal is free lunches for me and any guests."

"Aha, now I understand your generous offer to treat."

"You know I was born in Israel," said Abrams, and they both laughed.

"Okay, so what's the better news?"

"I think I've discovered who the mysterious Methuselah is."

Murphy stopped in his tracks and his jaw fell open. He stood in stunned silence for several seconds.

"Hello? Michael? Are you there?"

He finally recovered enough to speak. "That's . . . that's great! Who is he?"

"At lunch, Michael. At lunch."

"Are you kidding? You drop this bombshell, and now you're going to keep me in suspense until lunch?"

"That's the idea, Michael."

It was hard for Murphy to concentrate on his class lectures. Methuselah's true identity was a mystery he'd been trying to solve for years. And now Levi had the answer.

Even though he had never actually gotten a good look at Methuselah, Murphy did know a few details about him. He knew that he was a large, gray-haired man in his sixties who walked with a limp. Tyler Scott, a prisoner at the Cannon City Penitentiary, had shared that information with him. He knew that he had a habit of clicking his tongue and also had a high, cackling laugh—that sadistic sound that had taunted Murphy on numerous occasions.

He also knew that Methuselah had a vast amount of knowledge about the Bible and biblical artifacts. And he knew that he had to be very wealthy to be able to plan the types of elaborate games and tests of skill that he had put Murphy through.

Levi was waiting outside the restaurant when Murphy arrived. They shook hands, went inside, and sat down at a table.

"Well?" said Murphy.

"Well, what?" replied Levi with a big smile on his face.

"Who is he?"

"Let's order lunch first."

"You really know how to torture a man, don't you, Levi? Did they teach you that in the Mossad?"

"Yes, and much more. Demolitions, marksmanship, mind control . . ."

"Okay, okay. I give up."

"So easily? Just when I was having so much fun."

Murphy made an exasperated sound, but they ordered their meal, and at last Abrams became serious.

"The fingerprint you sent me was a right index finger. I ran it through all of our criminal files and came up empty. I then ran it through our civilian files and found a match."

"Is he an Israeli?"

"Actually, he's an American who has dual citizenship . . . as well as Taiwanese citizenship."

"That sounds strange."

"It gets stranger. According to our records, he, his wife, and three children were on an Israeli plane that was blown up in 1980."

"I vaguely remember that."

"As I dug deeper, I found out that he and his family were on their way from New York City to Tel Aviv for a vacation. Also on the plane were some up-and-coming Israeli leaders. It is our belief that a terrorist group wanted them dead and smuggled a bomb on board. Methuselah and his family were just innocent passengers that happened to be at the wrong place at the wrong time."

"How did he survive?"

"The bomb was detonated while the plane was on its final approach into the Tel Aviv airport. We believe the terrorists were hoping that the pilot would lose control and crash into the terminal building, killing thousands of people. However, it didn't happen that way.

"Sounds like the attacks on the Twin Towers in New York."

"Similar . . . except no one tried to take control of the plane. The terrorist was a suicide bomber. The bomb exploded near the right wing, blew out the side of the plane and caught the engine on fire. The whole plane dipped to the right but the pilot was able to stabilize it and bring it in for a landing."

"Heck of a pilot."

"He was, but even so, he overshot the runway and skidded across a road and into a field. They might have made it if it weren't for a steel transmission tower. The left wing caught it and sent the plane into a spin. The plane spun into another tower, breaking off the rear section of the plane. Methuselah's seat was near that area. He and about a dozen people were tossed out of the plane while still in their seats. He was one of only three survivors."

"What happened to the rest of the passengers?"

"The plane burst into flames, and everyone in the front of the plane, including Methuselah's family, was burned alive. Those in the broken-off rear section were electrocuted when the electrical transmission lines dropped on the plane."

"Tragic."

"It was a terrible disaster. Our records indicate that Methuselah was in a Tel Aviv hospital for nearly three months recuperating."

Murphy thought about Laura, and the pain he had felt at losing her. He felt a strange kinship for Methuselah, having lost his wife and three children. But he still wanted answers.

"So who is he?"

Levi leaned in close and spoke quietly. "Have you ever heard of the Zasso Steamship Lines, the Zasso Bank of International Trade, or Zasso Enterprises, Inc.?"

"Who hasn't? The Zasso companies must be worth billions."

"The fingerprint you gave me matches Markus M. Zasso. He is the owner and president of all the Zasso corporations. He survived the plane crash. And get this: His middle initial 'M' stands for Methuselah."

"Are you sure about all this? Where did he get a name like Methuselah? Zasso is an Italian name."

"I thought you might ask. I found out that Methuselah inherited the steamship lines and all of the other companies from his father, Mario Zasso. During the 1930s and 1940s, Mario Zasso became very wealthy in shipping and international trade. His ships were used by the United States in the Pacific during World War II."

"What about the name Methuselah?"

"I'm not sure, but I think it must have come from his grandfather, Marcello Zasso. The grandfather became a naturalized citizen during the 1920s. He underwent some type of spiritual conversion and joined a theological seminary and later became a missionary to China. His son Mario was born in Taiwan. I think that the grandfather must have had a strong influence on his son and on his grandson. Maybe that's the source of Methuselah's interest in the Bible and biblical artifacts."

"Makes sense. And his wealth gave him the opportunity to study about archaeology. I guess he got bored and had nothing to do but set up traps for me to escape from."

"There may be more to it than that, Michael. There must be some method to his madness. Markus Zasso does not do things haphazardly. He is a hard-driven businessman that has something he wants to accomplish."

"Did you find out anything else about him?"

"Well, obviously he owns homes and businesses around the world. He even owns a chain of fancy hotels in exotic places. But did you know that he also owns a home about two hundred twenty miles from Raleigh?"

"Here in North Carolina?"

"No. Down at Myrtle Beach."

"Do you have the address?"

"It's an out-of-the-way estate off Arrowhead Road, just off of North Kings Highway and south of Briarcliffe Acres and the Dunes. It's between the Arcadian Shores Golf Club and the Dunes Golf and Beach Club." He smiled. "You want me to draw you a map?"

"I don't think that will be necessary."

"I assume you plan to pay him a visit?"

"The thought had occurred to me. But I'll bet he's pretty well protected."

"That's putting it mildly. He's better protected than Howard Hughes ever was. He always has highly paid bodyguards close by. You can't get within fifty feet of the guy. He makes anyone bringing his meals taste the food . . . just in case there's poison in it."

"It's probably impossible to get into his estate then."

"Pretty much. But there is still one possibility. Every day, he likes to go down to the beach and sit in a lawn chair and look at the ocean."

"How did you find that out, Levi?"

"We have our ways."

"Do you also have ways of obtaining a recent photograph of him?"

"As a matter of fact, I do. What's it worth to you?" he said with a smile.

Murphy counted the money in his thin wallet. "How about a dollar fifty?"

"That's just the price I had in mind."

Abrams pulled out a picture of Methuselah sitting in a lawn chair on the beach, surrounded by six large bodyguards. They were in swim shorts and Hawaiian shirts, with telltale bulges under their armpits.

"Do those bulges under the shirts mean what I think they mean?"

Levi nodded. "Most of them carry automatics. They are very well paid for what they do, and they take their job seriously. Even if you didn't recognize Methuselah from a picture, the small army of bodyguards would probably tip you off."

"Since he has so many homes around the world, do you know whether he would be there now or not?"

"Our sources indicate that he has been there for the last twenty days. We have no way of knowing how long he will remain there. He has his own private jet, and several assistants that travel with him and help to keep his business running smoothly."

"I probably couldn't get close to him anyway. He'd recognize me."

"Has he ever met you in person? Close up, I mean."

Murphy considered this. "Not exactly. But he might have pictures of me."

"He probably does. Even so, I'll bet that you could get real close to him."

"Why do you say that?"

"Because you have the element of surprise. He thinks he's safe and no one knows who he is. You can exploit his false sense of security. In the Mossad, we use the element of surprise to throw the enemy off balance. Remember the raid on Entebbe in Uganda, when they hijacked an Israeli airliner and held the passengers hostage? No one expected us to sweep into a foreign country and rescue the prisoners. They were taken completely off guard. I think you could do the same thing with Methuselah."

"That's a thought, Levi. There's nothing I would like better than to leave right now and go confront him. But I have a few things to do first. You were right. You had some good news and some better news. Maybe I can put an end to the life-threatening bouts with Methuselah."

The food arrived and Levi dug in. "So who says there's no such thing as a free lunch?" he said between mouthfuls.

Murphy wasn't sure if he was talking about the food or the priceless information he'd just received.

NINETEEN

MURPHY PULLED INTO the twenty-four hour parking lot at the airport. He let out a sigh as he got out of his car. He didn't like the idea that he would only be able to spend part of the day with Isis. His schedule just permitted him to book a quick turnaround flight to Washington and back to Raleigh late that same night.

He longed to spend more time with her. Ever since their time together searching for Noah's Ark on Ararat and their hunt for the Handwriting on the Wall in Babylon, he had found himself thinking about her constantly. It was wonderful to begin to care about another person. He still wore his wedding band, a reminder of Laura. But maybe it was time . . .

When he was settled in his seat, and the plane began its ascent,

Murphy slowly slipped the ring off his finger and read the inscription on the inside. OUR LOVE IS FOREVER. He closed his eyes and saw Laura's face.

The airplane hit some slight turbulence and Murphy opened his eyes. The plane bounced for a few moments and then leveled off.

That's what I've been doing . . . bouncing in emotional turbulence for a while. I think Laura would have wanted me to level off.

He caressed the wedding band between his fingers, and then slipped it into his pocket. His finger bore a band of lighter-colored skin where the ring had been.

Guess I'm officially in a transition period.

He laid his head back on the seat and closed his eyes.

The direct flight from Raleigh to Washington was quick. It just seemed long to Murphy.

At dinner Murphy could hardly take his eyes off of Isis. Her beautiful long red hair cascaded down the shoulders of the black dress that so perfectly accentuated her petite, well-toned body. Her green eyes sparkled, and as he listened to her soft Scottish accent, he couldn't help but smile.

"What?"

Murphy stared into her eyes. "I think you look beautiful tonight."

She smiled shyly and, for the first time, seemed to notice his bare ring finger. "Michael, I'm glad you came. I know we could have talked over the phone, but this is so much better."

"I agree," he replied. "Besides, I'll use any excuse I can find to see you."

Murphy noticed a slight blush in her cheeks. She quickly changed the subject.

"You asked me about someone named King Yamani. I went to volume two of the *Records of Assyria*. They were collected and translated by Lukenbill. In paragraph sixty-two it mentions King Yamani."

Murphy smiled. It was one of the things he liked about Isis. She was like a bulldog when it came to discovering some detail in an ancient manuscript.

"In the seventh year of King Sargon's reign, he was requiring that tribute taxes be paid to Assyria. That same year, a man named Yamani seized power in the town of Ashdod. The name Yamani means 'the Greek.' He proclaimed himself king and attempted to start a rebellion against Sargon and his taxes. He approached Pir'u, the king of Musru, for help."

"I'm not familiar with his name."

"Yamani was Pharaoh, king of Egypt. Yamani also solicited aid from the nation of Judah. Hezekiah was king at the time. It seems that Isaiah the prophet urged him to not get involved and he did not join Yamani."

"That all makes sense."

"What does, Michael?"

"There is only one mention of King Sargon in the Bible. I was just reading about this the other day while doing some research. It's in the book of Isaiah. It suggests that one of Sargon's supreme commanders was sent to attack Ashdod and captured the city."

"You're right. The name for the commander is 'turtan.' It is not a personal name, but a title that refers to a high military and administrative official, second in rank to the king."

Isis removed a piece of paper from her purse and unfolded it. She began to read. "Listen to what it says in the *Records of Assyria*. The rebellious king Yamani fled to Ethiopia to seek a safe haven but ran into trouble. 'The king of Ethiopia, who lives in a distant country, in an inapproachable region . . . whose fathers never—from remote days until now—had sent messengers to inquire after the health of my royal forefathers, he did hear, even that far away, of the might of Ashu, Nebo, and Marduk. The awe-inspiring glamour of my kingship blinded him and terror overcame him.' It seems that the Ethiopian king did not want trouble with Sargon. It goes on to say, 'He threw him [Yamani] in fetters, shackles and iron bands, and they brought him to Assyria, a long journey.' "

Murphy's face lit up with sudden realization.

"What is it, Michael?"

"It's Methuselah. His note said, 'In the town of King Yamani a great mystery has been solved—I Kings 8:9.' It all makes sense now. The reference in I Kings refers to Aaron's Rod that budded and the Golden Jar of Manna. They were missing from the Ark. The town of King Yamani is the city of Ashdod. Ashdod is where the Philistines first took the Ark of the Covenant after they captured it, the city that was the home of the Temple of Dagon. I think that Methuselah is trying to say that Aaron's Rod and the Golden Jar of Manna were taken out of the Ark in Ashdod . . . and that we may still find them there."

Murphy sat forward, his eyes wild with excitement. He looked like a little boy in a candy shop trying to decide which piece to eat first.

"The second note Methuselah left me said, 'Thirty degrees northeast of the altar . . . press the king's head.' That must refer to some sort of secret passage or hiding place." He looked at Isis. "What do you know about Ashdod?"

"Ashdod is the fifth largest city in Israel, founded in 1956 and located between Tel Aviv and Gaza on the coast. It's becoming a very important seaport for Israel. Over fifteen thousand tons of cargo pass through there each year. Its population is about a quarter of a million people."

"It's coming back to me now. In 2004, two suicide bombers killed ten people and injured sixteen at the Ashdod port."

"I remember that, Michael."

"As I recall, two eighteen-year-old Palestinians hid themselves in a container that was delivered by truck. The investigators found food remains and five unexploded grenades in the container. They were from the Jabalya Refugee Camp in the Gaza Strip. They detonated their bombs, killing ten people and wounding sixteen. The Hamas and Fatah claimed responsibility for the attack. . . ."

Murphy trailed off. Something Isis had said troubled him.

"But, hold on, if the city was founded in 1956, this can't be the location."

"The original site of Ashdod is about three to four miles inland. The city was conquered by the Macedonians under Alexander the Great. At that time it was known as Azotos."

"You're brilliant. I can't believe you're giving all this information from memory."

Isis blushed again. "In 163 B.C., Judas Maccabaeus came into the city and destroyed the Temple of Dagon. In 148 B.C., Jonathan and Simon burned down what was left of the temple. There have been a number of excavations at the site. They have discovered at least twenty-two strata of continuous settlements of the city. Maybe Methuselah has discovered something new there."

Isis caught Murphy's grin.

"What are you smiling at?"

"I was just thinking how archaeological findings keep pointing to the truth and reality of the Bible. The more we discover, the stronger our faith becomes."

Isis seemed to withdraw a little.

"What's wrong?"

"You keep talking about the truth of the Bible. And you get so excited about these new discoveries. I don't know how to relate to it all. I sort of believe that there is a God. Everything we see couldn't just pop into being without a Creator. But you seem to talk about God like you know Him personally."

Murphy hesitated for a moment. With a heavy heart, he remembered that Isis had not yet made a leap of faith.

"You can know Him the same way I do, Isis. All you have to do is believe that God revealed Himself through Jesus Christ. Jesus took upon Himself the burden of everyone's sins. With His death on the cross, He paid the penalty for everything we have ever done wrong. But then Jesus arose from the dead so that we too could have eternal life with him. All anyone has to do is to receive this information . . . and believe it by faith and ask God to come into his or her life and change it. That's what it means to be saved."

"I don't know, Michael. All that faith stuff seems to work for you but not for me. Jesus appears to be a nice person, a great teacher, and a wonderful example. But to believe that he is God is a big leap of faith. I don't know if I am ready to make that type of commitment."

Murphy found himself in silent prayer, asking God that he might have the right words to say.

"Each person must come to that decision by themselves. No one can take that step for you. I wish I could, Isis. Let me share a verse out of the Bible with you. It is found in the first chapter of the Gospel of John. It says, 'To all who received Him, to those who believed in His name, He gave the right to become children of God.' That's all a person has to do. Believe and receive. Isis, you're an avid reader. All of this is made wonderfully clear in the Gospel of John in the Bible. I'm sure that you would enjoy searching this out for yourself."

Murphy sensed her uncertainty. He didn't want to put on any pressure, so he changed the subject.

"I want to thank you for all the hard work and effort you have gone to in finding information about King Yamani. I'm going to ask Levi to get us permission to go to the Ashdod site and do some exploring. If we can find Aaron's Rod and the Golden Jar of Manna, it will be a terrific discovery. But if they should fall into the wrong hands, people might try to use those artifacts as objects of worship or believe that they have some sort of magical powers."

Murphy looked at Isis and smiled.

"How about some dessert?"

Murphy talked about the possibility of finding Aaron's Rod and the Golden Jar of Manna as Isis drove him to the airport. They also spoke of Talon, but she said she'd been careful and so far there'd been no sign of him. Other than that, she said little during the drive.

When they arrived, Murphy was surprised to see how many people were unloading vehicles and preparing to travel at that late hour. He got out and so did Isis. She came around to the passenger side to say good-bye.

"You're so quiet. Is there something wrong?"

She looked at him for a moment before she spoke.

"I don't want you to leave. I feel so lonely when you're not around."

Murphy reached out and pulled her close, drowning in her green eyes. He leaned in and kissed her, and she responded with equal passion. Time seemed to stand still as they held each other tightly.

Suddenly there was the honking of a car and a man's voice.

"Hey, Mack! Why don't you just go to a motel?"

Murphy looked up to see a taxi driver leaning out of his window. Murphy looked at Isis, who was laughing. He held her again and kissed her. He didn't want to let her go. Slowly they parted and Isis got into the car. He watched from the curb as she drove away.

He turned and walked through the revolving doors and headed for his departure gate, in a daze all the while. He shook his head.

What's happening to you, Murphy?

TWENTY

The town of Shiloh, 1083 B.C.

THE POUNDING *on the door woke Hophni from a dead sleep.* Who could it be at this hour? *he wondered. He had just pulled back his blanket and was getting out of bed when he heard his front door being broken down.*

Before his feet touched the floor, soldiers bearing torches rushed into his room. "I am Captain Gaddiel. Get dressed quickly. You must come with us immediately."

"Certainly not!" replied Hophni with indignation. "Who do you think you are? I am the son of the high priest. You have no right to break into my home. I want you to leave this instant!"

Gaddiel's voice became stronger. "Get dressed now! We need to take you and your brother, Phinehas, and the Ark of the Covenant to the valley between Ebenezer and Aphek. We have suffered the loss of many lives. If we lose many more, our defeat is certain. We need the Ark to ensure our victory in the battle with the Philistines."

"You can take the Ark, but I'm not going to any battlefield! I don't want to be killed!" Hophni protested.

"You and your brother are priests. Don't you wish to serve your people? You will go and bless the troops. Half of my men are at your brother's house right now. They're getting him ready to leave with us. You will both go, or else."

"Or else what?"

"Or else I will expose you to the people for what you really are. I know that you both are corrupt. I know that you both take the best meat sacrificed to God for your own families' consumption. You act so religious and pious. You both are nothing but frauds. It makes me sick to even look at you. You and your brother claim to know the Lord but your actions deny it."

Hophni hesitated. He did not want his surreptitious activities to come to light, but that still seemed preferable to marching onto a battlefield. But the captain wasn't finished yet.

"I also know that you both lay with the women who assemble at the door of the tabernacle of meeting. Suppose your wife were to learn of your activities once she returns from visiting relatives? Doesn't the law require that those who commit adultery should be stoned?"

Hophni was speechless. He had no idea how Gaddiel had gathered so much information about him and his brother. He did not say a word while he dressed and went with the captain.

When the Ark of the Covenant arrived at camp early in the morning, the people cheered so loudly that the ground shook. Many danced around the Ark as it moved toward the battlefront.

The noise from the camp of the Israelites startled the Philistines. "What does this great shout in the camp of the Israelites mean?" asked Commander Jotham. He ordered that spies be sent to determine what was going on. Within a couple of hours the word came back.

"God has come into the camp of the Israelites. Woe unto us! Nothing like this has ever happened before. They have brought their Ark of the Covenant to help fight their battle with us. It is the home of their God Jehovah, the same God who struck the Egyptians with all the plagues in the wilderness."

Commander Jotham tried to calm the fears of the soldiers. "Be strong and conduct yourselves like soldiers, you Philistines, that you do not become servants of the Israelites. You need to act like men and fight for your country and families!"

He had barely gotten the words out of his mouth when a runner approached.

"Commander! The Israelites are on the march!"

Jotham knew he would have to go to battle whether he wanted to or not. He gave the order to assemble and encouraged his warriors to fight with all their heart and soul.

"Do not fear the God of the Israelites. Is not the great god Dagon more powerful? He will deliver us from these weak and cowardly warriors. We defeated them yesterday and we will do the same today!"

It was an impressive sight to see the Israelites marching to battle. The golden Ark of the Covenant stood at the front of their ranks. Flags and banners flapped around the Ark, and Hophni and Phinehas cut impressive figures in their formal priestly robes.

Jotham and his aides were too far away to see the terror in the eyes of Hophni and Phinehas. They had always lived a life of luxury and sensuality. They had never set foot on any battlefield. They would have run away and hidden in a cave if Gaddiel and his elite soldiers had not kept them next to the Ark. But the men in the Israelite army never suspected the extent of the priests' fear and corruption. They blindly trusted and followed their priests.

Jotham spoke. "Take one hundred of the bravest warriors and seize the Ark. Be sure to kill the two priests following it. If we can capture their precious religious relic, it will demoralize the entire army."

One hundred of the bravest Philistine warriors snuck into the ravine of a riverbed that ran through the valley. They were able to work their way to almost the center of the battlefield undetected by the Israelites. They camouflaged themselves with bushes to conceal their ambush.

And then they waited.

As the Israelites reached the middle of the valley, Jotham gave the signal for the trumpets to blast. The Israelite army was focused on the approaching conflict and did not notice the concealed warriors. When the Philistine arrows began to fly, the Israelites put up their shields, and the one hundred warriors in hiding launched a surprise attack on the Ark and the soldiers surrounding it.

The surprise overwhelmed the Israelites near the Ark. Within a few minutes, the Philistines had captured the Ark. To the horror of those nearby, they watched as the Philistines beheaded Hophni and Phinehas. One of the Philistine warriors picked up the two heads, held them high in the air and bellowed a victory scream, sending chills down the spines of the Israelite soldiers.

The capture of the Ark turned the tide of the battle. It was a slow retreat at first . . . but it didn't take long before it was an absolute exodus of Israelite warriors. They dropped their weapons and ran for their lives in stark terror.

The Philistines quickly sensed the fear and took advantage of it. They chased after the Israelites, yelling and screaming at the top of their lungs. They soon began to gain on the ranks in the back and slew them as they attempted to flee. It became an exciting game of hunt, chase, and kill for the Philistines. When the great slaughter at last came to an end, thirty thousand foot soldiers lay dead.

Jotham and his aids commenced dancing and shouting as they surrounded their trophy. The Ark was now theirs. The general raised his arms and yelled at the top of his voice.

"The Israelite God is powerless against our great god Dagon!"

A cheer went up among the Philistines. It was a glorious day.

TWENTY-ONE

SHARI DIDN'T HEAR the door to the lab open and then close. The latest CD from her new favorite band blasted from a nearby boom box. In addition, she was deeply engrossed in a papyrus manuscript that Murphy had found in an out-of-the-way curio shop in the seedy part of Cairo some time ago.

She had just taken some pages out of the humidifier and begun to carefully unroll them. The normally porous white paper had turned brown and was still a little brittle. She bit her lower lip as she carefully unrolled and separated the pages. This was one of the things she liked about her job. She had a curious mind and could hardly wait to discover the hidden mysteries in these ancient pages.

Paul Wallach watched Shari in silence. His face was expressionless as he observed her . . . but deep inside his emotions ran wild.

It had been several months since he had seen her and during that time he had come to realize what a fool he had been. He missed her warm smile and playful spirit. The lure of a job offer by Shane Barrington had clouded his thinking as he was overcome by thoughts of wealth, fame, and power.

Wallach had come to believe that Barrington really cared for him. He looked at Barrington as a father figure and mentor . . . especially since his own father was gone. At first, Barrington seemed to be genuinely interested in him. The visits to his hospital bed after the bombing at the Preston Community Church. The paying of his tuition at the university. Barrington had, on more than one occasion, indicated that Paul was like his own son, whom he'd evidently lost in an accident.

Paul watched as Shari bent over the manuscript and gently unrolled it. The two ponytails coming out of the sides of her head were almost touching the papyrus. Her jet-black hair was contrasted by her bright white lab jacket.

He thought back to the time in the hospital. Shari had sensed something about Barrington. She had told Paul that he wanted more than just a father-son relationship. Her intuition had told her that Barrington was a phony and a hypocrite, even though Paul couldn't—or wouldn't—see it. Of course she had been right.

Paul was ashamed now of his own greed. Barrington didn't care about his desire to become a writer for his news network. All he wanted was someone on the inside to write about Murphy and what he was teaching. It had never dawned on Paul that he was being used as a spy . . . until now. He felt angry, cheap, and used.

For a moment, Wallach flashed back to that fateful day in Barrington's office. He had felt like Barrington was looking through him rather than at him.

"I was curious as to what my responsibilities would be. We really haven't had a chance to talk much about it after you gave me the assignment of reporting on Dr. Murphy's archaeology class. How have you liked my writing so far? What does the future hold for me with Barrington Network News?"

Paul remembered how Barrington had just sat there in silence for the longest time. It was almost unbearable.

"Well, Paul, I have a reputation for speaking frankly. Are you ready for a man-to-man talk?"

Paul had the same feelings come over him as he did when Barrington first said those words. He felt scared and helpless in the face of such a powerful man, a man who controlled millions of dollars and the lives of thousands of people.

"We're going to have one today. Your writing stinks. I only needed you to get information on Murphy, but I no longer care about him and I have no use for you anymore. And, oh, by the way, your scholarship is discontinued."

In an instant, Paul felt his whole world come crashing down.

"But, Mr. Barrington, you told me that you thought of me as a son."

Barrington's response destroyed him.

"Oh, grow up, Paul. If you want to know the truth, you haven't got skills enough to drive a nail—let alone survive in this kind of business. I'll spell it out slowly so you'll understand: You're fired."

Paul's attention was drawn back to the lab as Shari started singing along with the music. He smiled to hear her voice. He had missed hearing it.

Shari finally sensed his presence and turned. A look of shock came over her. Paul Wallach was the last person she had expected to see. The last time they were together it had ended in tears. Shari could hear her last words as she looked at Paul.

"Let me try to explain. You and I think differently about God, eternal values, how to conduct one's life, and what's important in life. It's like water and oil. They can't be mixed together. Try as hard as I would like to, it's just not going to happen. If we were to continue our relationship you wouldn't be happy

with me and I wouldn't be happy with you. I think it's best if we stop seeing each other. It's evident that you and I are walking down separate roads. I can't reject all that I believe in, no matter how much I care for you. Trying to do so will only end in disaster. I wish it didn't have to end this way, but in the long run it will be the best for both of us."

"Hi, Shari. I was in the area and thought I would drop in and say hello."

Shari was tongue-tied. "Hello, Paul," she finally managed.

"I know you're busy . . . but can you break away for a little bit?"

"I . . . I guess so."

"Great. Could we go for a walk?"

Shari nodded her head and took off her lab coat.

What's this all about? she wondered.

They walked in silence for a little while, Shari trying to figure out what was going on and Paul trying to muster his courage. Finally he spoke.

"You know, you were right."

"About what?"

"About Barrington. He didn't care about me. I was just being used. He's an expert in using people."

Shari nodded her head in agreement.

"I don't work for him anymore."

"You don't? When did that happen?"

"A couple of months ago."

"What are you doing now?"

"Nothing. I have reenrolled at Preston and will start next semester. I'm looking for a part-time job until then."

"Why are you coming back here?"

"I guess there are two reasons. The first is that I need to find out who I am and what I would really like to do in life. The second . . ."

He paused for a moment. "The second is that I would like to see if we could possibly begin dating again."

"Well, I . . ."

"Don't say anything yet. I know I've acted like an idiot. You were right and I was wrong. I hope that you can forgive me for hurting you. I'm so sorry."

Shari hadn't expected any of this.

"I can forgive you, Paul. But just because I forgive you doesn't mean that we will go back to the way we were. My faith in God has not changed and we see life differently."

"I know. I guess what I am saying is maybe you were right. Life isn't just earning money and buying things. I've had a severe wake-up call. I'm trying to process everything and I think I'm more open-minded than I was before."

"Paul, I hope that's true. That would be wonderful. But if you're trying to adopt a belief in God to win me back, it won't last. Your decision to come to the Lord needs to be yours alone . . . regardless of whether we ever get back together or not."

"You're right, Shari. I'm not trying to pressure you. I just hope that you might consider it. I've gone through a tough time the past couple of months. It's been lonely, and I've had to do some heavy thinking."

"Have you been thinking about God?"

"Yeah. But if I'm honest, I guess I'm a little mad at Him."

"For what?"

"For letting this all happen to me."

"Maybe He didn't let it happen to you, Paul. Maybe He tried to stop you and you wouldn't listen. Maybe you brought it on yourself."

"What do you mean?"

"Did God tell you to take the job with Barrington?"

"No, I don't hear voices from heaven."

"Sometimes God uses the voices of other people."

"What do you mean?"

"Maybe God was using me to warn you of the danger ahead. Maybe I became His voice to you."

"I hadn't thought of it that way before."

"Paul, I know that you were angry when you lost your father. You didn't think it was fair that he died. Now you have lost another father figure in Shane Barrington. Not only did you lose him, but he used you and didn't give a rip about your feelings. That's enough to get anybody angry."

"You've got that right."

"I can understand why you've been depressed. I had some of those same feelings when I lost my parents. It took me a while before I realized that anger and depression are tied together. Of course, you can be angry and not be depressed . . . but you cannot be depressed without some form of hurt and anger. I wasn't able to pull out of my depression until I faced my anger. I had to admit it . . . own it . . . and choose to let go of it."

"That doesn't sound easy."

"No, it's not. It was one of the hardest things I had to do. Is it possible that you haven't dealt with your anger yet?"

"I think that's safe to say."

"That's only natural. I would be hurt and angry too. But will your anger change the situation?"

"No, but I'd like to punch him in the face!"

"What if you don't get that opportunity?"

"I don't know."

"Maybe then you will have to face your anger and let go of it."

"How can I do that?"

"By making peace with the things you cannot change. By learning to not get into the same type of situations in the future. By forgiving."

"By forgiving? I don't think I'll ever be able to forgive him."

"Didn't you ask me to forgive you a few minutes ago for hurting me?"

"Yeah, but—"

"No buts. What if I had responded to you the way you're responding to Barrington? Would you like that?"

"Of course not."

"What's the difference, Paul? You can't harbor hatred in your heart and expect to ever heal emotionally. That was one of the hardest things I had to learn. I have to keep reminding myself of it all the time. Hurtful thoughts have a way of haunting us. We have to keep giving them back to God. He's the only one who can give us the strength to do this, and the inner peace that comes from forgiving."

"Pretty heavy stuff, Shari. I'm going to have to think about what you've said. Thank you for not hating me."

"I haven't hated you, Paul."

"I hope that you might be open to talking again, Shari. I hope that we might be able to work through our differences. Would you be open to that?

"We'll see, Paul. That's all I can say for now."

Shari's eyes were fixed on the floor and she was deep in thought when she entered the lab. She didn't see Murphy sitting behind a microscope at the side of the room.

"So?"

She looked up, startled.

" 'So'? What do you mean?"

"I saw you walking with Paul Wallach over by the pond. Is he working on some story for Barrington News Network?"

"No. He was let go. Barrington really didn't have a job for him."

"It doesn't surprise me. He's the type of person to use someone and then throw them away. What's Paul doing now? Is he planning to come back to school?"

"He signed up for next semester."

"And?"

"And what?"

"And are you going to start dating him again?"

Shari felt a mix of emotions beginning to swirl within. "Now who's playing matchmaker?"

"I'm just asking."

"I'm not sure. I don't know if he has changed. I think I'll have to just watch for a while."

"You're wise to take it slow. If he has changed, you'll know it."

TWENTY-TWO

FASIAL SHADID TURNED the corner and drove toward downtown Cairo and Tahrir Square. He had been a professor of Ancient Writings and Ancient Culture at the American University for twenty years, and before that, a student at the university. He had witnessed the growth of the school to over five thousand students, especially after the addition of the "Greek" campus and the Jameel Management Center.

Fasial was a small man with a leathery complexion. However, he carried himself in a confident manner that made him seem almost imposing. There were large gaps between his teeth when he smiled and his dark brown eyes brimmed with enthusiasm. He enjoyed walking the campus, talking with the students, and looking at the majestic buildings that used to be a palace that dated back to the 1860s. He also enjoyed attending events in the Ewart Memorial Hall. It was one of the most culturally active auditoriums in Cairo. But his greatest joy was being part of the committee that designed and helped construct the buildings housing Special Collections and the Rare Book Library.

His curiosity had been greatly aroused when he received a phone call from his assistant Nassar Abdoo telling him to come quickly.

Nassar was sitting at a desk looking through a high-powered magnifying glass when Fasial arrived. They greeted each other and Nassar adjusted the magnifying glass with his bony sticklike arms and oily fingers. His sunken eyes had dark circles around them and a deep furrow of concentration was permanently etched into his brow.

"Fasial, look at this." He was pointing to the foot-long piece of brass on the table before him.

"Just what do you want me to look at?" he said as he bent forward toward the magnifying glass.

"Look, on the belly of the snake. On the smooth part just below the carved scales."

Fasial could make out faint traces of what looked to be early Babylonian writing.

"Yes, I see it. Have you been able to decipher what it says?"

"I can make out part of it. The rest has either been rubbed off or exists on the other sections of the snake."

Fasial looked more closely at the writing.

"It seems to suggest that the Babylonians believed that there was some type of healing power in the snake. Can you make out the word 'Nehushtan'?"

"Yes, I see it."

"Just recently I did some tracing back through the Old Testament of the Bible. The word 'Nehushtan' is mentioned in II Kings 18, in a description of Hezekiah's ascent to the throne. It says, 'He removed the high places, smashed the sacred stones and cut down the Asherath poles. He broke into pieces the bronze snake Moses had made, for up to that time the Israelites had been burning incense to it. It was called Nehushtan.'"

"That would seem to suggest that this is one of the broken pieces."

"Yes, and I did some more research on the word 'Nehushtan.' It was also mentioned by a Babylonian priest by the name of Dakkuri who had somehow gotten ahold of the broken pieces of the Bronze Serpent of Moses."

Nassar smiled at Fasial, exposing his yellow teeth.

"Now for the final proof. Look at the carved scales on the side, just right of the center. If you look carefully, you can make out faded letters, one letter in each scale. To the casual observer, they appear to be random markings on the scales. They spell D-A-K-K-U-R-I."

"This is a wonderful find, Nassar. I recall having come across something in my research about a cult that had been worshiping this piece of bronze. It would be interesting if we were able to reunite all three pieces, to determine if it truly does have some great power. Up for another late night?"

"I've already sent a student to bring us some kishk bread, milk, cheese, dates, and figs." Nassar smiled. "Let's get to work."

It was 11:00 P.M. when Nassar rose to stretch. He walked around the room nibbling a fig. Fasial was intently reading an ancient manuscript.

Nassar gasped and Fasial's head whipped around in his direction.

"You startled me, sir. I didn't hear you coming."

Nassar looked into the cold eyes of a stranger. The man had black hair and a black mustache and stood over six feet tall. He had a bone white complexion and wore gloves, which seemed strange for this time of year.

"I'm sorry to startle you. I'm looking for a Mr. Fasial Shadid and a Mr. Nassar Abdoo."

Nassar placed his accent as South African. "I'm Nassar and that is Mr. Shadid."

The stranger reached out his hand and greeted both of the men.

"May we help you, sir?" said Fasial.

"Possibly. I have been informed that you have a section of what might be the famous Bronze Serpent of Moses. Is this true?"

Nassar and Fasial exchanged frowns. They had informed no one of what they were doing.

"How would you know that?" asked Nassar.

The man shrugged. "Amazing how stories get around. I have something that might interest you."

Both of them looked at him quizzically.

The stranger reached into his briefcase and removed the tail section of the Bronze Serpent.

Both of their mouths flew open. Fasial put down the manuscript and went over to look at the tail section of the Bronze Serpent. They took it over to the large magnifying glass and began to study it. They noted the Babylonian writing and the similarity of the carved scales.

"Where did you get this?" asked Fasial.

"It recently came into my possession," the stranger replied evasively.

With a nod from Fasial, Nassar went to a file cabinet, unlocked it, and took out the middle of the Bronze Serpent.

"Bring it here, Nassar. Let us see if they fit together."

All three gathered around the magnifying glass. Nassar gently fitted the two pieces together.

"A perfect fit. The breaks are so fine that the pieces could easily be put back together and no one would know the difference," he said.

"Excuse me, sir," said Fasial. "We have introduced ourselves but we did not catch your name."

"My name is Talon," said the stranger as he began to take off his gloves.

"Is that your first or your last—?"

Nassar and Fasial's attention was drawn to Talon's hand.

"Did you have an accident?" asked Fasial.

"What, this?" He held up his odd-looking finger without a trace of self-consciousness. "As a matter of fact, I did. When I was a young boy I had a pet falcon. One day he attacked me and ripped off my finger. I had it replaced with this one."

"It seems quite sharp," said Nassar.

"Let me show you."

The words were barely out of Talon's mouth when he lashed out with a backhanded swipe under Nassar's chin, severing his larynx. Blood gushed everywhere as Nassar clutched at his throat and collapsed to the floor.

Fasial was frozen for a moment as his mind tried to absorb what had just happened. Then he ran to the desk and grabbed a sharp letter opener. His breathing came fast as he brandished it at Talon.

Talon stood like a statue, a sneer curling his thin lips. "Well, this ought to be fun."

Fasial was waving the letter opener back and forth in front of him, hoping the motion might ward off an attack. He was wrong.

Talon stepped forward, spun, and fired off a spinning back kick that sent Fasial into the wall. The letter opener flew out of his hand and across the room.

Fasial held his stomach. "I can't . . . breathe," he rasped.

Talon threw a punch into his chest, right over his heart. Fasial's eyes grew wide for a moment and then he collapsed to the floor.

"Problem solved," said Talon.

TWENTY-THREE

MURPHY HAD MIXED EMOTIONS as he walked up the meandering pathway to the Memorial Lecture Hall. His topic for the day was evil angels, and while it was good for the students to understand the influence of evil in the world, he hated to give Satan and his demons any credit and thereby add to their notoriety.

Forewarned is forearmed, he thought.

As he rounded the corner of the Science Building, he saw the students already making their way to his class. It was a sunny morning and the smell of magnolias was heavy in the air.

He nodded to some of the students as he entered the hall, stopping to field some questions about homework assignments. He noticed Shari setting up his PowerPoint projector on the stand near his desk.

No one could ask for a better assistant . . . a little kooky at times, but very supportive.

He hooked up his computer to the projector, pulled up his lecture slides, and arranged his notes.

He was about to call everyone to take their seats when *she* entered. This was the third time that Summer Van Doren had attended his lectures. And again, as before, the men in the back of the lecture hall also noticed her.

"Good morning, class. Last time we talked about good angels. Today we'll be discussing the other side of the issue. The dark side of evil angels."

Murphy saw a hand go up in the back of the room. It was Clayton Anderson. He knew that something crazy was coming.

"What is it, Clayton?"

"Dr. Murphy, did you hear about the angel that died?"

"No, Clayton. What about him?" He knew that he was being set up.

"He died of harp failure."

Everyone groaned. A few students rolled up paper balls and threw them at him. Anderson was giving the class his typical innocent "Who, me?" look.

"Is that part of your homework that you want me to grade you on, Clayton?"

Anderson gave a sheepish grin and shook his head.

"Smart lad."

Murphy caught Summer smiling at him with a twinkle in her deep blue eyes. It was very distracting. He gathered his wits and turned on the PowerPoint projector.

"Let's get back to our topic here. The Bible makes reference to demons and evil spirits. They are basically those angels that chose to follow their leader, Satan."

EVIL OR FALLEN ANGELS

- **Angels kept in prison**
- **Angels that are free**
- **Demons**
- **Evil spirits**
- **Satan—leader of the evil or fallen angels**

"These demons or evil spirits have been given a number of different common names. Some of the names will be familiar to you and others may be new. All cultures have terminology for angels and for some form of demonic or otherworldly creatures. As you look at the next slide, see how many of the names are familiar to you."

VARIOUS NAMES FOR EVIL OTHERWORLDLY CREATURES

Baba Yaga	**Ghoul**	**Puck**
Banshee	**Gnome**	**Specter**
Bogeyman	**Gremlin**	**Spook**
Bugaboo	**Hobgoblin**	**The Undead**
Doppelganger	**Imp**	**Vampire**
Dybbuk	**Incubus**	**Wandering Soul**
Evil Spirit	**Mombo Jombo**	**Werewolf**
Fiend	**Phantom**	**Witch**
Fury	**Poltergeist**	**Zombie**

"You wouldn't want to encounter any of these guys in a dark alley or spot them following you across campus. As you are no doubt aware, the movie industry has used the various names of evil spirits for horror films, in which these creatures wreak havoc, terrify, and murder people. There are a number of films that deal with the exorcism of evil spirits. Scary stuff."

Someone made a ghostly *oooooh* sound, and Murphy didn't have to see to know it was Clayton Anderson. The class had a good chuckle, which was okay with Murphy.

"Exactly. But not all otherworldly creatures are depicted as scary. Some have been portrayed as being kind or helpful in some way."

VARIOUS NAMES FOR GOOD OTHERWORLDLY CREATURES

Brownie	**Mermaid**
Elf	**Nymph**
Fairy	**Pixie**
Fairy Godmother	**Satyr**
Familiar Spirit	**Spirit Guide**
Genie	**Superhero**
Leprechaun	**White Witch**

"Think about the Aladdin films with the Genie in a lamp. Or how about superheroes, like Superman, Batman, and Spider-Man? There are also all of the Disney films with fairy godmothers, singing mermaids, or little elves that help Santa Claus at Christmas. If you want to find otherworldly creatures, all you have to do is turn on the television on Saturday mornings. Young children are indoctrinated at an early age into the world of ghosts, demons, wizards, witches, mediums, and the occult."

Murphy clicked up the next slide.

"The chief of the fallen angels is a being named Lucifer, but he goes by many names."

VARIOUS NAMES FOR LUCIFER

Abaddon
Accuser of the Brethren
Adversary
Angel of the Bottomless Pit
Apollyon
Beelzebub
Belial
Devil
Enemy
Evil Spirit
Father of Lies
God of This World
Great Red Dragon
King of Tyrus
Liar
Lucifer
Morning Star
Old Serpent
Power of Darkness
Prince of This World
Prince of Devils
Prince of the Power of the Air
Ruler of the Darkness of this World
Satan
Serpent
Son of Dawn
Spirit That Works in Disobedient Children
The Tempter
The Unclean Spirit
Wicked One

"The Bible suggests that this angel, Lucifer, was a very beautiful being who became filled with pride. He tried to engender a rebellion in heaven among all the other angels. The angels that followed him became evil spirits or demons, and to this day they attempt to hinder the influence of God in this world. From their influence have risen cults, false religions, and the worship of spirits that has affected mankind down through the centuries. Yet, each October we celebrate these spirits in an event called Halloween."

One of the students raised her hand.

"Dr. Murphy, is Lucifer as powerful as God?"

"No. He does, however, have great powers and influence in the political affairs of nations. His final end will come in what is commonly called the Day of Judgment. He and his fallen angels will end up in a place called the Lake of Fire. Most people call it hell. There is a popular conception about Satan, with his pointed ears, long tail, and pitchfork, ruling over this place."

Murphy noticed Summer quietly stand up and leave. *She must have a class to teach. She sure is easy on the eyes.*

Stay focused.

"In our class on biblical archaeology," he continued, "we have studied the influence of pagan gods on the lives of people from many nations. Often priests or other influential people commissioned artisans to make idols of gods and supernatural creatures out of wood, stone, clay, and metal. Many of these artifacts have been discovered and studied by universities and private groups around the world. The Israelites also did this with the Ark of the Covenant. This box contained the Ten Commandments given by God to Moses, Aaron's Rod, and a golden jar of manna from the wilderness. As you recall, manna was food that God provided for the Children of Israel while they wandered in the wilderness. The Ark had two cherubim, or angels, carved out of gold on the lid.

"Demons are also seen in the design of ancient and some modern constructions. Some buildings have included decorated waterspouts that project from the building to drain water off the roof. These waterspouts are formed to look like grotesque, otherworldly creatures and are called gargoyles. Many of the Gothic cathedrals and palaces have these features. Often they are half human and half animal or half bird. Rainwater is channeled through the mouths of these creatures and away from the buildings, and the word 'gargoyle' comes from the Latin word *gurguilo* . . . which means 'gullet' and has to do with drainage. Some of the early stonemasons must have had some fun with these gargoyles. They would occasionally portray their patrons or colleagues in a grotesque form. It is something that Mr. Anderson would really enjoy."

Everyone looked at Clayton and made an *ooooh*ing sound. Clayton happily soaked up all the attention.

"In some Asian cultures, the roofs curve up at the bottom to form a point, the thought being that the points would help to keep evil spirits away from the homes, places of business, or houses of worship. In cultural parades and events, Asians will often have a long, colorful costume that forms a fire-breathing dragon. This costume is carried by many people and weaves back and forth through the crowds of people. Just another example of the strong influence otherworldly creatures have had on society."

A hand went up.

"Dr. Murphy, does that include things like séances, card reading, and crystal-ball reading?"

"Yes, it does. In séances, mediums attempt to contact some type of spirit. They often suggest that they are human spirits of the dead but they can also be some form of supernatural creature, like a fallen angel. In card reading or crystal-ball reading the practitioner is attempting to tap into some otherworldly source that will predict the future."

Another hand went up.

"Dr. Murphy, what about people who worship Satan and fallen angels?"

"I suppose one of the most famous is a man by the name of Anton Szandor LaVey. In the late 1960s he wrote a book called *The Satanic Bible.* His book became very popular on college campuses and outsold the Bible for a period of time. He became the head of the Satanic Church."

A student spoke up.

"Dr. Murphy, did this LaVey guy have some sort of weird childhood?"

"I don't know if you would call it weird or not. But as a sixteen-year-old, he played the organ for a carnival, where he would observe men lusting after the half-naked dancing girls. He also played the organ for a tent-show evangelist who happened to have his tent at the other end of the carnival. He would see the same men who'd been lusting after the dancing girls sitting in the chairs with their wives and children, and he became very disillusioned as a result of their hypocrisy. He came to the conclusion that man's carnal nature will win out in the end. This helped him to form a philosophy that was based on indulgence of desires. He listed Nine Satanic Statements that he said helped to clarify his doctrines."

Murphy projected a slide with the information.

LAVEY'S NINE SATANIC STATEMENTS

1. Satan represents indulgence, instead of abstinence.
2. Satan represents vital existence, instead of spiritual pipe dreams.
3. Satan represents undefiled wisdom, instead of hypocritical self-deceit.
4. Satan represents kindness to those who deserve it, instead of love wasted on ingrates.

5. Satan represents vengeance, instead of turning the other cheek.
6. Satan represents responsibility to the responsible, instead of concern for psychic vampires.
7. Satan represents man as just another animal, sometimes better, more often worse than those that walk on all fours, who, because of his "divine spiritual and intellectual development," has become the most vicious animal of all.
8. Satan represents all of the so-called sins, as they all lead to physical, mental, or emotional gratification.
9. Satan has been the best friend the church has ever had, as he has kept it in business all these years.

Murphy glanced at the clock on the wall. "We have time for one more question."

"Dr. Murphy, do you have other examples of worship of angels or otherworldly creatures?"

"There are many. Not all of them focus on angels, demons, or other creatures. Some focus on demonic types of philosophy."

Murphy clicked up his last slide.

"Here's a list of some of the things that have grown out of demon-related thinking."

ALTERED STATES OF CONSCIOUSNESS

Astrology	**Ouija Boards**
Auras	**Parapsychology**
Blood rituals	**Psychic surgery**

Channeling
Crystal Work
Dreamwork
Dungeons & Dragons
Eastern gurus
Edgar Cayce
Exorcism rituals
Friday the 13th
Lucis Trust
Macumba
Mantras & mandalas
Psychics
Pyramid Power
Regression therapy
Santeria
Scientology
Shamanism
Tarot cards
UFOs
Voodoo
Wicca
Yoga

"As we end our class today, I would like you to think about two questions: One, to what extent have I been exposed to occult-type philosophy? And two, how has it affected my thinking and daily life? For example, even some Christians read their astrology charts. Some have little mantras that they repeat over and over. And some are deeply enmeshed in Ouija boards, tarot cards, and other occult objects.

"What about you?"

TWENTY-FOUR

MURPHY DEBATED for a moment as he stood in the line at the Student Center—should he go ahead and order the hamburger and French fries, or a tuna salad sandwich? He had been very faithful in his workout schedule. . . . a combination of running, lifting weights, and karate practice three times a week. And now, as the smell of the hamburgers frying on the grill wafted up to his nostrils, his entire body craved the burger.

I deserve a reward for doing my ninety push-ups a day.

"What will it be, Dr. Murphy?" asked the short-order cook.

Murphy hesitated for a moment, and then let out a sigh.

"I'll take the tuna salad."

"Would you like anything else with it?"

Murphy wanted a chocolate fudge sundae with it.

"Just water, Susan. Thank you."

He found his usual secluded spot, away from most of the other tables and hidden by some shrubbery. He sat down and stared out the window at the lush green campus. It was good to get a break from questions by the students. He had just taken a bite of his sandwich when he heard a voice behind him.

"Do you mind if I join you?"

Murphy turned and looked into the blue eyes of Summer Van Doren. He stood and pulled back one of the chairs, gesturing for her to sit down as he quickly chewed and swallowed.

"Please."

"I'm sorry that I had to leave your class early. I had a short meeting with the head of the Physical Education Department." She brushed a few stray hairs out of her face.

"That's quite all right. Are you feeling comfortable in your new position as women's volleyball coach?"

"I love it. The students seem eager and the Preston campus is a garden paradise. Just a little more humidity than I'm used to."

"Where do you call home?"

"San Diego, California. I was born and raised there."

"That's a beautiful place also. I've been told that the weather there is gorgeous year-round."

"Yes, it is. Just a little fog in the mornings if you live near the beach."

"Is that where you lived?"

"Yes. I lived in Del Mar just a couple of blocks from the beach."

"Did you surf?"

"All the time. It's a great sport. During the summers I was a lifeguard."

Murphy looked at her and nodded his head slightly. *She does look the part. A southern California beauty with blond hair.*

"Dr. Murphy, I find it interesting that you are talking about false gods, and good and evil angels in your class. At the Preston Community Church, Pastor Wagoner is also talking about false teachers and fallen angels."

"Please, call me Michael . . . and yes, you're right. Bob is a close friend and we've been talking a great deal about the rise of the occult, false teachers, and demonic influence in our society. It bothered him terribly that it had infiltrated the church. Some members have gotten involved with the occult, and he thought it wise to warn the people as to what to watch out for."

"I could tell that your students are very interested in the topic, and they really seem to enjoy your classes—especially Clayton."

"Maybe Clayton enjoys it a little *too* much."

"I like the way you integrate your faith into the classroom. It seems so natural."

"Well, not everyone likes it."

"Are you referring to Dean Fallworth?"

He raised his eyebrows in response.

"Is he one of the gargoyles you were talking about in your class?"

Murphy chuckled. "How did you guess?"

"I've heard some of the other teachers talking about him. They think he's wound a little too tight."

Murphy saw Summer cast a furtive glance at his left hand, reminding him that he was not wearing his wedding band. If she noticed, she did not mention it.

"Michael, you talked about fallen angels or demons in your class. Do you think there is much demonic activity today?"

"My guess is that there is more than we are aware of. Does the name Dennis Rader mean anything to you?"

"It doesn't ring a bell."

"Maybe you remember him better as the BTK Killer."

"Yes, that does sound familiar. . . ."

"Rader tortured and killed ten people. In his testimony, he said that demons told him to do it. A number of mass murderers have made similar claims."

"Do you think the demons always compel their subjects to commit murder?"

"I don't think so. Those are extreme cases. A number of Bible scholars believe that most demonic activity takes on more subtle forms. Things like extended depression, suicidal thoughts, debilitating anxiety, and doubts about God."

"Do you believe that all emotional problems are rooted in demonic activity?"

"Of course not, but when demonic activity takes place, it just exacerbates the individual's emotional turmoil. This type makes it very hard for counselors to distinguish between demonic attacks and psychological problems."

"How do people deal with this demonic activity?"

"Very carefully. In recent years there have been more and more discussions about exorcism or the casting out of demons. Some have even developed what are called 'deliverance ministries.'"

"It sounds a little scary."

"I think there has to be a balance. There is a danger in saying there is no such thing as demonic activity . . . and there is a danger in seeing demons everywhere. Jesus is a good example to follow. Most of the people He dealt with were normal people with normal problems. He did, however, occasionally encounter people under demonic possession. He effectively dealt with both kinds of people."

"I've heard that missionaries to non-Western countries have more exposure to demon possession. Have you heard that?"

"Yes. Many missionaries report that they see more outward manifestations of demonic or occult activity. This is especially true in areas where voodoo is practiced. In some countries people go into trances and some pierce their bodies with large nails and other items. People have been known to throw themselves onto fires or into the water or onto the ground in convulsions."

"What about in the United States?"

"I think the occult influence takes on the forms of séances, card readers, use of spirit guides, and various forms of cult worship. You might recall Sergeant Loye Pourner. He was the officer from Travis Air Force Base in California who fought for his faith. He claimed that he was a high priest of Wicca. I think that demons are smart enough to work within a culture to capture the thinking of people. In less developed cultures they use outward manifestations. In more advanced societies they modify their presentations."

"It seems like some people have adopted sensational methods for dealing with demons."

"Some have, Summer. They seem to think that every sin is prompted by demons. That simply is not true. We all are capable of doing wrong without the help of any demon. This type of thinking removes responsibility for one's actions. You know the popular saying 'The Devil made me do it.' Some people think that if they remove the demon they will be able to live a good life. Truly good living comes from a relationship with God."

"Michael, have you ever had to face a demon?"

"No, and I hope I never will. Demons are very powerful. However, they are not as powerful as God. If demons are to be cast out of someone, it must be in the name and power of Jesus Christ. The Bible suggests that if we resist the Devil and his followers, they will flee from us."

"I'm with you. I don't think I'd like to make an occupation of casting out demons. I'll think I'll stick with volleyball." Summer looked at her watch. "And speaking of which, I have a class in about ten minutes. I don't know where the time went."

They both stood up.

"Thanks for the stimulating conversation, Michael," Summer said with a smile that could melt the polar ice caps.

"Great talking to you too."

Murphy sat back down and watched Summer depart as a growing

confusion gnawed at him. Both Isis and Summer were strikingly beautiful women, warm and well spoken and intelligent. The one difference was that Summer shared the same faith as Murphy. They could connect on a different level than he and Isis. Until now, he hadn't realized how much he missed that.

Still, it bothered him that he could be attracted to Summer when he had such strong feelings for Isis.

TWENTY-FIVE

MURPHY AND WAGONER were amazed as they drove the rented panel van onto the field. If the overfull parking area was any indication, the crowds attending J. B. Sonstad's Faith in God Crusade had increased. They noticed that two smaller overflow tents had been set up to accommodate the extra people. The men in orange vests had their hands full trying to get everyone to park in an orderly fashion.

Murphy briefly followed the traffic and then turned back toward the large tent. He went past the first row of parked cars and maneuvered to a spot not far from the semi truck housing Sonstad's television equipment. There were also a couple of smaller vans parked nearby belonging to local television stations.

Murphy stopped near the vans. He and Wagoner got out and placed two antennas on top of their van.

Murphy was the first to speak.

"Have you come up with anything on Sonstad since our last visit?"

"Yes, I searched on the Internet and discovered that Sonstad is married and has three children. His only daughter, the youngest of his children, got married last year."

"Nothing unusual about that."

"You're right, except for one thing. I ran across a newspaper article that said that Sonstad put on a massive wedding for her at an exclusive country club. Dignitaries and important businesspeople from around the globe were in attendance. It was a formal sit-down dinner with well-known vocalists and musicians as entertainers. Cascading flowers, gourmet food, expensive champagne. And the article even tallied up the total cost. Care to hazard a guess?"

"Fifty thousand dollars?"

"He spent one point two million dollars for the wedding."

"You've got to be kidding! How long does it take to earn that much money, let alone spend it on a wedding? And where did the money come from?"

"What do you mean, Murphy? Doesn't every pastor of a church spend one point two million dollars on his daughter's wedding?"

"I guess I shouldn't be surprised. My own research indicated that the Sonstads own homes in Atlanta and San Diego, not to mention their ranch in Montana and their holdings in a television network."

"Well, at least we know that his preaching that God wants you to be rich works for him."

Murphy and Wagoner continued to make preparations and then went into the main tent. It seemed totally packed so they joined a number of people who were standing in the back.

They watched the people get worked up as the music played.

Sonstad's entrance onto the platform was even more flamboyant than the last time. He quieted the audience and began his supposed conversation with God.

"Yes, Lord. I'm listening. . . . What's that you say? . . . There's going to be an end to the conflict between the Palestinians and the Jews. . . . They are going to live in harmony. . . . When will this take place, Lord? . . . In a year and a half . . . Praise God! Thank you! . . . I'll tell the people."

By now the people were on their feet yelling and cheering. The noise was deafening.

Wagoner leaned over and yelled into Murphy's ear.

"Oh, that reminds me. While I was doing my research on Sonstad I discovered that he often prophesizes on future events."

Murphy yelled back to Wagoner.

"Have any of his prophecies ever come true?"

"A couple. But they were so general that you or I could have made them. At least a dozen of the ones I looked at never came to pass."

"Doesn't the Bible suggest that a prophet, if he speaks for God, has to be one hundred percent accurate?"

"True."

"Didn't they stone prophets that did not tell the truth?"

"Yes, they did. But I don't think you'll see anyone throwing stones at Sonstad here today."

"Well, Bob, I have to admit he is a great speaker. He knows how to manipulate a crowd. He would do well selling used cars, or refrigerators to Eskimos."

Murphy left Wagoner for a few minutes and went out to the van.

"What did I miss?" Murphy asked upon his return.

"Not much."

The crusade continued, with Sonstad having conversations with God and calling out the names of people with diseases. When their names were called they came to the platform, were touched on the head by Sonstad, fell to the ground, were helped up by the catchers, and returned to their seats. By the time the twentieth person was healed in this manner the crowd was beside itself. It was time for a good offering.

While the offering was being collected, Murphy and Wagoner quietly discussed what they had seen.

"Bob, have you noticed how Sonstad works some wonderful disclaimers into his talks?"

"What do you mean?"

"The first is that if you have enough faith, you will be healed. That gives him a great out if nothing happens and the person isn't healed. It's because they didn't have enough faith. It's not Sonstad's fault."

"But Jesus healed a number of people that didn't exercise any faith in His healing."

"Right, Bob. The second is when he says, 'The Lord doesn't always heal in the meeting. Many times He does the healing at home when you are alone.' This gives him another out for anyone not healed during the meeting.

"The other thing I was aware of was that most of the supposed healings were for problems or diseases that you could not see. Things like liver disease, kidney disease, or diabetes. How could anyone at the meeting tell if anyone was truly healed? They couldn't see it."

"That gives Sonstad another safety blanket, doesn't it, Michael?"

"Right. And did you notice that no one with a withered arm or leg was healed? That would really be something to see. There were no blind people whose sight was restored. No lepers who were cleansed. And no physically or mentally disabled people who were cured of their disability."

Murphy and Wagoner watched as the people left the meeting greatly excited about what they had seen. They could hear many people talking about how wonderful J. B. Sonstad was and what a great earthly messenger he was for God.

They made their way back to their rented van.

"Do you think it worked?" asked Wagoner.

"We'll soon see. Everything was on and functioning when I left."

They opened the van, climbed in, and shut the door. Murphy could see that the red lights were still on and the recording device was running.

"Let's rewind the tape and see what we've got."

"Where did you get all of this equipment?" asked Wagoner.

"I borrowed it from Levi Abrams. He said that it would pick up any conversations broadcasted within a half mile."

Murphy turned on the tape. They could clearly hear the voice of a woman speaking.

"Look toward your left. The third section. The man in the blue shirt. His name is Carl and he has been suffering with diabetes for three years."

"You've got to be kidding, Michael. When you told me that you thought that Sonstad had a receiver attached to his headset microphone, I thought you were crazy. Who is that woman speaking?"

"It's Sonstad's wife. I saw her when I came back to turn on the equipment in the van. The back door to the semi truck with all the television equipment was open and I could see her looking at the monitors. I recognized her from her pictures on the posters outside of the tent."

"How did she get the information about the people in the audience with problems?"

"It was fairly easy. Remember when we went into the tent? We were given prayer cards asking if we needed healing and what the ailment was so that their staff could pray for us. They would single out certain people and write down what they were wearing and where they would be sitting. Sonstad's wife would then pick up one of the cards and relay the message with the information to Sonstad while he was onstage."

"So he really was having a conversation with someone . . . only it wasn't God."

"You've got that right, Bob. Let's see if the rest of the tape is clear."

Murphy and Wagoner listened to the entire tape. There were twenty clear messages from Sonstad's wife to him on the stage. They could even hear her final words before she stopped broadcasting.

"Don't go so long tonight. We have a late dinner appointment across town. I'm hungry. By the way, the last lady that you're going to deal with has been in a mental hospital before. You might tell her that she will never have to go there again."

"This is unbelievable!" Wagoner fumed. "We've got to expose them somehow."

"I think we should give the tapes to Steven Bennett at the *Raleigh Gazette*. He's a hard-hitting, no-nonsense, investigative reporter who will take the information and run with it. I'm sure that he'll do a whole exposé that will put an end to Sonstad's charlatan crusade."

"Michael, is what he's doing illegal?"

"I'm not sure. At the very least, it is misleading, unethical, and brings negative publicity to all the ministers and organizations that are doing the Lord's work. I'm not sure that the general public will be able to tell the difference, though. They might just throw the baby out with the bathwater. As far as I'm concerned, people like that cause great harm and should be held accountable for it."

A week later, Murphy received a phone call from Wagoner.

"Did you see Steven Bennett's television interview of J. B. Sonstad?"

"No, Bob. What happened?"

"Well, Bennett confronted him with sound bites of his wife talking to him. He said, 'Yes, that was my wife. We weren't doing anything wrong. We were merely trying to strengthen the weak faith of some of those in the audience. When they think that God is speaking directly to them, it ignites hope in their hearts. The seed of faith sprouts in their minds and for the first time they believe that God cares about them enough to heal them of their illness. That, in turn, motivates them to stand and come forward to be healed. When all is said and done, God gets the glory and everyone is joyful.' Sonstad then invited Bennett to come to the meetings himself."

"Unbelievable," said Murphy. "Unbelievable."

TWENTY-SIX

"UTTERLY MAGNIFICENT, Jakoba! It's incredible," said Viorica Enesco as they walked around the statue.

"Yes, it is true. The Academy has many works of art, but I think that Michelangelo's statue of David is the grandest. The architect Emilio de Fabris constructed the *tribuna* in 1873 just to house it."

Viorica cocked her head to one side and then the other, and stared for a long time at the thirteen-and-a-half-foot-high naked body.

"Wouldn't it be wonderful if all men looked as good as this statue?"

They both laughed.

The portly Sir William Merton waddled up beside them. He was wearing his usual jacket and collar of the English cleric. Viorica thought it was too bad that Sir Merton's body didn't match his brilliant mind.

"What are you two laughing at?"

"Oh, nothing," said Viorica, brushing her fingers through her red hair and giving Jakoba a knowing look.

They both giggled.

Women! he thought. *Who will ever understand them?*

He continued to speak. "Isn't it delightful that John Bartholomew chose Florence for our meeting? Italy is always so charming, especially at this time of year. How I love to meander around the Piazza Annunziata and do a little people watching. And have you ladies noticed all of the colorful and elegant scarves that the women are wearing?"

Viorica and Jakoba nodded their heads. They both thought it unusual for a man to notice such things.

"Oh, there you are," said Señor Mendez. "I've been looking for you. John would like the meeting to begin in one hour. He asked me to round everyone up. Have you seen General Li and Ganesh Shesha?"

"Yes," replied Jakoba. "I believe they're in the cathedral looking at the dome."

"I'm glad you are all here. We need to make a decision with regard to Reverend De La Rosa. We will be seeing him in Rome in a few days. Shall we give him the go-ahead?"

General Li nodded his head and spoke. "I think that the time is right. We should encourage him to put the program into full swing. The world is ready for a religious leader to unify all of the religions into a one-world church. People are tired of all the conservative religious right hogwash. Evangelical Christians are a danger to everyone."

"I agree," replied Ganesh. "In India, the people are tired of all the fighting and killing over religion. I think they would welcome a peacemaker."

"I concur," responded Sir William. "The people of Great Britain and the United States have had their fill of corrupt preachers, strange sects, and weird cults. I think they would be drawn to a religious leader who exuded integrity and honesty. Especially when he is able to back up his words with some bona fide miracles."

"We must instruct Shane Barrington to have his television crews follow De La Rosa everywhere he goes. They should be there to record all of his miracles for the whole world to see. Once the people hear his convincing message, it won't be long before everyone believes in him."

"I agree with Viorica. The media will be a powerful tool toward our goal," said Bartholomew.

"Are we ready for the mark?" asked Jakoba.

"I think it's a little early. De La Rosa needs to develop a strong following before he introduces the marking system for buying and selling. When the people trust his message of peace and unity, then we can institute the controls of the mark. He will need to provide sustenance for the poor for a period of time. Once the masses think he is the great provider not only of spiritual truth but also of food and clothing, it will be easy to persuade them to voluntarily take the mark. We will disrupt the flow of goods and services for those who do not have the mark, and blame it on the unbelievers. They will be forced to comply or become global pariahs. We will starve them into oblivion."

They lifted their wineglasses and drank a toast. John Bartholomew turned to General Li.

"General Li, have your informants any new information on the activities of Dr. Murphy?"

"Yes. He and a man named Bob Wagoner have begun to expose some false teachers in the United States. But I don't think it will garner much attention. These people have large and loyal followings as a result of their television programs and literature. Murphy and his ally will be rejected as religious wacko extremists."

"Perhaps," responded Sir William. "But I am a little tired of his continual irritating interruptions. He is like a bulldog that won't release its grip. Is there something that can be done about him? I'm afraid that when De La Rosa begins to gain popularity, Murphy will do what he can to discredit him. He will not see De La Rosa as a prophet."

"The answer is obvious," said Jakoba. "Send Talon to kill Murphy."

Barrington frowned. "Easier said than done. Dr. Murphy has proven most resourceful in the past. Furthermore, if Murphy becomes a martyr for his cause, it could do us more harm than good."

"I've got an idea," said Mendez. "We had Talon kill his wife and that slowed him down for a while. We instructed Talon to get rid of his girlfriend. That would have succeeded if the police hadn't shown up at the last minute. How about eliminating his assistant, Shari Nelson? They are very close and perhaps Murphy will get the message that no one he cares about is safe so long as he opposes us."

A grin crept across Bartholomew's face. *Perfect.*

TWENTY-SEVEN

MURPHY HAD HIS BACK to the counter and didn't notice the approach of the man in the tailored blue pin-striped suit. He was sipping his Starbucks coffee and daydreaming about finding Aaron's Rod and the Golden Jar of Manna. It would be an archaeological find that would stun the world and put Bible critics on the run. Physical proof of the Bible's authenticity.

"Dr. Murphy. Do you mind if I join you?"

Murphy turned and looked full into the face of Shane Barrington. His flint-gray eyes burned with intensity, and he'd gone a little grayer at his temples than when Murphy last saw him. Light reflected off the gold Rolex watch on his wrist as he brought his coffee to his lips.

"Be my guest."

Murphy's mind quickly shifted back to the last encounter they'd had. It was when he had asked Murphy to come do a show on archaeology for the Barrington Communications Network. It had turned less than cordial when he turned him down. Barrington wasn't used to people saying no to him and he demanded a reason.

"Because I don't want to be a part of your sleazy organization. Your late-night shows are nothing but pornography. Your prime-time shows are filled with sexual innuendos, distasteful language, and an assault on morality. Your comedy shows make fun of everything that is decent in America. Your reality shows don't even touch reality. And you support political leaders who are corrupt. If I've left anything out, I apologize. To quote a verse from the Psalms, 'I would rather be a doorkeeper in the house of my God than dwell in the tents of wickedness.'"

After that response, Murphy was surprised to see him and even more surprised that Barrington wanted to talk to him.

"I guess we both like a good cup of coffee."

Murphy nodded in agreement.

"You're a long way from home."

"I'm in town to close the deal on a television station. We recently bought KKBC Channel Twenty-four."

"I saw that on the news. How many stations do you now own?"

"Thirty-two, plus a number of radio stations. Have you seen our new religious program?"

"The one promoting Reverend Constantine De La Rosa?"

"Yes, that's the one. What do you think?"

Strange. Barrington doesn't care a whit for anyone else's opinion. Is it small talk or is he probing for something?

"He certainly has charisma . . . and the ability to use all of the catchphrases." Barrington looked at him quizzically, so Murphy began to rattle them off: " 'Unity in the midst of diversity,' 'a culture of peace and security,' 'honoring the environment,' 'discouraging absolutism,' 'encouraging tolerance for all sects, cults, and methods for worship'. . ."

"Don't you think those things are important?"

"Actually, Mr. Barrington, I think they're a little dangerous."

"Dangerous?"

"Yes. The Bible talks about what is called 'the last days.' During that time there will come many false teachers and prophets. They will say things that will tickle people's ears and will outwardly sound beneficial for all men and women. They will take on the form of being godly but inwardly they deny the truth of the Bible."

"But how about some of the miracles that De La Rosa has performed. There was a blind man that had his sight restored. And a woman who was deaf and can now hear. Those have to be acts of God, don't they?"

"Not necessarily. The Book of Revelation talks about a man who will come to prominence during the last days. He is referred to as the False Prophet. He will have great powers and will be able to perform miracles. He will have a plan to establish a world church and will gain control of global religious affairs. Let me ask you some questions: Does this De La Rosa talk about forming a worldwide church? Is he performing miracles? Do you think he might be deceiving people?"

Barrington was silent for a moment. He knew how corrupt he was . . . and he knew how corrupt the Seven were . . . and he knew that the Seven had forced him to give television coverage to De La Rosa. He had insight enough to know that Murphy might have put his finger on the truth. Barrington didn't believe in God like Murphy, but he did admire Murphy's ability to not mince words and to speak honestly.

"Are you saying that he is the False Prophet?"

"I don't know that for sure, but we can get some idea by looking at what he believes. Does he have an appreciation for the gospel? That means the good news that Christ died for our sins, was buried, rose from the dead, and was seen by numerous people."

"I don't know."

"Well, when I've heard him speak he does not refer to Christ at all. He talks about the brotherhood of man a lot. He talks about unity of beliefs and occasionally he will mention the name of God. But when he accepts everything from Wicca to UFO cults, I don't think he believes the gospel. In fact, there is an underlying current of rejection of Christianity in his speeches. He talks about tolerating everything and that there are no absolutes. However, there are absolutes. There is right and wrong. There is good and evil in this world."

Barrington couldn't say much. He knew there was lots of evil in the world and he hadn't seen very much good.

"But Reverend De La Rosa seems to want to do good for the poor people and help develop peace in the world."

"Well, then, Mr. Barrington. Since your communications network is promoting him, and since you seem to be trying to convince me, may I ask you a question?"

"I suppose."

"Are you becoming one of his followers? Do you believe in what he says? Are you going to follow his example?"

Barrington knew he should answer yes. He was a consummate liar, but somehow he didn't want to lie to Murphy about this. If he said no, he wasn't going to follow De La Rosa, he knew that Murphy would ask, *Then why are you promoting him?*

"My communications network covers all kinds of news. Constantine De La Rosa is news just like the pope, or Mother Teresa, or any other famous religious leader."

They both knew that Barrington had skirted the issue. Murphy approached it another way.

"You see, here's the difference, Mr. Barrington: When someone truly believes in something, that belief changes the way they live. I believe that Christ is God's son and that He came to rescue me from my sins, my wrongful thoughts and deeds. Because I believe this, I try to follow the teachings of Christ in my daily life. Are you suggesting that you believe in and follow the teachings of De La Rosa?"

Barrington didn't like to be pressed. He had to keep his temper in check.

"Frankly, I don't know that much about him yet. He is just starting his Religious Harmony Institute. Our plans are to cover his upcoming World Unity Summit. We'll see what comes out of all of that."

"I'll be watching and listening intently to what he has to say. If he is not the False Prophet, he will not contradict the Bible in any way. In my view he has already started to separate himself from the promises found in Scripture. Be careful, Mr. Barrington . . . you may be promoting the wrong person."

Murphy got in his car and drove back to the university. He wasn't concentrating on his driving as much as on his conversation with Barrington.

Lord, why did You bring him into my life today? Am I supposed to have some kind of influence in his life? He's power hungry, arrogant, and difficult to like. Help me to be tolerant. Please give me patience and the wisdom to have the right words to speak.

As Barrington rode back to KKBC Channel Twenty-four, he felt uneasy. He didn't like to admit it, but Murphy was right. There was something corrupt about De La Rosa. He also didn't like the fact that the Seven had threatened him into promoting this golden-tongued religious hypocrite. He was getting very tired of them pulling the strings of his life. His anger continued to grow as he reflected that it was the Seven who had ordered Talon to kill Stephanie Kovacs and his son. Barrington felt like he was going to explode as thoughts of revenge dominated his mind.

TWENTY-EIGHT

THE SUN WAS BEGINNING to set and the sky was filled with spectacular reds, oranges, and golden colors. The smell of steaks cooking on the barbecue made the mouth water. It was a typical warm North Carolina evening. Murphy and Isis sat in his backyard. They had decided to have a quiet dinner at his place rather than going out. There was something very appealing about just relaxing together and watching a rented movie.

After dinner, Murphy and Isis cleaned up the kitchen. Murphy washed while Isis dried the dishes. They laughed and joked through the process. It felt so natural to be together. In a word, it was comfortable.

It wasn't long before they were cuddling together on the sofa. Both their feet were on the coffee table in front of them. Murphy had his arm around her, and her head was snuggled into his chest. Murphy thought, *This is something I could get used to.*

As the movie ended, Isis got up to get a drink of water.

"Is there anything I can get you while I'm up?"

Murphy leaned back and watched Isis move about in the kitchen.

"I guess I'll have one of those apples."

He turned back and began flipping the channels. But nothing on the TV screen captured his interest. All he could think about was Iris.

"Here, catch."

Murphy's quick hands shot up to catch the apple that she had tossed. He fell back on the sofa in the attempt, and before he could sit back up, Isis had hopped over the back of the sofa and landed on top of him with a laugh. Surprised, Murphy looked at her. As their eyes locked, she leaned in and gave him a long, passionate kiss. They had been building to this moment the whole night. Maybe much longer than that.

Murphy dropped the apple and his arms enfolded her in a strong embrace. It felt so good to hold her and to show how much he cared for her. They exchanged one passionate kiss after another, completely lost in the moment.

The phone began ringing. Murphy tried to ignore it, but it wouldn't stop. He couldn't believe that after all this time, a ringing phone was ruining their long-awaited moment. And the phone just kept on ringing.

Murphy groped around with one hand for the receiver.

"This is Murphy!" he barked, sounding not exactly pleased with the interruption.

"What's the matter, Murphy? Did you get up on the wrong side of the bed? It's only ten-thirty at night."

Murphy felt like he was in a fog for a moment and then he recognized the voice. It was Levi Abrams. At the same moment he also realized something else. Isis was gone. He looked about the room. The television was on but she had vanished. Then it hit him like a ton of bricks. She was never there. He had fallen asleep and Levi's phone call had awakened him from a most pleasurable dream.

"Sorry, Levi. I fell asleep in front of the TV."

"Well, that's what happens when you get older. I hope that I didn't wake you from a good dream."

"As a matter of fact, Levi, you did. Anyway, what's on your mind?"

"My mind? I'm just returning your call. You left a message on my answering machine . . . or did you do that in your sleep too?"

"Oh, yeah. I did call."

"You're not becoming one of those absentminded professors, are you?"

"I guess I am . . . or I'm still enjoying my dream. Anyway, I need your help."

"Another fingerprint for Methuselah?"

"No. This has to do with Ashdod."

"You mean, Ashdod, the city in Israel?"

"Right. I got a note from Methuselah that indicates there may be some important artifacts hidden in Ashdod."

"But Ashdod is not that old of a city. You mean someone has brought artifacts into the city?"

"I'm sorry, Levi. I must still be half asleep. I mean the original Ashdod, located three to four miles inland. It was the city that housed the Temple of Dagon."

"I don't know much about the original site. In some of our Hebrew classes I remember that Ashdod was supposed to be the home of the Anakites. They were a tribe that produced people of extraordinarily large stature."

"Do you have a moment to talk about it?"

"Why don't we get together at the gym tomorrow and talk about it. I could use a good workout, and I need to practice my karate on someone. How about doing a little sparing?"

"You're on. What time?"

"I've got an eight o'clock meeting. How about six A.M., if you can tear yourself away from your dreams."

"You're on. I'll see you there."

Murphy batted aside the large fist and snapped a swift kick with his left leg. Levi gamely deflected the move and the two circled around each other on the mat.

"Getting slow, Murphy," Abrams taunted.

"I'm just going easy on you. I know what a crybaby you are."

Levi unleashed a fierce volley of punches and kicks, but Murphy blocked or dodged every one, and then went on the offensive. They were perfectly matched. After a half hour of intense sparring, Murphy and Abrams sat down to rest.

"Levi, your reverse punches are like hammers. How did you develop them?"

"With paper."

"Paper?"

"A reverse punch comes from the hip position. The fist is made with the fingers and thumb facing upward. As the fist comes forward, it rotates with a twisting motion. At the end of the blow, the fingers and thumb are facing downward. The final twist happens at the last split second before impact. The purpose of the twist is to tear the skin and shatter the bone."

"I don't think you shattered my ribs but it certainly felt like it."

"Actually, I pulled the punch a little or it would have. It works sort of like a bullet shot out of a gun. The barrel of the gun has ribs inside that cause the bullet to twist. As the bullet enters a person's body, it is spinning. It is that motion that shatters bones. Although the reverse punch doesn't travel as fast as a bullet, it operates on the same principle."

"What's that have to do with paper?"

"You practice with paper. You take an eight-by-eleven sheet of paper and suspend it from two strings. The paper is hung about shoulder level. You then throw a reverse punch at the center of the paper. If you are throwing the punch correctly—that is, twisting the punch at the last second—it will tear the paper where the knuckles hit it. If you twist the knuckles a fraction of a second too soon or too late, the paper will not tear. It will just move with the punch. The object is not to tear the paper away from the strings holding it, but to tear it in half with the twisting motion of the knuckles while it is still attached to the strings."

"That sounds very difficult."

"It is. It takes a lot of speed. The body must remain completely relaxed throughout the movement. Tension in the arm will slow down the blow. With practice, you can begin to do the twisting necessary at the last second. It will tear the paper if done properly."

"I'll try that at home."

"Enough of the karate lesson. Tell me about Ashdod. What are you looking for?"

"Well, do you remember from your Hebrew classes that the Ark of the Covenant was captured by the Philistines and taken to Ashdod?"

"Yes. They took it before the statue of Dagon and left it there overnight. The next day the statue of Dagon had fallen on its face. Wait a minute, Michael. Are you saying that you might find the Ark of the Covenant in Ashdod?"

"No, I don't think so. But we may find what was inside the Ark."

"Inside?"

"Yes. We may find Aaron's Rod that budded and the Golden Jar that contained manna from the wilderness journey."

"That would be incredible, Michael. That would be an astounding find. I would be glad to help you any way I can."

"That would be great, Levi. Do you think you can push through the paperwork for an archaeological dig in Ashdod?"

"I don't think that should be a problem. The Israeli government and the Israeli Archaeological Society would be most interested in this project. I'll call Moshe Pearlman tomorrow."

"Who is Moshe?"

"He's one of the men who worked with me in the Mossad. I will ask him to go to Ashdod and check it out for us. In the meantime, I'll start the paperwork. We'll try to eliminate as much red tape as possible."

"Maybe you can suspend all the forms from two strings and just tear them with your nasty reverse punch."

"That does it," Levi said. "Back on the mat. You're about to see my reverse punch up close and personal."

Murphy grinned and took a defensive posture. "Bring it on, tough guy."

TWENTY-NINE

In a field near the town of Ebenezer, 1083 B.C.

MISHMANNAH THE BENJAMITE *had been with the soldiers guarding the Ark of the Covenant when the Philistines unleashed their ambush. He was one of the first to spot them coming, and yelled to alert Captain Gaddiel. The captain had turned to look at Mishmannah an instant before an arrow entered his chest. Without a word, the captain fell forward to the ground, breaking the arrow that had pierced his heart.*

Mishmannah, along with his fellow soldiers, had fought valiantly, but it was too little, too late. He ducked as a spear was thrown, just missing him by inches. He turned and raised his sword a moment too late. A Philistine sword slashed his stomach and he collapsed in the throes of death.

Neziah and Bazluth saw the attack on the Ark and rushed forward. A wounded Philistine reached out and grabbed at Bazluth's foot as he ran by.

He tripped and went down. Another Philistine raised his spear to drive it into the downed Bazluth.

Neziah saw the move and swung his sword with all of his might into the Philistine's side. The Philistine screamed and dropped his spear and fell on top of Bazluth. Bazluth's eyes were wide with terror as he pushed the body off and struggled to his feet. He was covered with the Philistine's blood.

Neziah was relieved to see his younger brother was not injured. He turned to rejoin the battle, when a battle-ax glanced off the side of his head.

The blow rendered him unconscious. Blood from his wound flowed down across his face and pooled in front of his nose as he lay on the ground. The Philistines assumed that he was dead and went on to capture the Ark.

It was late in the evening when Neziah awoke with a very painful headache. Instinctively he reached his hand up to touch the wound and winced as his fingers felt the gash on his head. The blood had clotted and dried in his black hair.

He slowly sat up, listening for any sounds or indications that he was still in danger. As he tried to focus his eyes in the dark, he became aware of many bodies on the ground around him.

He staggered to his feet, struggling to keep his balance. He tried to grasp what had happened in the battle. Even in the dark, he could recognize the markings on the uniforms of the Israelite army. Most of the bodies on the ground were his fellow warriors.

Then the thought hit him, What about Bazluth? *He began to look over the bodies around him. Ten minutes later he found his brother. There was a gaping wound on his neck and his eyes were frozen open in terror. Neziah let out a deep cry of anguish and fell weeping next to his brother. He held him and cried until no more tears would come.*

Neziah knew that it would be dangerous to linger on the battlefield. He guessed that the Philistines would return at the light of dawn and begin to strip the soldiers of any valuables and kill any of the enemy that might still be alive. He lifted his brother up and began to carry him.

Neziah had no idea where his army had gone. He was alone. He was tired and in pain and emotionally drained. He carried Bazluth's body to a spot near a tree and laid it down. He then found a sword from a fallen soldier and used it to dig a shallow grave. He gathered some rocks and covered the fresh earth in an effort to discourage any animals from digging there. The tears returned as he sat still in the darkness. The night had grown chilly and he began to shiver. Close by he saw a robe from a fallen soldier and wrapped it around his shaking body.

I will head back to Shiloh, *he thought to himself,* and hope that the enemy has not gone in that direction.

He looked at the sky and stars to get his bearings and then began his twenty-five-mile journey to Shiloh. He had to step over the bodies of several hundred Israelites before he left the battlefield. He was sick with grief as his thoughts dwelled on Bazluth.

No one could persuade Eli the high priest to stay at home. He had worried about the Ark of the Covenant being taken to the battlefront by Hophni and Phinehas. They had not asked his permission. In fact, they no longer asked his permission about anything pertaining to the operation of the tabernacle of meeting. They did whatever they liked.

Hophni and Phinehas had always been willful children and Eli had been too permissive with them. Now that he was ninety-eight years old, very fat, very tired, and blind, he did not have the energy to confront them. He had heard about their taking sacrifice meat offered to God and using it for their own families. He had also heard about their laying with many women. He knew it was wrong, but as always, he was powerless to do anything about their behavior.

Eli had one of his servants take him to the rock wall that lined the ramp leading up to Shiloh. He wanted to sit there all day until some word about the Ark of the Covenant reached him.

It was late in the day when Neziah arrived at Shiloh. As he started up the ramp to the city he spotted the high priest sitting on the wall. With great consternation he approached the blind patriarch.

"Sir," said Neziah to Eli.

Eli turned in the direction of the voice. "Yes, my son."

"I bring news from the battlefield."

"Yes, yes. Please tell me."

"I fled the battlefield last night. I was wounded and separated from the rest of the army."

"Go on, my son."

"The battle was lost and Israel has fled before the Philistines. There has been a great and terrible slaughter of our people."

Neziah saw the look of fear come over Eli's face . . . his blind eyes seeing nothing.

"And what news do you have of my sons and the Ark of the Covenant?"

Neziah hesitated. His thoughts went back to the battlefield and the death of his brother and the horror of what he had seen. He felt nauseated.

"Go on, my son. Please tell me. I have been sitting here worrying."

"I am so sorry to have to bring you such sad news. Your two sons, Hophni and Phinehas, are dead; and the Ark of God has been captured by the Philistines."

The old man was silent, but the shock was too much for him. He fell backward off the rock wall. If the horror of Neziah's words did not take his life, then the fall that broke his neck certainly did. Neziah stood there, stunned. He could only look up at the sky and silently ask, Why?

Nimrah had called for the birthing stool and the midwives. The labor pains were growing stronger. Her pregnancy had not been an easy one. Added to her pain was her emotional displeasure that the soldiers had taken Phinehas and the Ark of the Covenant to the battle with the Philistines.

A husband should be with his wife when she is giving birth, *she thought.*

Another sharp pain hit and she cried out. Nimrah knew that it was time to give birth to a new life. She was about to bear down when a commotion arose from her servants.

"What is it? What are you . . . crying about? Birth is a time . . . for happiness, not sorrow," she said between breaths.

One of the midwives spoke.

"News has just arrived. The Ark of the Covenant has been captured. The news of its capture caused your father-in-law, Eli, to fall off the wall at the entrance to the city and he broke his neck. And . . ." she hesitated to share the last piece of bad news, "your husband Phinehas has been killed in battle."

Nimrah bowed her head. The baby was coming, but there was a lot of blood. Too much. *The midwives could tell that something was wrong. They tried to encourage her, and after much pushing and crying, the baby emerged.*

"Do not fear, for you have borne a son. He will bring you new joy."

Nimrah did not respond. She closed her eyes and turned her head away from her newborn child. The midwives continued to try to direct her mind back to the baby.

"What would you like to name him?" they asked.

Nimrah whispered, "Name him Ichabod. For the glory has departed from Israel because the Ark of God has been captured and my husband and father-in-law have died."

With the utterance of those words she died.

THIRTY

AS SHARI PASSED OUT printed notes on false teachers, Murphy noted with disappointment that someone was missing. Summer Van Doren was not in attendance, and he had begun to get accustomed to her presence in the back of the lecture hall.

Get your head in the game, Murphy. You've got a class to teach. Anyway, how could you be thinking about her after you had that wonderful dream about Isis?

"Let's all take our seats. We're going to begin."

Murphy was about to speak when he saw Paul Wallach in the back row. It had been quite some time since Paul had dropped out of his class.

I guess he and Shari are really trying to put their relationship back together.

Murphy smiled and nodded at Paul, who returned the nod.

"Today we'll be expanding on the concepts we discussed in the last few lectures. We've looked at the influence that the concept of God has had throughout the ages. It has spawned many cultures to create pagan gods and idols for the people to worship. It was believed that these gods would provide food for the people, oversee the birth of children, give sexual pleasure, protect the people in times of war, and benefit their followers in many other ways. They had gods for the earth, sky, and almost every place imaginable."

Murphy could see that many students were beginning to take notes.

"We also examined the thinking about both good and evil angels. The concept of some type of devil and of fallen angels exists in almost all cultures. While most people would agree that there is evil in the world, there is much debate as to its cause. Some people, of course, do not believe in angels or demons or Satan. But there are more people worldwide that believe in some type of evil spirits than those who do not.

"Today we are going to take a look at what we call 'false teachers.' Through the ages, people have preached a multitude of religious views that do not always agree with one another. Even Jesus addressed this concept when He said, 'Watch out that no one deceives you. For many will come in my name, claiming, "I am the Christ," and will deceive many. . . . At that time if anyone says to you, "Look, here is the Christ!" or, "There he is!" do not believe it. For false Christs and false prophets will appear and perform great signs and miracles to deceive even the elect if that were possible.' "

Murphy clicked up the first slide.

"Here are the names of people who actually claimed to be Christ or suggested that they were sent by God to speak to the people. Many of them gained a large following."

FALSE CHRISTS AND TEACHERS

A.D. 30	Theudas
A.D. 30	Judas the Galilean
2nd Century	Simon Bar Kokhba
5th Century	Moses of Crete
A.D. 591	Wandering Preacher
A.D. 720	Abu Isa from Baghdad
8th Century	Aldebert
A.D. 832	Moses—Risen from the Dead
A.D. 1110	Tanchelm of Antwerp
12th Century	David Aloroy

"Theudas and Judas the Galilean are mentioned in the book of Acts in the Bible. They persuaded people to follow them in an attempt to overthrow the Roman government. Simon Bar Kokhba tried to set himself up as the Messianic king called 'Son of the Star.' He commanded over a half million trained warriors until the Roman army massacred them. Saint Gregory wrote about a nameless wandering preacher who claimed to be the Messiah and had a woman companion called Mary. Moses of Crete was an interesting man who claimed that he would lead the Children of Israel like Moses did. The people followed him to the sea, but it did not part. He ordered the people in and many drowned. He somehow disappeared from the scene and was thus believed to be some sort of malignant spirit who had been sent to destroy the Israelites. Aldebert was known to have distributed his nail-clippings and hair-clippings among his followers. Oh, by the way, Tanchelm of Antwerp claimed to be the Messiah and passed out his bathwater to his followers. Some drank it as a holy drink in substitute for the Eucharist."

Murphy could hear the students moaning and muttering "Yuck." He clicked up the next slide.

FALSE CHRISTS AND TEACHERS

A.D. 1240	Abraham of Abulfia
A.D. 1490	David Reuveni
A.D. 1523	David Reubeni
A.D. 1542	Hayyim Vital
A.D. 1543	Isaac Luria
A.D. 1626	Shabbatai Zevi
A.D. 1726	Jacob Frank
A.D. 1774	Ann Lee
A.D. 1792	Richard Brothers
A.D. 1800	Baal Shem Tov

"The followers of Isaac Luria believed that he could perform exorcisms and miracles, speak the language of animals, and read faces to look into people's souls. Shabbatai Zevi possessed an uncontrollable sex drive. He claimed to be the Messiah at twenty-two years of age and publicly married a Torah Scroll. His followers were involved in sexual orgies. The movement became known as Shabbetianism. Jacob Frank was an arrogant practical joker. He was also involved in religious sexual orgies. He appointed twelve apostles and twelve female concubines to serve him. Ann Lee was unique. She was called the 'Elect Lady.' She asserted that she spoke seventy-two languages and conversed with the dead. She instituted shivering and swooning and falling down as acts of devotion."

Murphy was about to click on the next slide when he saw Clayton Anderson's hand go up.

"Dr. Murphy, speaking about ministers with great power. Did you hear about the minister that wired all his pews with electricity? On the next Sunday he said, 'All who will give a hundred dollars toward the new building, please stand up.' He then pressed a button and twenty people shot to their feet. Then he said, 'Now all who will give five hundred dollars, please stand up.' Again he touched the button and twenty more people sprang up. Then he asked, 'How many will give a thousand dollars each?' He threw the master switch and electrocuted fifteen deacons."

Murphy had a hard time regaining control of the class.

"That's very good, Clayton. Clever idea to wire the seats with electricity. By the way, will you be sitting in the same seat next week?"

Again the class broke out in laughter.

"Now, if we can continue."

FALSE CHRISTS AND TEACHERS

A.D. 1919	Father Divine
A.D. 1959	Maitreya
A.D. 1993	Ca Van Lieng
A.D. 1993	Aum Shinri Kyo
A.D. 1997	Marshall Applewhite
A.D. 1997	Sun Myung Moon
A.D. 1998	Nancy Fowler
A.D. 1998	Hon-Ming Chen

"Father Divine had a large following from the 1920s to the 1940s. His original name was George Baker and he was born around 1877. He stopped preaching in 1960. His wife, known as Mother Divine, then picked up where he left off. The followers of Maitreya claimed that he was the Messiah and took out many newspaper advertisements to this effect. Ca Van Lieng was a Vietnamese cult leader that instituted a mass murder-suicide that killed fifty-two people. Marshall Applewhite became famous with his partner Bonnie Nettles. They were leaders of the Heaven's Gate UFO Cult. His followers considered him to be the reincarnation of Christ. Applewhite convinced his followers that they were going to ride away on a spaceship that was following the Hale-Bopp Comet. They all committed suicide. Nancy Fowler was involved in the Cult of the Virgin. She claimed to have conversations with the Virgin Mary."

Murphy turned off the PowerPoint projector.

"There are many more that have made such claims or been touted as Messiahs by their followers. People like Maharishi Maheshi Yogi, the Great I Am, Charles Manson, Jim Jones, and Maharaja Ji."

Murphy picked up the handout entitled False Teachers and waved it back and forth.

"Take a look at some of the predictions made by various groups or individuals. You will find them on the sheet that was handed to you at the beginning of the class."

Murphy then went over the list of false teachers with the group.

"I have given you only one page of predictions and false teachers. I have nine more pages that essentially say the same thing. We call these people false teachers because what they predict does not come true."

One of the students raised her hand.

FALSE TEACHERS

PERSON / GROUP	PREDICTION
Watch & Be Ready	This Mormon literature stated that the New Jerusalem will descend from heaven in the year 2000.
Ruth Montgomery	The earth will shift on its axis and the Anti-Christ will reveal himself in 2000.
Sun Myung Moon	The Kingdom of Heaven will be established in the year 2000.
Shoko Asahara	By the year 2000, 90 percent of the world's population will be annihilated by nuclear, biological, and chemical weapons.
Bhagwan Shree	By the year 2000, the world will be devastated by AIDS. After that, the world will be rebuilt by a peaceful matriarchal society.
Ca Van Lieng	There will be an apocalyptic flood during the year 2000.
Bobby Bible	At the stroke of midnight in the year 2000, Jesus will descend from Heaven and take home believers.
Cerferino Quinte	The world will be destroyed by a rain of fire on January 1, 2000. To survive, his cult members built an elaborate series of tunnels and stockpiled a year's worth of supplies for 700 people.
Ola Ilori	In the year 2000 the earth will shift, causing a crack in its crust—like an eggshell.
Joseph Kibweteere	Predicted the end of the world in June of 2000. He had 600 of his followers sealed into a church, which was set on fire, and they all burned to death.
Gabriel of Sedona	Between May 5, 2000 and May 5, 2001, the destruction of humanity will take place. Only his faithful group will be saved by UFOs.

"Dr. Murphy, hadn't there been predictions about Jesus Christ . . . like where He was going to be born and how He would die, for hundreds of years before the event?"

"Good question. There were over three hundred predictions concerning Christ's first coming. What would be the odds of a person fulfilling all of those prophecies?"

Murphy paused for a moment to let the concept sink in.

"Let me help you out. A mathematician named Dr. Peter W. Stoner applied the theory of probability to Christ fulfilling just eight of the prophecies. He documents this in a book entitled *Science Speaks*. He had twelve different classes—about six hundred college students—work out the mathematical odds. The final conclusion was that Christ would have a one in ten to the twenty-eighth power of fulfilling eight prophecies."

Murphy walked up to the white board. "To give you some idea, let me write out ten to the twenty-eighth power for you."

He wrote a *10* on the board and began adding zero after zero. The students began to laugh at the absurdly long figure. When at last he had finished, the number read: 10,000,000,000,000,000,000,000,000,000.

He could see the shock on the faces of some of the students. Murphy shook out his fingers theatrically, as if they were cramped from writing all those zeroes.

"Dr. Stoner attempts to help the reader of his book comprehend the staggering odds with a visual illustration. He suggests that it is sort of like covering the entire state of Texas two feet deep in silver dollars. Paint one of the silver dollars blue. Mix up all of the silver dollars with a big spoon. Blindfold a man and let him walk anywhere he wants and have only one grab for the blue silver dollar. Those would be the odds."

Murphy again paused to let the enormity sink in.

"Dr. Stoner went on to consider the odds of Christ fulfilling forty-eight of the prophecies concerning him. The odds were one in ten to the hundred-and-fifty-seventh power. He said that you could no longer use silver dollars. You would have to use something far smaller, like an electron. Imagine a ball of electrons extending in all directions from the earth six billion light-years into space—light traveling at over a hundred eighty thousand miles per second, times the number of seconds in a year. Paint one electron blue. Mix up all the electrons with a big spoon. Blindfold a man and let him walk anywhere he wants and have only one grab for the blue electron. That's just to fulfill forty-eight prophecies. Remember, Jesus Christ literally fulfilled over one hundred nine predictions of his first coming. There are three hundred twenty-one predictions of his second coming!"

Murphy glanced at the clock. The bell was just about to ring.

"With odds like that, when Christ returns, I don't think there will be any doubt about it. So think about the importance of following a true teacher as compared to a false teacher. It could affect the future of each and every one of you."

The bell rang and the students treated Murphy to a standing ovation for a particularly inspired lecture. He blushed and gave a nod of gratitude.

He looked over at Shari. She was beaming and clapping right along.

THIRTY-ONE

MURPHY ENTERED THE LAB and found Shari deep in concentration over an old manuscript. She was oblivious to his presence. As he watched her, her frown changed into a smile.

"That's it!" she exclaimed.

"That's what?"

She looked up with a gasp.

"Murphy! You almost scared me to death!"

"Sorry. What are you so excited about?"

"It's the papyrus manuscript that you discovered. You know, the one from the curio shop in Cairo."

Murphy nodded his head.

"What about it?"

"I discovered that it was written by the historian Mamonte."

"I knew that it was old, but not two centuries before Christ. Were you able to read it?"

"Most of it. It basically records various events in history. Things like fires, floods, and other disasters. There's something that I think you'll find very interesting."

"What's that?"

"A brief mention about the Philistines capturing the Golden House of God of the Israelites."

Murphy drew in a quick breath. "The Ark of the Covenant?"

"So it seems. It indicates that two magical objects were removed from beneath the cherubim. It then records that a number of people died from a strange illness. Do you think it could be alluding to the events that occurred in Ashdod and the Temple of Dagon?"

"It sure sounds like it. Let me take a look at it."

"You might want to hold off on that until later. You have a command performance right now."

"What do you mean?"

"You got a call from your best friend at the university."

Murphy looked at her quizzically. "You don't mean Dean Fallworth?"

"Good guess! And he didn't sound happy."

"I guess I'd better get it over with." Murphy was not looking forward to this.

"Oh, by the way, did you hear the news about him?"

"I don't think so."

"Since President Carver is retiring, the trustees are considering making him the new president of the university."

Murphy felt sick to his stomach. "I think that would be a colossal mistake."

"No argument here," Shari said.

Murphy went into his office looking for a couple of pieces of paper. If he had to go into the lion's den, he would at least not go unarmed.

Fallworth was all business. "You may not have heard yet, but President Carver is retiring and the trustees will probably select me as the new president."

Murphy was glad Shari had tipped him off. In his arrogance, Fallworth wanted to get some kind of reaction out of Murphy. But Murphy refused to give him the satisfaction. He simply said, "Oh."

Fallworth looked a little disappointed. "I want to go on record with you that if I become president you may not be teaching your course in biblical archaeology."

"Would you care to tell me why, Archer?"

"I've told you before. Religion has no place in the classroom!"

"Does that mean anything that has to do with religion?"

"Yes, it does."

"Well, let me see if I understand you correctly. In teaching U.S. history, we should leave out the influence of Father Junipero Serra and the early Catholic missions? In teaching European history, we should omit all references to the great religious controversies of the Middle Ages? We should ignore the Protestant Reformation? We should eliminate any comments about the struggle for religious freedom in colonial times? We should discard Da Vinci's *Last Supper,* Michelangelo's *Moses,* Beethoven's *Missa Solemnis,* or Wagner's *Valkyrie*? Do I understand you correctly?"

Fallworth rolled his eyes. "You know what I mean, Murphy."

"No, I'm afraid I don't. How can any teacher separate himself from what is part of history? What is there to fear in teaching what people believe and how it has influenced humanity? If I hear that someone believes in UFOs, that doesn't threaten me. Or if they believe that a large meteor hit the earth and caused the dinosaur extinction, I don't have to agree with them. What are you afraid of . . . intellectual honesty?"

"Religion should be taught in churches only."

"Really. Then may I ask you a question? Do you believe in obeying the legal rulings of the U.S. Supreme Court?"

"Of course I do. But they don't say that you can teach religion in schools. The First Amendment to the U.S. Constitution states that 'Congress shall make no law respecting an establishment of religion, or prohibiting the free exercise thereof. . . .' "

"I thought that we might have this conversation, Archer, so I pulled some information from my files for you. With regard to the First Amendment you quoted, there's a case that addresses it. It is found in *Abington School District* v. *Schemmp*. In his comments on opposition to religion and the study of the Bible, Justice Clark states the following:

> '. . . Of course . . . the state may not establish a "religion of secularism" in the sense of affirmative opposing or showing hostility to religion, thus, "preferring those who believe in no religion over those who do believe" (*Zorach* v. *Clauson*). . . . In addition, it might well be said that one's education is not complete without a study of comparative religion or the history of religion and its relationship to the advancement of civilization. It certainly may be said that the Bible is worthy of study for its literary and historic qualities. Nothing that we have said here indicates that such study of the Bible or of religion, when presented objectively as part of a secular program of education, may not be effected consistent with the First Amendment.' "

Fallworth did not respond. Murphy could tell he didn't like what he was hearing.

"In referring to teaching about religion and the social sciences and the humanities, Justice Brennan made these comments:

> 'The holding of the Court today plainly does not foreclose teaching about the Holy Scriptures or about the differences between religious sects in classes of literature or history.

> Indeed, whether or not the Bible is involved, it would be impossible to teach meaningfully many subjects in the social sciences or the humanities without some mention of religion.'

"Justice Goldberg spoke to the passive and active hostility to religion and religious teaching on legal, political, and personal values:

> 'Neither the state nor this Court can or should ignore the significance of the fact that a vast portion of our people believe in and worship God and that many of our legal, political and personal values derive historically from religious teachings. Government must inevitably take cognizance of the existence of religion and, indeed, under certain circumstances the First Amendment may require that it do so. And it seems clear to me from the opinions in the present and past cases that the Court would recognize the propriety of providing military chaplains and of teaching about religion, as distinguished from the teaching of religion, in the public schools.'

"Evidently, Archer, we don't see eye to eye."

"That's putting it mildly," he said with a sneer.

"I respect your right to disagree with me. I'm not trying to force you to accept what I believe. All I'm asking is that you have the same respect for me and my beliefs."

"Well, don't you sound like the loving Christian now."

"That's interesting, Archer. Whenever you have a difficult time defending your views, you resort to personal attacks."

Murphy got up and started to walk to the door.

"Archer, as you have gone on record . . . let me go on record. You are on shaky ground. If you choose to make a battle over this, so be it. I will not roll over and play dead on this issue."

He stormed out, slamming the door behind him.

Murphy felt the adrenaline pumping through him as he walked back to his office. There were not too many issues that he would fight for, but this was one of them. He started thinking about a proverb: *The dogs bark but the caravan rolls on.*

Over the centuries men have tried to put down the teachings of the Bible. They have barked like dogs at a caravan and yet the caravan of truth keeps moving forward in spite of them. God help me to remember this when under attack.

As he neared his office, he noticed Shari and Paul Wallach sitting on a bench under a magnolia tree and wondered if they were back together again.

THIRTY-TWO

MOSHE PEARLMAN had traveled many places in the world and throughout most of Israel, but he had never been to the original site of Ashdod. He took the highway leading south from Tel Aviv for about twenty miles and then headed west. He estimated that he was about ten miles north of the Gaza Strip. He was driving an old 911 Porsche from West Germany. It had given him many good years of service. It was also an old enough car that it didn't attract any attention.

Before long he entered a large, low plain. Rising up from the plain he could see terraced hillsides covered with olive orchards and vineyards. He had heard that this area produced much olive oil. It was also famous for large quantities of the murex shell, which was valued for the purple dye it produced.

He stopped his car, leaned over, and grabbed his binoculars. He had been told by one of the archaeologists at Tel Aviv University that he would find the original site of Ashdod located on a small mound. He was also told that there had not been much interest in the site in recent years. The archaeologist was sure that there was more to be discovered there, but that archaeological interest had shifted to other locations in Israel.

Off in the distance he saw the ground rising and figured that it might be the spot. Focusing his binoculars, he scanned the area. His attention was soon focused on four vehicles parked to the north side of the mound. He could also make out the remains of an ancient block wall.

I'll bet that's the place. But what are those cars doing here?

He got back into his Porsche and drove toward the mound. He saw no one.

Strange.

Pearlman's training with the Mossad made him very alert and very suspicious. He parked his car about a hundred yards from the other vehicles, behind an outcropping of rocks. He double-checked the clip in his automatic and put it back into his shoulder holster. He got out, donning a light jacket from the backseat to conceal his gun. He surveyed the area for any sounds or signs of movement. There were none.

I wonder where they are?

The closer he got to the vehicles the more curious he became. Carefully he looked into each car. There was nothing out of the ordinary except that these were not the type of vehicles one would take on an archaeological dig. They were too new, too nice, and too clean.

Again he looked around. *They have to be here somewhere.*

He examined the numerous footprints around the cars. He could clearly see the impressions they'd left in the light drifting sand. He followed the tracks away from the cars and toward the broken wall.

On the other side of the wall he saw another wall about twenty feet away. It had an opening in it about four feet high and about two-and-a-half feet wide. Pearlman approached, peering in, but he could only see a few feet into the dark.

He unhooked a Mini Maglight that he carried on his belt, hunched down, and entered the hole. Once inside, he found that he could stand up straight. He shined his light around the passageway. It was about six feet wide by about seven feet tall. It angled slightly downward and to the southwest. He followed it as it made several turns.

At one point he turned off the light and froze as he heard the muffled sound of voices ahead. He crept forward silently, keeping one hand on the side wall while the other felt in front of him. Eventually a light appeared in the distance and the two voices became clearer. To his surprise, he heard English.

"You two go back to the entrance while the rest of us go on. We don't want any uninvited guests."

Pearlman's heart began to race. It might have been a mistake to come alone but it was too late now. Who were these people and what were they doing? He realized that if he didn't hurry, he'd be meeting them real soon.

He began to back away from the light. He hoped that he could make it to one of the turns, where he could switch on his light and move more quickly. He didn't like the idea of being caught in a dark passageway with two strangers in the middle of nowhere.

He had just reached the turn when he heard them coming. He switched on his light and began to exit more rapidly. But it was too late.

"Rafi, look! There's a light."

The words echoed to Moshe and he heard them running toward him. His heart beat faster. He had a quick decision to make.

Do I keep running and have them shoot me in the back or do I stop and face them and try to talk through the situation?

He chose to stop.

He turned around and shined his light in their direction. They slowed and approached Pearlman cautiously, their flashlight beams in his face blinding him.

A voice spoke in a thick Arabic accent. "Who are you and what are you doing here?"

"I'm a tourist," Pearlman said brightly, hoping his acting chops were up to snuff. "I saw some cars and I stopped to look at the ruins of Ashdod. I then discovered the hole in the wall and entered. Are you archaeologists?"

The two Arabs moved closer.

"Why, yes, we are. We are exploring for ancient artifacts."

Moshe had heard enough lies during his career to quickly discern truth from falsehood by the tone in one's voice. All of his senses were alert. He didn't like them getting closer. Then he saw it—the quick reflection of light off a steel blade thrusting forward toward his stomach. He instinctively jumped back and at the same time brought a knife block down on the forearm of his attacker. It came with such force that it momentarily paralyzed the man's arm and he dropped the knife.

Pearlman then gave a sharp front kick into the Arab's chest. It sent him backward with such power that he collided with his compatriot, knocking both men to the ground. Pearlman then took off running. He didn't like fighting blind, with no room to maneuver. He heard them yelling. Their cries attracted the rest of their party in the passageway. They came running toward the commotion.

When Pearlman came out into the light he was a good ninety feet ahead of his pursuers. He took off running across the open plain at full speed toward his car.

He could hear the men shouting in Arabic as they burst out of the passageway. He shot a quick look over his shoulder. He had a good head start and was only sixty feet from the protection of the rocks. They'd never catch him now.

Talon calmly walked to the trunk of his car. He opened it and took out his Russian Dragunov SVD gas-powered semi-automatic sniper rifle. The silencer was already on it, and he always carried it fully loaded with all ten rounds.

He lifted it to his shoulder and focused the sights of the powerful scope. Everything he did was with patience and precision. He lined Pearlman up in the crosshairs and fired.

Moshe did not hear the sound. All he felt was a scorching pain in his right thigh as the bullet penetrated his leg and exited somewhere in the sand. He fell face-first to the ground, kicking up dust.

Talon laughed at the sight. It was a perfect shot . . . enough to slow him down but not enough to kill him. He handed the rifle to one of the Arabs. There were ten of them watching in awe as Talon performed what he did best.

Talon stepped forward and looked to the sky. He then opened the palm of his left hand and hit it twice with his right fist. The Arabs looked at one another in confusion.

In the meantime, Moshe was crawling toward the rock outcropping. He was not more than twenty feet away from the safety of his car. It was agony as he dragged his wounded leg along. His hands were bleeding from pulling himself forward over small rocks and cacti.

He was just reaching his hand up to the door handle when the first falcon gouged his claws into his neck. He felt the pressure of 200 pounds per inch deeply penetrate his flesh. Moshe rolled to his back, trying to strike the powerful bird away, but to no avail. The second falcon struck his exposed throat. A look of absolute panic came over his face as the sharp claws dug deep into his flesh again and again.

Murphy heard a ringing sound. He leaned over and checked his alarm clock . . . 3:00 A.M.

Who would be calling at this hour?

"This is Murphy."

"Michael, this is Levi. I've got some terrible news."

Murphy was wide-awake now. When Levi sounded like this, something serious was going down.

"What is it, Levi?"

"It's Moshe Pearlman. Some worker in the olive orchards around Ashdod found his body. If it hadn't been for his wallet and car, no one would have been able to identify the body."

"I'm so sorry, Levi. I know he was one of your friends. Did he have a family?"

"Yes. His wife and two daughters are devastated."

"What happened?"

"Something completely ripped his face and throat apart. The doctors say that all the wounds look like the clawing and pecking of birds. There wasn't much left of him, but they did find something else very strange. A bullet hole all the way through his right thigh. No one can figure out what happened. Someone brushed away all traces of footprints. There were only the car tracks of four different cars."

"It sounds like the work of Talon and his falcons. This is not the first time he's turned them on humans."

"Michael, if Talon is involved, you know there's something very important going on in Ashdod. It sounds like he might be after the same things you are. Do you still want to go to Ashdod?"

"More than ever."

"Good! I want to join you, to avenge Moshe's death. It would be my joy to turn those falcons on Talon."

"How soon can you work out the details?"

"I don't know. But with the death of Pearlman, I'll put everything into high gear. Even putting on the pressure, it may take a couple of weeks."

"Then put on the pressure!" Murphy said. "Talon already appears to have a big head start."

THIRTY-THREE

THE WEATHER FORECAST called for a bright and sunny day along the coast. It was just the kind of day that might draw Methuselah off of his estate near Myrtle Beach. Murphy guessed that he would go to the shores below Briarcliffe Acres.

He was not sure when Methuselah might go to the beach, so he left early in the morning. He decided to take State Highway 40 from Raleigh toward New Hanover and Wilmington. There he would join Highway 17 to North Myrtle Beach.

The trip was pleasant and he reflected upon the resort area he was driving to. Myrtle Beach had been named by Mrs. F. E. Burroughs, whose husband was the founder of the Burroughs & Collins Company. She called it Myrtle Beach because of the many wax myrtle trees growing wild along the shoreline. The building boom of the 1960s had brought an influx of people to the area. Many came to play golf in one of the over 120 courses that were scattered along the coast. Murphy wondered if Methuselah played golf or not.

Probably not. It wouldn't be exciting enough for him. He likes to see blood and guts, not a little white ball rolling into the water.

Murphy arrived at the beach area near 9:00 A.M. He found a place to park, grabbed his backpack, and headed toward the beach. He thought that he might try the area near the Dunes Golf and Beach Club. It was not far from Methuselah's estate.

Very few people were on the beach.

A little too early, he thought. *More people will arrive when it gets a little warmer.*

The sky was crystal clear except for a few puffy clouds in the distance. A slight offshore breeze was blowing toward him. He sat down on the sand and watched the breakers. It had a very calming effect. It had been ages since he'd allowed himself time to just sit and take in the glory of God's creation.

A passing jogger with a dog caught Murphy's attention and brought him back to the purpose of his trip. He consulted his watch. It was almost 10:00 A.M. He looked around the beach and noticed that a few more people had put out blankets and were sunning themselves. Murphy opened his backpack and took out a picture of Methuselah. It had been taken at a distance with a high-powered telephoto lens. Murphy thought he could make out his features well enough to identify him if he came to the beach.

He put away the photo and took out a book and began to read.

Might as well do something productive, Murphy thought.

It wasn't until 11:30 A.M. that Murphy saw something to indicate that Methuselah could be coming—two large men wearing Hawaiian shirts. They were sauntering along the beach, talking and stopping every now and then to look around. Murphy watched as one of them unhooked a two-way radio from his belt and spoke into it.

It wasn't long before he saw five other men strolling toward the beach. Two of them were carrying lawn chairs. One of them was older, with gray hair and a limp. Murphy whipped out the photograph and compared it with the man on the beach.

It was Methuselah. There was no doubt about it.

Murphy's heart began to race. Now what would he do? How would he be able to get close enough to talk with him? He couldn't believe that he was about to meet the mysterious Methuselah face-to-face . . . and on Murphy's terms, not his.

For a moment his attention was drawn away from Methuselah. He spotted two other men walking up and down the beach. Then Murphy had an idea.

"Excuse me, do you work for the Dunes Golf and Beach Club?" asked Murphy.

"Why, yes, I do," said the young man with a big smile. "Would you like to order something? We take orders for drinks and meals at the club. We'll bring them to you on the beach if you like."

"That's swell. How much do they pay you to do this job?"

The young man was caught a little off guard.

"Why . . . they . . . they pay us ten dollars an hour and we can keep any tips we earn. It's not a bad deal."

"No, on the contrary, it sounds great. How would you like to make a big tip?"

"Sure, I'm up for that."

"How about two hundred dollars?"

"What? Are you pulling my leg?"

"No. I just want to borrow a uniform like the one you're wearing for a couple of hours. There's someone I would like to talk to on the beach and your uniform might make it a little easier."

"I know what you mean," said the young man. He spoke in hushed tones. "I meet lots of good-looking young ladies this way. For two hundred dollars I can get you a uniform. Follow me."

Murphy could feel the adrenaline starting to pump as he walked toward Methuselah and his bodyguards. He was dressed in the Dunes Golf Club uniform and was carrying a small tray and an order pad.

All of the bodyguards became alert as he approached. Two of them got out of their chairs and started to move toward him. Methuselah was engrossed in a book and not paying any attention. It was evident that he had total confidence in his men.

"Hold it right there!" said one of the guards. He blocked Murphy while the other man came behind him and began to wand him for any metal weapons he might be carrying.

Murphy looked at the men and smiled casually like it was an everyday occurrence.

"Would you gentlemen like anything to eat or drink?"

Murphy saw the other bodyguards nodding their heads up and down. He could also tell that they would not order anything unless Methuselah ordered something. One of the guards spoke to him.

"Mr. M., there's a man here to take our order. Would you like something?"

Methuselah lifted his head to look at the bodyguard. He didn't even glance at Murphy standing about ten feet to his left.

"Yes, I'll have an iced tea and a tuna-melt sandwich."

Murphy was about to explode inside, his curiosity mingling with a great deal of anger. Methuselah had sicced a lion on him, almost killed him when he cut loose a cable in the Royal Gorge, and hired a host of professional killers to try to take him out. He hoped that Methuselah would not do much to him on a public beach.

He found it impossible to restrain his impatience any longer. He spoke in a firm and loud voice.

"How about some rattlesnakes for lunch?"

At these words, the other bodyguards exploded out of their chairs. The two near Murphy grabbed him, and he was down on the sand in a matter of seconds.

Methuselah was shocked, to say the least. What was one of Golf Club's employees doing talking to him like that? It was outrageous. He would have the man fired at once.

He rose from his chair and told the bodyguards to make Murphy stand up.

"Did I hear you say 'rattlesnakes for lunch'?" Methuselah asked with irritation.

Murphy now stood face-to-face with Methuselah. Levi was right. Caught off guard, the old man did not recognize him.

"You heard me right! Rattlesnakes for lunch. Just like you dumped on my head in the Reed Gold Mine!"

It took Methuselah a moment to process what had just been said. Then he smiled and began to laugh in his high, cackling way.

"Dr. Michael Murphy. My, my, my. Aren't you the industrious one, finding me here. You're more clever than I gave you credit for."

Murphy sensed the bodyguards' confusion over Methuselah's reaction.

"You can let him go. I don't think Dr. Murphy will do me any harm. You see, he believes in the Bible . . . that you should forgive those who trespass against you. . . . Turn the other cheek . . . and all of that stuff. Right, Dr. Murphy?"

Murphy just stood there. He had long imagined what he would say if this day ever arrived, and now he found himself at a total loss for words.

Methuselah motioned with his hand.

"Please. Please, pull up a chair and sit down. After all the trouble you've gone to, you deserve a rest."

He then looked at his bodyguards.

"It's all right. You can move back. Dr. Murphy and I are just going to have a little chat."

Murphy sat down and looked closely at Methuselah for the first time. His weather-beaten face was lined with wrinkles. He looked like an unhappy man who had been carrying the weight of the world on his shoulders.

"This is a surprise, Dr. Murphy. You must have done some heavy-duty investigation to find me."

"I have some friends."

Methuselah looked at Murphy contemplatively.

"Ah, yes, your friend Levi Abrams, no doubt. He must have checked the airplane crash records. But how?"

"You left a fingerprint."

"Impossible. I always wipe everything off or wear gloves."

"Except for one time. Even the best make mistakes."

"Pray tell me, where?"

"In the Reed Gold Mine on the back of the signboard."

Methuselah began to cackle. "Of course. It must have been those infernal rattlesnakes. They distracted me and I forgot to wipe off the back of the board. Good job, Dr. Murphy. I always appreciate competence wherever I find it. I suspected you had the qualities I was looking for. I just needed to test you to be sure."

"Did I disappoint you?"

"Oh, no. Far from it. You have been most entertaining, Dr. Murphy."

"Well, I'm not sure how to address you. Is it Methuselah or is it Markus Zasso?"

Methuselah smiled again.

"Mr. M. will do."

"It just doesn't have the same ring. I think I'll stick with Methuselah."

"Of course. Now, what's on your mind? You've gone to a lot of effort to find me."

"What's on my mind? Do you really have to ask? I can figure out how you know so much about the Bible. Your grandfather was a missionary and your father was an active Christian. But what's with all the games, the riddles, the attempts on my life?"

Methuselah nodded his head. "Fair enough. You have passed all the tests."

"Tests? Tests for what?"

"The story starts back with the plane crash. As you know, my wife and children were killed in the crash. I myself barely survived. That is why I walk with a limp today. It took me months to regain my health but I could not regain my family. I went into a deep depression over my loss, and the depression turned into anger . . . and the anger into hatred. Hatred for the people who killed my family."

Murphy hung on every word.

"I began to do my own investigation. I wanted to find out who was responsible for their deaths. I wanted revenge. Not just by killing them . . . I wanted to destroy everything they cherished before I took their lives."

Murphy detected the flash of rage in Methuselah's eyes as he spoke. "Do you know who they are?"

Methuselah paused for a moment and looked deep into Murphy's eyes. "Yes, and they will pay." There was something cold and final in his words. "I know more about them and their goals for world conquest than they realize. I have someone on the inside who passes information on to me. I am going to thwart everything they are attempting to do, or die trying!"

"Okay, you hate them. But what does that have to do with me? How do I fit into the picture?"

"The archaeological artifacts I've told you about. They help to prove the truth of the Bible. These people would like to see the Bible destroyed and believers in Almighty God eliminated. I am simply using you to help prove them wrong."

"Then why all the games and threats to my life? Why not simply help me to find these artifacts?"

"Two reasons, Dr. Murphy. One, you need to be battle-ready for these people. You have no idea how wicked and powerful they are. You need to be able to physically take care of yourself."

"And the second reason?"

Methuselah began to cackle again in his irritating manner.

"Call it boredom. You have added some much-needed excitement to my dreary days."

Methuselah's warped logic indicated to Murphy that the old man had all but lost his grip on reality. He'd become so focused on revenge that it was slowly destroying him. His vendetta completely consumed his thoughts, and nothing else mattered.

"You could have killed me several times!"

"That would have been regrettable, Dr. Murphy. It would, however, have shown me that you weren't the man for the job."

"A job I never exactly applied for!"

"You're wrong, Dr. Murphy. You did apply. With every riddle of mine that you solved and every trap that you wriggled your way out of. You could have refused. You could have turned back at any time. But instead, you persisted. I merely created the gauntlet," he grinned. "It was you who decided to run it."

"So now what?" asked Murphy. "Who are these people you're out to get? And just how do I fit in all of this?"

Methuselah looked at his watch.

"Well, it's time for me to get out of the sun. I have passed my normal time limit. Thank you for your visit, Dr. Murphy. It was a most refreshing break in my ordinarily routine schedule. You never fail to entertain."

"Wait a minute!"

Methuselah started to rise. With the merest of glances, his bodyguards came running.

"Will two of you please escort Dr. Murphy back to his vehicle?"

They nodded and two of the larger men stepped forward.

"Oh, I suppose you'd better return that uniform first. It really doesn't suit you."

Murphy had completely forgotten about the uniform. Small wonder.

"Perhaps someday we can continue our conversation. I have pressing business in Italy. I hope that you will have a pleasant drive back to Raleigh."

With that, Methuselah turned and left with four bodyguards in tow. Murphy couldn't believe what had just happened. It wasn't anything like he had expected. He looked at the two silent bodyguards. They followed him back to the Golf Club.

He desperately wanted to know more about these people Methuselah hated so. He had found out only enough to pique his curiosity. It was so typical of Methuselah to just walk away. It always had to be on his terms. He had to be in control.

No doubt about it. Murphy was ticked off.

THIRTY-FOUR

MURPHY WAS SITTING at his desk when Shari came into the office with a preoccupied look on her face. He glanced at his watch. It was 8:30 A.M. She usually arrived before he did.

"Rough night?"

"What?"

"I asked if you had a rough night."

"I don't know if I'd call it rough but it certainly was different."

Shari put on her lab coat slowly. She didn't seem to be in her typical humorous mood. Murphy eased up on the jokes.

"What happened?"

"Well, for the past two days I've been a little paranoid. I've felt like someone's been watching me and following me. It's hard to describe. I haven't actually caught anyone doing it but I have this eerie feeling."

"Do you think it might be Paul Wallach? Since he's back in town, has he turned into a stalker?"

Shari wrinkled her nose and frowned.

"I don't think so. He has his faults but I don't think he would follow me around. He'd have nothing to gain by it. But that's not all."

"What do you mean?"

"Last night I was home alone in my apartment. I watched some TV and got ready for bed. I was not quite asleep when the phone rang. It was Paula Conklin from the church. She was crying. She told me that her father had just died from a heart attack. He was only fifty-seven. Her parents live in Portland and she couldn't get a flight out until eleven o'clock this morning. I told her that I'd be right over. I know what it's like to lose your father. I thought I might be able to comfort her."

Murphy was ready for Shari to say that she was followed to Paula's but she didn't.

"We talked until about two A.M. and I ended up spending the night at her place. I got up early and came back to my apartment to get ready for work. As I opened my door, there was an extremely strong odor of gas. I had to hold my breath as I ran to open some windows. I went back outside for a bit while it aired out, and then went into the kitchen. Two of the burners on the gas stove were on but there was no flame."

"Did you accidentally leave them on?"

"I don't think so. I did have a cup of tea before bed but I think I turned the gas off. And besides, I only used one burner to heat the water."

"I don't like the sound of all this. Maybe you should call the police."

"I had the same thought. But what could I tell them? 'I have no real evidence, but I feel like someone's following me and turning my gas on when I'm not there'?"

Murphy nodded. She was right. Without more to go on, the cops couldn't do anything.

"Anyway, that's why I'm late. It was just a very strange incident."

"It was a good thing you went to Paula's. Her tears saved your life."

Shari looked at Murphy thoughtfully. She hadn't considered that.

Shari looked at her watch. It was 8:10. *Wow! I guess I do get involved in my work. I've skipped dinner and didn't even realize it.*

She took off her lab coat, gathered a few items, and put them in her backpack. She turned off the lights and locked the door. All of the other lights in the building were off, making her feel a little apprehensive. She didn't like being alone at night.

Shari, get a grip. Life isn't going to be much fun if you get scared at every little thing.

The only sounds she heard were her footsteps as she walked down the hall and pushed open the door to the outside. She waited until it closed and rattled it to be sure it was locked.

She looked around the campus. It was empty and growing dark. Only a few lights were on in the other buildings. She walked around to the side of the lab and unlocked her ten-speed bike. She was grateful that the walkway lights stayed on all night. It would be a scary trip across campus without them.

She felt a little more comfortable when she got to the road, where the streetlights were on and cars were passing. She began peddling the ten minutes to her apartment.

She reached the grocery store and thought, *Oh, I need to get some eggs and milk. I'll have breakfast for dinner.*

After locking up her bike, she went into the supermarket, feeling rather hungry.

This is not a good time to go shopping. Everything looks so good. Especially the sweets.

As she walked the aisles, she began to have the feeling that she was being watched. She turned around but no one was there.

Shari, stop thinking like that. You've seen too many scary movies.

She picked up her milk and eggs and slowly walked by the cookies, eyeing each package.

No. I'll get some microwave popcorn instead.

The clerk was smiling as she approached.

"Did you find everything all right?"

"Yes, thank you. By the way, could you please double the plastic bag? I'm on my bike."

"You bet."

When biking at night, Shari had a habit of riding on the sidewalk. She didn't like the idea of cars not seeing her and possibly hitting her from behind. When she came to intersections she would follow where the curb dropped down for handicap accessibility, ride across the street, and back up onto the sidewalk. She was not far from her apartment when it happened. She was just approaching an intersection and the light was green. She wanted to get across before it turned red, so she started to peddle faster. As she came to the corner of a building, a calico cat darted out in front of her.

She squeezed the front handbrake as hard as she could, trying not to hit the cat. The sudden deceleration threw her forward before she reached the curb.

She tumbled to the ground, her head narrowly missing a vehicle that ran the red light at about forty miles per hour. She sat there shaking. If she hadn't slammed on the brakes because of the cat, she would have been hit.

Then came the tears. When she fell, she had scraped some skin off both hands, bruised her right shoulder, and hit the back of her head on the pavement. No one was around to help her.

She crawled away from the street, rocking back and forth until she regained her composure. She looked at her bloody hands coated with sand and gravel. She could see the cat over by the building meowing as if nothing had happened. Her carton of milk was spilled all over the sidewalk and the dozen eggs were destroyed. The cat went over and started to lick the milk. Her bike lay half in the street and half on the sidewalk.

As she stood, she realized that she had sprained her ankle. She didn't feel like riding. She picked up the popcorn, put it into her backpack, righted her bike, and used it like a crutch to hobble home.

The next morning, Paul Wallach was walking across the campus when he saw Shari limping toward the lab with her backpack on and both hands wrapped in bandages.

"What happened to you?" he asked.

Shari looked at him and tried to smile through the pain she felt all over.

"I almost ran into a cat last night on my bike. It darted out in front of me."

"Looks like you got the worst of it."

"You could say that. At least the cat still has eight lives left."

Paul helped her over to a bench and they sat down. Shari explained how the accident happened.

"It sounds like the cat may have saved your life."

"It certainly did. Another split second and the car would have hit me. That's two times my life has been spared in two days."

"Two times?"

She told him about the incident with the gas burners and he looked very concerned.

"I think that you've had enough excitement. You should go home and get some rest."

"It's probably a good idea but I have some test papers Dr. Murphy needs today. I had to bring them to him."

"Here, let me take them for you. You sit right here and I'll be right back."

"I doubt that Dr. Murphy is in yet. Just put them on his chair behind the desk."

Within a few minutes, Paul returned.

"I've got an idea. You drive back home and rest for the day. Don't plan on doing any cooking. I'll get a pizza and bring it for dinner. I'll also pick up a movie and we can watch it after dinner. You can't beat good food and some entertainment. Will you let me do that for you?"

"It sounds very good, Paul. I don't feel like cooking or going out." Plus, she was starting to feel like she didn't want to be alone in the evenings.

"Shari, you go on home and I'll go back and leave a note for Dr. Murphy explaining why you won't be in to work. What time would you like to have dinner?"

"How about six-thirty?"

"I'll be there."

"Thank you, Paul."

THIRTY-FIVE

SHARI'S HEART JUMPED when she heard her doorbell ring. The uneasy feelings she had about being followed and two near-death experiences had made her jumpy. She reached over the edge of the couch and grabbed a baseball bat. Earlier in the day she had taken it out of the closet for security. She hobbled to the door and peered through the peephole. It was Paul Wallach holding two pizza boxes and a bag. She unlocked three latches and let him in, then quickly locked all three behind him.

"These are hot, right out of the oven. I've also got drinks in the bag and some cheese bread and dressings."

"It sounds great. I'm starving."

He looked at the bat in her hand.

"Planning a little batting practice tonight?"

Shari laughed.

"No. It's sort of a security blanket for me. I just feel safer when it's around."

Paul went into the kitchen and got down a couple of plates. Shari paused at the door and looked outside. Even though she did not see anyone she still had that eerie feeling that something was wrong. She shook her head.

You are getting paranoid.

She leaned the bat up against the back of the couch and went into the kitchen to help Paul. He wouldn't let her do anything but go sit down at the small dining table.

Dinner was pleasant and yet a little uncomfortable. Paul wanted to talk about their relationship but held everything inside so as not to pressure Shari. She, on the other hand, was trying to determine if Paul really wanted to change or if this was some kind of passing phase.

At one point Shari shared with Paul her thoughts about being followed and the two close calls.

"Well, aren't you a Christian? Won't God protect you?"

"Yes, to both of those questions, Paul. But even Christians pass away at some point. I'm not afraid to die, but that doesn't mean I'm ready to go just yet."

"Shari, I don't mean to make things worse, but what if your apartment filling with gas and the near-miss with the car weren't accidents? What if they were deliberate?"

"That's a terrible thought!"

"Can you think of anyone who is mad at you or wants to do you harm?"

"No. I don't think I have any enemies."

"How about an angry ex-boyfriend?" Paul was fishing to see if Shari had been dating other people during his absence.

"No. I've been too busy helping Dr. Murphy to do any dating."

Paul visibly uncoiled. "Well, let's try to put recent events behind us and think of something else. How are things going at the Preston Community Church?"

Shari noted that Paul was trying to get into her world and her concerns. In the past, his conversation seemed to focus more on himself. *This is new. Maybe he has changed.*

"Pastor Wagoner is doing a series of messages on false teachers and things involving the occult. It's quite interesting. You ought to come. I think you'd enjoy it." Shari was putting out a feeler to get Paul's reaction to spiritual matters.

"That sounds good. I would like to start going back to church. The people there are certainly more honest than those at the Barrington News Network." He was obviously still bitter.

"That would be great, Paul. If you really mean it."

Paul hesitated and then spoke candidly. "Shari, I am not putting on an act for you. I do want to change. And I do want to turn my life around. I just hope you'll give me a chance to do that."

"And how about spiritual matters, Paul?"

"I want to see that change also. I may not believe everything you do yet, but I am keeping an open mind."

"It's not that complicated, Paul. The Bible tells us that all you have to do is believe in Jesus. That He's God's son . . . that He died for our sins, and that He was raised from the grave to give us new life. And then, just invite Him into your heart."

Paul nodded his head.

"A person can do that anywhere, anytime. It doesn't have to be in a church. It could be in a car, or while you're walking, or even all alone in your bedroom."

Shari realized that she should not put pressure on Paul. It had to be his decision. Even though she had plenty more to say, she thought it would be best to take it slowly.

"Let's clean up the dishes and watch the movie you brought."

"No. You turn on the TV and relax and I'll clean up. You should stay off that ankle."

Shari smiled. "You're the doctor."

This is a nice change, she thought.

Partway through the movie, Shari thought she heard a noise. But she couldn't tell if it came from her bedroom or from the television. Paul didn't seem to hear it. He was deeply involved in an action scene in the movie.

Shari started to get up.

"Where are you going?"

"I was just going to check something in my bedroom."

"Can I do it for you?"

"No, I'll be right back."

Shari limped over to the doorway of her bedroom and turned on the light. She couldn't see anyone, and everything was in its place. The window was slightly open and the wind was blowing a curtain back and forth against the lamp shade by her bed. She laughed to herself.

You're going to go to the psycho ward if this keeps up.

She went over to the window and looked outside. She saw no one. She closed and locked the window, turned out the light, and left the room.

What she failed to notice was that her closet door was slightly open.

THIRTY-SIX

PAUL HAD GOTTEN UP for another soda while Shari remained on the couch. He was rummaging through the refrigerator trying to decide what to drink. Cherry Coke, Dr Pepper, or a Pepsi.

Shari was still feeling jumpy, so when she heard the slight squeaking sound, it registered that she had a loose floorboard just outside of her bedroom. She glanced in the direction of the squeak and let out a blood-curdling scream. It startled Paul and he dropped the Cherry Coke he had in his hand. He followed her gaze and his heart skipped a beat.

There in the hall stood a large, thin man dressed all in black, with bone white skin and a black mustache. His eyes burned with evil, sending a stab of fear into Shari. She had never seen eyes like that before. It was like looking into the face of death.

The man entered the living room and something flashed in his right hand. Something sharp. Something deadly.

The stranger's cold eyes coolly appraised the two of them like a predator deciding which of its prey to devour first. As Shari scrambled up off the couch, the man in black sprung into action, leaping forward and planting a fist into her face.

The blow struck her on the cheekbone and she went backward over the couch and onto the floor. She seemed disoriented and lay there defenseless.

Paul's ignored the instinct to run to Shari, and instead rushed to the back of the couch, grabbed the baseball bat, and came up swinging. The man in black ducked in the nick of time and Paul hit the lamp on the stand at the end of the couch. The lamp went flying across the room and shattered against the wall.

Paul cocked his arms back, preparing for the next swing. He knew that he couldn't afford to miss this time. Something about the man told him that he was a trained fighter. He would have to make every blow count or he and Shari were done for. They danced around each other, the man in black first going one way and then the other, looking for an opening. Paul was doing the same thing, mirroring the stranger's moves and blocking each feint. One good swing, that's all he needed.

Paul caught a glimpse of Shari on the floor and shouted, "Get up, Shari! Get out! Run!"

His words penetrated her stupor and she struggled to her feet, limped to the door, and fumbled with the three locks. Blood dripped from her cheek and tears streamed down her face. She tried to move faster but it seemed like one of those dreams where you're trying to escape from a monster but cannot move.

She heard Paul calling out behind her, "Get out, Shari! Run! Run!"

The man in black did not like the idea of her leaving. He circled around the other side of the couch to get her. Paul blocked his way, brandishing the bat. He could hear Shari behind him screaming and crying and struggling with the locks.

"You stay away from her!" Paul warned.

The standoff continued a few moments more, until Shari unlocked the last latch. As the attacker lunged toward her, Paul swung. The man ducked, reaching for Shari. Paul swung the bat around blindly and connected with the man's right index finger, crushing it against the molding of the door.

The man in black screamed in pain. Blood spattered all over Shari as she finally got the door open and ran the best she could with a sprained ankle. She was yelling for help at the top of her lungs.

The bat had completely ripped Talon's artificial finger off his hand. The pain was excruciating and as he stared at his deformed hand, Paul swung one more time and caught him on the back. He slammed hard into the door but was up like a shot. That was the final straw. This kid was dead meat.

He spun around and fired off a side kick into Paul's gut, making him gasp and fall to the ground. His brain told him he had to get up and he had to breathe but nothing was working. His eyes were wide with fear.

Talon could hear Shari's voice disappearing down the street. She was screaming and crying for help.

"Call the police! Somebody, help! Call the police!"

People began to open their doors to see what all the commotion was about. Two men approached Shari and she tried to stop sobbing and tell them what was happening. One elderly lady called 911.

Talon had never been this angry before. All he could think about was inflicting the maximum amount of pain.

Paul somehow struggled to his feet. His only thought was to try to escape, not stay and fight. Talon kicked him in the chest, breaking several ribs and knocking Paul over a footstool. He went down hard and was really hurt this time. It was an effort to catch his breath, and the broken ribs almost made it unbearable.

Talon could hear sirens in the background, but he wasn't through with this punk yet. He kicked him repeatedly until Paul coughed up blood. Talon then struck a downward blow into Paul's face with his left hand. The wound started to bleed profusely and Paul felt light-headed. He was finished.

Talon strode into the kitchen, grabbed a dishtowel, and wrapped it around his throbbing stump of a finger. The sirens grew louder and he heard car doors slamming. Talon walked toward the door and retrieved the metal finger that had been effectively amputated by the bat. He walked over to Paul.

"You're dead. You hear? Look at me! You are dead!"

He grabbed Paul by the throat and held the sharp steel edge of the finger close. Paul's head lolled to one side. Talon heard footsteps on the stairs, close now. One swift motion and it would be done. He searched for fear in his victim's eyes, the terrible certainty of his imminent demise, the knowledge that Talon's sneering face was the last earthly sight he would ever see. . . .

He found none of these as Paul lapsed into unconsciousness. *I could still do it,* Talon told himself. *I could still end his worthless life.*

The footfall of the police storming down the hallway thundered in Talon's ears. *No,* thought Talon, *why put him out of his misery? Let him suffer a while longer.*

The two police officers made all of the neighbors wait outside. Shari was sobbing in the arms of Mr. and Mrs. Krantz. They lived two houses down from Shari's apartment and had become like second parents to her.

Several police officers cautiously entered the apartment with their guns drawn. They were shocked at the state of the living room—furniture overturned, the shattered remains of a lamp—clear signs of a massive struggle. Then they saw Paul's body on the floor, his blood soaking into the thick white carpet.

One officer knelt down beside him and felt for a pulse.

"His heart is still beating but it's extremely slow. He's in bad shape. Call for the paramedics at the Kings Crossing firehouse. They're only a couple of blocks away. We have to get him to the hospital as soon as possible."

"Do you think he'll make it?"

The officer frowned and shook his head.

THIRTY-SEVEN

WHEN MURPHY GOT WORD about Paul and Shari being attacked in the apartment, he rushed to the hospital. It had been one-thirty in the morning when Bob Wagoner called and woke him up with the news. Several nights a month, Wagoner would work as Police Chaplain for the Raleigh Police Department. They had asked Wagoner to come down to the hospital to be with Shari. As Murphy arrived, he could see there were still three police cars outside of the emergency room. He recognized one of the officers.

Barry Miller was a large man who was definitely in shape. He had a buzz haircut and was clean-shaven. His arms bulged out of his short-sleeve police uniform like they were about to explode. He was taking notes for his report when Murphy came up.

"Barry, how are they?"

"Hello, Doc." There was no smile on Barry's face. He stopped writing.

"Shari has a few bruises and contusions, but she'll be okay. I'm not sure about Wallach. They're working on him in intensive care. I think it's pretty much touch and go. Most of his vital signs had dropped by the time he arrived in the ambulance.

Murphy headed to the emergency room entrance and stopped. There were about ten people in the waiting room, but Shari was not one of them.

The night nurse, Clara Jane Moline, was behind the counter filling out some insurance forms. Murphy remembered her well from the day Laura had been brought to the hospital.

"Hi, Clara, I'm looking for Shari Nelson and Bob Wagoner."

She smiled. "Oh, hi, Doc. They're down the hall in a small waiting room that families use." She pointed with her pen.

"Thank you. Good to see you again," he added as he rushed off.

"You too," she called after him.

When Murphy got to the waiting room he could see Bob Wagoner and Shari sitting in silence. She lifted her head when he entered, thinking he might be one of the doctors with some news.

She looked a mess. Her hair was disarranged. One eye was black-and-blue and very puffy. There was a bandage on her cheekbone with a large red bruise surrounding it. She looked worn out, like she had been crying half the night, and she started crying again when she saw Murphy. He went over and held her for a few moments. Finally, he asked: "How is Paul?"

Through her tears she tried to speak.

"We don't know. He's still in the operating room. We overheard the nurses talking about internal bleeding."

That was all she could get out before she was crying uncontrollably.

Wagoner looked at Murphy and shook his head. "It doesn't look good, Michael. There must have been a terrible fight. Paul was beaten severely. He protected Shari and gave her time to escape. If he hadn't been there and fought the way he did, I'm sure she wouldn't be alive. He's been unconscious ever since they brought him in. They say he's in very serious condition."

"Excuse me, Dr. Murphy, but could I see you for a moment?" It was Officer Miller. He was motioning for Murphy to follow him.

In the hallway, and out of earshot of Shari, Miller spoke. "Do you know anything about what happened last night?"

"Only what Pastor Wagoner told me when he woke me up at one-thirty. Why do you ask?"

"After they took Wallach to the hospital, we stayed around and searched her place for clues. We found a bloodstained note that said 'Back off, Murphy!' Do you have any idea what that's all about?"

"Maybe."

Miller began to write as Murphy shared what he knew about Talon. He gave a description of what he looked like, and reported that he spoke with a South African accent. He tried to explain his artificial razorlike finger and how Talon used it to assassinate his victims. Miller was shaking his head back and forth as he wrote. This was quite a story.

"Thanks, Doc. I think the crime lab people were able to get a number of bloody fingerprints. They're also doing a DNA blood analysis to see if there are any matches. With all the blood in there, there's a good chance that not all of it belongs to Mr. Wallach and Miss Nelson. We think that Wallach may have injured his attacker in the struggle."

"I doubt if you'll find any fingerprints or DNA that will match. He's too clever for that. If someone had ever taken his fingerprints, I'm confident that he would have killed them and destroyed the evidence. This is an extremely ruthless and evil man."

THIRTY-EIGHT

MURPHY KNEW THAT Shari would be at the hospital sitting at Paul's bedside. This was the second time for her. The first was when he was injured in the bombing of the Preston Community Church. And now that he was in critical condition as a result of trying to save her life, there was no way that she would leave his side. Shari was one of the most loyal people Murphy had ever met.

When he got to the room, he hesitated for a moment. Shari was sitting in a chair next to Paul's bed. Her eyes were closed.

Maybe she's sleeping. She's been through a lot.

Tubes were running out of Paul's nose and arms. Electrical wires were attached to his body and to monitors, which were registering his blood pressure and heart rate. He lay unconscious and motionless.

I'll let her sleep, she needs the rest.

He turned and started to go when his shoe made a slight squeaking sound on the polished floor. Shari opened her eyes.

"Dr. Murphy."

Murphy stopped and turned around.

Shari smiled a soft smile. He could tell that she was still in pain from her injuries.

"I was just praying for Paul."

Murphy saw more black-and-blue marks on Shari's arms and hands. He came over and gave her a hug.

"Any change?"

"No. The doctors still don't know if he will pull out of it. The attacker kicked him severely and did internal damage. They also think he has a concussion."

Murphy pulled up another chair and sat down beside Shari.

"I don't know why the man tried to kill me and Paul."

Murphy tried not to wince. He knew.

"I think he was trying to get to me by hurting you. Paul just happened to be in the wrong place at the wrong time for him. But he was in the right place for saving your life. I think the same man that killed Laura tried to kill you."

Shari had a shocked look on her face. "Do you think he'll try again?"

"I don't think so. Things didn't work out for him the way he planned. He'll know that the police will be watching for him. I think he'll leave you alone. He made his point."

He was about to continue, when he heard a soft voice behind him. "Dr. Murphy."

Murphy turned around. It was Summer Van Doren.

"I had dropped by the church to get some study notes when they told me about Mr. Wallach. The whole church is praying for his recovery."

Murphy stood and offered her his seat.

"Let me introduce you to Shari Nelson. She's my assistant. Shari, this is Summer Van Doren. She's the new women's volleyball coach at Preston."

They shook hands.

"I'm so sorry to hear about your friend, Shari. Have you heard anything about his recovery?"

"No, not yet. He's hurt very badly."

Summer and Shari talked for a while and Murphy listened. Summer seemed so warm and sincerely caring. It was a nice gesture. After about ten minutes she stood up.

"I'll let you be alone with him."

Murphy glanced at his watch. "Shari, you've been here for a while. It's almost six-thirty, how about getting a bite to eat? Miss Van Doren, we would love to have you join us."

Summer hesitated for a moment, looked at her watch, and then said, "I think that will work. My Bible study doesn't begin until eight."

Shari did not get up.

"You know, I'm sorry but I really don't feel hungry. If you don't mind I think I would rather stay here with Paul."

Both Summer and Murphy nodded sympathetically.

Murphy now felt a little strange. What was meant to be a nice gesture for both of the women was turning into something more like a date. He could tell that Summer was just a little apprehensive also. He tried to ease the pressure.

"You know, there's a little Mexican place just across the street from the hospital. We could leave our cars in the hospital lot and walk to it. We wouldn't have to drive around town. Do you like Mexican?"

Summer seemed relieved. The thought of driving somewhere to a restaurant, waiting in line, and eating with an 8:00 deadline made her uncomfortable—especially since Shari had declined to join them.

"I love Mexican."

During dinner, Murphy questioned her about her life in San Diego, her hobbies, athletic activities, and how she ended up at Preston University. She, in turn, asked about biblical archaeology and some of the things that Murphy had discovered. She was especially enthralled with the stories of his adventures in foreign countries and meeting strange and exotic people.

As the evening progressed they became more relaxed and free in sharing their thoughts and dreams. As Summer took a drink of water, she noticed her watch. It was ten minutes to eight.

"Oh, I didn't realize the time."

Murphy looked at his watch. They both stood up.

"Please feel free to go. I know you have a meeting. I'll get the waiter and take care of the check."

"That's very nice. I'm sorry to run. Thank you for dinner."

"It was my pleasure."

Summer reached out her hand and Murphy shook it. There was a slight pause as they looked at each other.

"I'll see you around the campus," she said with a warm smile.

"I'm sure you will."

As Summer walked out of the restaurant, Murphy noticed a number of men looking at her as she walked by.

Murphy paid the check and strolled back across the street to his car. He got in, started the engine, and turned on the radio. It was playing an old love song.

As he pulled out onto the street, the song on the radio made him think of Summer's beautiful face, blond hair, and deep blue eyes that sparkled while she talked. She had a cute smile and a laugh that was infectious.

He then found his mind wandering to Isis. Murphy had begun to develop feelings for her . . . and now a new woman had come onto the scene and he had mixed emotions. Again Murphy came back to the fact that Summer was a believer and Isis was not.

Murphy was torn. He knew that the Bible said not to have a mixed marriage with someone who didn't share the same faith. He began to realize that he might be called on to make a decision. He didn't like that thought.

How can you just let go of someone you genuinely care for?

He snapped off the radio. That stupid song had wrecked his evening.

THIRTY-NINE

The Cave of Markalar, 1083 B.C.

GENERAL ABIEZER *was hiding in the Cave of Markalar when one of his aides gave him the news. "Ocran the scout arrived a few minutes ago. He says that the Philistines have ended the pursuit of our army."*

"Where have the men gone?" inquired Abiezer.

"Most of them fled east in the direction of Shechem. Others escaped to the north toward Mount Gerizim. Some may have hidden in caves. There is no order to the retreat. They are in complete disarray."

General Abiezer hung his head in disgrace. He too had turned and run for his life. Guilt was now overpowering him for not leading his army. Thoughts of suicide crossed his mind.

The aide continued. "Ocran is a very brave and loyal man. He clandestinely followed the Philistines back to the battlefield and says that they stripped our warriors of their valuables and killed our wounded."

General Abiezer winced at the thought of his brave soldiers being killed in their vulnerable condition.

"What about the Ark of the Covenant and the priests?"

"Ocran says that they put the heads of Hophni and Phinehas on the tops of two spears and displayed them as trophies. They took the Ark of the Covenant and headed in the direction of Ashdod."

Runners had already reached Ashdod with the news of the victory over the Israelites in the valley between Ebenezer and Aphek. The slaying of over 34,000 of their enemy caused jubilation in the city. However, the most exciting news was the capture of the Israeli God named Jehovah and his house called the Ark of the Covenant.

When the Philistine army entered Ashdod, the people went wild. Great cheers went up as the Ark of the Covenant was paraded through the city streets. Curses were hurled at the home of Jehovah and praises were sung to the great god Dagon who had provided this great victory.

The soldiers ended their march in front of the Temple of Dagon. The priests opened the large doors and the Ark of the Covenant was carried inside.

It was placed to the right of the thirty-foot, half-fish/half-man statue of Dagon.

It was presented as a praise offering for the victory over the Israelites.

The priests bowed before the statue and offered prayers. They rolled on the ground and cut themselves as a sign of loyalty to Dagon. Trumpets sounded and great rejoicing occurred throughout the entire city. People danced and sang and drank much wine.

Late in the evening, Kadmiel, the high priest, entered the Temple of Dagon. Several other priests bearing torches accompanied him. They surrounded the Ark and admired its beauty.

Kadmiel spoke: "Let us open the Ark and see what is inside."

A look of fear coupled with anticipation came over the faces of the other priests.

"Take off the lid and we will see what makes this Ark so special."

Carefully the priests removed the lid and set it on the floor. They then raised their torches and looked inside. Kadmiel noticed four items in the Ark.

He removed two of the articles and examined them in the torchlight. He again peered into the Ark and studied the two remaining items.

"Put the lid back on."

One of the priests standing near Kadmiel asked, "Don't you want to take out the other two objects?"

"They are of no value. They are just two stone tablets with Hebrew writing on them. Something to do with their moral laws."

Kadmiel then bent down and picked up the two articles he had removed.

It was early the next morning when the priests entered the Temple of Dagon for their daily prayers. To their shock and dismay, the statue of Dagon had fallen with its face to the earth, as if it were bowing down to the Ark of the Covenant.

A great discussion took place as to how the statue could have fallen over. There was no explanation. The temple had been locked during the night and the usual temple guards were on patrol. No one could have possibly entered. No one felt an earthquake and the statue had been secure in its place for over twenty years. They couldn't believe a statue that large could fall without alerting the guards. It was an absolute mystery.

The statue weighed many tons and it took almost one hundred men to put it back in place. All the engineers of the temple were called to inspect the statue. Even small wedges were pounded under the front to insure that the statue could not possibly fall forward again.

Early the next morning the priests went into the Temple of Dagon for their prayers. To their shock, Dagon had again fallen to the ground before the Ark of the Covenant. Only this time, Dagon's head was broken off along with both of his hands. Only Dagon's torso was left in one piece.

Fear struck all of the priests. Could it be that the God of the Israelites was angry and striking back at the god of the Philistines? Was the Israelite God more powerful than Dagon? Was Jehovah sending a message? The priests ran from the temple and were afraid to return at peril of their own lives.

Kadmiel complained to his wife, "Something is wrong! I do not feel well this morning. I have an unexplained growth. I never noticed it before and I think it may be getting bigger."

"I have the same thing happening to me. I too have an unknown growth." Kadmiel could hear the fear in her voice. "The children are also complaining that they are not feeling well. Do you think it might be a plague of some kind?"

It did not take long for the devastating news to spread. The whole town of Ashdod, and the territory surrounding it, was stricken with growing tumors. From the infants to the elderly, a miserable cry of pain could be heard.

Kadmiel called all the priests of Dagon and the lords of the city together.

The chief lord spoke. "Do you think that this plague has come about due to the rats that are overrunning our city?"

Kadmiel responded, "I am not sure if the rats are spreading it or not. But I believe that this plague is a result of capturing the Israelite Ark. It may be a punishment sent by their God."

"What shall we do with it?" asked the priests and lords.

Kadmiel responded: "The Ark of the Israelite God must not remain here. Their God is angry with us and has struck the great statue of Dagon. Their God, Jehovah, has brought on a plague to torture us. Let the golden Ark be carried away to the city of Gath. They have giants in their city. Maybe they can deal with the God of the Israelites."

FORTY

THE SWISS ALPS looked majestic as the sun broke through the clouds. A fresh blanket of snow sparkled on the roof and turrets of the castle. Everything was covered in white, while a terrible darkness festered deep below the ancient structure.

Sir William Merton's face was so red that his head looked like a rocket about to explode off a launching pad. His fist came down hard on the table in front of him and he yelled.

"I told you! I told you! I told you before! He is a danger to our mission!"

The other six members winced. Even Talon, who was used to just about anything, was taken aback slightly by the strength of Merton's emotions. His left hand grabbed the gargoyle on the arm of the chair and squeezed. His right hand was wrapped in bandages.

"You are correct," replied John Bartholomew. "We all knew that it was a risk. He has not let the cat out of the bag yet. There is still time to resolve the matter."

Merton shook his head. "I hope so! I hope that it has not gone beyond the point of no return. What do you think would happen to us if the Master found out that we could not do our job?"

This hit a nerve. The Seven burst forth with a litany of excuses and opinions, talking over one another in their desire to place blame and escape responsibility. Talon could almost taste their fear, and it delighted him. He didn't like any of them and it gave him pleasure to see them squirm.

John Bartholomew tried to gain control of the group and get them to refocus. He pounded a gavel twice and at length their murmuring ceased.

"Please, let us not lose our heads. We have a guest. Talon, thank you for coming on such short notice. I see your hand is bandaged. Is there anything we should be concerned with?"

Talon knew they were not concerned about the injury to his finger by Paul Wallach. They were only concerned as to whether it would affect his ability to kill.

"Nothing serious. I will be able to fulfill any mission you desire."

The Seven smiled their evil smiles and Bartholomew continued. "Underneath your chair is a folder with a copy of an editorial. Would you please take it out and read it. We would like to hear your comments."

Talon bent forward and pulled the folder from under the chair with his left hand. He opened it and read.

AN IMPORTANT BARRINGTON NEWS EDITORIAL

Since the founding of Barrington Communications, I have made it a practice to let other people write the editorial column. It has only been upon rare occasions and for momentous news stories that I have personally picked up my pen. This happens to be one of those significant and notable times.

If you have been reading our newspapers or have listened to our television broadcasts, the name Dr. Constantine De La Rosa will be familiar to you. Dr. De La Rosa is the founder of the Religious Harmony Institute based in Rome, Italy.

We have been writing numerous articles about his desire to unite the world with Religious Harmony. You may have even seen several television documentaries recounting his miraculous healing crusades. These reports have provided eyewitness accounts of crippled people being able to walk. You have also seen documented cases of the blind having their sight restored and the deaf being able to hear.

Along with physical healings, Dr. De La Rosa has also made some astounding political predictions that have come true. Even more importantly, he has warned of the coming of a number of natural disasters. His call to be alert has saved the lives of countless thousands of people from several tornados, three hurricanes, seven earthquakes, and two tidal waves.

Dr. De La Rosa is becoming a household name in all nations of the world. His crusades seem to be striking a chord of harmony between all peoples regardless of race or religion. His dynamic personality has a magnetism that can only be compared to the life of one other person who has ever lived: The man called Jesus Christ.

However, this author is not afraid to ask some hard questions. Who is Dr. De La Rosa? Not much is known about him. We have been unable to trace any history of his birth, childhood, or even much about his adulthood. He seems to have just broken into the course of history out of nowhere.

This author also asks the question, 'Where does Dr. De La Rosa get all of his money?' Try as we may, we have been unable to discover any businesses he has started, inheritances he has received, or how he is supported other than the contributions he receives from followers.

I am also concerned about his so-called nonprofit corporation called the Religious Harmony Institute. Nothing can be found about a board of directors or any overseers of his activities. He seems to be accountable to no one.

At first glance one could say, 'So what? Look at all the good he is doing!' But I personally think this is a dangerous position to hold. Could Dr. De La Rosa have ulterior motives? Is there a group of people behind him supporting activities of *their* design? Are *their* motives good and right and moral? What do we know about these individuals? Are there just two or three of them or as many as *seven*?

You may say, 'Are you trying to punch holes in the reputation of Dr. De La Rosa? Is he a man that does not have integrity? Is he trying to lead people like the Pied Piper of Hamelin down a path that may lead to destruction?' Those are fair questions.

At this writing I am not yet willing to make that strong of a statement. I am merely questioning who he is and why he is doing what he is doing. I will say, however, that a thorough investigation is being launched by the Barrington Communications Company into all of these questions. We will find out the answers. And if, as we suspect, there is some clandestine motivation, you will be given that information.

This is a promise, and a solemn pledge, or my name isn't Shane Barrington, Owner and President of Barrington Communications.

Talon placed the paper in his lap and looked up at the Seven. He could see all of their eyes focused on him.

"It looks like he's about to blow your cover."

The Seven sat there for a moment in silence as Talon's words sunk in. He was never one to mince words.

"May I ask you how you got a hold of this editorial? I haven't seen it in print yet."

General Li spoke up.

"You are not the only one who works for us, Talon. We have some other operatives within the Barrington Communications Company. They alerted us to the fact that Barrington was beginning to consolidate and move money around. He has opened several Swiss bank accounts and is in the process of transferring money. We believe that he is trying to protect himself in the event that we shut off the flow of funds to his organization."

Talon nodded.

"In addition, Barrington has purchased extensive security equipment for his home. He has ordered a bulletproof car and has put out feelers to companies who do bodyguard work for high-level executives. In light of this, we instructed our operatives to break into his office and access information off of his personal computer."

Talon smiled. *They don't miss a trick.*

"They opened up his computer and found the editorial you read. We are not sure when he is planning to run it. But it is evident that he is out to try and destroy us."

Talon knew what was coming next.

Bartholomew said, "Talon, we have a number of assignments on your To-Do List. However, we think that this one should rise to the top."

"I understand. And may I inquire as to when—"

Bartholomew cut him off.

"The money has already been deposited in your Swiss bank account."

A blast of cold struck Talon as he exited the castle. He took in a deep breath of the fresh mountain air and buttoned the collar of his coat as the driver without a tongue opened the door to the limousine.

The drive back to Zurich gave Talon plenty of time to think about Paul Wallach. How could he have been so careless to allow an untrained fighter to damage his finger like he did? It was stupid. He should have waited until the boy left and the girl was alone. But after two failed attempts on her life, Talon had grown impatient and made his move too soon. And now he had paid the price. He began to rub his right hand, which was throbbing because of the cold, damp air. It would take a while before it would heal enough to have a new metal finger replacement.

Talon felt the limousine slip a little as they rounded a corner in the fresh-fallen snow. He saw the driver's eyes glance at him for a moment in the rearview mirror and then back to the road ahead.

That would be an ironic end. To slip off the road and over the cliff to the deep canyon below. Not the way I thought I would go. But then death sometimes arrives when least expected. In his line of work, Talon knew that better than anyone.

His mind drifted back to all the people he had killed. How many had it been? Too many to remember. How long would it continue? Was it the money? He had enough to last several lifetimes. Why did he do it? Was it anger? Yes, it was. Was it for pleasure? Yes, it was. Would he continue as long as his health held out? Why not?

After all, he reflected, *how many people truly love what they do for a living?*

FORTY-ONE

MURPHY GLANCED AT the clock when he heard the telephone ring. It was 8:45 P.M. He had been channel-surfing and, unable to find anything that held his interest, he'd decided to go to bed a little early and finish a mystery novel that he'd been reading.

He was reluctant to answer the phone. Lately it seemed that every time it rang, someone else had been injured or killed.

"Murphy here."

"Michael, it's Bob. I hope that I haven't disturbed you."

"Not at all. What's up?"

"Do you remember when we were at J. B. Sonstad's tent meetings?"

"How could I forget? People like that stick in your mind."

"I mentioned to you that one of the men that came forward went to our church."

"Yeah, the one with the kidney disease."

"Yes. That was Clyde Carlson. Anyway, I met with him later and talked about what happened. He told me that he wasn't sure. It was a very emotional experience and he hoped that he was healed. I encouraged him to go back to his doctor for a checkup."

"Let me guess. He wasn't any better."

"Unfortunately you're right. He was discouraged, to say the least. His condition is deteriorating. But that hasn't slowed him down. He heard from a friend about another person who claims to be a psychic healer, someone named Madame Estelle. She lives in an old farmhouse on the outskirts of Raleigh."

"I've never heard of her before."

"Neither have I . . . but actually I don't run in those types of circles, so it's not surprising. He's asked that I go along with him. I really don't feel comfortable doing that but I want to help him work through the acceptance that he may soon die from the disease. He is sort of grabbing at straws and I don't like him fighting the battle alone. This is a long way of asking if you'd be willing to go with us. I would feel much more at ease if you were there."

"Sure, Bob. When people face death sometimes they'll try anything to escape the inevitable. If I were in his place, maybe I would seek any kind of help too. I'll do a little research on psychic healing. Maybe we could get together over lunch and discuss it."

"That would be great."

"How about the Adam's Apple at twelve-thirty tomorrow?"

"You're on. I'll see you there."

When Murphy entered the Adam's Apple restaurant it was busy as usual. He could tell that Roseanne was under a little pressure. Not only was she waiting on the tables but she was trying to train a new girl at the same time. When she saw Murphy she pointed to the back.

"Pastor Bob is in the corner. I'll be with you in a minute."

"Thanks, Rosanne."

"Do you want your usual, Doc?"

"That'll be great."

As Murphy headed toward the back he could hear Roseanne yelling in the order. As he slid into the booth he noticed a tear on the green vinyl seat. Murphy and Wagoner shook hands.

"Well, what do you think, Michael? Fake healing crusades, psychic surgeons, rise of the occult, false teachers . . . we're certainly living in interesting times."

"That's putting it mildly. I did some study last night on psychic healers. Not only do we have them in the United States but in many places around the world. I read that psychic healing is quite popular in the Philippines."

"What do they do?"

"Their activities vary a little but often they pretend to do bloodless surgery without a scalpel."

"That sounds like my kind of surgery," Bob laughed. "I'm a wimp when it comes to pain."

"You won't believe what I'm about to tell you. They will have the person lie on a table and they act like they are digging their hands into the person's body and taking out the disease or cancer from their body. After the imaginary incision, the psychic seems to pull out some kind of tissue and discards it. Then they wipe their hand back across the person's body and the incision is gone and everything is normal. Sounds great, right?"

"No. It sounds weird."

"That's for sure. There is a book entitled *Arigo: Surgeon of the Rusty Knife.* It's the story of a Brazilian peasant who operates with an unclean pocketknife. It's supposed to be done without pain, bleeding, or stitches. It is said that this Arigo could stop the flow of blood with a verbal command, and that he had the ability to read blood pressure without instruments. Apparently, over three hundred patients a day would visit him."

"Is that documented?"

"No. He died in 1981 before any scientific investigators could verify his claims. I also read about a magician named Henry Gordon who debunked what psychic surgeons did. In front of television cameras, he performed the same type of surgery and also pulled out some flesh from a patient. In actuality, it was tissue from a chicken liver that he had hidden in the palm of his hand. It did look impressive, though."

"Well, when we go with Clyde we'll look for chicken livers."

Roseanne came waddling toward their table with plates in her hands. Her gray hair was tied in a bun and slight beads of perspiration gathered on her forehead. She placed the plates on the table.

"Here you go, men. Have a good lunch."

Murphy smiled. "Thank you, Rosanne. By the way, are you aware of the rip in the vinyl seat?"

Roseanne put her hands on her hips and she looked where Murphy was pointing.

"Humph. It must have been those teenagers we had in here last night. They were a rowdy bunch." She turned and waddled away.

"You know, Bob," responded Murphy. "It seems like evil is on the increase. Not just from kids horsing around destroying property like this seat, but keying and stealing cars . . . and other things like violent crime, terrorist bombings, murders, and wars. There is much darkness in this world and it's only going to get worse."

"As you know, Michael, the Bible informs us that in the last days many people will leave their faith in God. Then the 'man of sin' will come. He will be someone who will bring strong delusion. Do you think it could be that guy . . . what's his name . . . Rosa something?"

"Do you mean Constantine De La Rosa?"

"Yes, he's the one."

"I don't know, Bob, but whoever he is he'll be a strong leader. Unfortunately many people will believe his lies. It also says that he will be able to perform miracles and wonders."

"Sort of like this De La Rosa that has been in the newspapers and television lately?"

"Yes. It has been reported that he has been doing some very powerful healings and giving predictions." The implications raced around in Murphy's brain. "Do you think he might be the coming Anti-Christ, Bob?"

"Actually, I don't think so. He sure could pass for the False Prophet though. He's supposed to have great powers and be able to perform miracles. The False Prophet will pave the pathway for the Anti-Christ. He will do this by a call for religious unification between all peoples and all cultures. If he tries to globally organize political and social life, it would be a definite sign that he could be the person. If he then begins to set up some type of economic control with a marking or registration system, he will certainly be the person. The False Prophet is the one who will oversee the 666 marking of people on their right hand or on their forehead."

"Hmm," Murphy said absently.

"Michael? Are you still listening?"

"Sorry, I was just thinking about Isis. I don't think she has come to a point of faith in her life. I'd hate to see her begin to follow someone like the False Prophet."

"Michael, may I speak frankly?"

"Of course, Bob."

"I've been a little concerned about you and Isis. It seems like this is beginning to develop into something more than just a friendship."

"It's moving in that direction."

"You know that your faith discourages getting involved with someone who does not hold the same belief. It can lead to many disagreements and disappointments with each other. More than one marriage has struggled over these issues. I would hate to see you in a marriage like that, especially after you and Laura were so happy and well-matched.

"I know you're right, Bob. It's just difficult when the feelings begin to grow."

"It might be best to end them before there's no turning back, Michael."

"I know. I've been thinking very seriously about it. It's just hard."

"There are other wonderful people who love the Lord and share your faith. For example, there is that new young lady who has been attending our church. She's the new women's volleyball coach for Preston."

"Summer Van Doren."

"You know her? I didn't realize that. What do you think about her?"

"She's quite impressive. She's got it all . . . looks, personality, talent, and a strong faith."

"Well?"

"Well, I have been thinking about it. Isis has it all also, except she doesn't share my faith. And that's really big to me. I have noticed the difference the few times I've talked to Summer. She's a very warm and caring person. There's a dimension with her that I don't have with Isis. I just don't like the idea of hurting someone else in the process."

"There is no easy way around that, Michael. You can't have your cake and eat it too. Life is filled with choices. Some are easy and some are very tough. You have to look at the big picture. Do you want to spend your life with the wrong person? I have a lot of people like that in my counseling office."

Murphy was quiet. Wagoner could tell that he was struggling.

"Michael, I will be praying that God will give you the right answer for your relationship with Isis. Remember what it says. *'Trust in the Lord with all your heart and lean not on your own understanding; in all your ways acknowledge him, and he will make your paths straight.'* I am confident that God will enlighten you with the right answer at the right time."

FORTY-TWO

MURPHY OPENED the taxi door and got in. The driver turned and looked at him.

"Where to?"

"The Parchments of Freedom Foundation."

"Okay. It may take a few more minutes than usual. The traffic is really heavy today."

"I understand," said Murphy as he settled back in the seat and stared out the window.

The flight from Raleigh to Washington had really seemed long. He hadn't looked forward to it as he had to previous trips. A dark cloud hovered over his thoughts. He did not want to face what lay ahead, and yet, he knew that it had to be done.

The whole process was made even more difficult by Isis's excitement over his visit. Murphy pursed his lips and shook his head. There was a dull pain in his stomach. He took a long deep breath and let it out slowly.

Isis was putting some papers into a filing cabinet when Murphy arrived at her office. Her back was to him as he entered and she was humming a tune. He hesitated in the doorway. She was wearing a black pants suit that was tailored to fit her shapely body. Her red hair had a hint of auburn in it.

Murphy softly cleared his throat. Isis turned at the sound.

Her face brightened with a big smile and her green eyes sparkled with delight.

"Michael!"

Isis moved toward him. They embraced and she kissed him.

"You're early."

"The plane had a tail wind and we arrived about twenty minutes early."

Isis gathered her things. "The reservations are for seven o'clock. I'm so glad you're here."

The conversation at dinner was very general and somewhat stilted. Isis could tell that Murphy was a little preoccupied. She thought that he must be tired from the trip or maybe that he was worried about Shari . . . or about Paul Wallach in the hospital.

It wasn't until they were at Isis's apartment that Murphy began to open up.

"Isis. We need to talk a little."

There was something in his tone that made her very uneasy.

"You know, we've had a lot of good times together. We've been through some real danger and I'll always be grateful for you nursing me back to health after the events on Mount Ararat."

Isis could feel that something was coming.

"I appreciate everything you've done for me. Your research and translation work have been invaluable. You've helped in the discovery of a number of important artifacts. It's been wonderful."

She thought to herself, *There's a "but" coming.*

"My feelings toward you have grown stronger over the past few months. But there is an issue that has been hard for me to face."

Murphy paused and took a deep breath.

"You know that I have a strong faith in Christ and believe the Bible. It is something that is a significant part of my life. I also know that you are not at the same place that I am in your spiritual journey."

Murphy's faith in God was one of the things Isis liked about him. It made him different from all the other men she had ever dated. It gave him a sense of purpose that had been missing in other men. It also seemed to change his behavior toward her. He had treated her with more respect and gentleness than anyone she had ever met. And if she was totally honest with herself, it was the one thing that caused her to begin to think about her own relationship to God.

"If two people are to develop a strong and lasting relationship, they really need to be on the same wavelength when it comes to faith in God. Divided families often have great struggles. Both parties are not able to share the same experience or values. It can bring about great stress."

Isis could feel it coming and she didn't want to hear what he was going to say. She knew that it wasn't going to be good.

"I care about you very deeply. However, I don't think it's wise for us to continue to see each other and have our feelings develop to an even deeper level. I think we might be headed for greater hurt if we do. I need someone who shares my same beliefs. I respect you so much, Isis. You are a beautiful person inside and out. And I have loved being with you. I just can't let my feelings go any further. I don't want to hurt you any more than I have to. It wouldn't be good for either of us. I also don't want you to feel pressure to believe what I believe. Nor would I want you to try and create some type of experience to please me. Everyone's faith must be his own. Each person has to individually come to a relationship with God."

Isis felt like she was going to cry.

"It might be good for both of us if we began to see other people. You have so much to offer someone and I don't want to stand in the way of you meeting someone who will love you with all of his heart."

Isis felt like the rug was being pulled out from under her. Tears were close to the surface but she held her composure.

"Michael, I don't know if I agree with you. I think that two people can still see one another and have a relationship grow, and still talk about faith. I don't think it has to end."

"But what if the relationship grows and the faith does not?"

"There's risk in every relationship, Michael."

He did not respond. She could tell that his mind was already made up and that nothing she could say would make any difference now.

"I hear what you're saying and I can tell that you're uneasy," she said at last. "I wouldn't want you to be in a relationship that didn't meet your spiritual expectations."

Isis didn't want to press the issue. She didn't want to come across as begging for the relationship to continue. She had too much self-respect and pride to do that. All she wanted to do was escape from the emotions she was feeling. She felt sick inside. She knew that this was hard for Michael and she loved him so much that she was willing to let him go. She could only hope that he would change his mind and come back to her.

Murphy knew that what he had said had destroyed the evening and maybe even their friendship forever. He took her hand.

"Isis. The last thing I want to do is hurt you. I just think that with the gap of faith between us, we could be in for even deeper hurt in the future. I'm so sorry to do this to you."

Murphy could tell that she was close to tears.

"I'd better go, Isis. I'll take a taxi back to the airport." Murphy stood.

Isis wiped a little tear from her eye and stood as well. She was trying desperately to hold herself together.

Murphy took both of her hands and looked into her eyes. He then embraced her and whispered in her ear, "I'm so sorry."

She felt so good in his arms and he didn't want to let her go. Finally, he knew that he had to. He let go and slowly backed away.

Both of her hands came up and she began to wipe away the tears that were beginning to flow uncontrollably.

Murphy walked to the door, turned around, took one last look at Isis, and left.

The flight back to Raleigh was worse than the flight going to Washington. Murphy felt terrible. He knew that he had deeply hurt Isis and he truly hadn't wanted to do that. He played the conversation back in his mind, and the more he did, the sicker he felt. Had he made the wrong decision? His emotions made him want to catch the next flight back to Washington to try and repair the damage he'd caused. He wanted to hold her in his arms again.

The stewardess came by and offered drinks and a snack to everyone on the plane. Murphy ordered a Coke and began to mindlessly eat the pretzels.

Even though Murphy knew intellectually that he had made the right decision, everything else inside him screamed in protest. Now what was he going to do? There was a large, empty void in his heart. He had lost Laura when Talon killed her and now he had driven Isis out of his life.

Murphy felt angry, depressed, and terribly lonely.

God, why is all of this happening?

FORTY-THREE

WHETHER IT WAS curiosity, a hunch, or just wishful thinking, something motivated Murphy to again drive down Highway 40 to North Myrtle Beach. He had to get more information about the mysterious Methuselah. There were too many unanswered questions about the reclusive billionaire.

This time there would be no deception, no putting on a waiter uniform. He would simply approach Methuselah directly and let the chips fall where they may. He was tired of all of the games. Besides, it would save him another two-hundred-dollar tip.

Murphy parked his old Dodge, grabbed a book, and walked down to the beach. This time he came a little later, figuring that Methuselah would not come until after 11:00 A.M., when the sun's rays became warmer. There were a couple dozen people scattered about. A couple was fishing, several were jogging, and the rest were just relaxing.

Murphy had no idea if Methuselah would show up or not, but he thought he would play the odds. At the very least, if he did not come, Murphy would get a little relaxation at the beach with a good book. Plus, it would help keep his mind off Iris.

At 11:30 A.M., Murphy stopped reading and began looking around. Methuselah was nowhere to be found. *Maybe he's not even in the country.*

About 12:15 P.M. he got up and stretched. He was beginning to believe that this trip would turn out to be fruitless. He was heading back toward his car when he saw three men in the distance walking along the beach near the water. They were wearing Hawaiian shirts. Behind them was one man who was followed by three more men in Hawaiian shirts. The man in the center had a slight limp. No one had any folding lawn chairs.

Murphy's heart began to beat a little faster. He decided that he would join Methuselah in his stroll along the beach. As he drew closer to the group, he could see the lead bodyguards going on the alert, intently watching him approach. One was already starting to reach for the automatic that was bulging under the brightly colored shirt he wore.

Murphy could hear one of them say: "Mr. M.!"

Methuselah turned to his bodyguard and then spied Murphy. The three bodyguards behind were moving forward, closing the distance between them and Methuselah.

The older man began to smile and then let out a little cackling laugh.

"Well, well, well. Dr. Murphy. Curiosity killed the cat and satisfaction brought it back."

The whole group had stopped and two of the men moved toward Murphy and began to frisk him for weapons.

"It's all right, gentlemen. I think Dr. Murphy would like to join me for a stroll."

Methuselah started to walk and Murphy joined him.

"I still have some unanswered questions," Murphy began.

"I'm sure you do, Dr. Murphy."

"I don't understand your game. Why do you keep revealing the location of biblical artifacts to me? What's behind all of this?"

"A combination of reasons, Dr. Murphy. Part of it has to do with my grandfather, Marcello Zasso. As you know, he was a dedicated missionary and a devoted student of the Bible. He also had a passion for biblical archaeology like you do. He wished to explore for biblical artifacts but never had the opportunity. Instead, he spent countless hours researching obscure historical texts and experts' papers. As a child I would listen to his stories and his theories about where certain items might be hidden. I used to keep a little notebook of my grandfather's thoughts."

Murphy was listening intently.

"Do you mean he had figured out where Nebuchadnezzar's golden head might be located?"

"Yes, and much more. He had done research on the three pieces of the Bronze Serpent of Moses, the location of Noah's Ark, the Handwriting on the Wall, and even the site of the Temple of Dagon."

"You left me notes suggesting that Aaron's Rod and the Golden Jar of Manna could be found. Have you found them?"

"Not personally, Dr. Murphy. I just use my grandfather's notes. I am leaving the discovery of the various items up to you."

"You also mentioned that my discovering various biblical artifacts would hamper the activities of a group of people who killed your family."

"Yes, yes. These are evil people who do not believe in God or the Bible. I get great joy out of trying to destroy their plans. Revenge, as they say, is sweet."

"Plans? What do you mean? Who are these people?"

"They call themselves the Seven. They are extremely wealthy and power-hungry. Together, they control the largest banks in the world.

They have influence over the richest oil fields ever discovered. They have infiltrated many governments and have countless political leaders in their pockets. They promote corruption wherever they can. They also influence the movement of the European Common Market and have designed a clandestine conspiracy to control the economies of the entire world. They are the force behind the rebuilding of the city of Babylon."

Murphy was trying to process the enormity of what Methuselah was saying.

"This group of people wants the United States to become a lesser power in the world. They will try and turn the United Nations against the U.S. They will help to foment war and turmoil within countries, like the crisis between Pakistan and India. They are the financial supporters of a number of leading terrorist organizations and helped to coordinate the attack of 9/11. They have contacts in many of the sleeper cells. And they are rejoicing that America has been stretched financially between the war with Iraq, natural disasters by hurricanes, and the expense of homeland security."

"How do you know all of this?"

"Being a billionaire does have its advantages, Dr. Murphy. There is a great deal of information for sale if you can afford the asking price. Besides, I have infiltrated their organization."

"You get information from one of the Seven?"

"Oh, no. But I have an informant who gets me the information."

"What if they catch him and make him talk?"

"That would be impossible. He cannot talk. He has no tongue. He lives deep within their headquarters in a solitary room. Little do they know, but an air duct runs from their meeting room past the room of my informant. He can hear everything they talk about. It has been a wonderful turn of events."

"If they're so powerful, how can you stop them?"

Methuselah stopped walking and picked up a starfish that had been washed ashore. He held it in front of Murphy.

"You see this starfish, Dr. Murphy?"

Methuselah tossed it back in the water.

"I'm sure that you've heard the story of the little boy who was tossing starfish back into the sea which were stranded on the shore. When asked what he was doing he said, 'I'm saving the life of this starfish.' 'But,' replied the questioner, 'there are so many starfish on the shore. How can you possibly make a difference?' You'll remember the little boy responded, 'I'm making a difference to this one,' as he tossed it into the sea. So, I may not be able to stop all the evil actions of the Seven . . . but any action I can stop gives me great joy. I love to be a thorn in their side or a pebble in their shoe. I'm making a difference in hindering them."

"And what if they try to kill you to put an end to your harassment?"

"Oh, they've tried that on several occasions. But my informant has gotten word of their plans to me before their assassin could carry them out. He's a strange man who has an addiction for killing people with his pet birds."

Murphy's heart almost stopped. *Talon.* But if he worked for the Seven, then they were responsible for killing his wife and the attempts to kill Isis and Paul Wallach, plus many others. Murphy suddenly realized that he and Methuselah had common enemies in the Seven.

"You see, Dr. Murphy, I have been using you to hamper the work of the Seven. Your discoveries help to prove the validity of the Bible, which in turn helps to destroy their plans."

"What does this all have to do with the Temple of Dagon and Aaron's Rod, and the Golden Jar of Manna?"

"Well, Dr. Murphy . . . just think about it for a moment. Aaron's Rod that budded was a miracle. What if someone had Aaron's Rod and used it to lend credibility to so-called miracles they might perform? People would follow that person. And suppose that same person had the Golden Jar of Manna. Manna was a symbol of God providing food for the hungry. What if the person began to feed the starving people of the world? Do you suppose that they might generate a big following? I think that this is all part of the plan of the Seven."

"And how about the Bronze Serpent of Moses?"

"That could become a symbol of the healing of all forms of illness and disease. Remember, Moses lifted up the Bronze Serpent on a rod or pole and the people were healed. I think that someone could do the same thing today using the Bronze Serpent. People would begin to think there was healing power in the snake. Even King Hezekiah knew of the danger in worshiping the snake, which is why he had it broken in three pieces."

Murphy was amazed at all of Methuselah's knowledge of the Bible.

"With you knowing so much about the Bible . . . have you ever come to faith?"

Methuselah began his cackling laugh.

"Just because someone knows the facts about the Bible doesn't make one a believer. I just listened carefully to my grandfather and my father. They were believers. But not me. I'm too old and bitter for that. God wouldn't want to have me in heaven."

"But God—"

Methuselah cut him off before he could finish.

"Enough talk about God."

Methuselah sounded irritated. He stopped walking and looked at Murphy.

"I know that you are a man of faith. That's fine. So were my father and grandfather. But don't try to push your thoughts on me. I think we are through talking. In fact, since you persist in taking away the pleasure of the surprise element of our relationship, I can no longer involve you in my little games."

Incredibly, Murphy was disappointed to hear it. He certainly had no desire to face any more of Methuselah's little death traps, but did that mean the old man would no longer provide information on hidden biblical artifacts? Murphy started to ask him, but Methuselah was clearly through for the day.

"Good day, Dr. Murphy," he said curtly. "Perhaps our paths will cross again someday. Two of my men will escort you back to your car."

With that, Methuselah turned and headed away with four of his bodyguards. Murphy watched silently for a moment and then looked at the two large men. They wore sunglasses on their expressionless faces and walked in silence beside him.

Murphy had mixed feelings as he headed back to his car. He had uncovered some startling information about the power wielded by the Seven, and learned who was responsible for his wife's death. But he'd also managed to offend Methuselah somehow, depriving himself of his considerable help just when he needed it most.

FORTY-FOUR

THE RALEIGH HEALTH and Fitness Gym had been open twenty-four hours a day for more than two years. The owners wanted to meet the athletic needs of a broad range of working folks. Murphy usually went to the gym around 6:00 A.M. three days a week. He was glad that he had kept this routine for quite a while. He felt like he was in pretty decent shape. And with Talon and Methuselah in his life, he never knew what to expect. But at least he felt up to the challenge.

The first part of his hour-long workout started with some stretching exercises. He would then proceed to a step machine and begin to work up a little sweat. That was followed by the use of free weights. He would bench-press his usual two hundred pounds and intersperse a number of routines with dumbbells and other equipment.

He had just finished his last set of repetitions on the bench press when he heard a voice behind him.

"That looks like a lot of hard work, Dr. Murphy."

He sat up and turned around, taken off-guard by the sight of Summer Van Doren. She was wearing gray jogging pants, a lighter gray tank top and a gray sweatband around her blond hair. She held a towel in her left hand and she'd evidently been working out. Despite the perspiration, she looked quite attractive. He noticed that the other guys lifting weights around him had slowed down a little and he could see them trying to get a better glimpse of her. He thought that they might want to change places with him.

Did she ever look bad?

He grabbed a towel and wiped his forehead. "Remember, it's Michael . . . not Dr. Murphy."

"Okay, Michael," she said with a slight smile.

"I didn't know you worked out here, Summer."

"I have been for several weeks. But I usually come in the evening. This is my first time early in the morning. I really don't like to get all sweaty before going to school but sometimes it's just more convenient to do it in the morning. Are you all through with your workout?"

"Just about. I always like to finish with about a twenty-minute jog in the park across the street."

"I've thought about doing that, but didn't feel comfortable running through the park at night alone."

Murphy nodded. "That's understandable. Our world is not always safe. There are some real weirdoes in it. You made the right decision."

He stood up.

"Are you all through?"

Murphy was still quite aware that he was the envy of every guy in the room.

"Yes, I just finished."

"Well, I'm going to finish with a jog. Would you like to join me?"

Summer smiled a cute smile and said, "That sounds like fun. Why not? I've got plenty of time before I need to be at school."

Murphy was impressed how effortlessly Summer kept up with him. They held a pretty good pace for fifteen minutes and then began a slow jog for another five minutes. Eventually they started walking.

"How is Paul Wallach doing?" Summer asked.

"Not real well. His condition hasn't improved. He had some severe internal damage from the beating he received."

Summer grimaced. "That's terrible. Do the police know who was responsible for the attack?"

"Not for sure. But I think I know who it might be."

"You do? Have you shared that with the police?"

"Yes. They're attempting to check into it."

"Who would do such a thing?"

"A man named Talon. He's a highly trained assassin. He seems to get great pleasure in hurting and killing people. He's a true sociopath without any moral compunction for his behavior."

They both sat down on a park bench and continued their conversation.

"Why would he choose to hurt Paul and Shari?"

Murphy proceeded to share with Summer some of his experiences and battles he had with Talon. She sat there dumbfounded at the tales of danger and adventure coming from Murphy's lips. She had no idea how perilous a life the Preston University archaeologist led.

She finally spoke. "I've been praying for Shari and for Paul, but now I think I need to add you to my list. God has graciously spared you on a number of occasions. Have you ever thought about changing occupations to something a little less dangerous?"

Murphy laughed.

"As a matter of fact, I have. But I feel like I'm on some kind of mission. I think that God has allowed me to become involved in all of this for some purpose. There are powerful evil forces at work in our world. The Bible suggests that in the last days, moral and spiritual darkness will increase. We are only beginning to see the edge of this darkness. Somehow I think He wants to use me in battling these evil forces."

"What you're talking about is similar to what Pastor Wagoner has been talking about in his sermons at church. He has mentioned that there would be an increase of crime, wickedness, and deception from false teachers. When he talks about the danger of the occult, it disturbs me. I have to admit I'm really fearful of the occult. Have you had to face these kinds of things also?"

Murphy shared with Summer the story of his encounter with J. B. Sonstad. She sat there on the bench with her mouth slightly open and never took her eyes off of him.

"Where do you think all of this is going to lead?" she finally asked him.

"I'm not sure. My friend Levi Abrams and I will be leaving soon on an expedition to a spot in Israel. It's the site of the ancient Temple of Dagon."

"What do you expect to find?"

"I'm not sure. But it could be of great significance. I think it may have something to do with what the Bible calls the False Prophet."

"When will you be leaving?" For some reason, Summer felt just a little sad that he wouldn't be around.

"It looks like it'll be just after school ends for the summer."

"That's just a few weeks away."

Murphy and Summer walked back to the gym, gathered their things together and said good-bye.

On his way back to school, Murphy replayed his conversation with Summer. She seemed very interested . . . they had a common faith . . . she was athletic and very attractive . . . and she was very easy to talk to.

Where is this leading? he wondered, and not for the first time.

FORTY-FIVE

EUGENE SIMPSON was excited when Shane Barrington's bullet-proof car arrived. He had been a chauffeur for a number of years but had never driven something quite as exotic as this. It was a black Mercedes with tinted windows that bullets could not shatter. The metal on the sides of the vehicle could withstand a medium bomb blast. The car could even ride on the heavy-duty tires if they were pierced and the air was let out. It had all the bells and whistles.

This is pretty cool. But why does Mr. Barrington need a car with so much protection? He's not the President."

A group of security experts went through every detail of maintaining the car and checking it out before it was driven. They provided

Simpson a long pole with a mirror on it, to slide under the car to check for any bombs that might be placed on the frame. It was to become a daily routine before he would pick up Mr. Barrington.

Simpson wondered why Barrington was so concerned about his safety. He had never seemed worried about such things before. He had noticed that two bodyguards had been hired within the last two weeks. They traveled everywhere with him.

Oh, well. It's his money. Rich people are strange.

On the tenth day of driving the new car, Simpson received a phone call from Barrington's assistant, Wilson Dewitt.

"Eugene, this is Wilson. Mr. Barrington will be going to the office at his regular time of nine A.M. He would like to be picked up then. He has an important meeting at ten A.M. and would like to arrive in plenty of time to prepare some last-minute papers. Don't be late."

"Yes, sir."

Nine A.M. That gave Eugene plenty of time to pick up the package his parents had sent him from California. Especially since it was on the way to Mr. Barrington's penthouse.

At ten minutes after nine, Wilson Dewitt's phone began to ring.

"Wilson here."

"Mr. Dewitt, this is Eugene."

"Eugene where have you been? Mr. Barrington's in the lobby waiting for you. His patience is running very thin."

"I'm sorry, sir. There's been an accident."

"With the new car?"

"No, sir. A taxi ran into a bus in front of me and it is blocking traffic. I haven't been able to move forward or backward. It's just now clearing up. I should be there in about seven minutes."

"I'll tell Mr. Barrington. . . . Uh-oh . . . here he comes, Eugene. He doesn't look happy. Just a minute . . . he's asking me a question."

Simpson was very nervous waiting for Dewitt to come back on the line.

"Eugene."

"Yes, sir."

"Mr. Barrington wants to talk with you."

Simpson's heart began to sink.

"Eugene. This is Barrington. What's going on? Where are you?"

"I'm sorry, Mr. Barrington. After I picked up the package, I got stuck in a traffic jam. There was an accident in front of me."

"What package are you talking about, Eugene?"

"My parents sent me some fruit from California. I picked it up at the bus station. But I left extra early, sir. This accident is just—"

"Do your parents usually send you packages of fruit?" Barrington interrupted.

"No, sir. This is the first time."

"How did you hear about the package?"

"Some man from the bus station called and told me it was in."

"What does it look like, Eugene?"

"It's a small wooden crate. It's the type that you send oranges in. You know, the type with wooden slats nailed on the top and a picture of oranges on the side."

"Where are you, Eugene?"

"I'm at a stop light on Seventy-third. I'm waiting for the light to change."

"Eugene, can you reach the wooden crate?"

"Yes, sir. It's on the passenger seat next to me."

"Pick it up and hold it to your ear, Eugene. See if you hear anything."

"I can hear a very soft whirring sound."

"Eugene, get it out of the car. Do you hear me? Get rid of that box as fast as you—"

An enormous blast put an immediate end to the conversation. A ball of fire blew out all four doors as the flaming vehicle lifted off the street and flipped upside down.

Fortunately no one was in the crosswalk. Drivers in the cars waiting for the light to change were blinded by the flash of light. Debris from the Mercedes rained down on the windows and hoods of the waiting cars.

Eugene Simpson never knew what hit him.

Wilson Dewitt's phone rang. It was the news desk at Barrington Communications. They informed him that they had just received several cell phone calls from citizens in the downtown district. They said that there had been a tremendous explosion just past 73rd Street. No one knew the cause yet. The police were on the way. There were fears that it might be a terrorist bombing. Dewitt shared the news with Barrington.

Barrington shook his head back and forth.

"Wilson, it's not a terrorist bomb. It was Eugene Simpson."

"What? We were just talking with Eugene. I thought your car was protected against bombs."

"Yes, if the bomb came from *outside* of the car. It wasn't built to withstand a blast from *inside* the car. If Simpson had been on time to pick us up, we wouldn't be talking right now."

Dewitt's expression registered shock. The two bodyguards with Barrington overheard the conversation and began to look around with apprehension.

"Wilson. Call the office and tell them to cancel my meeting. I'm going back upstairs to the penthouse. I'll work out of there for the next few days. I need to find out what's happening. That attack was meant for me."

FORTY-SIX

BY LATE AFTERNOON Barrington had all the details surrounding the death of Eugene Simpson. It was indeed a very powerful plastic explosive bomb that had destroyed the new bulletproof car. Police could not find any leads regarding the phone call notifying Simpson of the package at the bus station.

Barrington was nervous and increased his personal security and barricaded himself in his penthouse for the next week. Although he did not talk to the police about his suspicions, deep in his gut he knew that the Seven were behind his attempted assassination.

It was on Friday evening when his phone rang. He was all alone except for the bodyguards that were stationed outside his penthouse door.

"This is Barrington."

There was silence on the other end of the line.

"This is Barrington. Hello!"

"Mr. Barrington, are you having a pleasant evening?"

Barrington immediately recognized the South African accent.

"What do you want, Talon?"

"Just a little chat."

"Oh, yeah? About what?"

Barrington began to pace back and forth in front of his windows that overlooked the city.

"About the death of your driver. It's such a shame."

"I didn't know you cared about the death of anyone."

"No, no. It's not a shame about his death. It's a shame that I wasted good explosives and didn't kill you."

"Sorry to disappoint you. When I come after you, I'll try to do better."

Talon laughed. "You may be a cutthroat businessman but you're no killer."

"I'll make an exception for you."

"That sounds very brave, Mr. Barrington . . . coming from a man who has confined himself to his penthouse. Are you nervous?"

"Not at all. It's just very cozy up here. As a matter of fact, I think I'll stay here indefinitely. Sorry to ruin your plans."

"Mr. Barrington, I don't think my employers are very happy with you."

"What are you talking about? I'm doing everything they told me to do."

"Oh, really? What about Dr. Constantine De La Rosa?"

"What about him? I'm promoting him like they asked."

"And what about the editorial?"

Barrington's heart skipped a beat. How did Talon know about the article he had written? He hadn't shown anyone yet. He played coy.

"What editorial?"

"The one on your computer. The one that you haven't printed yet. The one that tries to discredit De La Rosa."

Barrington was nervous. What else did these people know? Did they know about his Swiss bank accounts?

"You're very thorough, Talon. How did you know about that?"

"Now, now. You don't really expect me to reveal all of my secrets, do you?"

"Okay, Talon. Let's cut through all this flack. What do you want?"

"Oh, my. Are we getting angry? There's no need for that. After all, you have the upper hand, sitting there all nice and safe in your penthouse."

Something in Talon's tone sent a chill up Barrington's spine. He feverishly searched around the room. There was no way Talon could have gotten in.

"Completely untouchable . . ." Talon continued.

Barrington rushed to the window and looked out across the street. On the rooftop of the high-rise apartment across the way, he saw a flash of red and then a tail of white smoke. In an instant he realized that he was in deep trouble.

He dropped the phone, turned and began to sprint away from the windows. He only got about fifteen feet across his massive living room when the rocket crashed through the windows and exploded.

Pedestrians on the street below heard the blast. They looked up in time to see flames shooting out from the windows far above. Their first thoughts were that maybe a plane flew into the building. They ran as glass and debris began to rain down on them.

Murphy's phone began to ring.

"This is Michael."

"Dr. Murphy."

"Yes, Shari. Is there some news about Paul? Is he getting better?"

"No, there's been no change. He's still in critical condition. I'm with him at the hospital. Have you seen the news?"

"No, I've been reading."

"It's Shane Barrington. He was killed in an explosion in his penthouse. I was down in the cafeteria getting some coffee when the announcement came over the evening news. The firefighters are still there trying to put out the flames. No one is sure how it happened. I thought you'd want to know."

"Thank you, Shari. Something very dark and evil is going on. You watch yourself."

"I will. The police still have a protective watch on me. One officer is here in the hospital with me. During the night they have a police car stationed in front of my house. I'm still scared."

"I know, Shari. I'm so sorry this is happening to you. I know it's all because of me. It seems so little, but I'll be praying for you and Paul. You go home and try to get some rest. Thanks for giving me a call about Barrington. I think I'll talk to Levi about what's going on."

FORTY-SEVEN

On the path from Ashdod, 1083 B.C.

PAINFUL ONLY SLIGHTLY *describes the ten-mile journey from Ashdod near the great sea called the Mediterranean. The inland march to Gath and the great village of giants was torture, to say the least. The priests from the Temple of Dagon could not ride horses or camels because of their tumors. They had to walk, and walking caused the tumors of some to bleed. Every face wore a look of misery.*

Kadmiel spoke to the other priests. "I wish we had never seen the Israelite Ark of the Covenant. We can only hope when it is safely in another town that the plague will be removed from Ashdod."

The other priests nodded in agreement and let fly some muffled curses.

The guard in the watchtower on the wall of Gath saw the strangers nearing the city. They were leading a team of oxen pulling something on a cart.

"There is a group of people approaching from northwest toward the city! It looks like they are coming from the direction of Ashdod," called the guard to the captain below in the courtyard.

"How many do you see?"

"I count fourteen. They are moving very slowly."

"Can you tell if they are friendly, or do they look like enemies?"

"They are carrying the banner of our people. They are too far away to tell for sure, but it looks like they are wearing the robes of the priests of Dagon."

"Keep your eye on them," called the captain.

It took another two hours before the priests from Ashdod reached the gates of Gath. They were allowed to enter and meet with the elders of the city. Kadmiel had heard there were giant Philistines in Gath but he couldn't get over how large the people were. The smallest men, and most of the women, seemed to be six feet tall. The majority were around seven feet, while there were some at eight feet tall. He even saw a few that he estimated to have been nine feet in height. He was awed by the sight.

"Those giants look fearsome. I'm glad they are Philistines."

Kadmiel explained the situation of the battle with the Israelites and the capture of the Ark of the Covenant. He described the mystery of the statue of Dagon and how it had fallen to the floor before the Ark. He concluded by telling them about the plague and asked if his fellow Philistines would take the Ark.

Trophet, the chief elder, began to laugh. The other elders joined him.

"That is quite a story," he said after his laughter had died down. "That golden chest with the cherubim on top could not have caused Dagon to fall. It sounds like poor engineers to me. And as for the plague . . ." He laughed some more. Kadmiel was in pain and not amused. "We have never heard of such

a thing. I think that the tumors have been forced out of your bodies because of fear."

All of the elders began to laugh.

"We will gladly take your 'fearsome Ark.' And we will give you a ride back home in a wagon. It is a long walk back to Ashdod."

Kadmiel felt a sense of relief as he left Gath.

They might be big, but I don't think they're very smart, *he thought to himself.*

Within two days the entire city of Gath was struck with painful tumors. No longer were the giants laughing. The size of their bodies only meant larger tumors. They did not wait long to get the Ark of the Covenant out of their city. They sent the Ark north to the village of Ekron. These Philistines had the reputation of cutting the hamstrings of their enemy's horses and enslaving the people they captured. Maybe they could deal with the Ark.

Word of the tumors had already reached Ekron when the Ark arrived. The leaders of the city were not happy.

"The giants have brought the Ark of the God of Israel to us, to kill us and our people!"

The Ark was in Ekron only one night before the city experienced the deadly destruction of the plague. A great cry went up among the people. They were in panic. The elders, priests, and diviners gathered the next day to devise a plan.

The chief of the elders said, "Let us send away the Ark of the God of Israel. Let it go back to its own place so that it does not kill us and our people."

Another elder spoke up. "Let us ask Zereida what he thinks. He is one of the magicians and a very wise diviner."

All of the heads turned toward Zereida.

He paused for a moment as if thinking and then said, "If you send away the Ark of the God of Israel, do not send it empty. We need to return it with a trespass offering. Then we may be healed. And if the plague does not stop after the return of the Ark and the trespass offering, then you will know that the God of the Israelites did not send the plague."

"What should be the trespass offering to the Israelite God?" asked the chief elder.

"I suggest five golden tumors and five golden rats, according to the number of the five lords and five major cities of the Philistines. For the same plague was visited on all of you and on your lords. Therefore, you shall make images of your tumors and images of your rats that ravage the land. You should also give glory to the God of Israel. Perhaps He will lighten His hand from you, your gods, and your land."

The priests did not like that suggestion. They did not want to give glory to the God of the Israelites.

Zereida continued, "Why then do you harden your hearts as did the Egyptians and Pharaoh? When the Israelite God did mighty acts against them, did they not let the people go?"

No one had any other suggestions.

"Now, therefore, make a new cart. Then hitch two milk cows that have never been yoked to the cart. Be sure to take away their calves from them. Next, take the Ark of the Covenant and set it on the cart. Put the trespass articles, the golden tumors and the golden rats, into a chest and place it next to the Ark. Then send the Ark away. Watch from a distance to see if the cows will pull the cart in the direction of the Israelite territory toward Beth Shemesh. You will know that the God of Israel directs them, if the cows leave their calves and walk a path completely unknown to them."

The men of Ekron followed the advice of Zereida. To their amazement, the cows headed straight for the road to Beth Shemesh. The cows did not turn to the right or the left or stop for water or grass. The lords of the Philistines followed the cart until it reached the border of Beth Shemesh and then disappeared down the road. They continued to follow at a safe distance.

FORTY-EIGHT

DARKNESS HAD STARTED to fall when Murphy, Wagoner, and Clyde Carlson approached the old farmhouse on the outskirts of Raleigh. It was located at the end of a dirt road about a quarter of a mile from the highway. It was a two-story frame house with three gabled windows on the second floor. A light was on in the center gable. A covered porch ran completely around the home. Lights were shining in the lower-floor windows. The drawn curtains prevented them from seeing inside. They could only see an occasional shadow moving about. The farmhouse looked like it must have been built in the early 1900s. There were five newer-model cars parked in front.

The wooden stairs to the porch looked like they had been in need of repair for many years. The paint on the round posts holding up the covered roof was peeling. The boards on the porch itself squeaked as they approached the door and knocked. There was a stained-glass window on the upper half of the door. No one spoke, but they all looked at each other with a little apprehension.

When the door opened they were greeted by a woman in her mid-forties. Her face seemed more wrinkled than normal for someone her age. She was dressed in an outfit that looked much like a gypsy's.

"Welcome. My name is Carlotta. I am the assistant for Madame Estelle. Please come in and join the others. We're about to begin."

They were ushered into a large living room with faint lighting. The furniture and appointments made them feel as if they were back in the 1920s. There were ten other people in the room, four men and six women. They watched Murphy, Wagoner, and Carlson enter but didn't say a word to them. Murphy couldn't tell if they were being rude or if they were embarrassed to be seen there.

The woman named Carlotta spoke.

"Please follow me. We will be performing the healings in the dining room."

In the center of the room was a large table with fourteen chairs around it, five down each side, three at the far end, and one chair presumably for Madame Estelle at the head. Over the table there was a dimly lit chandelier which cast strange shadows on the wall.

Murphy leaned over and whispered in Wagoner's ear, "It looks like a set from some 'B' horror picture."

"Please be seated. Madame Estelle will be with you shortly."

Soon music began to play in the background and then Madame Estelle entered, also attired in a gypsy outfit with a brightly colored scarf tied around her head. She had on heavy makeup with dark eye shadow and flaming red lipstick. For a moment Murphy almost laughed, she looked so ridiculous, but he restrained himself.

She sat down and immediately closed her eyes as if she were meditating or waiting for some spirit to speak to her. Everyone watched in silence. Finally, she opened her eyes and looked around the room.

Murphy, Wagoner, and Carlson were seated at the far end of the table opposite Madame Estelle.

As soon as her eyes met Murphy's, he seemed to notice a slight flash of fear in her face. She then looked at Wagoner and the look of fear turned to a look of anger.

"What are you men doing here?"

Everyone was shocked at her opening and sat in silence.

"You are not believers! You have no part in this meeting! You will hinder the spirit of healing."

Then her voice seemed to deepen.

"You must leave our presence! You are a negative force!"

Wagoner and Carlson, who were already uncomfortable, started to move. Murphy did not budge. He did not like being challenged in public, and his Irish temper began to flare.

"We're here to see if what you claim is real. Let's see you perform your so-called healings."

"No! You must leave this house."

Murphy came on a little stronger. "By what power do you perform your healings? Is it by the name of Jesus?"

There was a hideous screeching laugh that startled everyone. The eyes of all the guests were wide with shock.

Madame Estelle's head bent forward and slammed onto the table with a loud thud. Everyone jumped. For a moment her face lay on the table and she did not move, as if she'd been knocked out.

Then her head shot up and her eyes were bulging. She had the look of a wild animal that was in some kind of trance. As she opened her mouth and began to speak, what came out was a deep, male voice that sent chills down everyone's spine.

"Unbelievers! Enemies of the Master!"

As she spoke, she grabbed the large table, stood up, lifted her end off the floor and tossed it. The table rolled onto some of the guests who were scrambling to get out of the way. Others screamed and headed out of the room.

Murphy, Wagoner, and Carlson seemed to be glued to their seats at the far end. Wagoner yelled to Murphy.

"Michael! This is for real!"

"I know!" he responded as he jumped to his feet.

Murphy took a step forward. "What is your name?"

The deep, manly voice began to swear and Madame Estelle picked up a wooden chair and tossed it at Murphy. He ducked as the chair flew by. Wagoner moved sideways in time but Carlson was not as fortunate. It hit him, knocking him to the ground. He was bleeding from his nose.

Wagoner joined Murphy and spoke. "What is your name, demon? In the name of Jesus we demand your name!"

"Leave me alone!"

Wagoner reached into his pocket and took out the small Bible he always carried with him. By now, all the other guests had fled the house.

Madame Estelle's assistant Carlotta fearfully approached and touched her on the shoulder from behind.

"Madame Estelle, please . . ."

She didn't have time to complete the sentence. Madame Estelle struck her with such superhuman force that her feet left the ground and she flew back, slamming against the wall and crumpling onto the ground. She was bleeding from the mouth where she had been hit.

"Enough, demon!" Murphy yelled. "In the name of Jesus we command you to sit down."

Madame Estelle looked like she was struggling with some unseen force as she stumbled toward a chair that was still upright. She sat down with a fierce, wild look in her eyes. Her head was shaking from side to side and guttural sounds burst forth from her lips.

Murphy and Wagoner looked at each other. They couldn't believe what was happening. They had only heard stories about such events. They had never come face-to-face with the real thing.

"What is your name? In the name of Jesus we demand that you speak."

Madame Estelle's head went back and forth rapidly and finally she spoke with the deep, male voice.

"Deception."

Wagoner joined in.

"Are there any other demons?"

"Yes."

"What are their names? We command you to speak."

Madame Estelle twisted violently in her chair. "The Black Healer," came another voice.

"Corruption," was the response of a third strange voice.

"Are there any more?" asked Murphy.

"No."

"We command that you three leave this woman at once."

Madame Estelle squirmed and screamed and arched her back and collapsed onto the floor in spasms and finally lay still.

Carlotta, the assistant, was holding her mouth and whimpering in the corner of the destroyed dining room. Carlson was still on the floor with a look of shock on his face. Murphy looked over at Wagoner, who was breathing heavily. Wagoner looked back.

"Bob, are you all right?"

"I am. I'm just shaking inside. This was like a nightmare. I've never done anything like this in my life."

Murphy shook his head. "Me neither."

"I don't think I'd ever like to do that again. It was like coming up to the edge of darkness and facing the devil. There are forces going on in this world that I never really dreamed of."

Madame Estelle began to cry. Murphy and Wagoner approached her.

"Are you all right?" asked Murphy.

She sat up and looked at them. She no longer had a harsh distant look in her eyes. Her whole countenance had seemed to soften.

"How long have you been under their control?" Wagoner inquired.

"As far back as I can remember. I think it began when my mother took me with her to a card reader. That sparked my curiosity. I started to read books about the supernatural and the occult, and I began to have terrible nightmares. I became a very angry and rebellious child. Later I got deeper into the occult and even joined the Satanic Church. In my twenties I began to discover that I seemed to have the ability to foresee the future. In my late twenties I began to have people come to me for healing. I thought I was helping at first. But before long I began to have deep depressions come over me. I battled with evil thoughts and soon the nightmares became night terrors."

"How are you feeling now?" asked Wagoner.

"I'm not sure. I feel like a great burden has been lifted from my shoulders. I feel a peace like I have never felt before. Please tell me about what just happened to me."

Murphy smiled kindly. This was going to require some delicacy.

FORTY-NINE

ISIS HAD MIXED emotions as she dialed the Preston University number. In some ways she wished that Murphy would answer the phone. She longed to hear his voice and talk with him. She missed him deeply. On the other hand, she was nervous and half hoping that he wouldn't answer. What if she called and he didn't want to talk with her? She tapped her fingernails on the desk as the phone was ringing.

"Preston University. This is Susan. May I help you?"

"Yes, Susan. Could I please have the office of Dr. Michael Murphy?"

"Just a moment, please, and I'll connect you."

Isis continued to tap her fingernails as she listened to the ringing. She couldn't believe how nervous she was. Her heart was beating as if it would pop out of her chest. After the fifth ring, she felt a pang of disappointment. She began to put the phone down when she heard someone answer.

"Dr. Murphy's office. Shari speaking."

Isis brought the phone back up to her ear. "Hello, Shari. This is Isis McDonald."

"Oh, hi, Dr. McDonald. I'm sorry for the delay in answering the phone. I was in the laboratory with a fragile manuscript in my hands."

"I understand, Shari. You just can't drop an ancient manuscript."

"I was placing it back in the humidifier."

"Shari, while I've got you on the phone . . . I was so sorry to hear about your terrible encounter with Talon. That must have been frightening."

"It was. And I still wake up in the night thinking about it. I came close to losing my life."

"I know what you mean. I still have nightmares about him choking me to death. I don't think those emotional scars heal so quickly. Michael also told me about Paul Wallach. How's he doing?"

Shari sounded sad. "I'm afraid that he's still in critical condition. If anything, he seems to be going downhill."

"I'm sorry to hear that. I've been thinking about both of you. I know that you were very close."

"Everyone at church has been praying for him. I'm not sure what God has for us to learn through all of this. Dr. Murphy has been very supportive through this tough time. I know he feels terrible."

"Is he there?"

"Not right now. He had a faculty meeting to attend. I can have him call you."

Isis felt disappointed and yet somewhat relieved at the same moment.

"No. That's all right."

"Is there something I can help you with?"

"You could leave him a message. Would you tell him that I found out a little more information about King Yamani. I did some additional research and discovered that one ancient historian wrote about the destruction of the Temple of Dagon. In a few brief sentences, he mentioned that after the temple was destroyed, the priests of Dagon constructed a passageway leading from the temple to another building nearby. This building became the temporary worship place. It was believed that the priests moved all the sacred articles from the temple to this other structure. Maybe what Michael is looking for is in this other building."

"Did it mention in which direction the passageway ran?"

"No. That was all that was written about it. I thought it might be helpful for Michael to know before he leaves on his exploration of the site. He might be able to discover where it was."

"I'll pass it on to him. Is there anything else you would like me to say?"

There was much more that Isis wanted to say but it would have been for Murphy's ears only.

"No. Thank you, Shari. That's all."

"Okay."

"I hope that Paul will get well soon. I'll be thinking about you."

"Thank you. I hope he will too."

As Isis hung up she found herself wanting to say more. She wished that she could have told Shari about what happened to her after Murphy broke off their relationship.

It nearly devastated her. She went into a depression that was noticeable to the people who worked with her at the Parchments of Freedom Foundation. A colleague named Lisa had asked her what was wrong. It was then that Isis broke down and began to sob, releasing all the sadness that she had been holding back. Isis began to tell her why she was so depressed.

Lisa listened with such compassion that Isis really felt like she cared about her. Over the next few weeks, her new friend shared advice and counsel. One day, Lisa invited Isis to join her in a singles Bible study. It was there she became more involved with the Bible and began to understand what it was to be a Christian.

One evening when Isis was alone in her bedroom, she finally came to the point where she cried and poured her heart out to God. She knelt down by her bed and asked Christ to come into her heart, to take hold of her life, and to change her. She knew this was what was missing in her life.

It was after that experience that Isis felt a flood of peace come into her life. Yes, she was still hurting at the loss of Murphy, but somehow she knew deep inside that she would be all right. She also found that she had a strong desire to begin reading the Bible, which brought much comfort to her.

Isis longed to tell Murphy about the change and what happened but something wouldn't let her. She didn't want him to think that she had made the decision of faith just to win him back. She didn't want to seem to be begging him to come back to her. She wanted him to come to her of his own accord. She wanted it to be his decision, not something that was cajoled or forced.

Isis had also resigned herself to the fact that they might never get back together. She knew that she would have to become a woman of God on her own. Because of this, she began to immerse herself into her work and attending the Bible studies with her friend Lisa.

On several occasions, she had been approached by men who wanted to date her, but she declined. They were attractive but she didn't want to be caught up in any kind of rebound relationship. She knew it was best to let herself heal without adding any complications.

Isis had given herself to God and began to trust Him for focus and direction. It wasn't easy at first, but with each passing day it had become more comfortable.

Isis sat there in her office after talking with Shari. She stared into space as many thoughts raced through her mind.

Dear God. Please help me through the tough days. Please help me to be honest with my feelings and not be overrun by them. Help me to trust You more each day. God, do You make house calls? I could sure use one. . . .

FIFTY

GABRIEL QUINTERO had been a policeman for thirteen years. He'd had many assignments during his career, from working behind a desk to pounding a beat. The hardest ones for him were to sit on stakeouts waiting for criminals to possibly commit a crime or guarding someone while they were in the hospital. The inactivity was difficult for a man who craved movement. He was pacing in front of the door to intensive care when Murphy arrived at the hospital.

"Good evening, Gabriel. Long day?"

"Feels that way, Dr. Murphy. I don't mind the responsibility of guarding people, but just sitting around can get pretty dull. My body wants to go for a run."

"Well, thanks for what you're doing, even though it's not easy for you."

"That's my job, Doc." He moved away from the front of the door and let Murphy in.

Shari was in a chair sitting beside Paul's bed. Murphy went over and gave her a hug. He looked up at all the monitors and electrical wires attached to Paul's body registering his breathing, heart rate, and brain activity.

"Any change?"

"No. Not really. It does seem like the doctors and nurses are coming in and out more frequently, though." She looked worried.

"Maybe I'll go out and talk with one of them, see if they can give me an update."

Murphy found Dr. Thornton talking with a nurse down one of the halls.

"Evening, Don."

"Hello, Michael. I haven't seen you in a couple of days."

"I've felt bad about that, but I've been swamped at work. How is Paul Wallach? Shari mentioned that the doctors and nurses have been coming in and out of the room a little more frequently."

Thornton shook his head. "I'm sorry, Michael. He could go at any time. His systems are shutting down. There's nothing we can do. I understand that he doesn't have any living relatives. It's been good that Shari has been with him. I'm glad you're here now to comfort her."

Murphy nodded his head gravely.

"I understand. Thanks, Don."

Murphy reentered the room and pulled up a chair next to Shari. He put his arm around her.

"Dr. Thornton says he doesn't have long. They've done all they could."

Shari began to cry. Murphy handed her some tissues. She blew her nose and tried to speak.

"I think Paul was trying to turn his life around after working for Shane Barrington. He had begun to come back to church and he seemed to be more caring than he'd ever been."

"Do you think he made any type of decision regarding faith, Shari?"

"I don't know. He certainly knew all about it. We had talked a number of times. I'm just not sure. That's what bothers me the most."

Shari took hold of Paul's hand and rubbed it.

Murphy prayed with her and they sat together for about ten minutes. He looked at the cabinet next to Paul's bed. It had a number of cards stacked on it.

"It's nice that so many people sent cards to Paul," Murphy said.

"Most of them have come from people at the church. I've opened them and read them to Paul. I don't know if he has heard me, but I read them anyway. Those on the top arrived today. I haven't opened them yet. There are more in the drawer."

Murphy picked up the stack and looked at the return addresses. Many of the names he recognized. One card, however, did not have a return address. Out of curiosity he opened it and began to read.

Roses are red
And violets are blue
Because of the baseball bat
Paul Wallach got the shoe.
. . . and I kicked him with much pleasure.

Murphy couldn't believe what he was reading.

I'm terribly sorry for all of the
inconvenience. They usually die
quickly and painfully. However,
I must say that there's a certain
pleasure in seeing others suffer.

His pain, and your pain, does help
to take away the pain in my finger.

Until we meet again!

Murphy was furious. He wanted to yell. He wanted to strike out. He gritted his teeth and looked at Shari. Her attention was focused on Paul. He quietly put the card into his jacket. He didn't want Shari to have to read that. He hoped that he hadn't messed up any fingerprints that might have been on it. Murphy's Irish temper was raging inside. He took several deep breaths to calm down.

His eyes were then drawn to one of the monitors. A little red light had begun to flash. It was soon followed by a beeping sound. He looked over at the heart monitor. The spikes began to separate and then there was a flat line with just a constant tone. There were no more beeps.

Shari's eyes were wide with disbelief. She knew that it was just a matter of time, but still it caught her off-guard.

Two nurses rushed into the room followed by a third pushing a cart. The code blue signal had alerted them. Murphy and Shari quickly moved out of the way as they applied the defibrillator pads to Paul's chest.

"Ready!"

"Clear!"

Paul's body jerked, but the only sound was the dull drone of the heart monitor. They tried three more times and then Dr. Thornton entered the room. He injected something in Paul's arm and they tried one more time to restore his heartbeat.

Dr. Thornton bent over Paul and placed his stethoscope on his neck and then on his chest. He finally stood up and shook his head. There was silence in the room except for Shari's sobbing.

The funeral was well attended. Most of the people were from the church. A few people from the community who had heard about it on the news were also present. Because it had been considered a murder, three television stations were covering the service. A half dozen policemen had been assigned to watch over the crowd.

Pastor Bob Wagoner performed the service and presided at the graveside. Shari was dressed in black and Murphy sat beside her with his arm around her. She kept wiping tears the entire time.

Murphy tried to distract himself from his own grief and kept surveying the crowd. Would Talon attempt to wear some disguise and come to the funeral? He didn't think so but he was on the alert. Inside he felt mounting anger. Talon had to be stopped. He couldn't be allowed to continue to kill innocent people. Murphy's resolve to end Talon's reign of terror began to consume his thoughts.

He looked over at Shari and gave her a hug. She just stared at the coffin. She was out of energy and felt numb, like she was stuck in a bad dream. She kept hoping that she would wake up and all this would have been just a nightmare. Reality struck home when the casket was lowered into the ground. Their relationship would never have a chance to develop. But, most of all, she ached inside because she knew Paul's eternity was settled.

Shari stood up and went over to the edge of the grave. She looked down and dropped the red rose that she held in her hand.

Good-bye, Paul.

She turned and buried her weeping face into Murphy's chest.

FIFTY-ONE

THE TAXICAB SLOWED and came to a stop. The driver started swearing in Italian about the traffic and all the people crossing the street. Talon just smiled. Long ago he had learned that patience was a virtue . . . especially in pursuing people. Earning top wages as an assassin made it a little easier too.

He busied himself by looking out the window at the beautiful Trevi Fountain in front of the Palace of Neptune. It had been several years since he had been to Rome, but he remembered it well.

The light changed and it wasn't long before traffic picked up and they passed one of the oldest buildings in Rome, the majestic Pantheon. As Talon recalled, it was built in 27 B.C. by Marcus

Vipsanius Agrippa and later rebuilt by Hadrian in A.D. 118. He stared up at the dome-shaped roof 144 feet off the ground.

Amazing.

It wasn't long before they drove by his favorite building in all of Rome . . . the Colosseum, built by Vespasian and Titus.

The driver of the taxi looked at Talon through his rearview mirror and spoke in broken English.

"It is big, *signore*, no? They say it could hold forty-five thousand spectators."

It would have been quite interesting to see all the slaughter that took place there.

The taxi turned onto Via Vittorio Veneto.

Hmm, thought Talon. *This is a fine location. His office is not far from the Piazza Barberini. He made a good choice.*

The taxi stopped in front of one of Rome's traditional buildings, and Talon got out with a single piece of luggage resembling a guitar case. The bronze sign next to the double-door entry read in large letters:

RELIGIOUS HARMONY INSTITUTE
Dr. Constantine De La Rosa, Founder
Welcome all who love peace and religious unity

Talon noticed that the reception area was crisp and classy but not ostentatious. He thought that De La Rosa was very smart to not look like he was spending all of his donated money on buildings and furniture. He wanted the people to believe that he was out to help the common man and not grow rich himself.

"May I help you, sir?" said the receptionist with a big, warm, and friendly smile. "We're glad you're here today."

They've got her well trained. "Yes, I have an appointment to see Dr. De La Rosa."

"Thank you, I'll let his assistant know. You may have a seat over there. Feel free to take some brochures about our upcoming World Unity Summit. We will be holding it here in Rome in September."

"Mr. Talon? My name is Gina. I am Dr. De La Rosa's assistant. He will see you now."

Talon followed her down the wide polished-tile hallway and entered a modest waiting area. She knocked and then opened the door to his office.

"Dr. De La Rosa, I would like to present to you Mr. Talon."

De La Rosa was behind a large desk that looked too clean to be the average working CEO's desk.

Talon was immediately struck by his looks as he stood and came around the desk to shake his hand. De La Rosa seemed to have a radiant, sun-browned face. It was devoid of any freckles, moles, or blotches. He was clean-shaven with a strong jaw. His eyes were almond-shaped and had a strange autumn leaf color of reddish brown. He had a high Roman-shaped nose set against black hair peppered with gray above the ears. It gave him a very distinguished look. When he smiled, his teeth were stunningly white and well-formed. There was something about him that made you want to just stare at him.

He looks like Apollo.

De La Rosa reached out his hand to Talon, who put down his case and offered his left hand, his right hand still being bandaged. As Talon shook his hand he could feel the strength of his grip. Even though Talon was a big man, he had to look up to Dr. De La Rosa. He was maybe six foot six and muscular.

Dr. De La Rosa's every movement displayed a commanding presence. His voice was deep and filled with conviction, and his speech had an air of wisdom and knowledge.

"Mr. Talon, it is so nice to meet you. I have heard a great deal about you."

"Have you?" Talon was always cautious of anyone who knew anything about him. He tried to keep his life a mystery.

"Yes."

De La Rosa hesitated for a brief moment, looking at Talon's right hand.

"Did you have an accident?"

"A little encounter with a baseball bat."

"Team sports can sometimes be dangerous," said De La Rosa with a smile. "You are an important player. You must take care of yourself."

Talon wasn't quite sure how to respond.

"I believe that we have some mutual friends. A group of people called the Seven."

Although Talon was able to control his outward response he felt a tightening of his stomach muscles. The Seven paid him well for his services but he would not consider any of them friends by a long shot.

Talon had never been one for small talk. He jumped right to the point of his visit.

"I have something that I think you will want."

"And what might that be?"

Talon opened the case that he had been carrying.

De La Rosa was curious to see what was inside. His eyes brightened when he saw the Bronze Serpent of Moses. All three pieces had been refitted together and polished to such a degree that the human eye could not tell where any of the seams had been.

"This is marvelous! I was told about this relic, but to handle it in person is indeed an extreme privilege. It will become a most useful symbol in my future work. As you know, in my line of work, credibility is everything. Thank you for your diligence. How did you get all three pieces?"

"The tail and center section were very easy to find. They were held by fools not dedicated enough to protect them. The head section was lost in a deep pit deep in the Pyramid of the Winds. I had to find a small man who would descend on a rope into the pit. He finally found it a few inches under the sand."

"And the man in the pit?"

"Unfortunately the rope broke and I was unable to pull him back out of the pit," said Talon with a sinister smile. "Archaeology is a risky business."

"I understand. I trust you have been well compensated for finding the pieces and putting the serpent back together?"

"Yes, the money has already been wired to my Swiss bank account."

"Good. I want to be sure that you are well taken care of. We may have need of your services in the near future. I would like you to be happy."

"I'm always happy to receive money, Dr. De La Rosa."

FIFTY-TWO

AFTER THE GRAVESIDE service, Bob Wagoner invited everyone to come to the social hall of the Preston Community Church.

"The women of the church have prepared a luncheon for all of you. We know some of you have traveled a great distance to honor the memory of Paul. And we count it a privilege to provide food and a place for you to visit with one another. They should be ready to serve you in about fifteen minutes."

Murphy was standing toward the end of the lunch line when Summer Van Doren approached. She was wearing a tailored black pantsuit, which was enhanced by her beautiful blond hair.

"I saw how broken up Shari was at the funeral. I understand that she and Paul had been going together for quite some time and then went through a period of separation. How is she doing?"

"It's been hard on her. She really has no family close by for support. The church members have been quite kind."

"Do you think it would be all right if I asked her to come to my place for the weekend? At least she wouldn't be alone. We could talk and do some girl things together."

"I think that would be wonderful. I know that Shari would be open to that. She's had a tough time. She hardly left Paul's side because she didn't want him to be alone. She's got to be exhausted."

Murphy's cell phone began to go off.

"Excuse me," said Murphy as he stepped out of line to get some privacy.

"Murphy here."

"Michael, this is Levi."

"Where are you calling from?"

"I'm in Tel Aviv. I just got the word about Paul Wallach and the attack on Shari. How is she holding up?"

"The shock of him dying has finally settled in. Besides being half scared to death by Talon, I think she'll do okay. She is a very strong person and has a firm faith in God."

"Please tell her I'm thinking about her."

"I'll pass that on for you."

"About another matter, I have finally received permission from the Israeli government to explore the Temple of Dagon at the original Ashdod site."

"That's great."

"I'm sorry for the delay. There has been a lot of red tape because of the murder of Moshe Pearlman. Investigators locked up the murder site while they tried to figure out what happened. They scoured the area for any evidence. All they could find were a few tire tracks."

"Did you go to the site?"

"Yes, I did."

"What's there? Can you see much of the temple?"

"Not really, Michael. There are only a couple of stone walls and several mounds of dirt."

"That's it?"

"As far as I can see. I don't know why anyone would come to this location. Do you still want to come?"

Murphy thought for a moment. It sounded like a lost cause, but his gut told him to go and see for himself. "Yes. There must be something there that everyone is missing. I'll schedule a plane flight and let you know when I'm coming. Can you send me some digital photographs of the site?"

"I'll e-mail them to you tomorrow. I'll look forward to seeing you. By the way, did you ever get in contact with Methuselah?"

"As a matter of fact, I did. I met with him twice, and it wasn't easy getting past his six bodyguards. If he hadn't given the okay, I never would have gotten near him. There's no question that he is quite eccentric. He'll talk freely with you for a while and then he just shuts down the conversation and walks away."

"It sounds like he likes to be in control."

"There's no question about that. He did provide some new information, however. Talon is not acting alone. He's employed by a group of people known as the Seven. Have you ever heard of them?"

"No, I've never heard them mentioned before. I'll check into it for you. Maybe someone else with the Mossad has information on them. Did you get any other information about them?"

"Nothing else was mentioned other than the fact that Methuselah hates them and is trying to get revenge on them for killing his family."

"We never did get any leads on who was responsible for the Israeli plane crash that killed his family and the up-and-coming Israeli leaders. If he believes it is this same group, I'm sure that our intelligence people will want to hear about it. I'll let you know what we find out. In the meantime, you be careful."

Murphy stepped back into line with Summer.

"It was my friend Levi. We were discussing an upcoming expedition."

"Is it the one you mentioned to me about the Temple of Dagon?"

"Yes. I'll be leaving shortly for Israel."

"Is there anything I can do to help?"

"Not really . . . other than being a friend to Shari while I'm gone."

"No problem with that. It'll be fun to get to know her better. Don't worry about her. I'll make sure she's okay."

There was a warmth in Summer's deep blue eyes and her gentle smile that stirred something inside of Murphy.

She is one amazing lady.

FIFTY-THREE

MURPHY ALWAYS CHOSE an aisle seat when traveling by plane. In case of an emergency, he didn't like the idea of being boxed in. He also hated to climb over people or make them move if he wanted to go to the restroom or simply stretch a little on a long flight. Sitting in the same seat for ten to twelve hours was not his idea of fun.

He was standing in the aisle when the flight attendant walked by.

"Excuse me, miss. How much longer before we arrive in Israel?"

She paused and looked at her watch. "About another five hours, sir."

Murphy stifled a groan and thought, *People who like to travel just haven't traveled enough.*

He sat down and began to piece together the events that had been occurring. The Seven had used Talon to sabotage his efforts to discover Noah's Ark. They had stymied him in his efforts to ascertain information from Dr. Harley B. Anderson about the birth of some boy. They had ordered the death of Laura, Stephanie Kovacks, and Shane Barrington. Isis, Shari, Vern Peterson the helicopter pilot, Levi Abrams, and he had narrowly escaped death at the hands of Talon or his hired men. Many other people like Paul Wallach had inadvertently stepped into the line of fire. But the question remained: What was the extent of the Seven's dark plans?

His thoughts turned to Methuselah. Why had he wanted Murphy to discover the Temple of Dagon? How would it really damage the Seven even if Murphy were able to retrieve the Golden Jar of Manna and Aaron's Rod? Unable to solve that riddle, Murphy began to think about his recent experiences with J. B. Sonstad and Madame Estelle and the demons.

Evil seems to be increasing and the Seven are right in the middle of it.

Eventually Murphy dozed off and fell into a restless sleep.

The cabin speakers startled Murphy.

"Please stow away your tray tables . . . straighten your seat backs . . . and be sure that your seat belts are securely fastened. We are on our final decent to the airport. We should be arriving in about twenty minutes. You may want to adjust your watches; the time in Israel is now seven thirty-two A.M."

Murphy was glad the trip was over. His large body was crying to get out of the cramped seat. *Someone out of the Spanish Inquisition must have designed these things.*

The plane tipped slightly to the right and he could see the tall buildings of Tel Aviv-Yafo, the largest city and major commercial center in Israel. It had become one of the most modern cities in the Middle East. As they descended lower, he saw the many rows of modern apartment buildings that lined the shore of the Mediterranean Sea. It had been several years since he was last in Tel Aviv.

Levi Abrams met Murphy just inside the terminal. He had on a big smile when he saw him. They embraced and patted each other on the back.

"How was your flight?"

"Long, as usual. I'm glad to get my feet on the ground."

"Give me your passport. I'll get you through customs without having to stand in line."

"I do like your style, Levi."

"Michael, I know you've had a long trip and are a little tired. Do you want to get a motel and rest a little bit, or are you game to move on toward Ashdod?"

"Let's get some breakfast and then drive on to Ashdod. I feel like time is of the essence."

"Do you have some more information about something that's going to happen?"

"No. I just have a gut feeling that this is an important expedition. Have you discovered any information about the Seven?"

"No one has ever heard of them. There's absolutely no record of their existence. Are you sure Methuselah isn't just playing games with you?"

Murphy had considered that possibility. "I doubt it. Not this time."

"Well, I've assigned another Mossad operative to watch the Temple of Dagon site. His name is Gideon. He's observing the area from a distance. He's a good man who knows how to stay out of sight."

It did not take Murphy and Levi long to go through customs. Almost everyone knew Levi, and those who did not recognized the identification of the Mossad.

"Better order a big breakfast, Michael. There are no fast-food restaurants where we're going."

FIFTY-FOUR

THE TRIP SOUTH from Tel Aviv to modern Ashdod took about thirty minutes. From there Levi and Murphy headed east about four miles to the site of the Temple of Dagon.

"What do you think is going on, Michael?"

"I'm not sure, Levi. It all started when we began searching for the Bronze Serpent of Moses. You know, the one that was broken into three pieces. We found a manuscript written by a Chaldean priest named Dakkuri that mentioned the Bronze Serpent. This led us to a map that described a place called the Horns of the Ox. Laura had an uncanny ability to read and understand maps, some sort of an intuitive sense of geological transformation through time."

Levi was listening intently.

"We eventually discovered a cave that was filled with ancient clay amphora jars. They're the kind that are bulbous in shape with two handles that stick out like ears from their narrow necks."

Levi nodded his head in acknowledgment.

"Laura found one that had been sealed with a plug made out of wax. We took out the plug and found a coarsely woven cloth. Wrapped inside of it was a preserved piece of cast bronze about twelve inches long and two inches in diameter. It was tapered like a snake at one end and broken off at the other. It took us a while, but we eventually discovered it was the tail end of the Bronze Serpent of Moses."

"What an incredible find!"

"Yes, we could hardly believe that we found something so ancient and so meaningful to us. We were so excited we could hardly contain ourselves. I thought we'd both need sedatives to calm down."

"I would have been excited, too. What did you do with it?"

"We took it back to the Parchments of Freedom Foundation."

Levi had a strange look on his face. "Did you find any other sections of the Serpent?"

"Yes, we did. It was Isis McDonald that helped discover it. It was found in the town of Tar-Qasir, south of Babylon. We discovered a way into the sewers that ran under the city. The middle piece was being worshiped by a group of cultists. We retrieved the middle section at the risk of our lives."

"What happened with the middle section?"

Murphy was beginning to wonder why Levi was asking all of the questions.

"The middle section eventually made its way to the American University in Cairo. It is under the care of Fasial Shadid, a professor of ancient culture and ancient writings, and his assistant Nassar Abdoo."

Levi continued with his questioning. "And that's the end of the story?"

"Not quite. The tail section was stolen . . . twice."

"Twice?"

"Yes. It was housed at the Parchments of Freedom Foundation. One day Isis's assistant, Fiona Carter, decided that she would clean up Isis's office. She came back to the Foundation and found two dead guards. They had been killed by falcons. She then searched the storage area where valuable antiques were kept. The tail end of the Serpent had been stolen."

"That's the first time. And the second?"

"Well, after several months, a strange package was dropped off at the Parchments of Freedom Foundation. It had been hand-delivered and had no return address. It was addressed to Isis McDonald. Inside the package she found the tail section of the Bronze Serpent. There was no note and no one knows who returned it or why. I personally think it sounds like something Methuselah would do. The second theft just occurred recently. Three guards were killed. One by a falcon, one had his throat slit, and the third had a broken neck. We know it was the work of Talon. Why are you asking all of these questions, Levi?"

"Michael, have you heard about the middle section?"

"What do you mean?"

"Our operatives in Egypt got word that the middle section of the Bronze Serpent had been stolen from the American University. Both Fasial Shadid and Nassar Abdoo were killed."

Murphy didn't need to hear the details. He knew. It was Talon's handiwork.

"I'm so sorry to hear that. That must mean that Talon has two of the sections of the Serpent. I wonder if he will try and get the head section? It's supposed to be somewhere at the bottom of a shaft in the Pyramid of the Winds."

"What would he want with all three pieces?"

"I'm not sure. The Serpent may have significance to evangelical Christians, but I'm not sure it does to anyone else. They believe it is a talisman with mysterious healing powers. My guess is that Talon will try to put the pieces together somehow. I think the Seven must have some plan for it. Maybe it will become a symbol of worship. In the wrong hands, it could be used to make people believe that they may be healed from all types of illness and disease. Pastor Bob Wagoner and I have been talking about that possibility."

"It's good that you came, Michael. My bet is that if he has two pieces of the Bronze Serpent he'll try to get the third. Maybe we'll have some opportunity to catch Talon and put an end to his killing."

Levi paused for a moment and reached for his cell phone.

"We're getting close to the site. Let me call Gideon and let him know we're almost there."

"Gideon. This is Levi. We're almost at the site. Have you seen any activity?"

"All is quiet around the broken-down walls. No one's been around other than some farmers in the nearby olive groves and vineyards. About an hour ago three vehicles drove up to an olive grove about a quarter of a mile away. Seven people got out and went into the grove. They may be workers. I don't know."

"Where are you located?"

"My car's parked out of sight in a vineyard. I have binoculars and am positioned where I can see what goes on at the site and in the valley."

"Why don't you get in your car and meet us near the broken walls. We should be there in about five minutes."

FIFTY-FIVE

THE VALLEY WAS QUIET as Levi and Murphy drove in. They could see a large mound in the distance with some ruins. There was a car parked there and a man leaning against it. They turned off the highway onto a dirt road that led toward the mound. As they got closer, Levi spoke.

"That's Gideon. He's been with the Mossad for thirteen years."

As they got out of the car, Levi went up to Gideon and gave him a hug. He was about five foot eight inches tall with a dark complexion, jet-black hair, and thick, dark eyebrows. Although he was not an exceptionally large man, he seemed very powerful. The muscles on his forearms and biceps rippled.

"Gideon, this is my good friend Dr. Michael Murphy from the United States."

Murphy shook hands with Gideon. He had an iron grip and a big smile that made his bright white teeth stand out.

While Levi talked to Gideon, Murphy began to look around. To the north of the site he saw the three cars that Gideon mentioned. They were parked next to the olive orchard. No one could be seen.

"What do you think, Michael?" Levi asked. "Looks deserted. Nothing but temple ruins. It doesn't look like there's anything here."

Murphy checked the outer wall. "Nothing out of the ordinary." He turned and looked at the other wall, which was about twenty feet away, and he became more animated.

"Levi. Look at the other wall. See anything unusual?"

"I'm no archaeologist, but it looks just like an old stone wall to me. They all look the same."

"Look how the hillside rises behind the wall. The hillside looks like it was cut out. I wonder if there might be something behind the wall."

Levi and Gideon walked forward, looking at the wall with new eyes. The three began to carefully examine all of the stonework.

Gideon was the first to speak. "Dr. Murphy. Come and look at the mortar around these rocks. It looks different."

"Good work! You're right. Whoever put the mortar in did a fairly good job of trying to make it look like the original but the color is just slightly off."

Murphy took out a knife and began to chip away at the mortar.

"This is fresh. It hasn't had time to harden to its full strength."

Levi went back to his car and took out a short shovel. He began to knock loose the mortar and pry away some of the rocks. Within about five minutes there was a hole in the wall. Murphy took a small flashlight out of his backpack and shined it into the hole.

"It looks like a fairly large cavity behind the wall, maybe six feet wide and at least that tall. Let's tear out some more rocks."

The discovery made them all excited and they began to work

harder. After about ten minutes they had a hole large enough to crawl through. Gideon got two more flashlights out of the trunk of his car.

"Are you ready to go in?" asked Murphy.

Levi hesitated. "I don't know if we should all go in. It might be good for Gideon to remain outside and watch our backs."

"I agree," said Gideon. "I think I'll go check out those three cars and talk to the workers in the olive orchard. After that, I'll return and guard the opening while you and Dr. Murphy do some exploring in there."

Murphy led the way through the rock wall and Levi followed.

"This is not a cave," said Murphy as they shined their lights around. "It's a passageway that leads into the hillside. It must have taken many men to build this tunnel."

They followed the passageway as it sloped at a slight downward angle. They also saw metal rings in the side of the wall about every thirty feet.

"I'll bet those rings held torches to light up the passageway."

"I would prefer electric lights," Levi responded. "Remember the last passageway we were in, we almost lost our lives."

"Well, at least I'm not dragging your body along this time. It looks like the passageway angles off to the left." Murphy tried to get his bearings. "It seems like it might be going under the olive orchard on the low hillside."

Shining their lights on the floor of the passageway, Murphy and Levi could see a number of footprints on the dusty floor.

"It looks like this has recently been a popular spot."

"Maybe it's for underground rave parties," said Levi with a smirk.

It wasn't long before they passed under an archway that led into a large chamber. Murphy shined his light around.

"I'll bet you this was some kind of secret room that led from the Temple of Dagon."

Murphy paced off the room. "It's about forty feet long . . . twenty-five feet wide . . . and about twelve feet tall."

Levi shined his light on some amphora jars in a corner. All of them were empty.

"What do you think this room was used for, Michael?"

"It was probably some type of storage chamber for the temple. I don't think anyone would live in this room. There's not much ventilation."

"Do you think that this is the room that Methuselah wanted you to find?"

"I doubt it. There's no king's head to push in this room."

They began to carefully explore the floor and walls.

"Look over here, Levi. The walls have been recently chipped like someone was trying to break through them."

"It looks like it didn't do them any good. Those walls seem very thick."

"They must have been looking for something. I wonder what it was?"

Suddenly Murphy and Levi froze in their tracks. And listened. They could hear muffled popping sounds.

Murphy turned toward Levi. "What do you think that is?"

"Those are gunshots. They're coming from the other side of the wall!"

"There has to be a way in there," shouted Murphy. "Quick, look around some more."

Murphy and Levi began to survey every inch of the thirty-foot-long wall. Nothing seemed to be out of place.

"Michael! Look!"

Levi's light was shining on the carved head of a lion. Murphy shined his light across the wall and saw eight-inch carved lions' heads about every six feet around the entire room about five feet off the floor.

"So?"

"Come on, Murphy! You're the archaeologist. Didn't Methuselah tell you to press the king's head? Maybe he was talking about the *king of the jungle*."

Murphy's eyes widened.

"That's it! Start pushing those lions' heads."

Murphy was at the next-to-last head on the wall when it gave way under his pressure. There was an echoing sound like a large stone rolling and then part of the wall began to slide slowly backward. Both Murphy and Levi shined their lights on the opening and then looked at each other in amazement.

FIFTY-SIX

The wheat field of Beth Shemesh, 1083 B.C.

PHUVAH AND HIS FELLOW *servants had been in the wheat field of Beth Shemesh harvesting since early dawn. The sun was now almost at half day and sweat poured from his body. He paused for a moment to straighten up his tired back and wipe his brow. As he mopped his forehead with the sleeve of his tunic, something curious appeared in the distance.*

He stared at the cart being drawn by milk cows with no one driving them. The sun reflected off of something on the cart so bright and shiny that he had to avert his eyes. He yelled to the other servants, who stopped their work to see what the commotion was about. They all stood speechless.

Phuvah finally realized what he was looking at. Although he had never seen it before, he had heard enough descriptions to recognize the Ark of the Covenant. He also knew that the Philistines had captured it in the battle of

Ebenezer. Was it truly being returned? His heart leaped with joy. He began to run in the direction of his master.

The wheat field of Beth Shemesh had been in Joshua's family for three generations. It had always been a very productive valley because of the year-round stream that ran through it and the canals that had been constructed.

Joshua was at the head of the canal talking with one of his workers when Phuvah ran up all out of breath.

"Master, you must come at once!"

"Has someone been injured, Phuvah?"

"No! No! It is something wonderful!"

"What are you talking about?"

"Look, Master! Look at what is coming into the valley!"

Joshua turned in the direction that Phuvah was pointing. His heart almost stopped beating. He couldn't believe his eyes. He and all of his workers began to run toward the cart.

The two milk cows had stopped when they reached the edge of the wheat field, as if they were just waiting for the workers to come.

Joshua yelled at the workers as he was running. "Do not go near the cart! Do not touch it or the cows! It is sacred and holy. We must not defile it in any way!"

Everyone stopped about a hundred feet from the cart. They stood for a moment and just stared at the Ark. Then, almost in unison, they all fell to their knees and bowed before it.

After a long silence, Joshua called to Phuvah. "Run as quick as you can and summon the Levites. They are the only ones who can touch the Ark."

It was around two o'clock when the Levites arrived. They danced for joy when they saw the Ark and then led the cart to a large stone in Joshua's wheat field. They had the workers gather smaller stones and the Levites made an altar. They took the Ark of the Covenant and the chest off of the cart and placed it on the large stone next to the altar.

The Levites broke the cart into pieces and placed the wood under the altar. Then they offered the cows as a burnt offering to the Lord. Everyone bowed and gave thanks for the return of the Ark.

Hidden behind rocks on the hills above Beth Shemesh were the lords of Ashdod, Gaza, Ashkelon, Gath, and Ekron. They were watching to see where the cows would go and what would happen to the Ark. They observed the Israelites slaughter the cows and offer them in sacrifice. They then noticed the Levites leaving and the field workers being stationed as guards around the Ark.

One of the lords, a giant from Gath, finally spoke.

"Their ways are certainly odd. Our god is so big and mighty. Their God is in a box. How great can He be? He certainly didn't give victory in battle to the Israelites. Our enemies now have their cursed Ark back. Let us return to our cities and see if the plague has been lifted."

All nodded in agreement and began their painful journey back in silence. An hour into the trip, the lord of Ashdod ventured a comment.

"I think we made the right decision."

They all stopped and looked at him.

"Why do you say that?" asked the lord of Ekron.

"The pain from my tumor is not as severe. I think it is shrinking."

Joshua had placed Phuvah in charge of the workers guarding the Ark. He had assigned them to different shifts so that someone would be awake at all times throughout the night.

Half a dozen of the workers had gathered around the fire to keep warm and talk about the Ark.

"What do you think is inside the chest along with the Ark?" asked one of the men.

"A good question. And what do you think is inside of the Ark itself?" responded another.

Their inquisitiveness grew until at last Phuvah looked at all of them and said, "Let us make a pact of secrecy. Let us agree to look inside the chest and the Ark, but we must agree to tell no one what we have done. Agreed?"

They all knew that the Ark of God was sacred and only the high priest was allowed to touch it. But their curiosity was greater than their fear, and they all agreed to the pact.

Excitedly they made torches and approached the large stone. The light from the torches reflected off the Ark in a distorted and ominous fashion.

"Let's open the chest first," said Phuvah.

Carefully he lifted the lid. They all held their torches over the chest and peered in. Phuvah reached his hand in and pulled out one of the golden emrod tumors.

"What is it?" asked one of the workers.

"I have no idea," said Phuvah. "I know only that it is pure gold."

He then pulled out one of the golden rats.

"Look at this! It must be an image of one of their gods."

The whole group broke into laughter.

Phuvah continued. "There are five of the golden rats and five of the globs of gold. It must symbolize the five great fortified cities of the Philistines. They're all rats!"

Again the group broke out in uncontrollable laughter.

"Let's look in the Ark," said another worker.

Carefully four of the men took off the lid and set it on the stone. They lifted their torches and looked inside. Phuvah started to grab for something in the Ark. . . .

It was early the next morning when Joshua arrived at the field of Beth Shemesh. He could not believe his eyes. His workers were all dead and lying in strange positions. A look of terror was frozen on each of their faces.

As he approached the large stone in his field, he looked at the six bodies lying around the Ark. He recognized the body lying closest to the Ark as Phuvah's. Joshua fell to his knees and put his hands over his eyes attempting to hold back the tears. "They knew better. They knew they shouldn't touch the Ark. Oh, my servants, how needless your deaths."

He could see Phuvah's right hand and arm were blackened, as if severely burned in a hot fire. The lid was off the Ark and the lid to the chest was also open. Next to the chest were two golden objects. One of them looked like a rat. He stayed about thirty feet from the large stone.

"I must get help from the Levites and priests!"

When Joshua arrived at the village where the Levities stayed, he found women and children in the streets weeping and wailing. The smell of death was in the air.

He approached one of the women. "What has happened? What is wrong here?" She did not respond. Even as he uttered those words he saw the dead men covering the ground. There were too many to count.

When he reached the home of the chief Levite he found that the door was open and he could hear noises inside. Peering in the door he saw the chief Levite on his knees, rocking back and forth, uttering prayers.

"Sir, what has happened?"

The Levite turned at the sound of a male voice.

"Joshua! You're alive. Oh, praise God. All of the men in the village are dead. Only the male Levites are alive. Levite runners from the other towns and villages around Beth Shemesh have reported the same thing. It is estimated that over fifty thousand men have suddenly been struck dead. No one has any idea why."

"I think I know why."

"Tell me, Joshua. What has gone wrong?"

"This morning I came back to the wheat field and the large stone where the Ark of the Covenant was placed. All of my men were struck dead and the lid of the Ark was open. I think they must have tried to look inside and see what was in the Ark."

"Then why didn't you die with them?" the Levite asked.

"I don't know why. Perhaps because I knew the Ark was holy and anyone unclean should not approach it. That's the only thing I can think of. The slaughter of my servants must be God's punishment for their disobedience."

"You may be correct, Joshua. Who can stand before a holy God? We must send Levite messengers to the town of Kirjath Jearim. It may be that they would be willing to take the Ark and put it into protection."

It took two days before the Levites of Kirjath Jearim arrived to transport the Ark. The process was quite involved as the men put cloths on their hands to pick up the lid of the Ark and put it into place. They were quite careful to not look inside the Ark during the process. They next covered the entire Ark with a scarlet cloth and then put it onto a cart drawn by oxen.

The Ark and the golden tumors and golden rats were taken to the house of Abinadab, who lived high in the mountains. It was there that his son Eleazar was consecrated to keep the Ark of the Lord.

One week had passed since the Ark of the Covenant had left Ashdod. All of the people had been healed from the plague. Their pain was gone and they had returned to their normal activities. Everyone except the priests of Dagon.

Kadmiel had gathered the priests together.

"Dagon has fallen to the earth twice. The second time his head and hands were knocked off. That is a terrible sign of doom. We will close and seal the doors of the temple. Our worship will be transferred to the underground building not far from the temple."

One of the priests asked, "What about the two items taken from the Ark? What will become of them?"

"We will carry them to the new place of worship. I think they may have great magical powers and could prove useful in the future."

FIFTY-SEVEN

LEVI TOOK his automatic out of his holster and carefully moved toward the opening. Both he and Murphy held their breath for a minute. They couldn't hear anything. All they could see was a flickering light dancing with shadows on the floor.

Levi cautiously entered the room, followed by Murphy. The structure they entered had a high ceiling of about twenty feet. It seemed much larger than the room surrounded by lions' heads. Along two sides and one end there were three rows of marble benches. They formed a horseshoe that focused toward the front of the room, where there was a large marble altar.

On two of the walls there were torches hung in rings protruding above the marble benches. They cast weird shadows. As Murphy and

Levi shined their flashlights around the room, they could see four bodies on the floor. One was in front of the altar, two were close to the center of the room, and one was lying near what looked like a passageway that led out of the room. All of them were dressed in gray robes and lying in pools of blood.

Levi went to the two men in the center of the room and felt for a pulse. Their bodies were warm but they were both dead of gunshot wounds. Murphy checked out the man by the passageway and the man in front of the altar. They were also dead.

Murphy shined his light on the robe of the man by the altar. It had a patch sewn onto the front just above the heart. On the patch there was a symbol of a half-man, half-fish.

"These men must have been priests or worshipers. They all have the symbol of Dagon sewn on their robes," said Murphy. "There must be another entrance to this room. Whoever killed them is not far ahead of us."

Levi searched the bodies for identification while Murphy walked to the altar to examine it. There was nothing on top. As he shined his light and looked more closely, he could see that the top of the altar was covered lightly with dust except for two areas in the center. The impression left was a round circle about six inches in diameter. The other impression was a straight line about six feet long and an inch and a half wide.

Murphy was both excited and exasperated. They seemed to have discovered the location of the rod and the jar, but too late. Whoever killed the men took the items from the altar.

Levi turned to Murphy.

"None of these men have any identification. Did you find anything?"

"Yes. Two items were on the altar. Unless I miss my guess, Methuselah was correct. The round impression in the dust was probably the Golden Jar that held the manna. The long straight line was most likely Aaron's Rod. These men must have been protectors of the two articles. I'm not sure how they got them but that's certainly why they were killed."

"There's nothing we can do for them, Michael. Let's go after whoever killed them."

"'Whoever'! You know as well as I do that it's got to be Talon. We're not far behind him. I wonder how he found out about the Golden Jar and Aaron's Rod?"

They stepped over the body of the man by the passageway and entered the dark corridor. They hadn't gone very far when they discovered two more bodies dressed in gray robes. As they shined their lights on them, they found that one of the men was still alive . . . but only barely.

Murphy leaned over the man. "Do you speak English? Do you understand me?"

The man only groaned.

"Do you know who did this to you?"

The man tried to speak but was unable to. Blood trickled from his lips and covered his chest.

His lungs must be filling, Murphy thought.

The man moved his arm and began to write in the dust with his finger. He barely finished two letters when his fingers stopped moving and he breathed his last. His brown eyes stared lifelessly at Murphy. Murphy shook his head gravely. It was never pleasant to see anyone die. He reached down and closed the man's eyelids.

He then shined his light on the two letters. They spelled *T U.*

I wonder what that means? It doesn't spell Talon.

Levi bent down and began to search the dead man. He found a wallet and examined the man's identification.

"His name is Karim Nandar. Nothing else here but a little money and a couple of pictures."

Murphy looked at the pictures. One was a group of seven men.

"Look, Levi! The man in the center with the dark mustache is Talon." He scrutinized the other faces. "The others are the dead men we just found. Either Talon is getting sloppy or he's in a hurry. It's not like him to leave evidence like this around. You can see in the picture that they're standing at the back end of a car and you can make out the license plate. Do you think you can get a trace on it?"

"Of course."

Levi took out a pen and a piece of paper.

"What are the numbers?"

"M72F355."

"Michael, we need to get outside where I can make a phone call. If this is Talon's work, we need to move fast before he has a chance to get away."

FIFTY-EIGHT

GIDEON LOCKED the doors of both cars and left them at the site of the two rock walls. He thought it might be best to walk the quarter of a mile to the olive orchard where he saw the seven workers get out of their cars and disappear into the trees.

As he approached the three parked cars, he became a little apprehensive. Something wasn't right. He couldn't see anyone in the orchard nor could he hear any sounds.

Strange. Where did they go?

He looked into the windows of the cars and did not see anything unusual other than the fact that the cars were immaculate.

He moved into the orchard and looked around. All he could see were rows of olive trees and a large formation of rocks. He was about to return to the cars when he thought he heard a sound. He paused and listened. It seemed to be coming from the rocky area.

He unhooked the strap on his shoulder holster and crept toward the rocks. As he approached, a stick suddenly poked its way out from between three of the large rocks in the pile, followed by a man with a mustache. In his left hand, he held a gunnysack with something inside. His right hand was bandaged and held on to a walking stick.

The man with the sack turned and looked into Gideon's eyes. Gideon had his hand on his gun. He could tell that the man was surprised to see him standing there. He noticed the man glance at Gideon's hand on the gun. His look of surprise changed to a smile.

"Hello, there," said the man. "How are you today?"

Gideon was still uncertain about the other man. "What are you doing in the rocks? And where are the other men?"

The man with the walking stick and gunnysack smiled again.

"We're exploring. We found an entrance into a chamber in the ground. It must have been hidden in the rocks for many years. The other men are inside. Come and see what we found."

Cautiously Gideon climbed onto the rocky area and over the three large rocks. In the center he could see that a stone had been removed, revealing a three-foot by three-foot hole in the ground. It looked like there was some kind of stairway that disappeared into the earth.

"Let me show you what we found inside," said the friendly man with the mustache.

He carefully set the gunnysack down and exposed a beautiful golden jar.

The sun reflected off it and made Gideon squint his eyes.

"Is that real gold?" asked Gideon as he knelt down to examine it.

"It sure is."

The next thing Gideon felt was a sharp pain on the back of his head. The blow from the six-foot walking stick sent him forward, knocking over the jar and smashing his forehead into a rock.

Although he was dazed and in pain, he instinctively reached for his gun. As he did, he felt an excruciating pain in his right hand as the man with the mustache swung the walking stick a second time, breaking three of his fingers.

Gideon knew he was in deep trouble. He tried to roll out of the way of the third blow but he wasn't fast enough. The stick came down, breaking his left collarbone. He let out a yell of pain. Then a strange thing happened. The man with the stick backed away and calmly rewrapped the Golden Jar. This allowed Gideon time to struggle to his feet. He was wincing in pain from all of his wounds.

The man put down the gunnysack and approached. He looked at Gideon and smiled again.

"This unfortunately has not been a good day for you. However, it has been a wonderful day for me."

With those words, he then drove the end of the walking stick into Gideon's throat, crushing his larynx. Gideon collapsed to the rocks, gasping for breath.

Murphy and Levi continued to follow the passageway, not knowing where it would lead. They began moving uphill at about a 30-degree grade. As they rounded a curve in the passageway they saw light up ahead. Soon they came to the base of a three-foot-wide stairway with about fifteen steps that led to the surface.

"Be careful, Levi. No telling what we will encounter up there."

They turned off their flashlights and climbed the stairs. Levi had his gun drawn and ready.

The bright light of the sun made them both squint as they came out of a hole in the middle of three large boulders.

Levi slowly looked over the large rocks.

"Oy gevalt!"

"What?"

"It's Gideon!"

They both scrambled to Gideon's side, looking for signs of life. Tears welled up in Levi's eyes as he looked at the beaten and lifeless body. He could tell that Gideon must have endured tremendous pain before he died. Levi suddenly realized that he would have to tell Gideon's wife and two children that he would not be coming home.

Levi swore loudly. "I'm going to kill that man!" he growled.

Murphy placed a comforting hand on Levi's back. They both ran the quarter of a mile back to their car.

"He's got a head start on us," said Murphy.

"I'll call in about Gideon and also try to get some information about the license number of the car in the picture. Michael, you drive. We will go back to Ashdod and then to Tel Aviv. My guess is that he will try to get out of the country as fast as he can."

Levi's phone began ringing about fifteen miles south of Tel Aviv. He talked for about five minutes.

"Our intelligence agency says the car was a rental. It was checked out at the Tel Aviv airport and was returned about twenty minutes ago. Step on the gas, Michael. He's probably still there. When we arrive, I'll have some copies made of the picture with the seven men. We'll have the airport police help us to try and find out which airline he may be flying out on."

"This time Talon is the one being pursued. I hope he experiences the same fear the fox feels when the dogs are on his tail. I would love to make him suffer in pain the way he makes others suffer. He's long overdue."

FIFTY-NINE

THE HEAD OF AIRPORT SECURITY, Ezra Talmi, was standing on the sidewalk outside the passenger loading area when Levi and Murphy drove up. He had six large Israeli airport policemen with him. They were all heavily armed.

He shook hands with Levi and they spoke in Hebrew for a moment. Levi then introduced Talmi to Murphy.

"It's nice to meet you, Dr. Murphy. I wish it were under better circumstances. Please leave the keys in the car. We will have someone from the rental agency come and pick it up. Grab your luggage and come inside. Levi, I understand that you have a picture. We'll get copies made and distribute them to all of the security personnel."

Murphy appreciated his straightforward, businesslike manner. It was good to see someone who clearly had leadership skills and understood the importance of timing. It wasn't long before the pictures were passed out to all the security checkpoints. All security personnel were put on a modified alert.

Talmi spoke to Levi and Murphy.

"We have a lounge you may sit in while our people go through the airport. They are very thorough."

"We appreciate everything you're doing, Mr. Talmi," Murphy responded. "But if you don't mind, I would like to walk around and do a little looking myself."

"As you wish. Just be careful. I don't think the person you are looking for will be armed. We have sniffer dogs moving through the terminal and our security checkpoints are very sensitive to anything that might be a weapon. If you do spot him, just contact any of our security personnel and they will respond instantly. Levi and I have a few items to discuss. By the way, let me give you a security pass. It will allow you to move about with a little more freedom."

"Thank you. I'll check in with you every twenty minutes."

Murphy began to wander through the crowds. The airport was packed with travelers. That made things a bit tougher. He meandered into the restrooms, looked into all of the restaurants, and walked through the shops. It was like looking for a human needle in a haystack of thousands of faces.

You're supposed to arrive at the airport at least two hours before international flights. He had about an hour head start on us. He's got to be here somewhere. Where would he be flying to?

Talon was also on the alert. He knew that Israel had very tight security. All bags would be hand-checked at some point. That's why he dropped the Golden Jar and Aaron's Rod off at a safe house that the

Seven owned. The person who managed the house would ship the items by special private jet to a location in Istanbul. They would arrive a day after he did.

As a precaution he used his platinum travel card and went into the executive lounge. He slipped into one of the shower stalls and quickly colored his hair and eyebrows. He also shaved off his mustache. He then pulled out his Swiss passport that had a picture of a clean-faced blond traveler named Emile Cornelle. He looked at himself in the mirror. The loss of the mustache and the switch to blond eyebrows and blond hair made a dramatic change in his appearance. He also changed into a blue pin-striped suit and took off the bandage on his right hand.

The skin on the tip of his stub of a damaged finger was bright red. He knew that he had a slight infection. He took out a skin-colored bandage and wrapped his finger. It was almost unnoticeable at first glance. The finger was still sore and he was still angry with Wallach for smashing it with a baseball bat. It was comforting to know that the brat had gotten what he had coming to him.

He then sat down and began to read through an Israeli newspaper. He would remain in the executive lounge until just before the flight. He was almost home free.

He was turning a page of the newspaper when he spotted Murphy at the welcome counter talking to the woman in charge. Talon could see him pointing to some card that he was wearing around his neck. The woman nodded and Murphy entered the lounge and started looking around.

He's better than I thought.

Talon lifted the paper a little to help cover the lower portion of his face. He pretended to read although his eyes never left Murphy. As Murphy drew closer he lifted the paper.

Murphy saw the man in the blue pin-striped suit but didn't pay any attention to him. He had never seen Talon in a suit before and he knew Talon had dark hair and a dark mustache.

Talon watched as Murphy made his way through the lounge. He disappeared into the restroom area and emerged a few moments later. He thanked the woman at the welcome counter and then left.

When Murphy rejoined Levi and Talmi they had nothing to report. Neither did he.

"What if he put on a disguise?" suggested Talmi.

"It's a possibility," said Levi. "But he wouldn't have a great deal of time to put on makeup and a false beard or anything too elaborate."

"What if he just cut off his mustache or made minor changes?" Talmi suggested.

"That would make more sense," responded Murphy.

"Let me have our artist draw in several different disguises. It may help us to find him."

An hour later Talmi presented a number of different drawings.

"What do you think?"

Murphy looked at all the pictures. One of them had a picture drawn in with blond hair and a blond mustache. Something about that picture caught his attention. He studied it for a moment and then placed his finger over the mustache.

"Wait a minute! I may have seen someone that looks like him in one of the executive lounges."

"Which one?" asked Talmi.

"The one on the second floor. I believe it was British Airways."

They all jumped up and ran up the stairs to the second floor, followed by four armed security guards. The woman at the welcome counter was surprised when everyone burst into the lounge and began searching. There were only seven people in the lounge. Three women, one child, and three overweight businessmen.

Murphy spoke to the woman at the counter.

"There were about twenty people in here about an hour ago. Do you have any idea which flights they might be on?"

She looked at a sheet of paper on her desk.

"We had three British Airways flights leave within the last hour. One went to Brussels. One went to London. And one went to Istanbul."

"That's it!" said Murphy with excitement.

"What are you talking about, Michael?" asked Levi.

"Remember in the Temple of Dagon. The one priest that was still alive tried to write something in the dust. He only got out two letters . . . *TU*. I'll bet he was trying to write out *TURKEY*. Talon is on his way to Turkey."

"Why would he go to Turkey? What's so special about Istanbul?"

"Levi, he has Aaron's Rod and the Golden Jar of Manna. He also has all three sections of the Bronze Serpent of Moses. I think he may be going after the backpack!"

"What are you talking about, Michael? What backpack?"

"Do you remember when I went on the expedition to look for Noah's Ark?"

"Of course."

"Well, we did find the ark. But we also found some other items in an old box on the ark. We found a sword and a dagger that Dr. Wendell Reinhold from MIT said were made out of tungsten steel. Somehow Noah had access to a smelting process that could melt steel at extremely high temperatures and produce metal of the highest tensile strength."

"Where would Noah get that type of technology?"

"According to the writings of Josephus . . . Jewish history suggests that Noah's wife's name was Naamah. She was the sister of Tubal-Cain, who is considered the father of metallurgy. We also discovered a number of other items. There was a curious bronze machine that had dials, pointers, interlocking gears, and wheels. We think it was a precision instrument that charted the positions of the stars and planets."

Murphy continued, speaking rapidly. "There were also weights and measures. And some colored crystals that were hot to touch. But, maybe most importantly, there were bronze plates that may prove to be one of the most important discoveries ever made."

Levi and Talmi were trying to follow Murphy's excitement and story about the ark.

"Dr. Reinhold believed that the bronze plates contained the secret of the Philosopher's Stone. The ability to change base metals into precious metals."

"You mean like changing lead into gold?" asked Levi.

"Yes. But even more important, the ability to change base metals into platinum."

"Why platinum?" asked Talmi.

"For the production of hydrogen fuel cells. As water passes through a thin layer of platinum it separates the protons from the electrons. This releases energy whereby we can take ordinary water and make it a clean-burning fuel that is a renewable resource. It would do away with the need for gasoline or any fossil fuels. This is already being done by a number of companies. The only problem is that platinum is very costly and very rare. If platinum could be created out of base metals . . . whoever had control of this process would have control of the fuel supply for the entire world. Now I understand why the Seven would want this. It's worth a bundle."

"But what's that got to do with a backpack?" asked Levi.

"The three bronze plates with the formula for the Philosopher's Stone are in the backpack. The backpack went overboard with Talon as we were traveling on a ship from Istanbul to Romania. It is somewhere in the Black Sea. I think that Talon is going to try and retrieve the backpack."

"How could he ever find it?" asked Talmi.

"I think it would be possible. The ship travels the same route every week and most likely it travels at roughly the same speed. All we need to do is look at the ship's log. I know the time Talon went overboard.

We only need to follow the same route for the same amount of time and we should be very close to the location."

"But, Michael," replied Levi, "it's still a large area. How could you ever find it?"

"With a mini-submarine used for salvage work. They're designed with very sophisticated metal-detection devices."

"It's still a long shot."

"I know it is, Levi. But considering the possibility of the Philosopher's Stone falling into the wrong hands . . . it's worth a try, isn't it?"

"Yes, you're right. It's worth a try."

"We're going to need the right hardware. Do you have any contacts, someone who could get us a mini-submarine?"

"I'm sure we do. I'll have to check with our intelligence people. I'll also alert our people in Istanbul to stake out the arrival gate and try to nab Talon before he can slip away again. In the meantime, Ezra, can you set Dr. Murphy up on the next flight to Istanbul?"

"Of course. I'll find out when the next flight is to leave. I think it's not for another five hours. The man you are pursuing will have at least an eight-hour head start. I wish you luck."

SIXTY

AS MURPHY DISEMBARKED the British Airways flight to Istanbul he looked over the crowd. Levi told him that one of the Mossad operatives would meet him at the airport. He noticed a dark-haired man of medium build eyeing him intently. The man then held up a sign that read, DR. MICHAEL MURPHY.

"Dr. Murphy, my name is Yosef Rozen. Welcome to Istanbul."

Murphy shook hands with the man. As they walked toward a waiting car, one thought was foremost in Murphy's mind.

"Did you get him?"

Rozen shook his head. "We discovered that there were five people who left Tel Aviv for Istanbul. But only one met your description. He has a Swiss passport and his name is Emile Cornelle. Unfortunately, he had already arrived before we got all the details together."

Murphy was disappointed, but far from surprised. Talon was a slippery one. "Istanbul is a very large and complex city. Do you think there's any hope of finding him?"

"It won't be easy, unless he checks into a hotel using the name Emile Cornelle."

Not likely. Talon didn't make stupid mistakes like that. "Were you able to get any information about the ship lines?"

"Yes, we were."

Rozen opened his briefcase, took out a folder, and handed it to Murphy.

"Inside you will find the routing for the passenger ship from Istanbul to Constanta, Romania. It is almost a straight line. It also lists the speed it travels, along with other navigational details. If you know the time when the man you were fighting with went overboard, you could be as close as a half mile from the spot."

Murphy looked at the route and calculated where the ship should have been at the corresponding time.

"It looks like the location is not far off the coast of Bulgaria, between Burgas and Varna. The navigational chart suggests that the depth of the water there varies from two hundred to six hundred feet. Was Levi able to secure the use of a mini-submarine?"

"Yes. You will also find that information in the folder. Much oil is shipped out of the ports at Constanta. Israel has been working together with the Romanian government in exploring some offshore drilling sites. We have two small Neptune class mini-subs stationed at the port in Varna. We have secured the use of one of them for you. The small submarine has enough fuel and oxygen for about seven days underwater.

They were letting him borrow a sub for a week? Levi sure knew the right people.

"And what about metal detection?"

"The submarine has a very sensitive metal-detection device. It can pick up readings from as far as an eighth of a mile. The meters can also determine the type of metal, from steel to silver or gold."

"How about bronze?"

"Of course. It has readings for most of the common metals. It can also tell the approximate depth of the metal in the event it has settled under the sand. It is quite impressive."

"It sounds just like what I'll need."

"One other thing. We have also checked out the port here in Istanbul to see if there are any mini-submarines in dock. There are three of them. One is in dry dock being repaired and the other two are down at pier number 103. We are still trying to contact the owners to see if anyone is scheduled to use them. That might provide one other possibility for finding the man you are searching for."

"I appreciate all of the work you have gone to. This man is very dangerous. Death and terror are his specialties. He must be stopped."

"We are pleased to help in any way we can, Dr. Murphy. We have also booked a room for you in one of the hotels south of the Golden Horn. It's in the older section of the city, at the top of one of the hills that leads down to the sea. It's not far from the Covered Bazaar. I'm sure that you will find it acceptable."

"Thank you. I think I'll settle in and then maybe explore the mini-subs at pier 103."

SIXTY-ONE

IT WAS ABOUT 6:00 P.M. when Murphy arrived at the hotel. He checked in and then went for a walk in the direction of the Covered Bazaar. It brought back memories of his time with Isis in Turkey. They had shared some wonderful times and some dangerous times together in their search for the Ark of Noah on Ararat.

Murphy let out a long sigh. He missed her.

After dinner Murphy took a taxi down to pier 103. The sun was just starting to set when he arrived.

"Do you want me to wait, sir?" asked the driver.

"No. That's all right. I'm not sure how long I will be. I'll catch another taxi later."

"Not a lot of taxis come down here at night, sir. There are not very many people around."

"I'll walk to a busier area."

"I don't know, sir. This is not a good place for an American to be walking around alone. Do you have an international cell phone?"

"Yes, I do," Murphy replied.

"Good. I'll give you my personal number. When you want to come back, you call me and I will come and get you. I would feel better if you did that. My name is Abd-Al-Rahim."

"Thank you for your concern. That's a good idea." Murphy wrote down the number. "You have been most kind."

"Be sure to watch your back, sir."

Murphy watched as the taxi drove away. He turned and looked around for a moment. No one could be seen in the dock area. Pier number 103 was about a block long and only had two light posts that were on, spaced quite a ways apart from each other.

Murphy walked down the pier until he found the two mini-submarines floating near each other. They both had white lettering reading CARSON OCEANOGRAPHIC on the side of their dark gray hulls.

I wonder who they are?

Murphy recognized the subs as the Ocean Ranger models. He had read about them in an issue of *Popular Science* magazine. They had an operating depth of 1,000 feet and were propelled by a combination of battery and diesel electric. They only needed one pilot and could carry up to four passengers if needed. Their surface speed was five knots and the submerged speed was three knots. Most importantly, they had a life support of 400 man-hours. If five people were on board they could last almost three and a half days. A single occupant could extend his stay to sixteen days.

Murphy wandered farther down the pier and sat on some crates in the shadows. A wave of pessimism settled over his thoughts. The pursuit of Talon seemed like a long shot and finding the backpack would be even more difficult. He was tired of battling against someone so evil who always seemed to come out on top. He was also physically tired after his adventure in the Temple of Dagon, the search for Talon at the airport, and his unplanned flight to Istanbul. He closed his eyes for a minute.

The sound of car doors closing startled him. He opened his eyes and looked at his watch. To his surprise, an hour and a half had passed since he had first closed his eyes.

I guess I was more tired than I thought.

In the poor light on the pier, Murphy could make out three men. They had just gotten out of a taxi, and as it drove away, the men began walking down the pier in his direction. He quietly slipped behind a large crate and watched.

As the three men passed under one of the lights on the pier, Murphy recognized Talon. His hair was back to its original dark color. He was clean-shaven. The two large men with Talon looked like Arabs. A combination of excitement and anger coursed through Murphy's body.

What Levi wouldn't give to be here now.

He watched as they stopped in front of the mini-submarines. They were speaking in Arabic. Every now and then Murphy could make out a couple of words.

After about ten minutes they walked back down the pier and into the street. Murphy followed, being sure to keep in the shadows. They turned right and walked toward a group of warehouses. Murphy waited until they rounded a corner before he went into the open street.

When he reached the edge of the building he carefully looked around the corner into a long alley between two warehouses. A light was on over a doorway on the warehouse to the left. Murphy saw no one, but he felt uneasy. He wished that Levi were with him . . . or at least Levi's automatic.

Murphy decided to continue his pursuit. He had moved about

halfway down the alley when one of the Arabs stepped out of the shadows about twenty feet in front of him, blocking his way.

The man said something in Arabic and Murphy heard a noise behind him. The other Arab had been hiding behind a garbage bin and was behind him about thirty feet away. Murphy was surrounded by warehouse walls on two sides and Arabs in front and back. Talon had disappeared.

He probably left them to do his dirty work for him.

Murphy quickly processed the situation. The words of a Civil War general flashed into his mind.

When surrounded on all sides . . . attack!

Murphy moved quickly toward the Arab in front of him. The man had not expected him to charge. He reached in his pocket, pulled out a switchblade, and pushed the button on the side. The blade shot straight out of the handle.

Murphy caught the flash of metal but kept moving forward. Just before he got within stabbing distance he quickly darted to the left. At the same time the Arab lunged forward with the knife. Murphy quickly turned back, using his right hand for a downward block on the Arab's forearm.

He let out a cry of pain and dropped the knife, his arm almost paralyzed from the force of the blow. Murphy raised his left arm high and then drove his elbow into the face of the Arab, shattering his nose. For a moment he tottered and then toppled backward like a giant tree that had been chopped down.

Before Murphy could shout "*Timber!*" the second Arab had closed the distance. He had a metal bar in his right hand and Murphy knew that he intended to split his skull open with it. As the Arab raised his arm, Murphy dropped low and charged into his stomach with his shoulder. He felt the bar glancing off his back muscles as they went down in a pile together.

The Arab was strong and was attempting to put a bear hug on him. Murphy made a fist with his right hand, his thumb sticking out a little. He then drove the extended thumb into the top of the Arab's rib cage just under his left armpit. The Arab yelped and released his grip.

Murphy then quickly drove his braced thumb a second time. This time it struck home in the Arab's left temple. He was stunned and disoriented. He was no longer on the attack but trying to retreat.

Murphy rolled away and bounced to his feet as the Arab attempted to get up. Murphy drove his right elbow into the upper back of the Arab and it was all over. The blow had rendered him unconscious.

What seemed like an eternity of fighting was over in less than a minute. Murphy was breathing heavy and shaking with adrenaline. He backed out of the alley, thinking it best to leave before any more of Talon's friends arrived.

He reached in his pocket for his cell phone. "Hello. Is this Abd-Al-Rahim? This is the wandering American in Istanbul. If you have a moment, I would appreciate a ride back to the hotel."

SIXTY-TWO

MURPHY RUBBED HIS FINGERS through his hair as the phone rang. He had a sense of urgency that he couldn't quite explain. It was just a feeling.

"This is Levi Abrams."

"Levi. Michael here."

"Michael. How's it going? Have you found Talon yet?"

"Yes and no."

"What do you mean?"

"I saw him at a distance last night but I have no idea where he is now. I lost him when two of his men jumped me in an alley."

"Are you okay?"

"I'm fine. Just a little tired. The two men who jumped me are a little worse for wear. Anyway, I saw him down at pier 103. He was standing next to a couple of mini-subs belonging to Carson Oceanographic. Do you know anything about them?"

"I've heard of them. They're a reputable company. They're helping in the search for possible oil sites in the Black Sea. My guess is that Talon is either going to steal one of the subs or rent one. Are you planning to wait for him and try to catch him?"

"I don't know, Levi. I'd like to catch him but what if he obtains a submarine from a company other than Carson Oceanographic? I'd be sitting around waiting while he was in the process of finding the backpack."

"You're probably right, Michael. You've got to find the bronze plates before he does. Then after that you could try to find him. Why don't you charter a plane to Varna and get the sub we have reserved for you. You could approach the site in the Black Sea from the north. Even if Talon used one of the Carson mini-subs, you might arrive at the site before he does. He'd be approaching from the south."

"Do me another favor, Levi. Call the people in Varna and let them know that I'm on the way."

The twin-engine charter plane banked in a wide circle over the city. Murphy was sitting next to the pilot. They both had on earphones so they could hear each other over the intense drum of the motors.

Murphy pointed. "What is that large building?"

"That's the nineteenth-century Cathedral of the Assumption of the Virgin. It is an important landmark in Varna," responded the pilot.

"The city is larger than I thought it would be."

"Yes. It is the third largest city in Bulgaria. However, it wasn't always called Varna. From 1949 to 1956 it was called Stalin after the Russian leader."

"How old is the city?" asked Murphy.

"It is quite old. The first colony was established in 580 B.C. In 1444 A.D. thirty thousand Crusaders came to the city awaiting passage by ship to Constantinople. However, they never did go because a hundred and twenty thousand Turks attacked them. This started a retreat from the advancing Ottomans."

"I notice a lot of ships in the harbor."

"Varna is the capital for shipping in Bulgaria. It's also the home of the Bulgarian Navy and the Naval Museum. Many of the ships you see are part of the Bulgarian Navy."

"Well, it sure is a beautiful city. Thanks for the information."

Murphy spent the rest of the day getting a crash course in the operation of the mini-sub and how to use the metal detector. The leader of the oil exploration crew spent time helping Murphy practice retrieving items off the floor of the ocean with the use of mechanical arms that extended from the ship and deposited the items in a watertight holding compartment.

They also discussed the underwater terrain, ocean depth in the search area, and escape procedures in case of an emergency.

"We've done some exploration in that general area," said the leader. "You need to be aware that there are a number of sunken ships at about a six-hundred-foot depth. We've seen four fishing trawlers and one cargo ship. Your metal detector will be sure to go off around them. You'll need to remember to switch from general metal detection to specific metal detection. Just adjust the setting to search for bronze."

"How long do you think it'll take for me to get to the general area?"

"Less than a full day. Maybe seven to eight hours, depending on where you begin the search. Your best bet will be to pick an area and utilize a crisscross pattern."

"And if I experience any difficulties?"

"Just use the radio unit and call our headquarters. We already have it dialed in for you. All you'll need to do is turn it on."

"I appreciate all of your help. My plan is to leave early in the morning."

"We'll have some men here to assist you with any last-minute details. I do hope you find what you're looking for, Dr. Murphy. We wish you the best of luck."

SIXTY-THREE

TWO MEN WERE at the dock when Murphy arrived. They helped load some of the food stores, checked the diesel fuel, oxygen tanks, and water supply. They also double-checked the underwater lights to ensure that they were all working.

Murphy shook their hands and then climbed into the mini-submarine. He screwed down the hatch to seal it tight and then slid into the driving seat. He started the engine and checked out all of the gauges. He said a little prayer and buckled his seat harness.

He looked out the window one more time at the men and gave them the go-ahead signal. They slowly lowered the sub into the water. He pushed the lever forward and moved into the harbor for the slow trip to the ocean. As he reached the breakwater he increased the speed.

About a mile from shore, Murphy began to experiment and test the ability of the sub to move forward and in reverse. He then practiced submerging the ship and resurfacing. He tested his ability to turn the ship quickly and the various functions of the underwater lights and grappling arms for picking up objects from the ocean floor.

He slowed to a stop and checked his charts one more time. Being satisfied, he set the directional gauges, which were hooked to the internal compass. It was now just a matter of time until he reached the possible location of the backpack. He began to feel some excitement and, at the same time, a healthy dose of fear. He knew there was a good chance that he might run into Talon.

The mini-sub was dwarfed by the vastness of the ocean. With each passing hour Murphy felt more and more alone. It was just endless ocean with only his own thoughts for company.

After about seven hours of monotony, Murphy noticed the flashing of a red light on the control panel. It flashed again a half minute later. It was the metal detector. The flashing increased in frequency until, after about ten minutes, the light remained constantly on. He leaned over and turned up the loudspeaker and heard a beeping sound. When he turned the sub to the left, the beeping got louder. When he turned to the right, it got softer.

This is not too hard.

He continued to move toward the spot where the beeping was extremely loud. The gauge registered "steel" at about twenty-five yards. Murphy turned on the outside lights for better viewing. He slowed the engine and effortlessly drifted toward the spot. Soon he could see the object coming into view.

It was a 55-gallon steel drum that must have rolled off a ship or maybe was thrown overboard. Murphy smiled.

At least we know the metal detector works.

Murphy went on for another hour and then slowed the sub to a stop. He reviewed the navigational charts and the gauges. He was now in the general area. He drew a half-mile grid pattern on the chart and began the slow task of piloting back and forth across the ocean floor in a standard search pattern.

I'll bet the pirates of old would have liked to have something like this ship. They could have found buried or sunken treasure.

After another half hour he began to pick up a slight beeping sound. He moved in the direction his gauges indicated. His heart began to beat a little harder when the metal detector registered a lot of steel and a little bit of brass. His excitement drained away when a sunken fishing trawler came into view. It looked like it had been on the ocean floor for many years and was extremely rusty. The registration of the brass on the metal detector must have come from the bands of brass around the decaying mast. As his lights shined on the vessel, a number of fish swam by.

This is a different world.

Another two hours passed as Murphy went back and forth in a grid pattern. He finally slowed to a stop and grabbed something to eat and some water to drink.

"I guess I can work any hours I want down here. There is no day. It's only night."

Time began to lose meaning in the darkness. It was only the hope of finding something that kept Murphy motivated. He made another grid pattern and continued the search.

Three hours later the metal detector indicated that something very large was nearby. He followed the gauges toward the object.

Murphy soon felt dwarfed in the mini-sub as it came next to a large cargo ship lying on its side. He slowed the engine and gently glided over the boat. He estimated that it was as long as a football field. He could see steel cargo boxes strewn about the ocean floor around the ship. They each looked to be about forty feet in length.

I'll bet they lost millions of dollars with the loss of the ship and cargo.

He began to wonder how many people had died when it sank. Had this boat become their tomb? It was a very strange feeling to move about in silence around this sleeping giant resting on a bed of sand.

Murphy maneuvered the sub around the cargo boat, appraising it from different angles. As he passed by the deck he could see the arm of a loading crane sticking out. It looked like the arm of a beggar asking for an offering. It seemed to say, Please, give me something I can pick up. I'm so bored down here.

Hey, Murphy, are you losing it? You must be tired.

Murphy slowed the sub and moved closer to the ocean floor. He allowed the sub to settle into a resting place on the sand.

As he looked out the curved window he could see strange fish swimming by the sunken ship. He watched for a few minutes and then his eyelids grew heavy and finally shut. He drifted into a weary sleep.

The next thing Murphy knew he was awake. Some noise had startled him out of his slumber. His heart was beating fast.

What was that?

The noise hadn't been loud. It was more like a thud against the outside of the small submarine. He turned on the outside lights and peered through the window. He watched for a moment and then he saw them. Three sharks were lazily swimming around the sub. It may have been the noise of the generator that had attracted them. Two of the sharks looked to be about twelve feet long and the third was very large at about sixteen feet long.

One of their tails must have hit the side of the sub.

Murphy started the engine and began to move away from the sunken ship and into the darkness of the ocean. He figured he was a hundred yards away from the ship when his metal detector began to sound again. He adjusted the meter. The gauges indicated brass.

Could it be?

Murphy's heart started to beat faster. He could feel a little bit of an adrenaline rush. Although he went back and forth over the spot he could see nothing.

I guess I'll need to pump some water.

He slowed the submarine to a stop at the point where the beeping was loudest and then turned off the sound so he could concentrate. He then maneuvered the mechanical arms down toward the sand. On each arm there was an attached tube through which water could be pumped. The flow of water under pressure would move the sand to expose objects that might be buried underneath.

Murphy started the slow process. If he pumped water too fast he would not be able to see. It would create something like an underwater dust storm.

After about ten minutes he saw something move in the sand. At first he thought it might be a fish, but it didn't swim away.

He stopped the pumping of the water and let the sand settle. The moving object looked like a strap of some kind. His hand shook as he maneuvered the mechanical arm toward the strap, opened the grips on the end, and then closed them on the strap. He slowly began to lift up the arm.

Murphy stopped breathing for a moment when it came out of the sand. It was the backpack. He just sat there and looked at it in the underwater lights, not believing what he saw. He closed his eyes for a moment and prayed.

"Thank you, God."

Murphy was so enthralled with what he found that he was not aware of the new reading on his metal detector or the dark gray shadow in the water moving toward him.

SIXTY-FOUR

MURPHY UNBUCKLED the harness and climbed out of his seat. He moved closer to the thick glass window to get a better view of the backpack. He wanted to see if it might have been damaged in any way. He wanted to be sure that none of the bronze plates had somehow fallen out. All three plates would be necessary for the formula of the Philosopher's Stone.

As far as he could tell, the backpack looked intact. There were no rips or tears. All the zippers were closed. He sighed in relief. Now the only thing to do was to work the mechanical arms and deposit the backpack in a watertight holding compartment.

Murphy turned and started to move back to the driving seat. His hand was on the arm of the seat when it happened.

The dark gray object that Murphy hadn't noticed was Talon in one of the Carson Oceanographic mini-subs.

Talon had spotted the lights of Murphy's sub and approached with his outside lights off. He had watched at a distance as Murphy had blown water into the sand and discovered the backpack.

Thank you, Dr. Murphy. You've saved me a great deal of time and effort. Now for your reward.

Talon moved the speed control to maximum on the Carson sub. He was going to be able to catch Murphy off-guard and blindside him.

The Carson sub rammed into Murphy's just behind the windows that wrapped around the front. Talon was ready for the impact but Murphy was not.

The collision sent Murphy through the air into the side of his ship. A lever that controlled the movement of the watertight holding compartment was sticking straight out. Murphy's body smashed into the lever, breaking three of the ribs on his left side. One of the ribs penetrated his lung and he cried out in shock and intense pain. He desperately gasped for air and collapsed to the floor.

Murphy had also hit his head on the metal side wall and was bleeding, disoriented, and confused. He had no idea what had just happened. The outside lights and inside lights on the right side of Murphy's sub flickered for a moment and then went out.

Talon, in the meantime, was putting the Carson submarine in reverse.

Murphy finally caught some air and struggled to his feet. He was holding on to his left side, fighting the sharp pain every time he tried to breathe. He moved his body in different positions to find some relief but there was none.

He staggered forward and attempted to reseat himself. He had lifted his right leg to get into place when Talon rammed the Carson submarine into the right side of the ship for a second time.

The impact caused Murphy's left leg to crack as he hit the floor and he shouted in agony once more. The blood from his head wound still flowed, soaking his shirt with blood. He felt water on his face, and as he lay on the floor of the sub, he saw a number of areas where water was leaking in.

His clothes were already wet with the cold salt water. He estimated that there was about an inch of water on the floor. He knew that it would only be a matter of time before his ship would fill.

Talon backed away from Murphy's sub a little distance and watched. Only a couple of small lights were still working. He could see the bloody and clearly injured Murphy on the floor.

I think that should take care of you for the time being, Dr. Murphy. Now I think I'll go pick up my prize. Cheer up . . . I'll return to finish the job. Your submarine will become your tomb.

Talon then began the task of retrieving the backpack.

Murphy's mind was spinning. He was aware that he was severely injured. If he didn't get help for his punctured lung, he knew he would eventually drown in his own blood. To make matters worse, his ship was rapidly filling with water. He would have to somehow get to the surface quickly.

He began to pray.

Yosef Rozen was pacing back and forth. Standing around in airports was not one of the things he liked to do. Finally, he heard what he was waiting for.

"British Airways Flight 9312 is now arriving at gate number forty-seven."

He turned and walked to the doorway and waited as passengers disembarked. Soon he saw the imposing figure of Levi Abrams in the crowd. They smiled and shook hands.

"Yosef. It has been a long time."

"Too long, Levi."

"How long have you been stationed in Istanbul?"

"Five years. Frankly, I would like to go home to Israel."

Levi nodded in agreement. "Have you heard anything from Dr. Murphy?"

"No. He took a chartered flight to Varna and boarded the submarine. Since that time we have not heard from him. We've tried to radio him several times but there's been no response."

"There must be something wrong with his equipment."

"Possibly, but everything was checked out before he left and was in good working order."

"Dr. Murphy had experience with mini-subs when he was in the armed services of the United States. I'm sure he'll be all right."

"Maybe so, Levi, but it's always a little dangerous to operate a submarine by yourself. If something should go wrong, there's no one to help you."

Levi considered this. "Maybe we should alert the Bulgarian Navy that we may need their assistance. At least they could be prepared to respond quickly if called upon."

"I'll have someone contact them."

"Have you any other information that might be helpful?"

"I think so. One of the mini-submarines belonging to Carson Oceanographic has been stolen. Two of the dockworkers were found floating in the water with broken necks. No doubt the person who stole the submarine also killed the men."

"Talon. It has to be. But what about Murphy? He may not know that Talon is already out there looking for the same object."

"There's not much we can do, Levi. We have only a general idea where they might be. The Black Sea is very large."

"I know, Yosef . . . I know!"

SIXTY-FIVE

WITH MUCH PAIN Murphy crawled through the water, dragging his leg behind him. He somehow pulled himself into the driving seat and buckled the harness. There was no comfortable way to sit with the pain of the broken ribs. Breathing was very difficult. His leg was numb. He knew that he was in mild shock but he had to forget the pain and do what he had to do, or he was dead.

Murphy could feel himself starting to shake, the first signs of hypothermia. His body temperature was beginning to drop from lying in the cold water. He glanced over to the side of the ship where it had been rammed. It seemed like the leaks had grown larger. He grabbed the radio unit, but it was dead, evidently damaged in the collision. Murphy was on his own.

He looked out the window and saw a sub with large white letters . . . CARSON OCEANOGRAPHIC.

Although he didn't see the person piloting the ship, he knew it was Talon. He could see the mechanical arms of the Carson sub holding the backpack and beginning to draw it inside. Murphy knew it would only be a matter of minutes before Talon would have complete possession of the bronze plates.

He reached down and turned the switch. The diesel engine made noise but would not start.

Oh, no.

Murphy tried it again. It still wouldn't start. He tried it a third time and it finally caught hold and turned over.

I hope it can still maneuver.

Talon had pulled in the backpack. He got out of the seat and unzipped the top part and looked in. All three bronze plates were there. He could also see two of the crystal lighting jars. He smiled smugly.

And now for Dr. Murphy.

He had just climbed back into the driving seat when he noticed some movement outside. He turned and looked out the viewing bay and saw a gray object filling up the window. Murphy was coming after him.

I don't think so, Dr. Murphy!

Quickly Talon pushed the lever in reverse and gave the Carson sub all the speed he could. It worked. He was able to go faster than Murphy's damaged sub.

The distance between the two subs grew. Talon briefly considered leaving with his spoils: the backpack and yet another clear victory over Murphy. But that wasn't enough. There was still a chance that the good doctor could make it to the surface. He wanted Murphy out of the picture for good.

Talon took the sub out of reverse. He could now maneuver into a better position to ram Murphy a third time.

His attention was fixed on Murphy's sub when he punched the Carson sub forward and to the left. What Talon didn't notice was that he had backed close to the sunken cargo freighter. As he turned and increased the speed, he ran into the crane arm that was sticking out from the ship. The outer point of the arm broke through the window of the Carson submarine like a dart going into a dartboard. Water began to rush in.

Murphy saw it all happen. He couldn't believe his eyes. He began to slow his ship. Finally Talon was getting what he deserved.

He was close enough to see a look of shock and horror on Talon's face. He watched as Talon struggled to undo his harness but couldn't get it to unlatch.

Murphy thought back to Talon choking Laura to death. How fitting that he would suffer the same fate. One of Murphy's outside lights was still working and gave him enough light to see the Carson sub fill with water.

Sweet Laura's justice has finally arrived.

Talon's eyes bulged with fear as the water level rose above his head. Then the lights in the Carson sub went black. Murphy watched as enormous bubbles of air escaped toward the surface. The weight of the water in the Carson sub caused it to slip off of the crane arm and drop into the sand next to the cargo freighter. A dust cloud of sand kicked up off the ocean floor, marking the spot that would forever be Talon's grave.

Murphy maneuvered a little closer and shined the light into the window. He could barely see Talon still strapped into the driving seat, his mouth and eyes wide open. The hair on his head was waving back and forth like grass in a gentle breeze. Murphy could see the backpack on the floor of the sub. Perhaps he could still retrieve it.

He heard a popping sound as the pressure outside the sub dislodged a rivet, further deforming the hull. Water began rushing in even faster.

Murphy knew he needed to surface quickly or this would be his grave also. The plates would have to wait.

Murphy felt a chill and his body began to shake some more. He pushed the lever to maximum speed and began the ascent to the surface.

Murphy looked around. The floor was now a pool of water six inches deep and quickly getting deeper. He glanced back at his oxygen gauges. They were deep in the red. His heart started to beat faster as he realized he had a punctured oxygen line.

Then Murphy noticed that the gauge registering his ascent was not working. He really wasn't sure if he was rising rapidly or not, and had no idea how far he had to go to get to the surface.

Between his injuries and hypothermia setting in, he could feel himself getting light-headed. Or was it the loss of oxygen in the ship? He couldn't tell for sure. He was trying to hold his thoughts together but things seemed to be slipping away.

Murphy began to pray . . . and then there was darkness.

SIXTY-SIX

SOMETHING INSIDE MURPHY began to stir. He tried to open his eyes but it seemed very difficult. Slowly his eyelids fluttered a little and then opened. He immediately closed them again. The bright light was painful. He tried again, squinting and blinking until his eyes began to focus.

He was disoriented. Where was he? What was going on? Was he dead? Was he in Heaven? Soon his mind started to clear. He was in a bed and there were tubes in his arms and an oxygen tube in his nose. The bright light he saw was the sun shining in the window of the room.

He look around and could tell that it was a hospital but certainly not a modern one. The room was small . . . there was no television . . .

the bed was old . . . and the green paint on the walls was chipping off. Out the window he saw some distant mountains.

Where am I?

As he took a breath of air, he felt a pain in his left side. He then became aware of bandages wrapped around his chest and his head. He tried to move a little, only to realize that his left leg was in a cast.

Then it all began to come back to him. He remembered the discovery of the backpack . . . the rammings and the breaking of his ribs and leg. He recalled the image of Talon harnessed into the seat of the sunken submarine.

But how did I get here?

An hour passed before anyone entered his room. The first person to come in was an older nun. She moved quickly over to the bed and looked at him and smiled. She was unmistakably excited. She then began speaking to him in a foreign language that he did not understand. Murphy shook his head back and forth.

"I'm sorry but I don't understand you."

She patted his arm and left the room.

It wasn't long before she returned with a doctor and a nurse. They too spoke to him in a foreign language. He again shook his head, indicating that he did not understand. The doctor then began to examine him, listening with a stethoscope and looking into his eyes. Soon they brought him food to eat. This continued for another day.

About midafternoon the next day, Murphy was occupied looking out the window at a bird circling in the sky when he heard a familiar voice.

"It's about time you rejoined the land of the living."

He turned and looked toward the sound. The large body of Levi Abrams filled the doorway. He had a big smile on his face.

"Levi!"

He came over and shook his hand. As he did, Murphy groaned a little.

"Oh, are we getting soft in our old age? Can't you take a little blow in the side?"

"It feels like one of your karate punches."

Levi laughed.

"Levi, what happened? Where am I? How did I get here?"

"Somehow you were able to maneuver to the surface with the mini-submarine. No one knows how you did it in your condition."

"All I remember is passing out."

"A fishing trawler happened to be in the area and saw something floating on the water in the distance. They motored in your direction and found the mini-sub. The fishermen opened the hatch and discovered you unconscious in the driving seat. They could tell that you were badly injured. They said that you had lots of blood on you. They loaded you onto their boat and brought you back to the port in Burgas and you were put in the hospital on the outskirts of the town. I swear, you must have nine lives like a cat."

"That explains the hills outside of the window. Those are the Bulgarian Mountains."

"We'd alerted the Bulgarian Navy and they had begun a search for you. When the fishermen found you, they also called the navy and the mini-sub was towed back to the harbor."

"How long have I been here?"

"Three weeks."

"Three weeks? You've got to be kidding."

"No. Your head wound caused you to go into a mild coma. The doctors set your leg, fixed your broken ribs, and repaired your lung. I asked them to contact me when you awakened from your coma . . . and here I am."

"I'm glad you're here, Levi. You've been a good friend."

"Well, that's the least I can do. Anyone who pulls me half-dead out of a collapsing tunnel deserves a vacation in Bulgaria."

"Some vacation. When do you think I can get out of here?"

"The doctors say you'll have to undergo physical therapy for the break in your leg. It was pretty bad. It will also take some time for that punctured lung to heal. They say that you will have at least another month before you can leave."

"A month?"

"Aren't you lucky? You get to relax and breathe fresh mountain air for a whole month."

"Well, I guess it will give me some time for reading and thinking."

"Michael, let me be honest with you. You will probably walk with a cane for a while and limp for several months afterward. However, the doctors think you will be able to make a full recovery after rehab."

"Thanks for being truthful. At least I know what I have to look forward to."

"Michael, I've got to ask you. Did you find the backpack? It was not on the mini-sub."

Murphy told Levi about finding the backpack and getting rammed by Talon before he got skewered like a shish kebab and drowned.

"I can't think of a better place for Talon to be," Levi said.

"Agreed. The backpack is still on the Carson submarine at the bottom of the Black Sea."

"Well, at least it's not in the wrong hands yet. We can mount a salvage operation to retrieve it if you tell me where it is."

Murphy just smiled.

"You're not going to tell me, are you?" Levi said.

Murphy shook his head. "After what I've been through, I want to be there when it's found. And I'm not quite up to the trip just yet. I still have a difficult time breathing."

Levi laughed.

"Oh, come on. Are you a wimp?"

Murphy laughed, but it hurt. "Have you found out any information about the Seven?"

"No. They are very elusive. But at least we know one thing about them now."

"What's that?"

"They no longer have their chief assassin working for them."

Murphy smiled and nodded his head in agreement.

SIXTY-SEVEN

GANESH SHESHA and Señor Mendez stopped to look at the Fountain of Apollo and the Grand Canal.

"Have you ever seen anything like this before, Señor Mendez?"

"No, I haven't. Nothing in all of South America could compare to this."

"I would have to agree with you. I've traveled throughout India and even the Taj Mahal can't quite compare to this. I think it was a wonderful idea for John Bartholomew to schedule our meeting here at the Château de Versailles. I have been to Paris many times but this is my first visit to this majestic place."

"Look, Ganesh. Bartholomew is waving for us to join the others."

Shesha and Mendez rejoined the group and Bartholomew commenced speaking.

"If I may have your attention. Today we will meander through the château grounds and the various buildings. Naturally I have arranged to have the entire area for our sole enjoyment, and no tourists will be admitted today. Every now and then we will stop and conduct a little business. I think it's a grand way to combine business and pleasure."

Sir William Merton was not quite as enthusiastic. Wearing his black cleric outfit in the bright sun was making him perspire. That, along with the fact that he was grossly overweight and it was almost a mile walk from the Fountain of Apollo back to the château. It was depressing.

It wasn't long before they reached the Fountain of Latona, with frogs and turtles spewing water out of their mouths.

Bartholomew spoke. "You see how all the animals circle the statue of Latona. This is what will happen when De La Rosa unites the various religions of the world. They will circle around him as the world's religious leader. They will look to him for leadership. Like spokes of a wheel all leading to the hub, he will lead them all to come to him for ultimate wisdom. And when Talon returns with more Christian artifacts, it will only increase his powers and influence."

"Very good," said Viorica Enesco. "May I add to your thoughts, John? Just as the animals of the fountain spout out water from their mouths . . . the religious leaders will spout out the same doctrines and the same orders from their leader."

"Well done, Viorica. You now see how to conduct business and pleasure."

After about an hour of walking through the fabulous gardens the Seven arrived back at the château.

When they came to the King's Bedchamber they stopped. General Li began the conversation.

"Look at all the gold in this room, on the walls, the fabric of the bedcovers, and the large hanging drapes. This reminds me of our plan to gain economic control of all the wealth of the world. Señor Mendez is assisting us by gaining control of all of the oil produced in South America. He has been doing a wonderful job in convincing the leaders of Venezuela to withhold sending oil to the United States."

"And don't forget our influence on Syria and Iran," spoke up Jakoba Werner. "By moving the United Nations to Babylon we begin to be able to influence how much oil is produced and who should receive it. It will enhance our ability to manipulate economies around the world. Besides, the environmentalists in the United States are so paranoid about drilling in Alaska and other places. They will hamper oil production in America. And if they have a few more hurricanes, they'll be in a real fuel crisis."

The next stop was in the Royal Chapel. The entire group gazed up at the ceiling high above. They were all silent until Sir William Merton spoke.

"As you look up in the central part of the chapel vault, you can see a painting by Antoine Coypel. It depicts the Heavenly Father in His glory announcing to the world the promise of redemption. It almost makes me sick to look at it. You are looking at our enemy . . . and the enemy of our leader, who is just about to make his presence known. Herein lies our struggle. We must do everything in our power to convince the world that redemption does not come through Christ. Redemption will only come through the power of 'the Boy,' who is now a man. He will come in all of his glory in just a few short days."

Everyone nodded his or her head in agreement. They continued the tour into other rooms.

"This is the Great Hall of Mirrors. Look at all the golden statues and the mirrors on the walls. They reflect the majestic paintings on the ceiling and the light streaming through the windows. It reminds me of the reflection of great power and miracles that De La Rosa is able to perform," said Jakoba. "Just as light comes in the windows, I think that he will seem like a spiritual light to the simple-minded followers. To them he will become an angel of light. They will not be able to tell the difference between the reflection of true light or false light."

The group moved on and Sir William Merton spoke again.

"This is the Hall of Battles. Louis-Philippe had artists produce thirty-five large paintings portraying fourteen centuries of French history through great military battles. I want to remind you that we have some great battles ahead of us. One battle will be to destroy the nation of Israel. They have been a thorn in the flesh of all nations around the world. Another battle is to diminish the voice of those who call themselves Christians. They pretend that they have a relationship with God and that God only cares about them. Ridiculous! The world would be a better place without those narrow-minded, judgmental hypocrites. We must renew our efforts against them."

John Bartholomew raised his hand.

"You know, I'm getting a little tired of walking. How about driving back into the city for a good meal and some fine wine. Besides, I'm a little tired of talking about the future. It will come soon enough. We all know what we have to do. We need a little break before we redouble our efforts."

"Hear! Hear!" said Sir William Merton.

General Li spoke. "I think that we all should show our appreciation to our meeting planner."

Everyone looked at John Bartholomew and politely clapped.

In the midst of their clapping, Bartholomew's cell phone rang. He answered but said little to the person who called. This made the others curious. They could not hear what was said but they saw Bartholomew's face grow red. He was not happy.

He finally flipped closed his cell phone and looked at the group.

"What's wrong?" asked Sir William Merton.

"That was one of our operatives in Istanbul. They've been waiting to hear from Talon but all has been quiet. They made some inquiries and found out that Dr. Michael Murphy has been hospitalized for a number of weeks in Bulgaria. They bribed one of the nurses, who told them that some fishermen on the Black Sea had rescued Murphy. With some further digging, they discovered information that suggests that Talon may have been killed. It seems that the secret of the Philosopher's Stone may be on a submarine at the bottom of the ocean."

"We must stop this Michael Murphy!" said Jakoba Werner. There was fire burning in her eyes.

"Yes, I agree," responded General Li. "But if Talon is dead, who will do our assassination work?"

John Bartholomew unleashed a sinister smile.

"This is not the first time I've had to think about a possible change in plans. For the last year and a half I have not been happy with Talon and his arrogance. During that time, I made discrete inquires about a possible replacement for Talon. I have found someone, and I have already placed this individual on a retainer. He has just been waiting in the wings for me to give him the green light. He was prepared to eliminate Talon and his murderous falcons. In fact, he can hardly wait to get started."

Ganesh Shesha seemed excited. "That is a wonderful backup plan, John. Who is this individual and where does he live?"

Bartholomew shook his head. "I'm afraid I must withhold that information for a few days . . . until some last-minute details can be worked out. Please trust me. You will be very happy with this individual. He has an excellent track record for mayhem and assassinations."

"What about our plans for conquest, John?" asked Viorica Enesco.

"I think the time has come for us to turn up the heat. De La Rosa needs to begin his program to control the economy of the world. It's time for him to put forth the marking system. He also needs to introduce our leader to the general public. Our time is almost at hand!"

SIXTY-EIGHT

MURPHY LOOKED FORWARD to his flight back to the United States. He had been gone for a little over two months during the summer. During that time he had grown to enjoy Bulgaria and its people. They had been very kind to him. And they had been very good with him in therapy. With his Irish temper and his struggle with weakness, he hadn't been the perfect patient. He had also appreciated his time to be able to think and read and plan while recuperating. It gave him an opportunity to reevaluate many things. *But,* he thought, *be it ever so humble, there is no place like home.*

As he stepped off the plane in Raleigh, he paused and took a deep breath. It was great. It took him a little longer than usual to get out of the airport. His limp and the use of a cane slowed the process. He even had to have a porter carry his bags. That was a new and humbling experience for him.

He took a taxi to his home not far from the university. The gardener had done a good job in Murphy's absence. Everything looked lush and green. He unlocked the front door and stepped in. The floor was piled with bills, letters, and magazines. *Too bad someone couldn't have taken care of all the bills too.* The postman had shoved two months' worth of mail through the mail slot.

That should be fun to go through. I wonder how many late charges I'll have?

He carried his luggage to the bedroom with much difficulty and a few more trips than normal. He was anxious to get rid of the cane. He unpacked and put the dirty clothes in the laundry room. He'd worry about washing them later.

He opened some windows to let the fresh air in. He then went and got a cardboard box from the garage. He hobbled back to the entry, filled the box with mail, and took it into the living room. He sat down in his favorite chair and set the box beside it. He put his left leg up on the ottoman. It was good to be home.

He then looked at the box of mail.

I don't think so. Not now.

He looked at the phone and sat there for moment, debating. Was he going to do it now, or was he going to put it off? He had thought about it all the time while he was recuperating.

Come on, Murphy.

He took a deep breath, picked up the phone, and dialed her number. He began to drum his fingers on the arm of the chair while he waited.

"Parchments of Freedom Foundation. May I help you?"

"May I please speak with Dr. Isis McDonald?"

"I'm sorry, sir, but she is in a meeting on the other side of town. May I take a message or would you like her voice mail?"

"I don't think that will be necessary. But would you possibly know what her schedule is this coming week?"

"Yes. Dr. McDonald will be gone Monday and Tuesday, but she will be giving tours here at the Foundation on Wednesday, Thursday, and Friday."

"Thank you very much."

Hmmm . . . Friday.

Murphy picked up his baggage and walked out the doors of the terminal, eschewing the help of a porter this time. He hailed a taxi.

"Where to, sir?"

"Hotel Carlton."

Murphy looked out the window as they drove by the Lincoln Memorial, thinking, *What a great man of character.*

"Here we are, sir."

Murphy paid the driver and went to the registration desk to check in. After dropping off the luggage in his room he went back to the registration desk.

"Excuse me. Is there a flower shop near the hotel?"

"Oh, yes, sir. You just go out the main doors and turn left. It's about half a block down the street." The man at the desk smiled. "Are you planning a surprise?"

"Yes, I think it will be quite a surprise."

Murphy picked up two dozen red roses and hailed a cab. He knew he wasn't being real creative getting red roses, but they were Isis's favorite.

"Where would you like to go, mister?"

"The Parchments of Freedom Foundation, please."

Murphy started up the stairs to the Foundation, then paused for a moment. He took a couple of deep breaths and continued up. His cane was in his left hand, the roses were in his right, and his heart seemed to be in his throat.

Inside the building he stopped at the information booth.

"Could you please tell me where the tour group might be right now?"

"Why, yes. They should be in the Hall of Egyptian Antiquities. It's down the corridor to your right, the third large doorway to your left."

The closer he came to the doorway the more nervous he felt.

Come on, Murphy. You don't get this anxious battling ninjas.

As he rounded the corner, he saw a group of people in front of a casket of an Egyptian mummy. He heard someone speaking but she didn't sound like she had a Scottish brogue.

Murphy waited until the young lady was through and the crowd was moving on to view the next object.

"Excuse me, miss. Is Dr. McDonald giving a tour today?"

"Oh, no. Dr. McDonald's not here. There was a change in plans. She left on Wednesday for Jordan. It seems that someone has discovered a cave containing a number of ancient manuscripts in some jars. They've asked her to come and translate the manuscripts." The young lady smiled. "They may turn out to be as important as the Dead Sea Scrolls."

With that, she turned and walked away.

Murphy stood there leaning on his cane for a moment. The crowd had moved on and he was alone. A deep sense of disappointment came over him.

I wonder if this will ever work out? Maybe we're just not meant to be.

He walked over to a trash receptacle and dropped the roses in. The echo of his shuffling steps was the only sound as he trudged back the way he had come.

ABOUT THE AUTHORS

DR. TIM LAHAYE is a renowned prophecy scholar, minister, and author. His Left Behind series is the bestselling Christian fiction series of all time. He and his wife, Beverly, live in southern California. They have four children and nine grandchildren.

BOB PHILLIPS, PH.D., is the author of more than eighty books. He is a licensed counselor and the executive director for the Pointman Leadership Institute.